BILLS

by

JOHN YELVERTON

This book is a work of fiction. Any reference to historical events, real people, or real places are used fictitiously. Other names, characters, places, and events are products of the author's imagination, and any resemblance to actual events or places or persons, living or dead, is entirely coincidental.

Fair Use Disclaimer: This work contains brief quotations and references to the life and writings of Ernest Hemingway. These uses are intended for literary and thematic purposes and are protected under the fair use doctrine as defined in Section 107 of the U.S. Copyright Act. All quoted material is limited in scope, used in a transformative context, and does not infringe upon the market value of the original works. The author makes no claim of ownership over any quoted material by Ernest Hemingway. All rights to Hemingway's works remain with their respective rights holders.

First hardcover edition, 2025

ISBN 979-8-9992477-1-1

LCCN 2025916932

For sales and marketing inquiries, contact:
Billsthebook@outlook.com

J.Y. Media
Fort Walton Beach, FL

AUTHOR'S NOTE

While the characters Jason Baymont, Soda, and Cricket in this story are fictional, this novel is inspired by the real-life fishing adventures of my brother, Jason Yelverton, Capt. Mike Noling (the real-life "Soda"), and Capt. Jimmy Crochet (the real-life "Cricket"). Their stories helped shape the heart of this book, though all events and characters are fictionalized for the purposes of storytelling.

CONTENTS

Many men go fishing all of their lives without knowing that it is not fish they are after.

— Henry David Thoreau

THE FAMILY TRADITION

He was a young man who fished the Gulf Coast. Jason Baymont had just returned to Destin, Florida, after a successful commercial fishing trip with his father. It was a beautiful late-spring day—the sun was shining, seagulls soared overhead, and a sense of excitement filled the air as people celebrated the arrival of warmer weather and the sea life that returned with it each year.

Nestled along Florida's Northwest Panhandle, known as the Emerald Coast, Destin attracted visitors from around the world, drawn by its stunning emerald-green waters, powdery white sand beaches, and legendary fishing. Upon entering the city, visitors were greeted by a billboard with an iconic blue marlin leaping from the water, alongside the message: "Welcome to Destin, The Luckiest Fishing Village in the World."

At the heart of Destin lay its harbor, located just inside the East Pass, which connects the Gulf to Choctawhatchee Bay. Known for having the largest private charter fishing fleet in North America, Destin Harbor was a hive of activity.

Most of the charter boats and other commercial vessels were docked along the north side of the harbor, which stretched nearly a mile and was lined with waterfront seafood restaurants, shops, and lively bars. Among the boats docked at the boardwalk was an old 55-foot steel-hulled fishing boat named the *Vanessa*, owned and captained by Jason's father, Jacob Baymont.

Years of exposure to the harsh marine environment and countless fishing trips had taken their toll on the *Vanessa*. Its hull, once a vibrant white with light blue trim, was now dull and weathered, marred by stubborn stains and dotted with rust spots. Old cut bait and fish slime clung to the vessel's exterior, permeating the air with a pungent odor that seemed impossible to wash away. In contrast to the sleek, modern boats and luxurious yachts surrounding it in the harbor, the *Vanessa* looked—and smelled—out of place.

Jason and three other fishermen, clad in dingy white bib-style slickers, were finishing the grueling task of unloading nearly four thousand pounds of fish from the boat's cold storage room below deck. They transferred piles of bright red mingo snappers, each weighing roughly one to three pounds, into round, orange plastic baskets.

One by one, the fishermen carried the baskets full of fish from the boat to the dock, where they placed them on a weight scale. The work demanded both strength and endurance. Being young, tall, and athletic, Jason was well-suited for the physically demanding job.

From the dock, Jacob oversaw the unloading operation and managed the financial aspects of the transaction. He was an earnest man with dark weathered skin and deep creases on his hands, face, and back of his neck. A small adhesive bandage adorned his left cheek, covering a potentially cancerous spot that had been biopsied just days earlier.

Despite his rugged appearance, Jacob's eyes radiated joy and purpose. Commercial fishing was his passion, and he had built a successful career around it.

"Alright, that's the last basket!" Jacob said excitedly. "What's that put our total at, Mr. Dan?"

Mr. Dan, the wholesale buyer, carefully inspected the quality of the fish, his expression serious and focused. As he recorded the total weight of the catch, the fishermen exchanged nervous glances, anxious to hear the final amount.

With an all-business tone, Mr. Dan replied, "I've got your total weight of mingos at three thousand eight hundred and ninety-two pounds, plus the ninety pounds of wahoo you had."

Jacob exclaimed, "Not bad, boys! Not bad at all!" He turned to Mr. Dan and proudly added, "My son Jason was the highliner this trip. He caught over a thousand pounds, plus the wahoo."

Mr. Dan responded matter-of-factly, "Yes, sir, I believe he's the highliner just about every time I buy your fish. I know you must be proud."

"I am! He did good. Real good," Jacob replied. "All these fellas did good this trip. I'm proud of 'em all."

The other three fishermen nodded with a subtle hint of envy over Jason's impressive catch. Each fisherman was compensated based on their individual haul, creating constant competitive tension among the crew. Unlike the rest of the men, Jacob earned a percentage of the total payout as captain, along with an additional share as the boat owner.

After writing a check to pay Jacob for the fish, Mr. Dan said, "Well, sir, here is your check, Mr. Baymont. I appreciate your business."

Jacob responded cheerfully, "Thank you, sir. I appreciate you doing business with us."

As Mr. Dan departed with the refrigerated trucks full of fish, Jacob called out, "Alright, boys! That's it for today—I'll have y'all's paychecks ready tomorrow."

With their work completed for the day, the other three fishermen said farewell and departed, while Jason and Jacob remained on the boat to finish a few tasks and lock up.

As they prepared to leave, a longtime friend, Soda, stopped by to chat. Soda worked as a mate on a privately owned sportfish boat that competed in marlin tournaments. It was an exciting but expensive sport where boat owners battled for bragging rights and cash prizes worth millions of dollars. Smaller payouts went to the largest tuna, wahoo, and dolphin—a fish widely known as mahi-mahi. But among all the pelagic game fish, the blue marlin reigned supreme. With some weighing more than a thousand pounds and capable of reaching speeds of sixty miles per hour, these magnificent creatures could test the limits of even the most seasoned anglers and their gear.

Soda greeted Jason and his dad with a warm smile, accentuated by his stubby chevron mustache. He had a stocky build and a round face framed by short, light brown hair. He wore a white long-sleeve T-shirt, shorts, and flip-flops. A pair of sunglasses hung from a lanyard around his neck, leaving a perfectly matched suntan line around his eyes. He had an easygoing, laid-back personality that complemented his drawn-out Southern manner of speaking. "What's happenin', fellas?" he asked.

Jacob beamed with pride. "Just weighed in nearly four thousand pounds of fish! How 'bout that?"

"Nice!" he said slowly, his eyes wide with amazement at the impressive haul.

Jacob continued, "And Jason was the highliner again this trip!"

Soda shrugged, a grin spreading across his face. "Not a big surprise."

"He's gonna be takin' over as captain in just a few years," Jacob added.

Jason nodded, a proud smile tugging at the corners of his mouth.

"He'd make a fine captain," Soda said with an affirmative nod. His gaze shifted to a pair of rod and reel setups by the cabin door. "Jason, I see you've got those trolling lures I gave you rigged up. Did you get a chance to try them out?"

Jason's eyes lit up. "Yeah, I caught three big wahoo on them trolling on the way in!"

"Nice!" Soda replied.

Jason continued, "Thanks for letting me try them out. It's definitely a lot more exciting to catch a wahoo on a rod and reel than a bunch of mingos on a bandit reel!"

"Mingos pay the bills, son! Mingos pay the bills!" Jacob said with conviction.

"I know, Dad, but there's just not a lot of sport in winching up a bunch of small fish on an electric reel," Jason replied, frustration evident in his voice. Each bandit reel was equipped with an electric motor that allowed fishermen to effortlessly haul in up to thirty mingo snappers at a time, using a vertical string of circle hooks with cut bait.

Jacob quipped, “Sport? Well, son, you could reel them up by hand on that bandit reel like we did in the old days. That’ll make it a little more sporting for you!”

Jason ignored his father’s ribbing and tried his best not to smile or laugh. “One of these days, I’m gonna catch a blue marlin like y’all do, Soda.”

Jacob couldn’t resist poking fun at his son again. “I don’t know what he’s gonna do with it! Can’t sell the damn thing!”

By that point, Jason was half smiling but still ignored his dad’s teasing. “So when is your next tournament?”

Soda responded, “We’ve got the Orange Beach Billfish Classic comin’ up at the end of May, so just about a week from now.”

“Sounds exciting,” said Jason.

“Yeah, I’m lookin’ forward to it,” Soda said with a lopsided grin. “I’m gonna be on a new boat this year, too.”

“Really? What boat?” Jason asked.

Soda responded, “It’s called the *Family Tradition* and it’s a brand new sixty-two-foot sportfish. It’s got all the bells and whistles, including a Seakeeper. And let me tell you, when that thing is turned on, it don’t matter how rough it is, the boat don’t rock. It might go up and down, but it don’t rock.”

“Sounds nice!” Jason replied. “Is the boat kept here in the harbor?”

Soda answered, “No, right now it’s being kept in a slip down the road in Sandestin at the Baytowne Marina. But the owner just bought a house here in Destin over in Joe’s Bayou and plans to keep it there once they get a dock built that can handle that size of a boat."

Jason's dad was now keenly interested and asked, "So, who's the owner?"

Soda replied, "His name is Mr. J.P. Gregory, and he's from Birmingham, Alabama. He bought the boat to go fishin' with his daughter who wants to go after big marlins. Neither one of them know anything about marlin fishin' or boats, but he's got deep pockets and is payin' me and Cricket good money. The kind of money we couldn't say no to!"

Cricket was the captain of the boat and had worked with Soda for many years tournament fishing.

Jason took the opportunity to poke fun at his dad, saying, "Wait a minute. He bought a new sixty-two-foot sportfish to take his daughter marlin fishing just for fun? I can't even get the old man over here to buy me a new rod and reel. He's so cheap, he gives me coupons for my birthday!"

Jacob laughed at his son's joke and responded in a defensive but playful way, "Well, it must be nice to have that kind of money to throw away gamblin' on marlin tournaments."

Soda chuckled. "All fishin' is a gamble. That's why they call it fishin', not catchin'!"

"You got that right! I prefer catchin', though!" Jacob said.

The three men laughed at Jacob's playful jab, and as the chuckles settled, he asked, "So, you think this new owner's gonna be a good fella to work for?"

"Yeah, super nice guy, real smart too," Soda responded. "From what Cricket told me, his family owned some big agriculture equipment business that he took over and expanded. He apparently did real well for himself, but he was workin' all the time and didn't see his family much. Then, about a year ago, his wife, Katherine, died in a car accident, and, uh..." Soda looked down for a moment. "Well, I guess he decided to step away from it a bit so he could do some things he'd been puttin' off."

"How old is his daughter?" Jason asked.

"She's probably about your age," Soda replied. "She goes to school at the University of Alabama, but she's gonna be stayin' in Destin over the summer break. She's a super sweet girl. I've only met her a few times, but she's got such a warm personality that I feel like I've known her a lot longer."

With a raised eyebrow, Jason curiously asked, "And she wants to spend her summer break fishing marlin tournaments with her dad?"

Soda smiled and shrugged his shoulders. "Yeah, it's gonna be a new family tradition for them, I guess. What Cricket told me was that Mr. Gregory and his daughter saw some interview with Warren Buffet's billionaire business partner, Charlie Munger, just before he passed away at the age of ninety-nine. The guy said his only regret in life was not catchin' a two-hundred-pound tuna, and that he just waited too long to get around to it. Said he would pay any amount of money to catch one when he was younger and had the strength to do it. After they saw that interview, Mr. Gregory told his daughter that he had always wanted to catch a big tuna. Then his daughter told him that she wanted to catch a big marlin. The next thing you know, he buys a three-million-dollar sportfish boat, a four-million-dollar waterfront home in Destin, and hires me and Cricket to take 'em fishin'."

Jason and his dad were completely captivated by the story, their faces reflecting a mix of wonder and disbelief.

Jacob said, "Dang. Well, I really hate to hear about him losin' his wife like that, but I'll tell you this, he couldn't ask for a better crew than you and Cricket to take 'em fishin' for marlins and tunas. That's a fact!" He then asked, "Is that boy Chip still gonna be fishin' with y'all as the second mate?"

"No," said Soda while he slowly shook his head and looked down. "Cricket had to let Chip go because he kept partyin' too much and was showin' up to work either still drunk or hung over. You know Cricket ain't puttin' up with that mess." He then added, "I tell ya, it's hard for a lot of these young guys not to get sucked into the party lifestyle when the liquor is flowin' freely at these tournaments and everyone around you is partyin' like there ain't no tomorrow. But as you know, we get paid to fish, not party, and that boat don't clean itself."

Jacob responded, "You got that right! You got someone else lined up for the second mate?"

"Not yet, but I'm workin' on it," Soda replied.

"Ten-four. Well, listen, man, I gotta run to a doctor appointment, but I'm glad you stopped by, Soda! It's good to see you, man," Jacob said.

Soda responded, "Yeah, good to see you too, Jacob." He then asked, "Is everything goin' alright with the Doc?"

"Oh yeah, the Doc just wanted to follow up with me on this spot he removed from my cheek," Jacob replied.

"Yeah, I seen that little bandage you got on there," Soda responded.

Jacob then playfully told Soda and Jason, "I told that joker, I said, 'Doc, if you're gonna go cuttin' on my face, at least give me a big scar that makes me look tough, you know! I want a cool lookin' scar I can make up a good story about! But no, what does he do? He gives me this little, tiny cut on my cheek that makes me look like a damn idiot that cut himself shavin'! I tell ya, man, I can't win for losin'."

The three of them laughed together while Jason shook his head at his dad's antics.

Soda told Jacob, "Alright, well, I'm sure it's nothin'. I've had a few spots removed myself. Ain't no big deal."

Jacob waved off the concern. "Yeah, it ain't nothin'." Then he flashed a half-smile and added, with a touch of sarcasm, "But I guarantee they're gonna send me a nice bill for it though."

"You got that right," Soda replied as he and Jason nodded their heads.

Jacob glanced at his watch, knowing he needed to leave soon. "Well, congrats on that new job, man. It sounds like a good deal! I'll give you a shout later on to see how things are going."

"Sounds good. Give me a shout!" Soda responded warmly.

Jacob shook Soda's hand and said farewell before walking to his truck parked at the boardwalk. As he closed the door, Soda and Jason waved goodbye.

Turning to Jason, Soda said, "Well, Jason, I actually stopped by to talk with you."

"Really? What's going on?" Jason asked.

"You know how I said I'm gonna need a second mate on this new boat?" Soda asked.

Jason squinted slightly, curiosity flickering in his eyes. "Yeah."

Soda continued, "Well, I told Cricket and the owner that you were the guy we needed."

"Really?" Jason asked, his eyes lighting up.

"Yeah, I mean, you're a hard worker, you've got your head on straight, and you were practically born with a fishin' pole in your hand. Are you interested?" Soda asked.

Jason's excitement quickly turned to frustration as he replied, "Well, of course I am, Soda. But you know I can't leave my dad. He wants me to take over as captain of the *Vanessa*."

"Do you wanna be captain of the *Vanessa*?" Soda asked.

Jason sighed, his shoulders slumping as he slowly shook his head. "Not really."

Soda then told him, "I think you'd enjoy marlin fishin' with us, Jason. There's nothin' quite like being in the cockpit, with a giant marlin dumpin' line from the reel, the boat backin' down on it, waves crashin' over the back of the boat floodin' the deck. Man, I love it!" He chuckled and nostalgically added, "This may sound silly, but sometimes when I'm wirin' a marlin, it kinda feels like I'm that character Santiago in *The Old Man and the Sea*. Y'know what I mean?"

Jason nodded with a subtle, knowing smile. "Yeah, that's one of my favorite books." His gaze drifted for a moment as he envisioned himself battling a giant marlin—the leader line wrapped around his hand, the fish leaping out of the water in front of him.

Soda added, “The owner is willin’ to pay you a base salary equal to whatever you’re makin’ now, plus a ten percent cut of the boat’s tournament winnings.”

Jason’s eyes widened as he heard the tantalizing offer, but then he sighed, his shoulders slumping again. “I don’t know, Soda. I just feel like it’s gonna break my dad’s heart. All he talks about is how glad he is to have me on the boat, how proud he is that I’m commercial fishing like him, and how he wants me to take over as captain one day.”

Soda replied, “Jason, I’ve been good friends with your dad for a long time. He’s gonna be proud of you no matter what.” He then added, “Just talk to him about it. Tell him you just want to try it out and see what he says. You can always go back to commercial fishin’ if it don’t work out.”

Jason gave a small nod, the weight of the decision evident on his face. “Alright. I’ll talk to him about it tonight and let you know how it goes.”

Soda smiled and nodded softly, a look of encouragement in his eyes as he extended his hand for a firm shake.

After the men exchanged goodbyes and Soda walked away, Jason pulled out his phone and texted his dad: “Going to stop by this evening. There’s something I want to talk to you and Mom about.”

Jason stood there, his mind swirling with conflicting emotions. Deep down, he knew Soda was right. He had the skills and passion for this type of fishing, but he felt torn between his own desires and his father’s expectations.

As he wrestled with his thoughts, his phone suddenly buzzed. He nervously glanced at the screen and saw his dad's response—a simple thumbs-up emoji.

Later that evening, as the sun was setting, Jason arrived at his parents' house, parking his truck next to his dad's in the gravel driveway. The home overlooked the Choctawhatchee Bay to the west. It was a modest home nestled amidst the tranquility of sprawling oak trees. On the left side of the yard, there was an old 20-ft fiberglass gill-net boat sitting on jack stands. Jason's father had used the boat to commercially harvest mullet in the past, but after the Florida gill-net ban in 1995 there was little use for it. The boat hadn't moved in decades and was filled with leaves and small plants that had made it their home. Various fishing implements were scattered across the yard, including crab traps stacked on top of each other, several boat anchors, and heavy ropes coiled on the ground. The home, with its maritime items, blended seamlessly with the surrounding natural beauty, giving it a distinct old Florida charm.

Behind the home was a wooden dock that extended gracefully into the bay. Jason and his dad had built it themselves when he was just a boy, and it had miraculously survived multiple hurricanes over the years with little damage. However, the harsh sun and salty sea had left their mark. The once-smooth planks were now worn and splintered, revealing deep ridges running between the intricate patterns of the wood grain.

At the end of the dock, Jason saw his parents sitting in Adirondack chairs facing the setting sun.

Jason's mom, Ellen Baymont, had blond hair, fair skin, and a thin frame. She was a kind woman who was quick to smile and always full of encouragement.

As Jason walked out onto the dock to greet his parents, he noticed several large blue crabs moving along the shallow sandy bottom. They occasionally raised their claws, ready to fight or feed on anything that ventured near. He spotted several more blue crabs clinging to the dock pylons, which were encrusted with oysters and barnacles.

Jason said to his parents, "I see the blue crabs are back. I'll never forget that time Dad and I caught a hundred and fifty of them in one day chasing them with dip nets." Poking fun at his dad, he continued, "Of course, Dad made me clean them all! I didn't even want to look at another crab after that experience!"

Jacob murmured in an uncharacteristically hollow voice, "Character-buildin', son. Character-buildin'."

As he continued toward them, Jason saw his parents' faces and could tell something was bothering his dad.

His mom was doing her best to smile, and said, "Well, hey there, Jason." As she got out of her seat to give him a hug, she added, "I heard y'all had a good trip!"

Jason beamed with pride. "Yeah, we crushed 'em and got a good price from Mr. Dan too. Probably one of our best payouts yet, right Dad?"

Jacob kept his eyes on the setting sun. In a quiet, distant tone, he replied, "Yep. It was a good trip. A real good trip."

"Is everything alright?" Jason asked.

There was an uncomfortably long pause before Jacob responded, “Doc said that spot he removed from my face was the c word.”

Jason’s brow furrowed in confusion, his eyes filled with concern. “Cancer?”

Jacob nodded, trying to conceal the worry in his expression.

Jason sat in stunned silence, a wave of uncertainty washing over him. He and his mom took a seat on either side of Jacob, their movements slow and heavy with concern.

“Well, they cut it all out, right?” Jason asked.

“The doc said he wants to run some more tests,” Jacob said, his voice tinged with a hint of worry and frustration.

Putting her hand on Jacob’s arm, Ellen supportively chimed in, “He’s going to be fine though. We’ll get those extra tests done, and see what’s next, but he’s going to be fine.”

Clearly uncomfortable with the discussion about his health, Jacob shifted the conversation. “So what’s going on with you? You said you wanted to talk to me and your mom about somethin’?”

Jason’s stomach churned with unease as he grappled with potentially burdening his dad with more unwelcome news. In a rush of anxiety, he blurted out, “It’s nothing. We can talk about it later.”

Puzzled by Jason’s response, Jacob turned his head to look at his son and could see the burden weighing on his mind. As he returned his gaze back to the setting sun, he said, “Son, you know spoiled milk don’t get any better if you leave it in your mouth. You just gotta spit it out, man.”

His dad's quirky saying broke the tension and made Jason chuckle. Taking a deep breath, he mustered the courage to spit it out. "Soda offered me a job as a mate on that new boat he was telling us about."

Surprised by the news, Jacob uttered a short, soft, "Oh."

"But we can talk about it another time," Jason replied.

Jacob asked, "I thought you wanted to become captain of the *Vanessa*. You went and got your license and everything."

"I did, but I've always dreamed about fishing for marlins—and at this point in my life, I just don't feel like my heart is in commercial fishing or being a captain."

Jacob nodded with a sense of understanding. After a brief pause, he told Jason, "Well, Soda is one of the best in the business. You could learn a lot from him."

Jason replied, "I just don't want you to feel like I'm abandoning you or anything, Dad."

As Jacob pondered his son's response, memories of his own past flooded his mind. He told Jason, "You know your grandad wanted me to be a commercial shrimper like him." A smile crept across his face as he continued, "I hated shrimpin'. First thing I did when he gave me the *Vanessa* was get rid of those damn nets and I bolted on some bandit reels!" Jacob laughed. "Boy, he was madder than hell when he found out!"

Laughing lightly, Ellen said, "Yes, he was, I remember that conversation very well."

Jacob sighed, "You only go around once, partner. You've got to follow your dream, not my dream, or anyone else's. If this is what you really want to do, then you should do it. You don't need my permission. You're your own man now."

Jason met his father's eyes. His voice was firm as he said, "This is what I want to do."

Jacob nodded, acknowledging his son's choice to go his own way. He reached into the cooler beside him and pulled out a beer. After twisting off the cap, he turned to Jason. "Alright then, it's settled. And since you're gonna be twenty-one in a few weeks, I wanted to offer you a beer for the first time tonight, son." He slowly extended the beer toward Jason, then abruptly stopped. "But—since you're quittin' on me, I'm gonna make you wait till your birthday." Grinning, he pulled the beer back toward himself and took a sip.

Jason chuckled, nodding at his father's teasing. "Fair," he replied.

Reflecting on the weight of his choice to venture down an exciting new path and the uncertainty of his father's health, Jason gazed out across the bay with his parents. They were captivated by the final moments of the sun disappearing behind the silhouettes of trees on the distant shoreline. The sky that evening was painted to perfection in various shades of orange, yellow, and blue, accented by blots of grey and wisps of white. Its reflection sparkled like tiny jewels in the gentle waves that rippled across the water's surface.

Ellen commented, "What a beautiful sunset. I never get tired of coming out here to watch them."

"Me neither," Jacob responded as he reached for Ellen's hand. He then commented, "You know, it's hard to see just how fast that ole sun is movin' across the sky until it sets on the horizon like that. It moves a lot faster than you think."

THE WIREMAN

After watching the sunset with his parents, Jason returned to his home on Holiday Isle, a narrow peninsula on the south side of Destin Harbor that serves as a barrier against the expansive Gulf. This stretch of land primarily featured luxury vacation homes and condominiums, although some locals, including Jason, lived there full-time. He owned an older yet cozy waterfront townhome that overlooked the harbor and the boardwalk to the north. The beach was just a short stroll to the south, and he could hear the rhythmic sound of the ocean most days as the waves crashed against the shoreline.

A slight chill hung in the air as Jason stood on the back deck of his townhome, overlooking the water and reflecting on the remarkable events of the day. The deck extended toward a short dock where he kept his 22-foot center console skiff. A few sailboats were moored toward the center of the harbor, their silhouettes dark against the evening sky, illuminated only by a single small white light shining at the top of their masts. On the other side of the harbor, the businesses along the boardwalk were brightly lit, and the faint sound of live music drifted through the air.

Though physically exhausted from a long day, Jason was eager to share his decision with Soda and couldn't wait until morning. He dialed Soda's number that night, a wide smile spreading across his face as he anticipated the conversation.

When Soda heard the news, his excitement matched Jason's, and they quickly arranged to meet the next morning at Baytowne Marina in Sandestin – just a short walk from the vibrant Village of Baytowne Wharf, a major attraction with upscale shops, dining, art galleries, and lively nightlife venues.

The marina sat in a quiet cove along the southern shore of Choctawhatchee Bay. Waist-high needle rush grass in shades of gray and green swayed in the coastal breeze. Schools of mullet – each about a foot long with sleek silver-gray bodies – glided along the sunlit shoreline. Occasionally one would leap into the air, twisting slightly before splashing down onto the mirror-like surface of the water.

The primary dock at Baytowne Marina extended far into the bay, flanked by four finger piers stretching north and three extending south. Though not as busy as Destin Harbor twelve miles to the west, Baytowne remained a premier destination with more than two hundred slips, many occupied by sportfish boats and yachts.

The next morning, Soda eagerly waited for Jason at the foot of the long marina dock.

Jason understood that his appearance would matter on this boat—unlike his time spent commercial fishing on the *Vanessa*. He arrived looking sharp in a crisp new fishing T-shirt, fresh shorts, and waterproof flip-flops that squeaked softly with each step. Sunglasses dangled from a neoprene strap around his neck, ready for the day ahead.

A broad smile stretched across Soda's face when he saw him. "What's happenin', buddy!"

"Hey, what's up, Soda!" Jason said as they shook hands, their grips firm and familiar.

"I'm excited that you decided to join our team!" Soda replied.

Jason shook his head, grinning with disbelief. "Yeah, me too, man! I can't believe this is really happening."

Soda gave him a hearty pat on the shoulder. "It's real, buddy, it's real! Let's go check out the boat."

As the two started walking down the lengthy main dock, Soda asked Jason in a concerned tone, "So when's your dad going back to the doctor to follow up on the skin cancer they found?"

Jason replied, "In about three weeks. The doc wants to do what's called a Mohs surgery on him, which will do the least amount of damage to his face."

The tension in Soda's posture eased. "Good deal, man. I was worried when you told me it was cancer. Is he handling the news okay?"

Jason replied, "Yeah, I could tell it was bothering him yesterday, but he seemed to be doing fine this morning when I called him. I asked if he was still going fishing this week, and he said, 'Does a fish crap in the water, Jason?'"

Soda chuckled, shaking his head. "Yep, that sounds like ol' Jacob, alright!"

As they approached the *Family Tradition*, docked at the end of the furthest finger pier extending to the north, Soda beamed, "There she is! Beautiful, isn't she?"

Jason's eyes widened at the sight of the *Family Tradition*, a stunning 62-foot sportfish with a sleek, shiny white hull and polished chrome hardware throughout.

At the back of the boat was a rectangular area called the cockpit, where the fishing took place. At its center stood a beautifully crafted fighting chair made of glossy dark mahogany. The chair gleamed in the sunlight, creating a striking contrast with the boat's white exterior and the light-colored teak of the deck and coverboards atop the sidewalls of the cockpit.

A wide step led from the cockpit to the mezzanine, where comfortable white outdoor bench seating was positioned against the bulkhead separating the mezzanine from the boat's interior. The bulkhead featured dark tinted windows and a rich mahogany door that opened to the living room, known as the salon.

Directly above the salon was the open-air flybridge, where the captain steered the boat. A tall fishing tower loomed above the flybridge, offering an even greater vantage point to help spot fish.

Despite having been around boats his whole life, Jason was awestruck by the beauty and craftsmanship of the *Family Tradition*.

Soda motioned for him to follow. "Come on aboard, and I'll show you the inside."

As Jason entered the salon behind Soda, he was captivated by the elegant white interior with glossy dark wood trim throughout. Even the ceiling was white and featured narrow strips of glossy dark wood trim spaced several feet apart, running the length of the salon. The boat's air conditioner kept the interior comfortably cool, and a distinct new boat smell filled the air, with hints of fresh leather and newly laid carpet.

A white leather couch ran along the port side (the left when facing forward) with a narrow wood side table opposite on the starboard side. Soda pressed a button on the table. With a soft electric hum, a large flat-screen rose from its hidden well.

Jason grinned. "Not too shabby."

Ahead of the couch, the galley had white granite countertops, a built-in bar — with a matching dinette on the starboard side.

Soda gestured toward the carpeted stairs leading below. "Come on, let me show you below deck."

While walking downstairs, Soda told Jason, "On the port side are the crew quarters and Mr. Gregory's master stateroom. Starboard side are the captain's quarters, a linen closet, and a washer and dryer." He then added, "There's another stateroom for Mr. Gregory's daughter in the V-berth," referring to the "V" shaped room in the bow of the boat.

Jason couldn't help but grin as he inspected each room, taking in the details with quiet amazement. The crew and captain's quarters featured two twin-size beds, while the master stateroom boasted a luxurious king-size bed. In the second stateroom located in the V-berth, there was a spacious queen-size bed. Each bed was fitted with an elegant beige bedspread, showcasing a striking white coral reef pattern. The walls were decorated with original paintings of various pelagic gamefish—like a blue marlin leaping from the water, a sailfish swimming with its dorsal fin proudly raised, and a vividly colored mahi chasing after flying fish.

Each room also had its own bathroom, referred to as a head, which included a shower.

Although the crew cabin was relatively small compared to the staterooms, Jason was used to much tighter quarters from his time working on the *Vanessa*, which featured five narrow sleeping bunks and a single head shared among four fishermen and the captain.

"I think this will do!" Jason told Soda.

"Yeah, I thought you'd like these accommodations." Soda pointed to a nearby door. "And the engine room is in here."

The two stepped into the expansive engine room. It was painted white and filled with ultramodern equipment. A steady, low-frequency hum from the generators filled the air. Raising his voice to be heard over the noise, Jason said, "I feel like I'm inside a spaceship right now! It's so clean in here too."

Soda chuckled. "Yeah, it's definitely full of advanced technology down here!" He pointed toward the two massive, head-high V12 engines. "These will put out about two thousand horsepower each. Cruisin' speed is forty-two knots, and she'll do forty-six at wide open throttle."

Jason let out a low whistle through pursed lips—clearly impressed that a boat that size could cruise at the equivalent of 48 miles per hour and reach 53 at full throttle.

Soda continued pointing out key pieces of equipment in the engine room. "That's the Seakeeper I was tellin' you and your dad about yesterday mounted over there." He turned toward Jason. "Have you ever seen one of these?"

Jason shook his head. "No. What is it?"

"It's called an omni sonar and is the latest advancement in side scannin' technology to help locate fish," Soda told him. "It's like an upside-down periscope that deploys from the bottom of the boat and scans a full three-hundred-and-sixty-degrees for fish up to a thousand yards away. If we see a good-sized fish with it, we can position our trollin' spread in front of its path."

Jason's face lit up with intrigue. As he continued to look around the engine room, his eyes were drawn towards two massive gaffs stowed near the entry way.

"Flyin' gaffs," Soda called out. "We use them when we need to boat a big marlin or tuna."

Jason nodded, struck by the sheer size of the flying gaff. Its large, stainless-steel barbed hook was nearly a foot wide, with a heavy-duty rope attached to it.

Soda explained, "When you gaff the fish, the pole is released, and the hook stays in the fish with the rope still attached. The rope is tied to the base of the fighting chair, and we use it to pull in the fish."

Jason's mind raced at the thought of battling a fish massive enough to require the flying gaff.

Soda leaned in. "Let's go check out the bridge."

As the engine room door closed, the sound of the generators became barely audible. Jason and Soda went back up the stairs and through the salon to the mezzanine, where the ladder to the flybridge stood.

The flybridge's open layout made it easy to spot fish all around the boat. It also offered access to a variety of sophisticated electronic devices and screens. On each side, bench seats with plush white cushions provided comfortable seating, with a walkway between them and the driving station in the center.

Although it had an open-air design, clear, flexible vinyl panels could be zipped closed, giving the captain some protection from inclement weather. Above the flybridge, a second, smaller driving station in the tower offered greater visibility but less protection from the elements and limited access to electronics.

Every detail of the flybridge was carefully considered and masterfully constructed to assist the captain while offshore fishing. The only item on the dashboard that wasn't built into the boat was an old, worn Bible with curled edges, resting beside the steering wheel.

"Cricket never goes fishin' without that," Soda told Jason, pointing to the Bible.

Jason nodded with a sense of reverence. As he continued to look around, he pointed to two large reels mounted in the ceiling above their heads. "What are these?"

Soda responded, "Those are the bridge teaser reels. Each reel has a line that runs to one of the outriggers. Have you ever used outriggers before?"

Jason shook his head, clearly interested in learning more.

Soda explained, "Okay. Well, we typically run two teasers and two lures from each side of the boat, and the outriggers help us keep the lines spaced apart. The lines go from the reels to a pulley system on the outriggers. The first teaser line on each outrigger is usually a dredge of some type that looks sort of like a chandelier and mimics a school of bait fish. You and I will control those teasers usin' electric reels in the cockpit. Cricket controls the next set of teasers, called the bridge teasers, which are positioned further out on the outriggers. We typically use lighter weight teasers like a squid chain on the bridge teaser lines, and they're run a little further back in the water than the dredges. The next two lines on the outriggers are lure lines. The lure lines are attached to the outrigger with clips that release the line when a fish bites. We don't use the terms port and starboard when we talk about the lure spread. Instead, when you're lookin' behind the boat, the first lure line on the left is called the left short rigger, and the second one is called the left long rigger. The ones on the right are named the same way, right short rigger and right long rigger. We also run one more lure line from the center of the boat, known as the center rigger. It's positioned the furthest back behind the boat."

"I gotcha. Makes sense," Jason replied.

Soda responded, "There's a lot that goes into the tackle. Every knot we tie has to be perfect, and every hook we use has to be razor sharp. Tackle failure for us mates is not an option."

Jason nodded. "Yeah, my dad always told me that you can either suffer the pain of being meticulous or suffer the pain of losing fish. You might get lucky and bring in some fish being sloppy with your tackle, but the attention to detail pays off every time when the paychecks are handed out."

Soda nodded, a satisfied smile spreading across his face. "Yep. Your dad taught you well, Jason."

"Yeah, I've learned a lot from my dad," Jason replied. "And I'm looking forward to learning from you and Cricket, too."

Soda adjusted his position to look behind Jason toward the dock. “Well, speakin’ of Cricket, here he comes now.” He then shouted a cheerful greeting, “What’s happenin’, Cricket?”

Cricket was walking down the dock carrying a bag in one hand. He called back, “What’s happenin’!”

Soda and Jason climbed down the ladder from the flybridge to greet Cricket in the cockpit.

Cricket was in his mid-forties—tall and lanky, with a distinctive presence. He wore khaki shorts, a faded navy-blue long-sleeve T-shirt, and flip-flops. A white visor rested on his head, blue-mirrored sunglasses hugged his face, and a gold necklace with a small cross hung around his neck.

As Cricket stepped onboard the boat, Soda introduced the two, “Cricket, this is Jason Baymont. Jason, this is Cricket.”

The two shook hands, and Cricket said, “Nice to finally meet you, Jason! I’m glad you decided to join our team.”

“Thanks, Cricket. I’m glad to finally meet you too. I really appreciate y’all giving me this opportunity,” Jason said.

“Whatcha got there?” Soda asked, pointing to the bag in Cricket’s hand.

“Oh! These are our new crew shirts. I just picked them up. Check ’em out!” Cricket said as he reached into the bag. He then handed both Soda and Jason a light-grey T-shirt. The two held the shirts out at arm’s length where they could see them better. The T-shirts had long sleeves and a hood. They were made from a synthetic quick-dry material that was breathable and would help the fisherman stay cool and dry. On the back of the T-shirt was a large, printed image of their new boat and *Family Tradition* name. As they turned the shirts over to the front, they could see the boat name was also printed on the front left chest area, accompanied by "Destin, Florida" in smaller font below it.

Soda exclaimed in his usual drawn-out manner, "Nice!"

Jason added, "These are awesome!"

"I got these matching camo gaiters for everyone too," Cricket said as he handed them to Soda and Jason.

Jason glanced at Soda, clearly thinking about his dad's skin cancer scare. "Definitely gonna be using this."

"Yup!" Soda responded.

"You got a nickname, Jason?" Cricket asked.

Jason thought for a moment. "Some of my surfing buddies call me J-Bay."

"Perfect!" Cricket replied, "Like the surf spot in Africa!"

"Yeah, exactly! Do you surf?" Jason asked.

"Every chance I get! I actually just went on a surf trip to Costa Rica this past April," Cricket replied.

Jason's eyes lit up. "That's awesome! Costa Rica is definitely on the list of places I want to surf one day."

Cricket chuckled as he turned to Soda. "A fellow surfer that wants to marlin fish with us, huh? I like him already!"

He then added, "Well, listen J-Bay, I do have three important rules you need to follow if you want to work with us.

Rule number one is don't use the Lord's name in vain on this boat. What you say off this boat is between you and God, but when you're on this boat, don't do it.

Rule number two is don't show up drunk, hung over, or on any types of drugs. We might have a few drinks every now and then, but just remember fishing is our job. It's how we pay the bills. We're here to fish, not party. Understood?"

"Yeah, of course," Jason replied.

Cricket continued, "The third rule is—don't be hittin' on the owner's daughter. Seriously, I need you to keep things professional, and don't be gettin' too friendly, alright?"

A flicker of surprise crossed Jason's face, but he quickly reassured Cricket. "Yeah, no problem."

"Alright! Well, again, welcome to the team, J-Bay!" As he reached out to shake his hand, Cricket added, "Let's get ready to catch some big fish and win some big money!"

Jason beamed as he shook Cricket's hand. "Thanks, man! Let's do it!"

Cricket turned toward the salon and made his way inside. As the door shut behind him with a soft click, Jason leaned closer to Soda and asked in a playful tone, "So, is the owner's daughter hot?"

Soda gave Jason a pat on the shoulder. "I would just try to avoid direct eye contact."

Jason stared into the distance, squinting as he tried to make sense of Soda's advice.

Changing the subject, Soda said, "Well, I guess we better start gettin' to work. We've got a lot to do this week to get ready for the tournament. I got all the new reels spooled up with fresh line and some of the tackle loaded up in my truck, so the first thing we need to do today is move all that stuff to the boat."

"Sounds good," Jason replied.

Soda had picked up an arsenal of fishing gear that included eight 80W reels, six 50Ws, and six 30Ws. These numbers followed an old naming convention, where each reel size corresponded to the yards of monofilament it could originally hold. The 80W—called an "eighty-wide"—was designed to spool 700 yards of 80-pound test and was the standard for trolling. However, thanks to advancements in line technology, Soda had the eighty-wides spooled with 800 yards of smaller diameter 200-pound braided line, topped with 300 yards of 100-pound clear monofilament for a total of 1,100 yards per reel.

The 50Ws—referred to as "fifty-wides"—were lighter and easier to handle, typically rigged with pitch baits like large ballyhoo or Spanish mackerel for targeting fish under 400 pounds. The 30Ws—"thirty-wides"—were usually paired with small dead ballyhoo to pursue white marlin, sailfish, and smaller blues under 250 pounds.

Jason and Soda spent the next hour making trips back and forth from the truck to the boat, pushing a cart loaded with gear down the long marina dock.

With everything aboard, Soda reached for one of the eighty-wide rods behind the fighting chair, pulled several feet of monofilament from the tip, and picked up a skirted lure in his other hand. "Alright, let me see you rig this for trolling. Use a Bimini Twist to make the double line and then connect it to the swivel using a Johnny Dukes Knot." Soda said.

Jason took the line and began tying, wetting each knot in his mouth before carefully cinching it tight. He threaded the leader through the skirted lure and crimped it to the hookset, then handed the finished rig to Soda.

Soda eyed it over and nodded approvingly. "Pretty work."

"Thanks," Jason replied proudly.

They spent the next several days getting tackle and provisions ready for the upcoming tournament. The morning before they planned to leave, Soda was teaching Jason how to rig a ballyhoo pitch bait while Cricket was upstairs in the flybridge talking on his cell phone with the owner Mr. Gregory.

Jason and Soda heard Cricket respond, "Oh, so the new dock is completed. That's great news, Mr. Gregory."

Cricket continued to listen to Mr. Gregory talk, then responded, "Uh, yeah, we can bring the boat over today. No problem."

Cricket hurried to the back of the flybridge and spotted Jason and Soda in the cockpit. Eyes wide, he silently mouthed, "Moving the boat today!"

"Can we be there by one o'clock?" Cricket replied, repeating Mr. Gregory's question with a skeptical expression.

Soda held up five fingers and emphatically mouthed, "Five!"—hoping for a little more time to finish preparing and clean the boat.

But it was too late. Cricket turned back and said, "Yeah, we can be there by one. No problem. We just need to give the boat a quick wash first, and then we'll be on our way."

Soda's head dropped, frustrated by the unexpected time crunch. The process of thoroughly washing and detailing the boat to Soda's preferred level of perfection usually took four hours, but now they would only have two hours.

Cricket ended the call with Mr. Gregory, and said to Jason and Soda, "Looks like we're gonna have to get the boat cleaned up in a hurry, fellas. Mr. Gregory really wants us to be there by one. I'll start working on the inside."

Soda told Jason, "I'll get this gear put away. You go ahead and get things ready to wash the boat. We'll start from the top of the tower and work our way down."

"Can I play some tunes?" Jason asked.

"Yeah, that's a good idea." Soda replied. "The boat has Bluetooth speakers if you wanna stream some music from your phone. Just be respectful of the folks around us and don't turn it up too loud."

"Yeah, of course," Jason said.

He then selected a playlist on his phone and began playing music through the boat's speakers. For the next two hours, he and Soda worked diligently washing one section of the boat at a time and then drying it with a shammy to prevent water spots.

As they dried the last section of the boat, a colossal 90-foot-long sportfish glided toward the end of the finger pier where they were docked. It was a magnificent vessel—more akin to a luxurious yacht—that dwarfed the 62-foot-long *Family Tradition*. The back deck featured a large cockpit and two expansive mezzanine levels with lavish couch seating. Two young men and five bikini-clad women, all in their early twenties, were having an exceptionally good time. They drank from red plastic cups, laughing, dancing, and singing along to crude lyrics that many would consider inappropriate for the setting. The loud music and their voices echoed throughout the quiet marina.

Jason glanced at Soda, who was also distracted by the commotion. "That boat is massive!"

Soda replied, "Yep, that's the *Trust Me*. It's a ninety-footer worth about eighteen million dollars. They just started competing in billfish tournaments last year."

"Are those the owner's kids?" Jason asked.

Soda shook his head. "Nope. That young guy by the salon door is actually the owner—the short, muscular one in the tiny yellow shorts and the snug white polo."

Surprised and humored by Soda's answer, Jason asked, "Really?"

Soda nodded. "Yeah, his name is Bill Murphy. His parents set him up with a trust fund, which is why he named the boat *Trust Me*, but everyone I know that has worked with him says he is not a guy you want to trust."

"Hmm. I'll definitely keep that in mind," Jason replied as they returned to drying the last section of the boat.

A short while later, Bill Murphy and his friends stepped off the boat and began making their way down the dock headed to the Baytowne Wharf for lunch. A few of the girls were heavily intoxicated, stumbling, laughing, and holding on to each other.

As they passed by the *Family Tradition*, Bill Murphy yelled out to Jason and Soda, "Hey, you missed a spot!" and started laughing.

Most of Bill Murphy's friends joined in the laughter, except for one of the girls who playfully told him, "Stop it," while tugging on his arm, trying to pull him away.

Jason and Soda looked at each other, dumbfounded and irritated by Bill Murphy's jeering.

Jason had grown up fishing alongside men who took pride in their hard work and had little tolerance for disrespect. When boundaries were crossed, things escalated fast—and fists often followed. He quickly fired back, "I was actually saving that spot for you. Thought you might enjoy the experience of doing a little work for once in your life."

Shocked by the audacity of Jason's response, Bill Murphy turned to his friends with an exaggerated, cartoonish expression. "Whoa!" he laughed. "Can you believe this loser? He's got a lot of nerve talking to me like that!" Still trying to belittle Jason, he added, "Clearly, this guy isn't the sharpest hook in the tackle box," as he gestured with an open hand toward Jason, mockingly drawing attention to him cleaning the boat.

Some of Bill Murphy's friends laughed, while a few of the girls became visibly uncomfortable with the escalation. Soda also looked concerned, unsure what might happen next.

Jason was furious but forced a smile. "Thanks, and you've got a lot of nerve wearing those short yellow shorts. Clearly, you're not the sharpest dresser, but hey—you do you, man!"

Bill Murphy's laughter quickly faded, replaced by visible anger as his face turned red. He raised his left fist, clenched tight, his oversized silver watch sparkling in the sunlight. Then, with a swift motion, he flicked out his middle finger—giving Jason the bird. The other young man with him joined in, mirroring the gesture.

After a brief stare down between the men, Bill Murphy said to his friends, "Forget this loser. Come on, let's go."

As the group slowly turned around and walked down the long dock, a few of the young women quietly whispered to one another.

Jason looked at Soda and said, “Yep, that guy is definitely a tool bag. He’d a got his ass kicked saying something stupid like that to any commercial fisherman I know.”

Soda replied, “Yeah, but this ain’t commercial fishin’, Jason. That guy is a prick, for sure, but you just can’t let people like that get to you in this business. You gotta play it cool, man. *Alright*?”

Jason nodded, his expression reluctant but respectful. “Yeah, alright,” his simmering anger still evident.

Cricket stuck his head out the salon door and asked, “Hey, are y’all ready to go?”

In a casual tone that masked the tension of the prior moment, Soda said, “Yeah, we’re ready. Just finished up.”

Cricket made his way to the flybridge to crank the engines, while Soda and Jason began untying the dock lines.

The Choctawhatchee Bay was calm that afternoon as the boat pulled away from Baytowne Marina and headed toward the owner’s new home in Destin. With each mile they put between him and Bill Murphy, Jason’s frustration faded like the wake fanning out behind the boat. Leaning against the transom, Soda said, “Well, Jason, I’ve been thinkin’ about this, and—I want you to be the wireman.”

Jason enthusiastically raised his arm to his chest and clenched his fingers into a celebratory fist. “Yes!”

Soda chuckled. “Yeah, I thought you might be excited to hear that.” From a tackle storage bin, he pulled out a pair of wireman gloves and handed them to Jason. "You'll need to wear these to protect your hands from leader burns and cuts. They'll also help keep your hands from gettin' crushed by the force of a big fish when you're wrapped up."

Jason eagerly looked over the gloves. "These are awesome, man! I can't wait to try them out!"

Soda responded, "Good! I'm lookin' forward to seein' you in action! But listen, Jason, wirin' a marlin is a whole different game compared to what you've done in the past. I know you've wired a few decent-sized fish, but a big marlin can easily pull you overboard in a fraction of a second if you're not careful. That's why I want you to start with fish under four hundred pounds first, and I'll handle anything bigger than that until I feel confident you're ready."

Soda paused for a moment, reflecting on a harrowing experience from his past, then continued in a more somber tone, "I was fishin' a tournament on the east coast many years ago, and a young wireman on another boat got snatched overboard by a marlin. The fish caught him off guard, and the leader line was cinched around his hand so tight that he couldn't let go. The crew on the boat said the fish pulled him under about 30 feet before it stopped, and they could see him down there strugglin' to get free. One of the crew members dove in to try to save him, but the line broke before he could reach him. The fish took off with the young man still attached to the leader, and they uh, they never recovered his body."

Soda then handed Jason a hook-shaped release knife. "This is called a mate saver knife. Always keep one of these on you. *Alright*?"

"Yeah, definitely," Jason replied.

Soda continued, "Wirin' a marlin is an experience unlike anything else, Jason. For those brief few moments when you're wrapped up on the leader, everything else fades away. There's no reel, no rod, it's just you against the full power of that fish. It's an awesome feelin', and I want you to have fun and enjoy this job, but you just gotta be careful with these fish. Even the smaller marlins can be dangerous. They're more prone to jumpin' in the boat with you and tryin' to stab someone with their bill! The point is, when you're wrapped on that leader, you need to be hyper focused on what that fish is doin' at all times. You gotta be able to anticipate its next move, so you can dump the wrap if you need to or get ready to duck for cover if it starts chargin' at you!"

Jason nodded with an understanding expression. "Thanks, Soda. I'll be careful, and I really appreciate you trusting me to be the wireman."

Soda nodded, lips tight—a silent acknowledgment of the risks Jason faced

A short while later, just before 1:00 PM, the boat reached Destin and approached the owner's new home—a sprawling two-story waterfront mansion in Joe's Bayou. Its white exterior and light brown Spanish tile roof stood out against the bright green, manicured lawn, complemented by an array of palm trees.

At the end of the recently completed dock, there was a young woman wearing a white bikini and black sunglasses sitting in a reclining lounger soaking up rays. As the boat neared the dock, she sat up with a radiant smile and gently pulled her white earbuds out. She stood up and called out to them in a soft southern accent, “Hey-ey!” drawing out the single syllable word into two.

Upon catching sight of her, Jason was thunderstruck. Paralyzed for a moment, he quickly came to his senses and averted his gaze fearing Cricket or Soda might see him.

Cricket waved back to the young woman from the flybridge and Soda affectionately shouted, “What’s happenin’?”

The young woman pulled her hair into a ponytail and slipped on a pair of faded cutoff denim shorts. She called toward the house, “Dad! They’re here!”

After Soda and Jason finished securing the dock lines, the young woman walked over to Jason and said in a friendly outgoing manner, “Hi, I’m Katie!”

With a bit of nervousness, Jason managed to utter, “Hey, I’m Jason,” as his eyes darted around, recalling Soda’s advice to avoid direct eye contact.

“Nice to meet you, Jason!” Katie replied warmly.

Jason tried not to sound too excited and responded curtly, “Yeah, nice to meet you too.”

Katie quickly turned to Soda with a captivating smile. “Soda!” she said, embracing him in a quick hug. “It’s good to see you, buddy! You been doin’ alright?”

Soda replied, “Yeah, doin’ great. We’ve just been busy gettin’ ready for this fishin’ trip and all.”

Katie bounced slightly on her heels. “I’m so excited to go! I can’t wait!”

Cricket climbed down from the flybridge and greeted her with a hug. “Hey Katie! How have you been?” he asked.

"Stressed! Oh my gosh, all I've been doing for the past few weeks is studying for final exams. But I'm finally finished, and so glad to be out of school for the summer!" she responded.

Mr. Gregory had just made his way down the dock to the boat. He was a handsome man—tall, with a lean muscular build and short dark brown hair. He had a stoic personality and spoke slowly with a deep voice, greeting them, "Hey fellas, good to see you."

Cricket replied, "Good to see you, Mr. Gregory! This is our new mate, Jason Baymont. He's gonna be our wireman."

With a curious look, Katie asked, "What does the wireman do?"

Cricket replied, "Well, once you or your dad reel in a fish close enough where he can reach the leader, the wireman fights the fish the rest of the way in by hand. If it's a marlin, he'll bring the fish alongside the boat where Soda can tag it if we plan on releasing it or gaff it if it's big enough to possibly win some money in the tournament."

"Oh," Katie replied with a sense of intrigue.

Mr. Gregory reached out to shake Jason's hand. "Sounds like an important job. Nice to meet you, Jason."

As the two shook hands, Jason matched his expression—firm and steady.

Mr. Gregory then asked Katie, "So, what do you think of the boat?"

Katie beamed with excitement. "Oh my gosh, Dad! I love it! It is so amazing!" She then gave her dad a hug, squeezing him tight. "Thank you for doing this, Dad. We're going to have so much fun!"

Katie and Mr. Gregory spent the afternoon exploring the boat and moving their belongings aboard. Their faces glowed with excitement as they prepared for their five-day trip the next morning, eager to embark on their adventure at sea and create lasting memories together.

THE CALCUTTA

It was the morning before their first tournament. The *Family Tradition* slowly cruised toward the Destin Bridge, navigating the minimum wake zone before heading out the East Pass toward Orange Beach. The tide was coming in, bringing with it the stunning emerald-green waters of the Gulf.

Mr. Gregory sat in the flybridge alongside Cricket. Jason and Soda were in the cockpit, while Katie stood alone at the top of the boat tower, her eyes wide with wonder as she soaked in the vibrant world around her. Everyone on the boat was proudly wearing their new *Family Tradition* T-shirts.

"This is so amazing!" Katie yelled excitedly down to her dad and the crew. She then leaned over the back rail and shouted, "Dad, you need to come up and see the view from up here!"

"I'm good right here. You be careful up there," Mr. Gregory replied in a light but protective tone.

A steady stream of fishing boats was leaving the Destin Harbor to the left as the *Family Tradition* glided under the bridge. Katie raised her arm, waving enthusiastically at them and cheerfully shouting in her characteristically southern accent, "Hey-ey!" A handful of fishermen on the other boats turned to look up, smiles breaking across their faces as they waved back.

Lured by her laughter, Jason looked up and was mesmerized by the warmth of her radiant smile, the sunlight shimmering in her hair. When she glanced back his way, he quickly averted his gaze, hoping she hadn't seen him. A surge of fear rocked him like a small boat caught in stormy seas, fearing she had noticed him admiring her.

Despite the turmoil brewing within him, the Gulf was calm that morning as the *Family Tradition* smoothly glided out of the East Pass. The soft lapping of the waves against the hull created a soothing rhythm, while the warm sun filtered through the gentle breeze. Katie and Mr. Gregory were thrilled to be underway on their new boat for the first time and enjoyed every minute of the trip, skirting the scenic coastline of sugar-white sand beaches. It took roughly two hours to reach the Perdido Pass, and another hour to travel the winding Intracoastal Waterway leading to the Wharf Marina, where the tournament was being held.

The Wharf was situated on a narrow stretch of the Intracoastal Waterway, featuring a marina with over 200 boat slips. A bridge elegantly spanned the waterway, running through the middle of the marina. In the background, an iconic Ferris wheel and several tall condominiums stood prominently. The Wharf offered a variety of dining options, unique boutiques, and specialty stores within walking distance, along with an amphitheater that hosted concerts and events, making it a popular hub for locals and tourists alike.

The marina buzzed with activity as Cricket skillfully backed the Family Tradition into the slip. The engine's low rumble merged with the clamor of forty-seven vessels from Florida, Alabama, Mississippi, Louisiana, and Texas—all eager to compete in the prestigious billfish tournament. A large tent had been erected for competitors to register and place their optional cash award entries in what was known as the Calcutta.

After Jason and Soda secured the boat, Cricket said, “I’m gonna take Mr. Gregory and Katie up to register for the tournament. After we finish up with that, I’m gonna show them around a little bit too, since they’ve never been here before.”

Soda replied, “Alright. Sounds good. Jason and I are gonna start testin’ the drags.”

In the world of high-stakes billfishing, there was no room for error, so the drags on the reels were meticulously checked before each tournament.

As they set up the reels, Jason asked Soda, “So how much does it cost to enter one of these tournaments?”

Soda explained, “Every tournament is a little different, but the registration cost for this one is seven thousand dollars, which is pretty standard. After that, it’s up to Mr. Gregory if he wants to place any side bets in the Calcutta.”

“How does the Calcutta work?” Jason asked.

Soda paused and leaned against the rich mahogany fighting chair, taking a moment to collect his thoughts. “Well, this Calcutta has seven different entry fee levels for both the biggest marlin and the billfish catch-and-release category. The lowest entry fee is five hundred dollars, and the highest is fifteen thousand. Mr. Gregory can pay to compete in any of those seven levels in either category, and he can enter all of ’em if he wants to. There’s also another five entry fee levels for the biggest dolphin, wahoo, and tuna, that ranges from five hundred to ten thousand dollars for each fish. So, basically, he has the option to enter twenty-nine different side bets in the Calcutta.”

Jason furrowed his brow. “Oh, so in the Calcutta, you’re competing against other boats that entered the same entry fee level for one of those five categories?”

“Yep, and there’s first, second, and third place winners for each entry fee level, except for the five-thousand-dollar winner-takes-all options for biggest marlin, and catch and release,” Soda answered.

Jason nodded slowly as he mentally processed the amount of money involved. “What do you think Mr. Gregory will enter in this Calcutta?”

Soda squinted and said, “Well, I don’t know for sure, but Cricket mentioned he talked to him about it earlier this week, and that he planned on entering the five-thousand-dollar entry levels for biggest marlin, catch and release, dolphin, wahoo, and tuna.”

Jason’s eyes widened as he asked, “So, twenty-five grand in the Calcutta, plus another seven in the main tournament?”

“Yep! It ain’t for the faint of heart or for people without deep pockets!” Soda chuckled.

Jason’s stomach tightened like a knot as he contemplated the staggering amount of money on the line and the heavy weight of his own responsibility. Just then, a deep voice boomed, “Well, look what the cat dragged in!” A tall, barrel-chested man strode toward them on the dock, momentarily distracting Jason from his unease.

Soda’s face lit up. “Hey! What’s happenin’, Bear? How’ve you been, man?”

Bear quipped, “I cain’t complain and wouldn’t do no good if I did!”

“Got that right!” Soda chuckled. “Bear, this is Jason Baymont, our new mate.”

"Baymont?" Bear's brow furrowed in curiosity. "You related to Jacob Baymont?"

"Yeah, that's my dad," Jason replied proudly.

A nostalgic glint flickered in Bear's eyes. "I know your dad from way back. He's a damn good fisherman. How's he doin'?"

"He's doing good. Still commercial fishing on the *Vanessa*," Jason responded.

"Well, tell him ole Bear says hello for me," Bear replied, a grin spreading across his face.

Jason gave a firm nod. "I will!"

Bear adjusted the visor on his head. "Well, Soda, I'm 'bout to run up to the tackle store to grab a few things. Y'all need anything?"

"No, I can't think of anything we need right now. I appreciate it though," Soda replied.

"Alright. Just give me a holler if you think of anything." Bear waved as he turned to leave, "I'll see y'all later. Nice to meet you, Jason."

"Yeah, nice to meet you too, Bear," Jason replied warmly.

As Bear walked away, Soda told Jason, "Bear works on a boat here in Orange Beach called *Old Habits*, but he's originally from Destin." With a smile on his face, he added, "There's a lot of good folks in these tournaments. It's like a big ole family reunion every time we compete in one of these things."

Jason nodded, a smile tugging at the corner of his mouth as he watched fishing buddies from across the Gulf Coast warmly greet each other throughout the marina. His nervousness eased, if only slightly, in the shared friendly spirit of the billfish tournament community.

Returning to the task at hand, Soda handed Jason a weight scale with a fishing line attached. “Alright, take this scale up on the dock and give it a good steady pull. We’re gonna set the drags on these eighty-wides at twenty-eight pounds for the strike position, which should make it around thirty-seven to thirty-eight pounds when pushed all the way forward to sunset. Then we’ll go back and make one more mark about halfway to strike at about eighteen pounds of drag, which is where we set it when we’re trollin’.”

Jason gripped the scale tightly and gave a steady pull on the line, causing the drag to give way with a “ZZZzzzzzzz...” sound.

“Alright, what’s the scale read?” Soda asked.

Jason glanced at the scale. “Right at twenty-four pounds.”

Soda made a quick adjustment and said, “Okay, try again.”

Jason pulled again, and the drag snapped free with a crisp “ZZZzzzzzzz...” He glanced at the scale and said, “Twenty-eight pounds. Right on the money.”

Soda grinned. “Good deal!”

There was a piece of blue tape on the right side of the reel where Soda wrote the resistance weight for the drag lever positioned halfway to strike, strike, and sunset.

After Soda and Jason finished setting the drag on all the reels, they were chatting in the cockpit when Soda spotted a sportfish named *Blues Man* from Mississippi cruising by. He cupped his hands around his mouth and shouted, “Skip!”

Skip looked their way, and cheerfully shouted back, “Hey, Soda! Good to see you, man! I’ll come over after we get things squared away!”

“Sounds good! I’ll see you in a lil bit!” Soda replied.

Soda turned to Jason and told him, "Man, I ain't seen Skip in almost a year, but he's just one of those guys where it don't matter how long it's been since we've seen each other—we just pick up right where we left off without missin' a beat."

Appreciating the depth of friendship, Jason sincerely replied, "I look forward to meeting him."

Jason and Soda then saw Cricket making his way back to the boat alone. He had a wide grin on his face and was shaking his head in amusement.

Soda curiously asked him, "What's going on?"

"Boss man just dropped fifty-five grand in the Calcutta! He went across the board at five thousand dollars and below on the biggest blue marlin, catch and release, dolphin, wahoo, and tuna!" Cricket told them.

Jason and Soda looked shocked by the amount of money Mr. Gregory had bet in the tournament.

"Yeah, he said he wanted to make it a little more—interesting," Cricket added with a grin.

Jason's eyes widened, and Soda let out a nervous laugh. "Well, that'll definitely make it a little more interesting."

"Time to catch some big fish and make some big money, fellas!" Cricket exclaimed.

"Yep," Soda said as Jason gently nodded, their eyes reflecting a mix of excitement and nervousness.

Cricket told them, "Mr. Gregory and Katie are gonna do some shopping and then go out to dinner. I'm gonna go meet up with my buddy Mick, but I'll be back in a little bit."

"Alright. Sounds good. We'll see you later," Soda replied.

A short while later, Soda's friend Skip strolled down the dock toward the *Family Tradition*, a bottle of wine in hand. He called out cheerfully, "What's goin' on, Soda!"

"Hey, Skip!" Soda said, eyeing the bottle curiously. "Whatcha got there?"

Skip grinned as he handed the bottle to Soda. "Brought you some homemade muscadine wine!"

Soda accepted the bottle, which was clear and contained a light golden liquid. He held it up to the light, inspecting it with great interest. "Awesome! Can't wait to try it out!" he exclaimed, giving Skip a hearty handshake before pulling him in for a quick hug. "Good to see ya, man!" He stepped back and added, "Skip, I wanna introduce you to our new mate, Jason Baymont."

"Nice to meet you, Jason," Skip said, extending his hand.

"Yeah, nice to meet you too," Jason replied, shaking his hand firmly.

"Where are y'all docked?" Soda asked, looking past him toward the boats.

"Oh, they got us situated all the way down there at the end, next to that boat, the *Trust Me*. And I'm gonna tell y'all this right now, I trust them about as far as I can throw 'em. They ain't friendly with nobody in here, and all they do is talk trash about anyone who beats 'em out of the tournament money. There's a bad vibe on that boat, and I don't even like bein' docked next to 'em."

Jason chimed in, "Yeah, I met the owner, and trust me, he's a prick!"

Soda chuckled. "Jason and I had a little run-in with the owner the other day in Sandestin. I thought I was gonna have to step in to keep Jason from givin' him an old-school attitude adjustment."

Skip burst out laughing. "I'd a paid good money to watch that with a bag of buttered popcorn! He needs a good old-fashioned whoopin', no doubt!"

"Probably so," Soda replied. "But you know we gotta keep it professional and all since we represent the owner and his boat. I've been in this sport a long time and have always found the best thing to do is just ignore guys like that. I've seen plenty of em' come and go over the years, and the ones that are in it just for the money usually don't last more than a season or two."

Skip replied, "Yep, that's right. If they ain't got a passion for billfishin', they ain't gonna make it long in this sport."

Cricket eventually returned to the boat, and the four men talked and laughed for hours, sharing stories about the ones that got away—some fish, others women. When it was time for Skip to leave, they exchanged heartfelt goodbyes, wishing each other good luck in the tournament.

After Mr. Gregory and Katie returned from dinner, everyone turned in early to get plenty of rest. Jason had felt the pre-tournament jitters earlier in the day—understandable for his first big event—but the news of Mr. Gregory's hefty bets in the Calcutta ratcheted up the pressure. He tossed and turned in his bunk that night, the weight of expectations heavy on his mind, at times feeling nauseous from the anxiety.

The next morning, the boats cast off from the marina, embarking on an hour-long journey through the intracoastal waterway and out the pass for the 12:00 PM tournament start. The Gulf was smooth as glass, shimmering under the bright midday sun. The sight of the boats lined up outside of the Perdido Pass was nothing short of spectacular. Suddenly, a shotgun blast pierced the air, signaling the start of the tournament. With a thunderous roar, the engines came to life, and the boats surged forward, slicing through the water with fierce determination as they raced toward their chosen fishing destinations. Saltwater sprayed high into the air as they sped ahead, their wakes fanning out, leaving frothy trails behind them. As Jason watched the sight of land fade, his pre-tournament jitters began to subside. He was in his element now. He knew the sea, he knew fishing, and he was eager to take on whatever challenges lay ahead.

As the *Family Tradition* made its way to the fishing grounds, Katie and her dad settled into the flybridge with Cricket, enjoying the scenic ocean view. Suddenly, Katie called out excitedly, “Look! Dolphins!”

Five dolphins appeared, racing alongside the boat, darting from one side to the other and leaping into the air.

Peering over the side of the flybridge, Mr. Gregory exclaimed, “Wow! They’re a lot bigger than I thought!” Together, they watched with delight as the dolphins leaped in the water beside the boat, their sleek gray bodies arching gracefully above the surface as they jumped, glinting in the sunlight.

Katie quickly grabbed her phone, eager to snap a few photos of the dolphins as they raced alongside the boat. Her voice brimmed with excitement as she asked, “Hey, isn’t it a sign of good luck when they swim alongside your boat like this?”

Cricket gave a sarcastic laugh. “Not really.”

Jason shook his head, with a sense of annoyance about the dolphins.

Soda told her, “Nope, they usually just steal our bait and scare everything else away!”

Unfazed by their lack of faith in maritime lore and their lack of appreciation for the magnificent creatures escorting them on their way, Katie cheerfully replied, “Well, I think they are a sign of good luck for us on this trip!”

Soda shrugged his shoulders and replied, "Maybe!" with a smile and a wink.

The dolphins eventually went their own way, leaping from the air a few more times as if to say farewell and good luck.

A short while later, a shimmer caught Katie's eye. "Look!" she shouted, pointing toward the water.

A grin spread across Mr. Gregory's face as he watched dozens of flying fish break the surface, gliding effortlessly through the air like silver arrows. His eyes widened in wonder as he took in the sight before him. "That's incredible," he said softly, his voice barely rising above the gentle hum of the boat's engine.

Katie's joy bubbled over. "That's so cool!" Her enthusiasm radiated through the crew, who had witnessed flying fish countless times before but felt their excitement renewed in the presence of Katie and her dad. Each leap of the flying fish seemed to draw them closer together, creating yet another shared moment of marvel. Smiles spread across their faces as they reveled in the ocean's breathtaking beauty.

The *Family Tradition* eventually arrived at a promising tideline at an area known as "The Spur." Cricket eased the boat to a stop, the engine's hum fading into the gentle lapping of waves against the hull. Katie and her dad exchanged knowing smiles, realizing that they had arrived at their first fishing spot.

The tideline stretched across the ocean expanse and served as a striking marker of life in the open water. A dense gathering of yellow-green sargassum, a type of seagrass, formed a narrow band, signaling the convergence of two bodies of water. On one side of the weed line, radiant cobalt blue water teemed with microscopic life that sparkled in the light, while on the other side, the water appeared dingy and was referred to as green water. Beneath the surface, the vegetation cast patches of shade that attracted smaller fish darting in and out, seeking refuge from the threat of larger fish. This dynamic interplay highlighted the predator-prey dance unfolding in the depths below and hinted at the potential presence of larger gamefish nearby.

Cricket steered the boat alongside the weed line at about 7 knots, roughly 8 miles per hour, carefully monitoring the omni-sonar for large fish. As the crew deployed teasers and lures in their hunt for big game, a few small flying fish, startled by something, leaped from the water, skimming the surface before disappearing into the depths.

Cricket called out, “There’s a school of chicken dolphins up ahead!”

Katie curiously asked Cricket, “What are chicken dolphins?”

Cricket explained, “That’s what we call young mahi. When they grow bigger, we call them bull dolphins. These little ones are fun to catch on light tackle and really good to eat, but we’ll need to catch one about ten times their size to have a chance at winning any money in the tournament.”

Katie gazed in amazement at the lively school of 20 to 30 young mahi-mahi, each weighing 2 to 3 pounds, darting around the weed line. Their bodies displayed a vibrant blend of electric blue and bright green on the dorsal side, fading into golden yellow. With long, flowing dorsal fins and deeply forked tails, they glided gracefully through the ocean, creating a stunning sight with their brilliant display of colors.

Soda cheerfully chimed in, “Seeing flying fish and chicken dolphins along a weed line like this is usually a good sign! Who knows, maybe we'll have some luck right off the bat this afternoon!"

As they trolled the weed line, however, luck was not on their side. Countless small pieces of sargassum had drifted away from the tideline, forcing Jason and Soda to constantly bring in the lines to clear it from the teasers and lures—a process they called "shagging grass." Sensing their frustration, Cricket reassured them, "The wind should shift later tonight, which will help push the grass together and clear things up for us by tomorrow."

Throughout the day, the team continued to troll along the weed line, hoping to find and battle a fish, but instead only battled the sargassum. While it had been an amazing first day for Katie and Mr. Gregory, the pressure to find fish was mounting for the crew. As evening approached, Cricket decided to move to another spot nearby known as "The Steps."

The next morning, the team began working the same weed line that extended all the way from The Spur to The Steps. The wind and current had worked together overnight to consolidate the grass into a more compact weed line and churn up a frothy white foam, which was often a telltale sign of productive fishing. Mr. Gregory was up early with the crew, drinking coffee, while Katie slept in a little later, taking her time to get ready for the day ahead.

When Katie emerged from the salon, her makeup perfectly applied and her hair pulled back in a sleek ponytail, she greeted Jason and Soda with a cheerful, "Good morning!"

Jason and Soda cheerfully responded in unison, "Mornin'!"

Jason's heart raced at the sight of her. He quickly shifted his focus back to the trolling spread, hoping to steady his nerves.

After climbing up to the flybridge and exchanging greetings with her dad and Cricket, Katie put on a pair of white earbuds and settled onto the bench seat, soaking in the beauty of the sea.

It was nearly 10:00 AM when Katie took her earbuds out and appeared somewhat restless.

Cricket asked, "So, what do you think so far, Katie?"

She replied, "It's really amazing being out here." Hesitantly, she added, "I thought the fishing part would be a little more exciting, though."

Cricket chuckled, "Yeah, it can seem a little boring sometimes until we get a fish on the line, but that's why they call it fishin', not catchin'!"

Katie smiled and playfully replied, "I'm ready to do some catchin'!"

Cricket laughed and said, "Alright, let's check the lunar calendar to see when the best fishing times are today." He pulled out his phone and quickly scanned the information. "Looks like the major feeding time is from 10:30 to 12:30 AM, and the minor feeding time is around 5:30 to 7:30 PM."

He turned to the cockpit and called out with a grin, "Soda! Katie's ready to catch a fish. Do some of your Soda stuff!"

Soda shrugged, unsure of what to do. He walked over to the reel for the left short rigger lure and made a few cranks, bringing the lure closer to the boat. As he reeled, the lure skipped across the surface, causing several splashes. Soda turned back toward Cricket and shrugged again, uncertain of what else to try.

Suddenly, the right long rigger line snapped free from the outrigger clip, and the reel's drag started screaming in a high pitch "ZZZzzzzzzz..."

Jason yelled out, "Fish on! Fish on!" He then looked at Soda and excitedly asked, "What did you do?"

Soda shrugged his shoulders, bewildered by the timing of the bite.

Cricket shouted from the flybridge, "Yes! That's what I'm talkin' about!" Turning to Katie with a smile, he told her, "This one's all yours, Katie!"

Jason, Soda, and Cricket turned on their respective electric reels to bring in the teasers as Katie climbed down into the cockpit and settled into the fighting chair. A bucket seat harness rested atop the chair, ready for her to connect to the bulky reel that would be too large to manage otherwise. Her eyes sparkled with a mix of excitement and uncertainty.

In the Gulf, billfish tournaments require participants to compete by International Game Fish Association (IGFA) rules, with one exception: the rod may be transferred (handed off) one time within the first minute of the fight. Jason carefully moved the eighty-wide from the rod holder on the right rigger side of the boat to the one in front of her as the line continued to rip out at a frantic pace. With swift motions and her heart racing, she clipped herself onto the reel, feeling the harness stabilize her as she prepared for the impending fight. Just as Soda had taught her, she placed her left hand on top of the eighty-wide reel to guide the line onto the spool, its golden metallic surface gleaming in the sunlight. With a firm grip using her right hand on the reel handle, she braced herself for the fight ahead.

Jason and Soda worked frantically to reel in the other lure lines, clearing them out of the way. Seeing that Katie was ready and the other lines were clear, Cricket shifted the boat into reverse using a technique known as backing down, which helped the angler gain line.

Suddenly, the drag fell silent as the boat reversed, and in an instant, the fish leaped into the air.

"It's a bull dolphin!" Jason yelled, his voice filled with excitement. The fish had a tall, blunt head and striking iridescent green, blue, and yellow colors that flashed brilliantly in the sunlight.

"Whoa!" Katie and Mr. Gregory exclaimed in unison, their eyes wide with awe.

"Reel, Katie! Reel!" Soda urged her.

Katie wound the line as fast as she could, keeping it tight as the fish leaped into the air. Its body twisted, revealing vibrant hues that shimmered in the sunlight. It landed with a splash, sending a cascade of water spraying around before launching into the air again and again, performing a series of dazzling acrobatics.

As the battle continued, Soda sprang into action, grabbing a straight gaff hanging from the tower. It was much smaller than the massive flying gaffs nearby, but was the right tool for the job. He positioned himself, ready to assist Jason in the final moments of the fight.

After ten adrenaline-filled minutes, the fish began to tire, allowing Katie to bring it close enough for Jason to reach the leader. Wearing his brand-new wireman gloves, he grasped the line firmly. Estimating the fish at around thirty pounds, he practiced his wiring technique, wrapping the line and pulling it in as if it were a giant marlin.

As the fish came alongside the boat, anticipation filled the air. Soda lunged forward with the gaff, expertly piercing the fish's flesh. With a swift motion, he pulled it over the side of the boat, and the crew erupted in cheers as it flopped on the deck.

"Way to go, Katie!" Jason shouted, offering her a high five, followed by everyone else. Their faces lit up with excitement, the thrill of the successful catch bonding them in shared exhilaration as they admired the stunning bull dolphin.

After the crew put the fish away on ice below deck, Cricket excitedly said, "Alright, let's get those lines back out! We've got more fish to catch!"

An hour later, still riding the high from their mahi catch, a dozen flying fish broke the surface of the water near the weed line, frantically trying to escape some unseen danger beneath.

Suddenly, the left short rigger snapped loose from the outrigger clip, and the reel's drag whined sharply, "ZZZzzzzzzzz..." as the fish tore away.

"Fish on!" Soda called out.

Katie leaped from the mezzanine bench where she had been sitting patiently and looked up at her dad in the flybridge. "Go ahead, sweetie, you got this one!" he said.

She quickly sat in the fighting chair, and Soda moved the reel into position. She snapped in and was ready to begin.

Cricket put the boat in reverse, but this time the drag continued its steady, high-pitched "zzzzzzzzzzz..."

"Whew! That fish is smokin' that reel!" Jason remarked, glancing at Soda as they continued to reel in the other lures.

Soda nodded, eager to see what was on the line.

The reel eventually stopped, but the fish stayed submerged, not wanting to reveal itself.

As the boat continued to back down on the fish, Katie reeled in as fast as she could. The battle was fairly uneventful until the fish was about 30 yards from the boat.

"I can see it! It's a big wahoo!" Jason shouted.

Suddenly, the fish made a powerful run, pulling out another 60 yards of line while staying just below the surface. After a few more intense minutes of struggle, Katie was able to bring it close enough to the boat for Jason to reach the leader.

Jason grabbed the leader line and excitedly told the others, "It looks like it's at least 50 pounds!" He then wrapped the leader line around his leather gloves and began pulling the fish toward the boat, feeling the intense pressure in his arms as the fish fought back.

Knowing that wahoo have razor-sharp teeth, Cricket hurried down from the flybridge to open the hatch to the fish box, ensuring Soda could quickly secure the catch below deck, safely away from everyone. With a precise jab, Soda gaffed the wahoo just behind its head. The long, slender body of the wahoo shimmered in vibrant blue and silver as it was hoisted over the side and into the fish box. The fish thrashed wildly, creating a rhythmic thumping sound that resonated throughout the floor of the cockpit.

After an intense 15-minute battle, the crew erupted in cheers, high-fiving and congratulating Katie on her impressive catch.

She humbly replied, "Well, I couldn't have done it without y'all! This was definitely a team effort!"

Mr. Gregory nodded proudly and declared, "Team *Family Tradition*!"

"Absolutely! Great work, everybody!" Cricket said enthusiastically. "Now let's get those lures back out and catch some more big fish!"

The *Family Tradition* continued trolling along the weed line for several hours without a single bite. Just before 6:00 PM, Cricket shouted from the flybridge, "I'm marking some big fish straight ahead!"—a common phrase used to indicate a fish sighting on the sonar.

Several hundred yards away on the port side, a school of massive yellowfin tuna, each weighing over a hundred and fifty pounds, erupted from the water, chasing bait. Some of them launched completely out of the water, their bodies resembling oversized footballs—blue on top, silver below, with a yellow stripe down the middle, and bright yellow sickle-shaped fins extending dramatically toward their tails.

Jason's heart raced as he exchanged hopeful glances with Katie and Soda, who were standing in the cockpit with him.

After a brief moment, Cricket called out, "I'm losin' 'em!" With frustration creeping into his voice, he continued, "They're moving too fast to keep on the screen."

The fish vanished as quickly as they had appeared. After several tense minutes passed, a sinking feeling began to settle over everyone, believing they had missed their chance to catch a tuna. Then, suddenly, the center rigger line snapped free, and the drag on the eighty-wide reel began to sing once again "ZZZzzzzzzzz..."

Cricket looked at Mr. Gregory and said, "I think you should take this one, boss."

Mr. Gregory quickly climbed down the ladder to the cockpit and readied himself in the fighting chair. Meanwhile, line continued to peel from the eighty-wide at a blistering pace as Jason carefully moved it from the rod holder behind the chair—referred to as a rocket launcher—to the holder in front of Mr. Gregory. Once it was in position, Mr. Gregory snapped his seat harness to the reel, and the fight was on.

With the teasers and other lures cleared away, Cricket backed down aggressively on the fish, sending water splashing over the transom coverboards. The tuna had already pulled out over 300 yards of line when the drag suddenly went silent.

Soda shouted, "Reel! Reel! Reel!"

Mr. Gregory began fiercely cranking the reel handle, quickly regaining line with the boat in hot pursuit. Suddenly, the fish made another blistering run, pulling line faster than the boat could keep up.

The battle wore on for the next fifteen minutes, with Mr. Gregory gaining and then losing line in a relentless back-and-forth. Eventually, the tuna dove deep, prompting Cricket to position the boat directly above it. This maneuver allowed Mr. Gregory to fully leverage the fighting chair to his advantage.

The drag on the reel was still set at 18 pounds, so Soda told Mr. Gregory, "Go ahead and push the drag to the strike position," which increased it to 28 pounds.

Mr. Gregory pushed the lever on the right side of the reel to the position labeled "Strike," noting a small button that prevented the lever from moving past this position unless it was pressed inward.

"Alright, just like we talked about, I want you to lean forward and wind yourself up. Then, use your body weight to pump the rod as you bring it back down."

Following Soda's instructions, Mr. Gregory leaned forward in his seat and cranked the reel handle, regaining line. He then leaned back, using his body weight to apply pressure to the rod. The tremendous force on the line was audible, creating a rhythmic, high-pitched sound—Tink, Tink, Tink—as the fish resisted. Eventually, the fish yielded to the pressure, allowing Mr. Gregory to lift it a few feet. This process continued for another twenty minutes before the fish began to show signs of tiring.

Soda and Jason could tell by the action in the rod that the fish was starting to "pinwheel," swimming in wide circles on its side—a hallmark trait of tuna, also known as the death spiral. But despite this, the fish was far from ready to give up.

Soda looked at Mr. Gregory and said, "Okay, when you feel the pressure in the rod start to go down, that means the fish is coming up. I want you to wind yourself up as fast as you can, until you can't wind anymore. Then, use your body weight to pump the rod, just like you've been doing."

Katie cheered him on, "You got this, Dad!"

With a determined nod, Mr. Gregory began to crank the reel handle, winding himself up as he sensed the fish swimming upward in a wide circle, still deep below the boat. This process continued for another twenty minutes, with tension building each moment. Suddenly, Jason called out, "I can see it! Wow! That thing is massive!"

Despite the high tension, smiles spread across everyone's faces, knowing the end of their long, hard-fought battle was near and that the fish would soon be in the boat. As the leader line came within reach, Jason reached out and made his first wrap. The power of the massive yellowfin tuna was immense. Jason locked his knees against the side of the boat, bracing himself as the fish pulled, feeling the line cinching tight around the leather glove on his hand.

When the fish began swimming upward again, Jason quickly made a few more wraps of the line, alternating hands as he pulled it closer. As the fish swam back down into the depths, he braced himself once more, holding his arms slightly inward in case he needed to let go. This continued until he finally brought the fish up to the boat, where Soda was waiting with the gaff.

Initially, Soda reached for the flying gaff but then opted for the straight gaff, believing the fish to be reasonably subdued, and that it would cause less damage to the fish and minimize weight loss for the weigh-in. With a swift motion, Soda jabbed the gaff under the tuna's chin, which jolted it back to life. He struggled to hold the fish steady as it thrashed its tail wildly at the surface of the water.

Meanwhile, Cricket had climbed down from the flybridge and quickly placed a second straight gaff into the fish's head, helping to get it under control. The two men worked together to bring the fish around to the hinged door built into the transom, known as a "tuna door," which Jason had opened for them. They carefully pulled the massive fish onboard, and Jason let out a celebratory, "Yeeaahhh!" High fives were exchanged all around as the crew erupted in cheers.

After packing the fish on ice below deck and tidying up the boat from an epic day of fishing, Jason and Soda began preparing dinner. Jason pulled out a small portable stainless steel marine gas grill to cook steaks for everyone—a celebratory feast for their successful day on the water. Meanwhile, Soda prepared baked potatoes and a fresh salad. When everything was ready to eat, Katie's eyes lit up with excitement. "Wow! This looks incredible!"

Soda gave Jason a playful nudge. "Compliments of Chef Jason."

Mr. Gregory nodded approvingly. "Nice work, Jason. These steaks look great!"

"Thanks! Hope y'all enjoy it," Jason replied, a hint of pride in his voice.

Cricket then told them, "Let's take a moment to bow our heads as I say grace."

Everyone bowed their heads and closed their eyes.

Cricket continued, "Dear Heavenly Father, we thank you for this precious time together and the countless blessings you have bestowed upon us. We humbly ask for your watchful protection as we journey through the waters ahead. Grant us the strength and wisdom to navigate any challenges that may arise. As we prepare to enjoy this meal, we ask that you bless the food we are about to partake, and let it nourish our bodies and strengthen our spirits. Amen."

"Amen," replied everyone as they raised their heads.

"Let's eat!" Cricket added cheerfully.

The galley was alive with laughter that night as they enjoyed dinner together, their hands gesturing animatedly as each one of them recounted the day's fishing adventures. The aroma of the hearty meal filled the air inside the boat, mingling with the sound of clinking utensils and shared excitement.

The next morning, on the final day of the tournament, they continued trolling down the weed line, which had broken up somewhat overnight. Soda and Jason periodically cleared grass from the teasers and lures while watching vigilantly for signs of fish. It wasn't until nearly 1:30 PM that they finally had their first strike. They hadn't spotted the fish visually, nor had it shown up on the side-scanning omni-sonar or the conventional downward-scanning sonar. So, it was a complete surprise when the left long rigger snapped free from the outrigger. Suddenly, line raced off the spool with a thrilling "ZZZzzzzzzz..."

"Fish on!" Soda shouted, excitement ringing in his voice.

Mr. Gregory glanced at Katie and gave her an encouraging nod. "It's all yours."

Katie had just settled into the fighting chair when the drag fell silent. The fish was gone. Soda reeled in the line, inspecting the lure and leader for any signs that might reveal what had caused the mysterious bite. He pointed out a rough patch on the leader above the lure to Jason—a clear indication that a billfish had attacked.

Holding the leader line, Soda called out to Cricket, "It looks like it was a billfish based on the leader, but we never got a look at it, so not sure if it was a blue or a white."

With a hint of frustration in his voice, Cricket replied, "Alright. Well, we're 'O' for one on billfish. Let's get those lines back out."

There was always some tension in the air when a chance to catch a billfish slipped away. It was the captain's responsibility to give them as many "shots" as possible, while the mates had to ensure the fish was hooked and stayed on until it could be counted as a successful catch.

Soda, still holding the leader line, pondered what, if anything, he could have done differently to keep the fish on the line, a frown creasing his brow.

They continued to work the area, searching for fish, but eventually had to head back to The Wharf for the weigh-in. The tournament rules mandated that boats clear the Perdido Bridge by 6:00 PM, making time management critical—

especially since they were holding three fish that could potentially bring in significant cash winnings.

The *Family Tradition* arrived back at the dock around 5:00 PM, greeted by a large crowd gathered near the weigh-in area. A white tower with a digital scale stood proudly at the center, flanked by massive stainless steel marlin statues, creating an impressive stage. Behind the weigh-in area, a sprawling condominium with an elegantly arched breezeway provided a striking visual backdrop. Guests leaned over their balconies, captivated by the unfolding drama of the tournament below. One by one, the fishing teams were called to the stage, each moment heightening the anticipation in the air.

When it was time for the *Family Tradition* team to weigh their fish, the announcer's voice boomed through the crowd. "Alright folks, next up we have Team *Family Tradition* from Destin, Florida, who will be weighing in a dolphin, wahoo, and tuna!"

Jason carefully maneuvered a wheelbarrow holding their fish to the weigh-in area, followed by the rest of the team.

As the weighmaster began hoisting the dolphin using a rope attached to a pulley system, the announcer told the crowd, "The lovely Ms. Katie Gregory here was the angler who caught this bull dolphin. This is Katie and her Dad's first time fishing in a billfish tournament and it looks like they are starting off strong with their new *Family Tradition*!"

The crowd looked on with great interest as the digital scale bounced up and down before finally settling at 32.4-pounds.

"Alright folks! Thirty-two point four pounds, which puts team *Family Tradition* in third place for dolphin," the announcer exclaimed.

The crowd erupted in cheers as the *Family Tradition* was added to the leaderboard, securing third place for their dolphin catch.

After the dolphin was lowered, the wahoo was hoisted up next, its long, sleek blue and silver body dangling from the scale. Speaking to the crowd, the announcer said, "Ms. Katie Gregory was also the lucky angler who caught this wahoo." After a brief pause for the scale to settle, he continued, "Wow! Look at that, folks! Fifty-two pounds even, which puts the *Family Tradition* team in second place for wahoo!"

Cheers and applause filled the air once more, celebrating the team's impressive catch.

The announcer continued, "What an incredible night so far for Team *Family Tradition*! They have one more fish to weigh in this evening, a very large yellowfin tuna that looks like a carbon copy of the one brought in by team *Cajun Baby* from Louisiana. The owner of the *Family Tradition*, Mr. J.P. Gregory, was the angler who caught this fish, which will need to weigh more than one hundred and seventy pounds to beat team *Cajun Baby* to win first place tuna. I'm tellin' you folks, this is going to be real nail-biter."

As the weighmaster hoisted the giant yellowfin tuna up on the scale, the announcer quietly joked to the crowd, "Wow, you could hear a pin drop in here right now y'all are being so quiet."

A ripple of quiet laughter broke through the crowd with everyone transfixed on the scale's digital display.

Speaking in a soft voice the announcer continued, "This is the type of drama we live for in tournament fishing, folks. Who will come out on top, Team *Family Tradition* or Team *Cajun Baby*?"

The scale finally settled, and the announcer excitedly shouted, "One hundred and seventy-one point four pounds and Team *Family Tradition* comes out on top for first place tuna! Wow! Talk about beginner's luck, folks! I can't remember the last time I saw a boat with three meat fish at the top of the leaderboard. What an amazing trip for Team *Family Tradition*! Let's give them a big round of applause!"

The crowd erupted with exuberant cheers and applause, their excitement echoing through the evening air.

The *Family Tradition* team posed for photos, beaming with joy as they showcased their first-place tuna hanging triumphantly from the white tower, flanked by massive stainless steel marlin statues. Although the tournament checks wouldn't be handed out until the awards ceremony the following morning, their total winnings in the Calcutta exceeded $120,000.

After capturing the moment, the fish were carefully loaded back into the wheelbarrow. With a wide grin, Jason began maneuvering the cart through the sea of spectators, making his way back to the boat with Soda and Katie behind him. Meanwhile, Mr. Gregory and Cricket remained behind, immersed in conversation with Team *Cajun Baby*, exchanging sincere congratulations, and sharing colorful tales of their epic battles on the water.

As Jason, Soda, and Katie made their way toward their boat, a familiar voice cut through the air.

"Katie! Katie Gregory!" the man shouted, working his way through the crowd to reach them.

She turned around, her face lighting up with a smile. "Hey, Billy!" Stepping forward with her arms open, she wrapped Bill Murphy in a quick hug. He was wearing short shorts again, this time blue, paired with a snug bright yellow polo shirt and oversized gold luxury watch.

Jason and Soda exchanged confused faces, trying to conceal their concern.

Bill Murphy exclaimed, "Wow! I can't believe you're actually here!" Puzzled, he asked, "When did you and your dad get a boat?" With an even more exaggerated puzzled expression, he added, "When did you start marlin fishing?"

"Oh, we just got it! And this is our very first fishing trip together," Katie said with a captivating smile. She then turned to Jason and Soda and asked, "Do y'all know Billy?"

Jason forced a casual smile. "I think we met briefly," he replied, being careful to keep his tone light.

Bill Murphy glanced at Jason and Soda as if he were looking past them, then replied with a hint of distraction, "Hmm, can't say I remember." His gaze drifted back to Katie, a warm smile breaking through. "Wow, Katie, it's really good to see you. You look absolutely stunning."

"Thanks, Billy," she replied, her voice softening with a touch of shyness. "So did y'all have a good trip?"

"Yeah, we caught and released six marlins, so I think we've got a pretty good chance at winning first place in that category. How many marlins did y'all catch?" he asked.

"We didn't catch any marlins, but we had an amazing trip! I caught my first mahi and wahoo, and my dad caught this huge tuna!" She stepped aside to show him their catch, while Jason and Soda beamed with pride.

Bill glanced at the fish, then back at Jason and Soda. A smirk crept onto his face as he taunted, "Hey fellas, y'all do realize this is a billfish tournament, right?" He then laughed in a teasing manner.

Katie smiled, rolling her eyes at the wisecrack.

Jason and Soda were clearly caught off guard by Bill's jab, which shattered their sense of accomplishment after their amazing string of victories in the meat fish categories. Jason turned red with embarrassment, while Soda forced an uncomfortable smile.

Bill Murphy quickly shifted his attention back to Katie. "Seriously, if you want to catch a blue marlin, you're welcome to join me on my boat anytime. It's a ninety-footer, so there's plenty of room. We usually catch two or three of them each trip, so you would definitely get a chance to hook up." He looked deeply into her eyes, a playful smile tugging on his lips, as if he were inviting her to share more than just the thrill of marlin fishing.

Soda, sensing the rising tension in Jason, casually slid an arm around the top of his shoulder, a subtle reminder to keep his cool.

Katie then playfully responded, "Well, that is very kind of you, Billy. But I'm gonna be giving you a run for your money on my boat!"

"Alright, alright. Game on!" Bill Murphy teased, his eyes sparkling with the challenge.

A man wearing a bright yellow *Trust Me* crew shirt approached Bill Murphy and said, "Mr. Murphy, they're about to call us on stage."

"Okay," Bill Murphy said, his voice tinged with frustration as he braced himself to leave.

"I'll come cheer you on!" Katie said, her bright smile lighting up the moment.

"Really?" Bill asked, stunned. He then smiled and added, "Okay, yeah! That would be great!"

Turning back to Soda and Jason, Katie said, "I'll catch up with y'all later!"

Soda forced a smile and said, "Okay, we'll see you later." Jason clenched his jaw as he and Soda waved goodbye, both trying to hide their concern.

THE GAMBLE

Just a few days after their remarkable first billfish tournament, the *Family Tradition* had returned to Destin and was docked at Mr. Gregory's home. It was a beautiful, sunny day just before noon, and Jason, Soda, and Cricket were standing in the cockpit talking.

"Listen, J-Bay. There's gonna be a lot of attractive girls your age on the boat today, so just remember to keep it professional, alright?" Cricket grinned, though his tone was serious.

Jason gave him a nod, fully understanding Cricket's expectations and ready to take on the day.

Katie had invited six school friends for the week, and they were eagerly getting ready to head out on the boat. Laughter spilled from the house as the girls made their way toward the dock, their carefree chatter blending with the sounds of boats and jet skis zipping by.

The smell of sunscreen filled the air as they climbed aboard, and Katie introduced her friends to the crew. The girls were excited to be going to Crab Island for the first time—a shallow submerged sandbar in Choctawhatchee Bay, just north of the Destin Bridge. Each day in the summer, hundreds of boats gathered at Crab Island, creating a massive party on the water.

It was nearly 1:00 PM when they were ready to cast off for the short ride over to Crab Island. By the time they arrived, several hundred boats were already anchored there, with people wading in the beautiful, waist-deep emerald water. Small boats weaved through the maze of vessels, selling everything from boiled peanuts and popsicles to pineapple drinks and Crab Island-branded T-shirts. The air was filled with music, each boat trying to outdo the others.

The *Family Tradition* had a draft slightly over five feet, so Cricket was careful not to take the boat into shallow water. He anchored it on the edge of the sandbar alongside several large sportfish boats. Meanwhile, Jason and Soda unfurled a large floating mat for the girls, securing it to the back of the boat and opening the tuna door for them to get in and out of the water.

As they settled in, Katie connected her phone to the boat's speakers and began playing music to which the girls danced and sang along. Their laughter and carefree joy were contagious, causing the crew to exchange quick, amused glances.

One of the girls, named Evie, shouted, "It's five o'clock somewhere, y'all!" as she cracked open a beer. The other girls laughed and quickly joined in, the crisp sound of cans popping open echoed in the air.

Another girl, named Anna, approached Jason with curiosity. "So, have you lived in Destin your whole life?"

"Yeah, that's actually my parents' house right over there where I grew up," Jason replied, pointing to his childhood home on the shoreline.

"Really!" the girls exclaimed, their voices in unison as they leaned in to get a better look. Katie added, "I didn't know that's where your parents live!"

Katie gazed out at the scenic shoreline. With a touch of envy in her voice, she replied, "It must have been so much fun growing up here. I bet you fished all the time, didn't you?"

Jason nodded, a nostalgic grin tugging at the corners of his mouth. "Yeah, even when I was just a little kid, I'd be out there catching small baitfish for my dad. I always wanted to be a fisherman just like him."

Suddenly, Katie's eyes lit up. "Oh! By the way, my dad grilled us some of that tuna he caught, and it was so good! Seriously, it was the best fish I've ever had!"

The other girls chimed in, their faces lighting up with excitement. "Oh my gosh, that fish was incredible last night!" one exclaimed. "Y'all need to catch some more of those!" another added, nodding eagerly in agreement.

As they continued to rave about the tuna, Jason felt a sense of pride swell within him. A smile crept onto his face as he listened to their lively conversation and laughter. While he enjoyed the moment and their attention, he remained mindful of Cricket's warning to keep things professional, trying to maintain a balance between friendliness and restraint.

Eventually, the girls made their way to the water through the tuna door. Katie and two of her friends perched on top of the floating mat with their drinks, while the others hung on from the sides, their spirited chatter mingling with the flotilla of activity around them.

Suddenly, a horn rang out, catching their attention. It was the *Trust Me* cruising by them on its way to Sandestin, with Bill Murphy standing in the cockpit, waving to Katie.

"Hey-ey!" Katie called out, waving back enthusiastically.

Jason and Soda exchanged quick glances, their eyes conveying a shared sense of annoyance.

Katie's friend Jessica rolled her eyes. "Ugh, Bill Murphy. He's such a creeper!"

Evie chimed in, "Yeah, but he's—loaded!"

As the girls laughed at Evie, Katie quickly defended him, "He's always been really nice to me. I hadn't seen him since we graduated high school, but I ran into him last weekend at the fishing tournament and he was a lot of fun to hang out with."

"Oh my gosh! Do you like him?" Jessica asked, raising an eyebrow.

Katie replied, "No! Not like that! We're just friends!"

Jessica smirked. "Well, he's known for being a player, Katie. I guarantee he wants to be more than just friends with you because he wants to be more than friends with just about every pretty girl."

Evie slyly added, "Sounds like I need to give him my number!"

The girls erupted into laughter, splashing water playfully as Katie shook her head and rolled her eyes. Jason and Soda again shared quick glances, their eyes signaling a sense of relief that Katie was not romantically interested in Bill Murphy.

The girls continued to enjoy their party at Crab Island for the next few hours while Jason, Soda, and Cricket sat in the flybridge discussing plans for the upcoming tournament. When it was time to leave, one of the girls named Taylor called out, “Jason, can you please give me a hand getting up?”

Evie began to laugh, squinting playfully. “I think I might need a hand too!”

Katie, with a friendly smile and a lighthearted tone, chimed in, “I think we all might need a hand, Jason.”

Jason glanced at Cricket and Soda, raising an eyebrow in acknowledgment while keeping a straight face. “Yeah, I’ll be right there,” he called back, his tone steady and purposeful.

Each girl thanked Jason as he helped them climb onto the boat. They laughed and chatted while drying off before disappearing through the salon door. Meanwhile, Jason and Soda pulled in the water mat and prepared to leave.

Back at Mr. Gregory’s house, the girls said their goodbyes and headed inside. Jason and Soda then set to work cleaning up the beer cans and leftover food before washing the boat.

The sun was setting by the time Jason was ready to leave. As he approached his truck parked in the driveway, Katie walked out of the front door and made her way toward him. “Hey, Jason. We’re going to Tripletails in about an hour to have a few drinks. You should come out with us!” She then leaned in slightly and coyly added, “My friends think you’re really hot.”

Jason was shocked, momentarily frozen like a deer in headlights. He slowly replied, “Well, I am definitely flattered, but Cricket told me earlier today to make sure I keep it professional with y’all. And, uh, this is like my dream job, so I really don’t want to do anything that might mess it up.”

Katie nodded understandingly. After a brief pause, she gave him a heart-melting smile and said, "Well, you wouldn't technically be on the job tonight."

"True," Jason replied with a sheepish smile as he thought it over.

Katie handed him her phone and said, "Tell you what, just give me your number, and I'll send you a text when we're getting ready to leave. If you can't make it, not a big deal."

Jason entered his phone number and handed it back to Katie.

"Well, I really hope you come out with us tonight," she said as she walked back to the house, looking back briefly to wave goodbye.

Jason's heart raced as he cranked the engine, his mind swirling with uncertainty.

Back at his townhome, he stepped into the shower, letting the warm water wash away the salt and sun of the day. Afterward, he changed into a crisp T-shirt and shorts, finishing off with a splash of cologne.

Standing on his back deck, he gazed across the moonlit water at Tripletails, an upscale seafood restaurant boasting a lively outdoor bar on the north side of the harbor. As he thought about joining Katie and her friends, a wave of nervous uncertainty washed over him, filling him with anxiety about the evening's possibilities. He felt his phone buzz. It was a text from Katie: "Leaving now."

He took a deep breath and decided to take the chance. Tripletails was always packed, and parking was limited, so he opted to travel by boat. After a short ride in his center console boat, he docked in an open slip and walked down the pier toward the bustling bar area. The crowd was especially large that night, but even with her back turned, Katie stood out to him as if she were the only person there. A smile spread across his face when she turned, her radiant personality shining like a star as she laughed and raised her glass for a toast with her friends. Suddenly, Bill Murphy appeared, joining in the toast.

Jason's heart sank, his smile receded, and his jaw clenched tight. The laughter around him turned into a dull roar as a wave of disappointment surged through him. He turned to leave, his shoulders slumping slightly as he made his way back to the boat.

As he finished untying his boat, he saw Katie walking toward him. "Hey, Jason! Why are you leaving? Everyone is up at the bar. You should come join us!"

Jason replied, "Yeah, I, uh, well, I saw y'all were hanging out with your buddy Bill Murphy, and I'm not really a fan of his, so I think it would be best if I just left to avoid any awkwardness."

Katie looked at him, her expression a mix of confusion and sadness, unsure of what to say.

Jason cranked the boat's engine. With a heavy heart and frustration in his voice, he turned to her and said, "I'm sorry, Katie. I shouldn't have come here tonight." He backed out of the slip, exchanging a brief wave goodbye, a hint of regret in his eyes. The lively chatter and music from the bar faded behind him as he headed home, his boat gliding alone across the calm moonlit waters of the harbor.

The *Family Tradition* crew had a few days off before their next tournament. Jason didn't see Katie again until the morning they were leaving Destin for Biloxi, where the tournament was set to take place.

While Jason, Soda, and Cricket stood in the cockpit, waiting for Katie and Mr. Gregory to arrive, Jason's friend Matt called.

"Hey, Matt," Jason answered cheerfully.

"Happy birthday, J-Bay! Whatcha up to?" Matt said, his voice brimming with enthusiasm.

"I'm just about to leave the dock. We're headed to Biloxi for our next fishing tournament," Jason replied.

"Nice! You gonna hit up the casinos?" Matt asked, a hint of mischief in his tone.

Jason chuckled. "Yeah, we'll probably swing by the casino for a bit tonight. Hopefully, I'll have some birthday luck! Speaking of luck, how did y'all do long lining this week?"

"Dude, we crushed 'em! I've never seen so many big tunas in my life!" Matt exclaimed, excitement radiating from him.

"Really? Where'd y'all go?" Jason asked, clearly intrigued.

"Loyd's Ridge, bruh! Blue water, tons of bait—it was going off!" Matt replied, his enthusiasm infectious.

"Dang! So, blue water and lots of big tuna at Loyd's Ridge, huh?" Jason glanced at Soda and Cricket, who both looked intrigued. He noticed Cricket's brow furrow in thought, weighing the implications for their upcoming tournament.

Just then, Jason spotted Mr. Gregory and Katie approaching the boat. "Hey, Matt, the owners are about to get on, so I gotta run. But I'll give you a shout when I get back."

"Alright! Well, happy birthday, bruh! And good luck in the tournament!" Matt said.

"Thanks, Matt!" Jason replied, ending the call with a wide grin.

As he hung up, Soda turned to Mr. Gregory and Katie, a beaming smile on his face. "It's Jason's twenty-first birthday today, y'all!"

"Oh my gosh! Happy birthday, Jason!" Katie exclaimed.

"Happy birthday, Jason," Mr. Gregory added.

Soda continued, "Now, I'm sure Jason has probably done some underage drinkin', but we'll have to take him out tonight so he can have his first legal drink!"

They all laughed as Jason stood there with a guilty grin on his face.

Mr. Gregory said, "Dinner's on me tonight. Steakhouse sound good?"

"Sounds great!" Jason replied, a smile spreading across his face as he felt a rush of excitement and gratitude at being celebrated on his special day.

The seas were choppy as they made their way out of the East Pass that morning, but the *Family Tradition* cut through the waves with ease. Jason spent most of the three-hour ride to Biloxi chatting and texting friends and family who wished him a happy birthday. Meanwhile, Soda, Katie, and Mr. Gregory sat in the flybridge with Cricket, enjoying the scenery. As they approached the mouth of Biloxi Bay several hours later, Cricket navigated eastward through the dark, tannin-stained waters toward Point Cadet Marina, where the billfish tournament was set to take place. It was the largest marina in Biloxi, with space for 241 boats. Sturdy breakwater structures, strategically placed around its perimeter, provided shelter from the waves, with several gaps allowing boats to enter and exit.

Behind the marina stood the Golden Nugget Biloxi Hotel and Casino. The area was bustling with fishing teams, all eager to test their luck in both the tournament and the casino.

After docking the boat, Cricket, Mr. Gregory, and Katie headed to register for the tournament and place their entries in the Calcutta. Meanwhile, Jason and Soda ensured all the tackle was squared away for the tournament the next day and then wandered along the docks, chatting with fishing buddies.

As the afternoon wore on, they all decided it was time to regroup and prepare for the evening's festivities. They planned to have an early dinner to celebrate Jason's birthday, ensuring they had enough time to visit the casino afterward.

The men had finished getting ready and were waiting in the salon for Katie. Cricket, Soda, and Jason were dressed slightly better than their usual fishing attire, while Mr. Gregory looked distinguished in a fitted black polo and slacks.

When Katie finally emerged from the stairway, she looked stunning in a simple black dress with heels and radiant diamond earrings that sparkled alongside a delicate diamond pendant necklace.

"You look beautiful," Mr. Gregory said to his daughter, pride shining in his eyes. The other men nodded in agreement.

"Thank you! And you gentlemen all look very handsome," Katie replied, her eyes sparkling like the diamonds she wore. She then playfully added, "Well, I don't know about y'all, but I'm ready to eat some steak and get this birthday party started!"

Laughter erupted from the group, and Soda teased, "Alright, birthday boy! Let's do this!" as he playfully put his arm around Jason's shoulder.

The steakhouse was just a short walk from the boat. Inside, the white tablecloths and soft lighting created an elegant ambiance that made Jason feel both excited and a little nervous. He ordered a drink "legally" for the first time and savored a glass of red wine alongside a perfectly prepared ribeye. As they dined, Jason, Soda, and Cricket exchanged tales of their outrageous fishing experiences and thrilling adventures at sea, while Katie and Mr. Gregory sat enthralled, their faces reflecting a mix of disbelief and delight. Jason loved seeing Katie smile and laugh but was careful not to look too long, even with the wine lowering his inhibitions.

When dinner drew to a close, the waiter approached with a beautifully presented dessert—a rich chocolate cheesecake adorned with a single lit candle. Jason's heart swelled as the group sang "Happy Birthday" to him. He focused on the flickering candle, intently contemplating his one wish. With a gentle breath, he extinguished the flame, a wistful expression crossing his face as he watched the smoke curl upward.

After dinner, they made their way to the Golden Nugget Casino, just a short stroll away. A kaleidoscope of colors greeted them as they entered, accompanied by the lively sounds of slot machines—some playing a catchy 8-bit tune reminiscent of 1980s video game after an unsuccessful spin, while others chimed with the sweet sound of victory: "Ding, ding, ding, ding..."

Eager to dive into the fun, they quickly moved to the craps table, enjoying complimentary drinks as they took turns rolling the dice. Each win was met with cheers, and every loss was met with playful teasing, creating a lively atmosphere. Later, at the roulette table, Jason hit a streak of good luck. His bets became bolder, and his stacks of chips grew ever higher. A small crowd of spectators formed around them, captivated by the excitement of Jason's bold bets and the lively interactions among the group. Almost all the numbers on the board were covered with chips, stacked precariously high, as if on the verge of collapse. Tension filled the air as they leaned in, silence falling over the group. Their eyes were wide with anticipation as they watched the wheel spin, waiting to see who would emerge as the big winner.

Suddenly, the ball came to a stop, and disbelief washed over them as it landed on the dreaded green double zero—the only square where they hadn't placed any chips. A collective gasp escaped their lips, and their expressions shifted from anticipation to dismay as the dealer slowly raked in their pile of chips, leaving them slumped in their seats.

Reeling from their loss and struggling to regain the momentum of their previous wins, they decided to try their luck at the poker table. The atmosphere remained lively, filled with laughter and friendly teasing as each player decided when to hold and when to fold, but as the clock ticked on, the initial buzz of excitement began to fade, and hints of fatigue crept in.

Noticing that the others were growing tired, Jason knew it was time to wrap up his birthday outing. Grateful for the wonderful evening spent celebrating with friends, he gently suggested that it was time to call it a night.

Together, they made their way outside, smiling and laughing as they stepped into the warm, humid night air. The bright lights and sounds of the casino gradually faded behind them as they headed back to the boat. It had been an incredible night, but the real adventure awaited them. The gamble they had come for would begin the next day when the tournament kicked off.

Jason, Soda, and Cricket were up early the next morning, sipping coffee in the salon as they discussed their plans for the day ahead.

"So where ya thinkin' about fishin' this trip?" Soda asked Cricket.

Cricket replied, "Well, I'm not sure yet. It sounds like almost everybody's going southwest to fish the rigs in Green Canyon. It's got blue water, and the fishin' reports have been good out that way. But—it's a long way to run, and I heard the sharks have been really bad out there lately."

"Yeah, Skip said they're headed to Green Canyon, and mentioned the same thing about the sharks," Soda responded. He then asked Cricket, "Where's the *Evening Star* headed?"

Cricket replied, "Mick's gonna run southwest to fish the rigs on the Shelf. He said he catches plenty of marlins in green, dirty water and didn't think it was worth it to run all the way out to Green Canyon just to fish blue water."

Soda replied, "Yep, we've caught plenty of 'em in green water too. I just always have more confidence fishin' blue water."

Jason chimed in, "What do you think about running southeast to Loyd's Ridge, where my buddy Matt caught all those big tunas? He said it had blue water, and was going off out there."

Soda turned to Cricket and said, "If there's a bunch of big tuna out there, there's probably some big marlins too."

Cricket sighed. "I mean, it does sound promising, but that's a really long way to run, and there's absolutely nothing else to fish near it. We'd be putting all our eggs in one basket. If the fish aren't still there by the time we get out there, we won't have enough time to go anywhere else on Friday. At least if we ran to Green Canyon, we'd have a lot more options and could fish our way back."

Soda took a sip of coffee, then said, "We've had pretty good luck in the past breakin' away from the pack."

Cricket chuckled. "True." He slowly took a sip of his coffee, his expression turning pensive as he contemplated his decision.

After a moment, he nodded, having made up his mind. He then turned to Jason and Soda and said, "Alright, fellas, I'm gonna roll the dice and give Loyd's Ridge a shot."

Jason and Soda grinned widely, their eyes sparkling with excitement. "Alright!" they exclaimed in unison.

The boats were cleared to leave the dock at 11:00 AM, marking the start of the tournament. When the hour arrived, the *Family Tradition* joined the procession of boats slowly heading toward the Gulf. The humid, salty air brimmed with anticipation as the crew prepared for the journey. However, the waves had intensified since the day before, now averaging 3 to 4 feet and approaching from the southeast—the same direction the boat was heading. Known as a head sea, the boat traveled directly into the oncoming waves, causing them to crash sharply against the bow. Each impact sent shudders rippling through the vessel.

Jason, Soda, Mr. Gregory, and Katie were settled in the salon, bracing themselves for the jarring ride out of Biloxi Bay toward their first fishing destination. They were cheerfully reminiscing about the fun they had together the night before when Jason felt his phone vibrate in his pocket. It was a text from his mom: "Call me when you get a chance." Realizing that he would lose cell phone reception once they ventured farther out to sea, he decided to call her back right then.

"Hey, Mom!" Jason greeted her cheerfully. "We just left Biloxi and are heading out to go fishing. What's going on?"

There was a pause on the line. He could hear the worry creeping into her voice. "I just wanted to let you know that your dad's out of surgery, but... the doctor said he wasn't sure he got all the cancer. He'll need another surgery—something more invasive—and they want to biopsy one of his lymph nodes this time."

Jason's expression turned serious. "So, when are they gonna do the follow-up surgery?"

Her voice began to break slightly, and he could hear her sniffles echoing through the phone. "We don't know for sure yet, but it'll be a few weeks."

He took a deep breath, trying to sound confident. "Listen, I know you're worried, Mom, but he's gonna be fine. This extra surgery is just a precaution to make sure they got it all."

"I know, I know. It's just... I'm scared it spread," she admitted, her voice trembling.

Jason clenched his jaw, determined to stay strong for her despite the pain and worry stirring within him. "He's going to be fine, Mom. Look, I'll be gone for a few days, but I promise I'll call you as soon as I'm back. Okay?"

"Okay. Just please be careful and call me when you can," she urged, her voice filled with concern.

"I will. Love you, Mom, and tell Dad I love him too," he said, trying to inject warmth into his words.

"I love you too," she replied softly.

As he hung up the phone, the lively chatter in the salon was replaced by an uneasy silence. Mr. Gregory, Katie, and Soda were all looking at him with great concern, their expressions a mix of sympathy and curiosity. Taking a deep breath and feeling the full weight of his worries, Jason told them, "The surgery my dad had this morning wasn't successful at removing all of his skin cancer. It was a little deeper than they thought. Now he'll have to go back in for another, more invasive surgery." Struggling to steady his voice while he fought back his tears, he continued, "They also want to biopsy one of his lymph nodes to see if it spread."

Mr. Gregory, Katie, and Soda's faces softened with sympathy upon hearing the news.

Soda reassured him in a steady sympathetic voice, "Your dad is about as tough a man as I've ever met, Jason. He'll get through this."

Jason nodded, trying to keep his composure.

As the boat continued to forge ahead through the rough seas, the weight of Jason's worries caused him to withdraw, isolating him like an island in a stream of turbulent emotions. They fished a few areas closer to shore that afternoon without luck. As night fell, they began the long journey to Loyd's Ridge.

To navigate safely in the dark, Cricket reduced the boat's speed to 14 miles per hour. However, even traveling at this slower speed, the steady jarring impacts of waves hitting the bow forced Katie to leave her room in the v-berth and move to the couch in the salon, where she hoped for a decent night's sleep.

That night, Cricket, Soda, and Jason took turns steering the boat in shifts known as "wheel watch." By the time they arrived at Loyd's Ridge the next morning, the seas had calmed, transforming into gently rolling one to two-foot waves.

Everyone was up early, eager to start the day. As the sun began to rise, the water revealed its stunning cobalt blue color, sparkling with microscopic life, just as they had hoped.

It didn't take long for Cricket to spot a weed line, which he began to follow.

Mr. Gregory and Katie settled in the flybridge with Cricket, while Jason and Soda sat in the cockpit. Jason still seemed distant that morning, lost in thought and clearly still concerned about his dad.

Hoping to take his mind off things, Soda reached into one of the storage coolers and pulled out a piece of belly meat they had saved from the bull dolphin Katie caught the prior tournament. Referred to as mahi belly, it was light green and shaped like a narrow taco, approximately 20 inches long. At the end of the piece cut from the fish's head, two short pelvic fins were still attached, along with the bony plate that sat just behind where the gills would have been.

"Hey, Jason. Remember that mahi belly we saved last week?" Soda said, holding the piece of meat up.

"Yeah," Jason responded, his curiosity piqued.

"Well, I salted it to help firm up the texture, and I wanna show you how to rig it for trollin' behind a teaser."

"Alright," Jason replied with a grin, eager to learn more.

Soda continued, "Now, this is an old-school technique that not many people take the time to do anymore because, frankly, it's just a lot easier to buy a frozen mackerel. But this is somethin' I still like to do, and I've always had good luck with 'em."

Soda continued, "The first thing you do is fold it over and cross-stitch it closed, goin' down one side, then come up the other."

Soda used a heavy-duty bridle needle and thick wax line to stitch the belly together. After finishing, he said, "The next thing you do is close up the head area to keep the meat from washin' out while you're pullin' it." He then began threading the needle under the bony plate on the head end of the belly meat, making several loops before cinching both sides tight.

Jason watched in fascination as Soda stitched the mahi belly closed.

Soda then showed Jason how to secure the meat to a line that ran through the head of a chugger lure, so that the mahi belly trailed just behind it. Once he completed the task, he held out the finished product, saying, "And that's what it looks like when it's all finished."

"Nice!" Jason replied, inspecting it with a mix of intrigue and wonder.

They added the mahi belly rig to the end of the squid chain on the right bridge teaser line. After it was deployed, they watched as the chugger head broke the surface of the water, with nearly two feet of mahi belly behind it, creating the illusion of a small predator chasing the squid.

"That should get their attention!" Soda exclaimed with pride and excitement.

Suddenly, with concern evident in his voice, Cricket shouted, "Big tiger, ten o'clock!" as he pointed toward a looming tiger shark.

Katie and Mr. Gregory rushed to the port side of the flybridge for a better view.

"Whoa!" Katie exclaimed, her voice filled with fascination.

"Wow! That is a big shark," Mr. Gregory added, his eyes wide with a mix of astonishment and fear.

They watched in silence as the massive tiger shark glided effortlessly through the cobalt blue water, moving along the weed line. Its sleek, muscular body boasted distinctive dark vertical stripes that faded into a pale underbelly. The shark exuded an aura of primal strength as one of the ocean's apex predators.

Jason and Soda held their breath as the shark passed the mahi belly that was splashing along the surface of the water. When the shark finally disappeared behind them, Soda let out a sigh of relief. "Whew! Let's just hope the ol' tax man keeps going that way, away from us."

A short while later, Cricket shouted, "I'm marking a big fish up ahead! Y'all get ready! It's about ninety feet deep and looks like it might be a marlin!"

The tension on the boat was palpable as they trolled toward the fish at a painfully slow eight miles per hour. As they finally closed the distance and their trolling spread passed over the fish, Cricket yelled, "It's coming up! It's at seventy feet!"

After a brief pause, he continued, "Twenty-five feet and rising!"

After another brief pause, he continued, "I'm losing him on sonar! Can y'all see him behind the boat?"

Everyone was scanning the surface of the water, when suddenly Cricket shouted, "There he is, behind the right bridge teaser!"

The marlin, raised from the depths, quickly zeroed in on the mahi belly. It looked like a torpedo just beneath the surface as it closed in on the teaser. Its body was a dark navy, while its pectoral and dorsal fins glowed an electric blue—a sign that it was excited and ready to attack. The water erupted as the marlin began slashing its long bill at the mahi belly, trying to stun what it perceived to be its prey.

But Cricket quickly activated the bridge teaser reel, pulling the bait away from the fish, angering it. The marlin swiped at the bait in vain as it skipped across the surface toward the boat. Frustrated, the marlin doubled back, aiming for the right short rigger lure.

As it attacked the lure, the line snapped free from the outrigger clip, audibly cutting through the air and water as it drew tight. The reel's drag began screaming in a high pitch "ZZZzzzzzzz..."

"Fish on!" Jason and Soda yelled in unison.

The fish immediately began leaping into the air, its tail fanning the surface of the water in a move often called tail walking.

"Whoa!" Katie yelled from the flybridge, while Jason, Soda, and Cricket shouted, "Yeah!" in unison.

The fishing line continued to stream into the water behind the boat. However, the fish was already several hundred yards to their port side, which created an immense bow in the line as it cut through the water.

Mr. Gregory settled into the fighting chair, and Jason quickly handed him the reel as the line raced from the spool.

Once Jason and Soda cleared the teasers and other lure lines, Cricket began backing down on the fish, yelling, "Reel! Reel! Reel!" as he tried to help Mr. Gregory regain the line.

The fish changed directions multiple times as the battle continued, leaping into the air and shaking its head in an attempt to dislodge the lure from its mouth. After nearly 30 minutes of fighting and chasing the fish in every possible direction, they had closed the gap to just 50 yards. Suddenly, the fish began porpoising directly away from the boat.

Mr. Gregory continued to reel frantically as the boat backed down in hot pursuit. Water sprayed upward with each impact of the blunt transom against the waves.

"Yeah!" Jason, Soda, and Cricket cheered, while Katie watched in amazement as the fish charged away.

Soda leaned toward Jason and softly said, "I know you've got a lot on your mind. You want me to take this one?"

"Nah, I got it," Jason replied with a confident grin.

Soda responded, "Alright, this one's still pretty green, so be ready to dump it if you need to. It might be a kill fish, so take it easy. We don't want to break it off before we get a chance to measure it."

Jason nodded, understanding what he had to do.

Eventually, he spotted the leader line and felt a surge of adrenaline–this was it. He glanced down at his waist, double-checking that his mate saver knife was secure in his tool belt. His heart raced, and his throat tightened as he extended his arm, ready to grab the leader. In the blink of an eye, the fish zipped to the starboard side, pulling the leader line away from his grasp.

Mr. Gregory managed to crank a few times as Cricket continued backing down on the fish, finally bringing the leader line back within reach. This time, Jason firmly grabbed the leader line, making his first wrap, then a second, before switching to his left arm for two more wraps. The power of the fish was unlike anything Jason had ever experienced. Suddenly, the fish caught him off guard and skyrocketed right in front of the boat.

Jason's eyes widened as he watched the magnificent creature leap completely out of the water, pulling him forward. It all happened so fast, but for a brief moment, it felt like time slowed down. He heard Soda shout with panic in his voice, "Dump it!" Jason felt the line continue to tighten around his hand, as the fish pulled him forward. He quickly grabbed onto the coverboard with his right hand, holding on tight. He then lunged forward, extending his left arm to reduce the tension on his hand, and pointed his fingers at the fish, allowing the line to slip smoothly off his glove. He could hear the leader line whiz by him as the tension returned again to the rod tip.

The fish crashed back down with a huge splash, then leaped several more times, pulling drag from the reel again.

"Yeah!" Soda and Cricket cheered. "Nice work, J-Bay!" Cricket added, while Soda nodded approvingly that Jason had managed to prevent the fish from breaking the line.

The fish suddenly changed direction again and started swimming toward the boat. Cricket quickly shifted into forward gear, creating a frothy plume of whitewash behind the transom. The fish appeared to be more subdued as it swam parallel to the boat, so Jason moved in for his next attempt to bring it in. Once again, he made a double wrap of the line around his right hand, then his left, repeating the process over and over again, gradually bringing the fish alongside the boat, which Cricket continued to keep in gear—moving forward. The fish had put up an incredible fight, but it was finally defeated and no longer displayed the bright electric blue on its fins.

"What do you think, Soda?" Cricket shouted, curious if he thought it was big enough to weigh in.

"It looks close," Soda replied, knowing this could be a contender for the tournament's largest marlin category.

Soda quickly set out to measure the fish from the bottom of its jaw to the fork of its tail. Tournament rules only allow one marlin to be brought on board, and it must measure a minimum of 110 inches at the dock. After taking the best measurement he could under the conditions, he looked up at Cricket and said, "It looks like it's right at one-ten and probably weighs at least four hundred pounds. What do you want to do?"

After a brief moment thinking about the potential for it to shrink over the next two days and the possibility of catching a bigger marlin, Cricket turned to Mr. Gregory and said, "I think we should tag and release this one and see if we can get a bigger one."

Mr. Gregory nodded in agreement, and replied, "Sounds good to me."

To tag the fish, Soda used a specialized tool called a tag stick to insert a small, flexible red tag the size of a matchstick near the dorsal fin. If the fish was caught again, this tag would help researchers track the marlin's movements and provide valuable data on the species' population and behavior. After carefully removing the hook from the fish's mouth, they watched as it gracefully disappeared into the depths of the cobalt blue water.

The boat erupted with cheers and high-fives all around as everyone congratulated Mr. Gregory on catching his first marlin. For Jason, the experience felt surreal as he replayed the sight of the marlin leaping in front of him while he held the wire. It was everything he had hoped for and more. As the cheers gradually faded, Cricket turned to Jason and Soda, and enthusiastically said, "Alright, y'all know the drill! Let's get those lines back out! We've got more fish to catch!" Jason and Soda eagerly set about deploying the teasers and lures again, excited for the chance to catch another blue marlin, hoping for an even larger one.

They continued to troll along the weed line for the next several hours. It was nearly noon when they saw a school of fish called rainbow runners leap from the water as the lures and teasers passed by. Each fish was roughly twenty inches long and was light blue with a bright yellow tail. Suddenly, the center rigger line popped free from the outrigger clip, and they heard the sound they had been waiting for—"ZZZzzzzzzz..." Almost immediately, a marlin began leaping from the water, and they could see it was roughly half the size of the one caught by Mr. Gregory.

Katie excitedly moved from the mezzanine to the fighting chair, eager to catch her first marlin like her dad. Jason grabbed the reel, which was placed in the rod holder behind the fighting chair, and moved it into position for Katie. As the teaser lines and other lure lines were being brought in, the marlin continued to pull line from the drag while leaping into the air, shaking its head over and over again.

"Whoa! Look at it go!" Katie exclaimed as she beamed with excitement. Suddenly, the drag fell silent, and a puzzled look spread across their faces.

After a brief pause, Soda turned to Cricket with a hint of disappointment on his face and said, "It spit the lure."

Katie was clearly let down and uncertain whether she had caused the fish to spit the hook. From the flybridge, Cricket shouted down with a big smile and an encouraging tone, "Don't worry about it, Katie. It just happens sometimes. We'll get you another one!"

Soda playfully added, "That one was too small for her anyway! We gotta get her a bigger one!"

"Exactly!" Cricket replied. "Let's get those lines back out so we can get her a real marlin!"

Their upbeat encouragement buoyed Katie's spirit, causing a timid smile to spread across her face.

After redeploying the teasers and lures, Cricket steered the boat alongside the weed line that stretched endlessly toward the horizon. The wind had died down, and the sun was scorching hot that afternoon. With no shade in the cockpit for Jason and Soda, they used their new gaiters and hoods to help protect themselves from the intensity of the sun.

They trolled for another two hours in the sweltering heat before Cricket called out excitedly, "There's some tuna up ahead tearing up a school of bait!" Everyone quickly scanned the horizon, eager to see the action unfold. Far off in the distance, a large school of baitfish rippled the surface of the water, spanning several football fields. Occasionally, they caught sight of the school erupting, along with the faint outline of a tuna briefly soaring through the air just above the surface.

The tension built steadily as the *Family Tradition* continued to troll toward the tuna at a painfully slow eight miles per hour. Cricket's voice suddenly rang out again, "I'm marking something big, five hundred yards away, about a hundred and fifty feet deep. Could be a marlin."

The prospect of a big marlin raised the stakes considerably, and was evident on everyone's faces as they moved at what felt like a snail's pace.

As the boat and trolling spread traveled above the fish, Cricket called out, "It's still at one-fifty, not coming up. I'm gonna circle around and make another pass."

After making a wide turn, Cricket began pulling the trolling spread back above the fish, this time approaching from the opposite direction. As the boat passed over the fish, Cricket's voice rang out excitedly, "It's coming up! It's at a hundred feet!"

Jason's heart raced as he waited for the next update from Cricket.

"It's at seventy feet and coming up fast!"

After another tension-filled pause, Cricket shouted, "It's at twenty feet and coming up on the left rigger side!"

A moment later, Cricket yelled, "I'm losing him on sonar! Y'all get ready!"

Suddenly, Soda called out, "There it is! Behind the left short rigger!"

The marlin was a dark, dull color and didn't display the brilliant electric blue on its fins like the previous one—a sign that the fish was not excited by what it saw. For a while, it lingered just behind the left short rigger, observing the lure intently. Then the marlin slowly swam toward the left bridge teaser, shifting from side to side, observing it carefully.

Cricket shouted with a hint of concern in his voice, “It looks like it’s just window shopping! Y’all try pitching it a bait!

Soda quickly grabbed a 50W rigged with a ballyhoo. Just as he began to drop it back, the fish slowly faded under the wake of the boat toward the trolling spread on the right. When it reappeared, it was just behind the right bridge teaser with the mahi belly. Suddenly, as if a light switch had been flipped, the marlin lit up with brilliant electric blue on its fins. It quickly accelerated forward, thrashing its bill at the mahi belly.

Chaos broke out on the deck as Soda frantically shouted to Jason, “Get the eighty pitch! Get the eighty! That’s a big fish!” Cricket turned on the right bridge teaser reel, pulling the teaser bait away. Unfazed, the marlin powered forward, determined to get what it wanted.

“He’s not dropping back!” Cricket shouted. Worried that the marlin might leave if it ate the mahi belly meat, Cricket reached above his head and began pulling the teaser line in by hand to bring it in faster. Suddenly, he shouted in pain, “Ahh!” as he jerked his hands back, gritting his teeth. The marlin had managed to grab the bait, pulling the line with so much force through Cricket’s bare hand that it caused a friction burn.

Everyone’s heads quickly turned to Cricket. Soda shouted with concern in his voice, “You okay?”

"Yeah! I just got my hand smoked!" Cricket replied, pain evident on his face.

The mahi belly had been pulled from the marlin's mouth when the teaser line drew tight, but some of the stitching was torn, and it appeared to be barely attached. Everyone anxiously watched as the mahi belly dragged along the surface of the water, with the marlin in hot pursuit.

With determination etched on his face, Cricket reached up again and began pulling the teaser away by hand as fast as he could. By this point, Jason had grabbed the cumbersome 80W setup rigged with a Spanish mackerel and dropped the bait behind the boat, near the marlin. However, he watched in stunned silence, mesmerized, as the massive marlin swam past him, his eyes wide. It displayed its brilliant electric blue colors as it closed in on the mahi belly, which was nearly at the outrigger. Just as the marlin was about to catch its bounty, Cricket yanked the entire squid chain teaser up to the outrigger, the mahi belly dangling just above the water.

Foiled, the fish faded away under the boat, turning in the opposite direction. They lost sight of it momentarily. Then, seemingly out of nowhere, the fish exploded on the mackerel pitch bait that Jason had dropped behind the boat, grabbing it with its mouth and disappearing below the surface. Jason dropped the rod tip and kept the reel in free spool, applying just a light bit of pressure to the spool with his thumb to prevent a backlash as the fish rapidly peeled away line.

Soda exclaimed, "Let him eat it, Jason! Keep lettin' him have it!" After a brief pause, he continued, "Okay, now slowly start pushin' the drag up." Jason felt the pressure building on the rod and reel as the line tightened, and the circle hook rolled securely into the fish's mouth.

"He's on!" Jason shouted as the fish shot away from the boat like a rocket, bending the rod over. Jason quickly moved the rod and reel to the fighting chair and positioned it in front of Katie, who strapped in quickly, ready for the fight.

The marlin continued to pull line from the reel at a blistering pace, staying just below the surface. As soon as the other lines were brought in, Cricket began backing down on it, yelling, "Reel, reel, reel!" However, the fish dove deep and stubbornly held its position beneath the boat, where the backing-down technique would not help Katie gain line.

Following Soda's instructions, Katie leaned forward, winding herself up from the seat using the reel handle. She then tried to use her body weight to apply pressure on the rod to bring the fish up. The tremendous force on the line was audible as the fish resisted, creating a rhythmic "Tink, Tink, Tink..." However, the marlin didn't budge. Instead, the drag gave way in short bursts, "ZZZ...ZZZ...ZZZ..." allowing the fish to hold its position.

Katie turned to Soda, frustration evident in her voice. "I can't seem to get any line in."

"That's okay. Just keep the pressure on him. You're doing great, Katie."

The stalemate lasted for at least 30 minutes before Katie slowly began making progress, bringing the fish up inches at a time. Crank by crank, she reeled the fish up from the depths. Nearly an hour into the fight, Katie had managed to bring the fish to just under 100 feet below the boat. With each pump of the rod, she grew more confident, knowing the end was near. However, the marlin had other plans.

Unexpectedly, the fish began swimming toward the surface again. “He’s comin’ up!” Soda shouted.

Suddenly, the massive marlin skyrocketed from the water. With adrenaline pumping, they all watched nervously as the fish unleashed its fury, leaping repeatedly and violently shaking its head in an attempt to dislodge the hook.

It then disappeared, diving deep into the dark abyss again, pulling drag from the reel with a high-pitched “zzzzzzzzzz...” It stripped several hundred yards of line before the tension on the rod eventually lessened, causing the drag to slow to a steady, low-pitched “ZZZZZZZZ...”

Soda quietly watched the action on the rod with concern. He turned to Cricket and said, “I think the fish died and is just sinking fast toward the bottom.”

Cricket dropped his head in frustration. “Can you stop it?”

Soda shrugged. “It had a lot of momentum divin’ down, so slowin’ it down is gonna be tough. We’ll run out of line long before it ever hits bottom out here, so all we can do is try.”

Soda turned to Katie and said, “I want you to push that small button right there on the side of the reel inward, which is gonna let the drag lever move past the strike position. Then, I want you to slowly—and I mean slowly—start easing it all the way forward toward the sunset position.”

As Katie nervously moved the lever forward, the stress on the line was audible. Each small adjustment of the drag created a higher-pitched “Tink, Tink, Tink...” sound, followed by short slips of the drag: "ZZZ… ZZZ… ZZZ…" The tension in the air was as taut as a fishing line. Katie's heart raced as she finally moved the lever to the sunset position, adjusting the drag resistance to its maximum of 38 pounds.

Everyone watched anxiously, their eyes fixed on the reel as the drag eventually stopped pulling and the tip of the rod slowly raised slightly. Katie had successfully stopped the fish from sinking further into the abyss, but the battle to bring it up nearly 600 yards had just begun.

To bring the fish up, they had to use a painstakingly slow process. Cricket would pull the boat forward to drag the fish, then quickly put it in reverse so Katie could gain line. At first, she was only able to gain back inches of line at a time, then feet, and eventually yards.

This process continued for nearly three hours before they could see the body of the fish beneath the boat. Jason excitedly called out, "I see color!" He turned to Katie with a big grin. "You did it, Katie!" With a throaty shout, Soda added, "Yeah! Nice work, Katie!"

Katie was exhausted. The battle and the summer heat had taken their toll on her, but when she heard the news, she perked up. A smile tugged at the corners of her mouth as she thought about her accomplishment. Suddenly, she felt the line pulling on the reel. Frantically, she braced herself as the drag began to slip. "ZZZZ….ZZZZ….ZZZZ…." The rod tip jerked, moving quickly up and down.

Puzzled and panicked, Jason and Soda turned to look behind the boat at the marlin. Their stomachs dropped as they watched a giant tiger shark attacking the marlin, violently shaking its head and tearing flesh from the fish.

Soda glanced at Cricket, a mix of fear and helplessness in his eyes, and said, “It’s a shark!”

Jason looked at Soda and asked, “What do we do?”

Soda sighed, and his shoulders slumped. Shaking his head, he replied, “There’s nothing we can do.”

They watched helplessly as the shark took several more bites of the marlin, then disappeared into the depths.

They were eventually able to pull the mutilated marlin alongside the boat. Cricket had come down from the flybridge and was looking over the fish with everyone. He turned to Mr. Gregory and Katie and said, “It’s a trophy fish for sure, but the bite marks are going to disqualify it from tournament.”

Upon hearing the news, Katie’s face dropped, and tears formed in her eyes, while Mr. Gregory’s expression remained steady.

Cricket continued, “Since we can only boat one marlin during the tournament, we’ve got two choices. First, we can take this one back with us. The tournament officials will likely give us a courtesy weigh in, and the fish will be donated to the University of Southern Mississippi’s Gulf Coast Research Laboratory. Scientists there will put it to good use, studyin’ it to learn more about older marlins like this one. The other option is to cut it free and try to catch another marlin that might win us some money in the tournament. The sharks will be more than happy to eat the rest of this one.”

Mr. Gregory thought intently about the two options. He then turned to Katie and said, “It’s your fish, Katie. What do you want to do?”

Tears streamed down Katie's face as she weighed her options. With a flash of anger, she exclaimed, "I don't want the sharks to have my fish! I want to bring it back!"

Mr. Gregory wrapped Katie in a hug and calmly said, "Let's bring it aboard." Cricket, Jason, and Soda nodded in acknowledgment, knowing they would miss out on the chance to win money if they caught another marlin large enough to bring in.

The mood on the boat was somber. The only words exchanged were brief and related to specific tasks. The crew used straight gaffs and a meat hook to pull the giant fish through the tuna door and onto the cockpit deck. Then, they worked together to move the fish into an insulated bag designed specifically for marlins, packing it with ice.

Once the task was complete, Cricket turned to Soda and Jason and said, in an uncharacteristically distant tone, "We've got about thirty minutes before it gets dark, so let's get those lines back out." He then climbed back up to the flybridge and began steering the boat across the vast, empty expanse of the sea. The horizon stretched endlessly before them, its surface desolate, as they headed toward the last spot where they had seen the tuna.

They took turns staring out at the horizon in silence as the last few minutes of light faded away. They had successfully boated a trophy marlin, but the mood on the boat was heavy with defeat. Katie sat on the mezzanine bench seat, sadness etched on her face, on the verge of crying.

Jason was upset that the shark had ruined their shot at winning prize money, but it pained him more to see Katie so distraught. Hoping to brighten her mood, he pulled out his phone and connected it to the boat's Bluetooth speakers. Turning to everyone, he said, "My dad would always play this song on the *Vanessa* when things weren't going the way we wanted." He pressed play, and "The Gambler" by Kenny Rogers began to fill the air.

Jason began to sing softly, a smile spreading across his face. He couldn't help but make silly, dramatic facial expressions as he continued his performance, hoping to bring a smile to Katie's face.

Soda smiled as he sang along softly with Jason, deeply reflecting on each line of the lyrics, as if they held the key to life.

Cricket shifted the boat into neutral and cranked up the music, singing along with enthusiasm. Even Mr. Gregory joined in, a subtle smile on his face. Their voices grew louder and their smiles wider as they belted out the famous chorus about knowing when to hold and knowing when to fold.

Katie watched with a mix of humor and bewilderment as the scene unfolded before her, while Jason teased, "Come on, Katie. Don't act like you don't know the lyrics!" With a playful grin, Katie joined in, singing humorously the line about not counting your money when you're sitting at the table.

As the song played on, their camaraderie radiated through every note. Leaning into the music, they exchanged glances and smiles, singing the lyrics a little louder as they reached the line about knowing what to throw away and knowing what to keep. They had gambled big at Loyd's Ridge and lost, yet they reveled in the unforgettable experience they shared.

After the song came to an end, the group settled into a comfortable silence, savoring the satisfaction of a day well spent. As they gathered around the dinner table that night, laughter filled the cabin as they recounted their adventures, their hands animatedly illustrating each tale. With every bite, the joy of their shared experiences deepened, and the worries of the outside world faded away, if only for a moment.

Later that night, Jason took the first wheel watch as they headed to the fishing grounds closer to Biloxi, where they planned to fish the next day. Despite the fun he had that evening, worries about his dad's cancer crept back into his thoughts, weighing heavily on his heart.

Unexpectedly, Jason heard someone climbing the ladder behind him. He turned to see Katie joining him.

"Hey-ey," she greeted him warmly.

"Hey, what's going on?" Jason replied, surprised to see her.

She then told him, "Well, I just wanted to thank you for cheering everyone up after the whole shark ordeal today. It's easy to forget just how lucky we are to be able to come out here and have these amazing experiences together. And I just wanted you to know that I'm really glad you decided to work on our boat, Jason." She then leaned in and wrapped her arms around him, squeezing tightly.

Initially unsure how to react, Jason gently returned the hug. As she slowly pulled back, their eyes locked. Attraction flickered in their gazes, mixed with a hint of fear, each aware of the potential risk if they dared to cross the line into something more. Yet, in that moment, neither wanted to let go, caught between desire and uncertainty.

Jason put all his chips on the table and leaned in, their lips meeting halfway. For that brief moment as they kissed, time seemed to stand still. It was just the two of them, surrounded by the vast emptiness of the sea and sky, illuminated by the stars above. The only sound Jason could hear was the heavy beating of his heart, echoing in the silence of the night.

Gradually, the hum of the boat's engine returned, and reality came back into focus, bringing with it an awareness of the risks their feelings posed.

Despite their concern, soft smiles formed on their faces as they looked into each other's eyes. Katie leaned in and whispered in his ear, "Don't stay up too late," then quickly kissed him once more before walking back toward the ladder.

As Jason returned his hands to the helm, looking out ahead, his heart raced. He was overjoyed but also in disbelief at what had just occurred. Thoughts of the kiss with Katie swirled in his mind, mingling with worries about his dad's health. As he steered into the darkness, uncertainty loomed regarding the future he was navigating toward.

The next day, neither Jason nor Katie mentioned their kiss. They moved through their routines with ease, carefully concealing their feelings from the others in a way that would have made any poker player proud.

Although they didn't catch any fish that day, the ride back to Biloxi was far from one of defeat. Mr. Gregory and

Katie beamed with smiles as they sat with Cricket in the flybridge, reminiscing about the thrill of catching their first marlins while taking in the breathtaking ocean views. In the cockpit, the conversation drifted from Jason's experience wiring his first marlin to the new fishing gear and techniques he and Soda were eager to try. Although the *Family Tradition* wasn't bringing back a tournament-winning marlin, they were returning with a true trophy fish—and a deeper appreciation and passion for their pursuit of something greater than victory alone.

They were one of the last teams to return to the marina that afternoon. The crowd watched with excitement as Katie's marlin was hauled from the boat to the weigh-in area.

The announcer addressed the crowd, "Next up, we've got team *Family Tradition*, who will be weighing in a big blue marlin. Ms. Katie Gregory was the angler, and this is her very first marlin!" A gentle wave of applause cascaded through the crowd.

The announcer continued, "Unfortunately, a shark attacked the marlin while they were bringing it in, and because the body was mutilated, it has been disqualified per the tournament rules." Gasps echoed through the crowd as they heard the news, with several spectators wincing and shaking their heads in disbelief.

"I know, I know—it's absolutely heartbreaking, y'all," the announcer said. "This fish looks like it's a good bit bigger than the only other marlin weighed in this tournament. However, team *Foolin' Around* will safely hold on to first place with their three hundred and ninety-two pound marlin that measured exactly one hundred and ten inches."

The large cookie-cutter bites on the fish's body became clearly visible as it was hoisted up, revealing jagged edges of torn flesh. A murmur spread through the crowd as people gawked at the massive fish, pointing at the giant bite marks and whispering in disbelief.

When the scale finally settled, the announcer exclaimed, "Six hundred and five pounds! What an incredible fish! Let's give Katie a big round of applause for her first marlin, everyone!"

The crowd erupted into roaring applause. Katie smiled wide, her eyes sparkling as she waved graciously, mouthing "thank you" to the cheering crowd. She then struck a proud pose for photos beside her trophy fish, while her dad, Cricket, Soda, and Jason stood beaming by her side, smiling from ear to ear.

THE BLUES

After taking photos with Katie's first marlin, the *Family Tradition* team began to navigate through the crowd away from the weigh-in area. The air was filled with the sounds of spectators and the announcer calling up the next team.

Suddenly, Bill Murphy emerged from the crowd, a wide grin spreading across his face. "Congratulations on your first marlin, Katie! That's awesome!" he exclaimed, his voice brimming with enthusiasm. He extended his palm toward her in a celebratory high five.

"Thanks, Billy!" Katie replied, her face lighting up with pride as her hand met his.

Bill's expression softened as he continued, "It's a shame it was disqualified, but that was still a really impressive fish!" He then turned to her dad, extending his hand for a handshake. "Good to see you, Mr. Gregory, and congratulations on landing your first marlin too, sir," he said respectfully.

Mr. Gregory returned the gesture with a warm smile, his firm grip conveying genuine camaraderie. "Thanks, Billy. It's good to see you too. Katie tells me you're going to school at Vanderbilt. That's impressive!"

Bill shrugged with a grin. "Well, I was really hoping to go to the University of Alabama with my friends, but dad, of course, insisted that I go to school at Vanderbilt, like he did."

"How is your dad?" Mr. Gregory asked. "I haven't seen him in ages."

"Oh, you know Dad—always working," Bill Murphy responded.

Nodding with a look of understanding, Mr. Gregory said, "Well, tell him I said hello the next time you talk to him."

"I will!" Bill Murphy replied. He then asked, "So, are y'all going out to the casinos tonight?"

"No, since we didn't place in the tournament, we're skipping the awards ceremony tomorrow morning and heading back to Destin tonight. Katie and I are flying up to Birmingham tomorrow to spend the week there. I need to check on our house and take care of some business."

"Really? I'm flying up there tonight. Y'all should totally ride with me!" Bill Murphy exclaimed, his eyes lighting up with excitement. "I've got my jet here, and there's plenty of room, and you can just have your pilot pick you up whenever you need to leave next week." A hopeful grin spread across his face as he eagerly awaited Mr. Gregory's response.

Unsure, Mr. Gregory replied, "Well, I appreciate the offer, Billy, but we wouldn't want to impose."

"Sir, you and Katie wouldn't be imposing at all. Seriously, you've got to ride with me! I want to hear all about the marlins you caught!" Bill Murphy said, enthusiasm shining in his eyes.

Bill Murphy's excitement brought a smile to Mr. Gregory's face. He glanced at Katie, gauging her reaction to flying home with her friend. Katie shrugged and smiled. "It's up to you, Dad. I'm just along for the ride."

After a moment of consideration, Mr. Gregory looked back at Bill, who watched them with eager anticipation. Nodding, he said, "Alright, then. Thanks, Billy. That will save me some time and give you two a chance to hang out. I know how fast summer break flies by—it won't be long before you and Katie have to head back to school."

"Awesome!" Bill said, a broad grin spreading across his face.

Katie smiled politely. Her gaze flickered toward Jason for a moment.

With a clenched jaw, Jason forced a smile, both he and Katie trying their best to hide their emotions from the others.

As the *Family Tradition* made its way home that night, Jason stared out at the dark sea beneath the inky sky, devoid of stars. His shoulders slumped, and his face was long as doubts clouded his mind. Could a relationship really work between him and Katie? After all, he was just a mate on her dad's boat, while she came from a world of wealth and luxury. Thoughts of Katie and her dad flying to Birmingham with Bill Murphy on his private jet gnawed at him. Mr. Gregory's voice echoed in his head: "It won't be long before you and Katie have to head back to school." The weight of his feelings deepened as he recalled Cricket's warning: "The third rule is—don't be hittin' on the owner's daughter. Seriously, keep things professional, and don't get too friendly, alright?" As these thoughts replayed in his mind, Jason found himself caught between desire and caution, wondering if pursuing Katie was worth the risk for what might be just a summer fling for her before she returned to school.

Sensing something was off, Soda asked, "You alright?"

"Yeah, it's just been a long day, and I'm ready to get back home," Jason replied, forcing a smile.

Soda nodded with a sense of understanding and patted Jason on the shoulder. With concern in his voice, he said, "Keep me posted on how your dad's doing this week, alright?"

Jason gave him a quick nod, his smile tight but grateful. Yet he kept his feelings about Katie under wraps, concealing the turmoil simmering just beneath the surface.

The next morning, Jason sat on the back deck of his townhome, holding his phone and typing a text to Katie: "Hey, what's up?" An unsatisfied smirk crossed his face as he considered sending it, but he quickly deleted the message. He tried again: "I can't wait to see you again." Squinting at the screen, he deleted that one too.

Message after message, he typed and erased, his agitation building with every failed attempt. Clenching his jaw, he felt a wave of frustration wash over him, knowing that if he kept the relationship a secret from Cricket, he would jeopardize not only his job but also a valued friendship. With a resigned sigh, he finally turned off his phone, mumbling to himself, "I can't do this right now."

Jason grabbed his truck keys from the kitchen counter and drove to his parents' house. Inside, the living room walls were lined with dark wood paneling, creating a cozy atmosphere that opened to beautiful views of the bay through sliding glass doors. Countless pictures adorned the walls and side tables, showcasing Jason and his dad proudly holding various trophy-sized fish they had caught together throughout the years. One photo showed them with baskets of blue crabs they had caught when Jason was just a boy. In another photo, he held a massive stone crab he caught while snorkeling as a teenager. There were also old photos capturing cherished memories of Jason's grandad and Jacob shrimping and running mullet nets, highlighting their family's fishing legacy.

Sitting in the living room, Jason's parents were enthralled as they listened to his stories about wiring his first marlin and how Katie's fish would have won if it hadn't been disqualified for being attacked by a shark. "I gotta admit, that does sound pretty exciting," Jacob said, a hint of nostalgia in his voice. "If I were a younger man, I might have to give that marlin fishin' a try too!" However, his smile slowly faded, the corners of his mouth drooping slightly as his lips pressed together, revealing the anxiety surrounding his upcoming surgery. The bandage on his cheek, where he had his most recent surgery, was slightly larger than before.

Sensing his dad's unease, Jason tried to lighten the mood, teasing, "So, it sounds like you're finally gonna get that big scar you wanted, huh?

Jacob chuckled and responded, "Yeah. I told that joker, I said, Doc, now you know I was just kiddin' about givin' me that big scar on my face, right?" He then emphatically added, "I'm gonna keep my damn mouth shut next time I go there, is what I'm gonna do!"

They all laughed softly and settled into a more comfortable silence. With the mood lifted, Jason asked, "So, when do you have to go in for the next surgery?"

Jacob took a deep breath and then exhaled slowly before responding, "Not this Friday, but the next. He said he should have the lab results for my lymph node biopsy the followin' week."

Jason told his dad, "I'm supposed to be fishing a tournament the day of your surgery, but if you need me here, I'll try to get someone to fill in for me."

With a squint in his eye, Jacob teased, "Does a fish need a bicycle to swim, Jason?"

Jason looked puzzled as he thought about the question.

"It's a rhetorical question, son," Jacob quipped. "Ain't nothin' you can do for me here. Plus, your team's countin' on you."

Jason nodded, understanding his dad's point, but he struggled with the feeling that he wanted to do something to help.

When Jason returned home later that day, he sat on his couch, staring blankly at the coffee table in front of him. He reached for his phone, pulled up Katie's name, then abruptly turned off the screen with a frustrated sigh.

As his week off from fishing dragged on, he never contacted her, and she never reached out to him. The shared silence and distance between them caused their romantic flame to dim. Like a lead weight, doubt about the future of their relationship pulled Jason deeper into a sea of uncertainty.

Their next tournament, the Emerald Coast Billfish Classic in Sandestin, was scheduled to start the following Thursday. On Monday morning, Jason, Soda, and Cricket arrived at the boat that was docked at Mr. Gregory's home in

Destin, so they could begin preparing for the upcoming trip. As the trio stood in the salon, Soda said, “The seas are looking pretty rough later this week,” his voice tinged with worry.

Cricket replied, “Yeah, word is they might have to delay the start until Friday, but at this point, it doesn’t look like they’re gonna cancel it.”

Soda said, “Well, I know the three of us can handle the rough seas, and I know the boat can handle ’em, but I ain’t too sure Mr. Gregory and Katie can handle ’em.”

“Yeah, I’m a little worried about that too,” Cricket replied. “A lot of the other boat captains I’ve been talkin’ to say their owners are probably gonna drop out, but Mr. Gregory said he and Katie still want to go if it’s not canceled.”

Soda nodded, but his worry was evident. “They might do alright.” He shrugged. “We just won’t know until we get out there.”

“Yep,” Cricket replied as the three men contemplated how well their anglers would fare in the rough seas. He then continued, “Well, the kickoff party is still gonna happen Wednesday regardless of whether they delay the tournament or not, so Mr. Gregory said he wants us to move the boat over there that morning. They’re gonna fly into Destin that afternoon and will meet us over there that night.”

On Wednesday morning, the crew arrived to move the boat to the Baytowne Wharf Marina in Sandestin. As Jason and Soda were untying the lines, Cricket called down from the tower, “I just got word that the tournament’s been delayed until Friday. Seas are forecasted to be around four to six feet that afternoon and continue dropping the rest of the weekend."

Jason and Soda nodded, eyebrows raised, knowing that it would be a rough ride out on the first day of the tournament.

After making the short ride over to Sandestin, they docked the boat in the same familiar slip they had used when Jason was first hired. At the end of the dock, the imposing silhouette of the *Trust Me* towered in the water, a stark reminder to Jason of Bill Murphy's looming presence.

That evening, Jason, Soda, and Cricket arrived at the banquet hall for the kickoff party. It was a casual affair, so they wore their usual fishing attire with flip-flops. After settling in, they sat on the far-left side of the room at a large round table draped in crisp white tablecloths as they waited for Mr. Gregory and Katie. The air was filled with the sound of a live band, the buzz of conversation and the enticing aroma of food from the buffet. Servers in pristine white chef coats expertly served dishes to guests. The spread featured roasted chicken with a rosemary-garlic glaze, beef tenderloin drizzled with red wine reduction, and a colorful medley of roasted seasonal vegetables, all complemented by creamy risotto. Guests eagerly filled their plates and enjoyed a variety of drinks from multiple bar areas.

"There they are!" Cricket called out, waving to signal where they were sitting.

As Jason, Soda, and Cricket turned their attention to the entrance, Katie walked in alongside Mr. Gregory. Dressed casually for the occasion, she exuded a beachy, coastal elegance in a light blue miniskirt paired with a white one-shoulder fitted top that accentuated her sun-kissed skin. Her hair was pulled back into a sleek ponytail, emphasizing the graceful length of her neck. The diamond stud earrings she wore caught the light and sparkled as she turned her head.

Jason's heart fluttered, and his eyes widened while he took in her presence. She always had a way of lighting up the room, and this time was no different.

"Hey-eh!" she greeted everyone with her usual warm and friendly tone. But as she spoke, it became clear to Jason that she was deliberately ignoring him, her gaze drifting past him as if he weren't there. He immediately regretted that he hadn't reached out to her during the past week while they were apart, but he was also confused about why she hadn't contacted him either. A storm of turbulent emotions swirled inside him, yet he managed to mask them behind a practiced smile, determined to hide his turmoil from the others.

After a bit of small talk, the team left the table to grab food and drinks. When they returned, Mr. Gregory settled into the seat next to Cricket, leaving the only open spot for Katie between him and Jason. Raising their voices to be heard above the lively band and the chatter around them, the team animatedly carried on, smiling and laughing as they enjoyed their food and drinks in the vibrant atmosphere. Yet, amid the camaraderie, Katie never looked at or spoke to Jason, her avoidance overlooked by the others but painfully obvious to him.

"That beef tenderloin is phenomenal!" Mr. Gregory exclaimed after finishing his last bite. "I'm going to get more," he added with a wide grin as he pushed back his chair and headed toward the buffet line.

"Yeah, I think I'm gonna have to grab some more of that myself!" Cricket chimed in as he followed Mr. Gregory toward the line.

Once they left, Soda turned to Katie and Jason. "I'm gonna grab a drink. Do either of you need anything?"

Jason and Katie both smiled and shook their heads politely as Soda made his way to the bar, leaving them alone at the table.

Surrounded by the lively atmosphere of the party, an awkward silence settled between Jason and Katie.

Finally mustering his courage, Jason blurted out, "How was your week in Birmingham?"

"Fine," Katie replied curtly, her tone leaving no room for elaboration.

Jason nodded, fully aware that "fine" was far from the truth and that she was clearly upset with him.

Softening her tone but still avoiding eye contact, Katie asked, "How's your dad?"

"He's doing okay. He's going in for his next surgery this Friday," Jason replied, trying to gauge her reaction.

Katie nodded, taking a sip of her wine without looking his way.

With sincerity in his voice, Jason apologized, telling her, "I'm sorry I didn't call or text you this past week."

"You should be," Katie shot back tersely.

With frustration evident in his voice, but still trying to maintain his composure, Jason defensively replied, "Well, you didn't call or text me either after you left with Bill on his private jet."

Katie turned sharply to face him, her frustration evident. “Is that why you didn’t call me? Because you were jealous that my dad and I flew back home with Billy?”

Initially bristling at her accusation, his posture softened with a heavy sigh. “No,” he replied, his voice steady but sincere. Jason thought carefully about his next words before telling her, “When I blew out my birthday candle that night in Biloxi, I wished I could find a girl like you one day. I just didn’t think I’d actually have the chance to be with you for real. I guess I’m scared of losing this opportunity with our team if it’s just a summer fling for you before you go back to school in a couple of months.”

As she listened to Jason’s heartfelt confession, Katie’s expression softened. A smile began to appear on her face.

Jason couldn’t help but smile back, curiosity gleaming in his eyes. “What?” he asked, unsure of what had sparked her smile.

With genuine warmth, Katie replied, “That night you played that gambler song and cheered us all up with your goofy singing, I remember looking at the stars above us and wishing I could find a guy like you one day.”

Jason felt a rush of emotions swell within him, disbelief mingling with joy at Katie’s confession.

She added, “I know there’s a few things we’d have to figure out to make a relationship between us work, but maybe after this tournament, we could at least talk about it.”

Jason’s smile grew. “Definitely.” They briefly gazed into each other’s eyes before the others returned to the table.

They spent the rest of the night enjoying the party with their teammates, continuing to hide their true feelings from the others. When Katie and her dad returned home that night, they didn't come back to the boat until Friday morning. Although Jason and Katie still had things to resolve, Jason's spirits were buoyed by the knowledge of how she felt and their plan to talk after the tournament.

Friday morning, a noticeable sense of nervousness hung in the air as the few teams brave enough to venture into the rough weather prepared to leave the calm, sheltered waters of the Baytowne Marina. The clatter of gear and shouts of hurried instructions echoed across the dock as crew members rushed to finalize their preparations.

When Mr. Gregory and Katie arrived, Jason and Soda were in the cockpit, making last-minute adjustments and organizing tackle. Meanwhile, Cricket sat in the flybridge, intently studying the weather forecast.

After exchanging warm greetings, Cricket climbed down from the flybridge, his expression a mix of concern and determination. "It still looks pretty rough out there," he told Mr. Gregory. "Only twenty-seven of the seventy-five registered boats are going out today."

Mr. Gregory and Katie exchanged glances, a brief look of apprehension passing between them, but Mr. Gregory responded with a reassuring smile. "Well, if it turns out to be too much for us, we'll just head back in. But I think we'll be fine."

Katie nodded, her face lit with excitement and ready to embrace whatever challenges lay ahead.

Cricket grinned, his confidence returning. "Alright! Sounds like a plan!" Jason and Soda, encouraged by Mr.

Gregory and Katie's optimism and their willingness to brave the rough seas, exchanged enthusiastic nods.

The team filed into the salon, continuing their discussion, except for Jason, who worked alone in the cockpit with his back turned toward the dock. Suddenly, he heard Bill Murphy's voice behind him teasingly call out, "Missed a spot!" It was a biting reminder of their first encounter in the same location, accompanied by a snickering laugh as Bill passed by.

It had been an emotionally difficult week for Jason, leaving him with little tolerance for Bill's antics. Ignoring Soda's advice to play it cool, he raised his left arm with a clenched fist close to his chest, careful not to let anyone inside the salon see. Then, pretending to slowly turn a reel handle with his right hand, he extended his middle finger mockingly, like a fishing pole emerging from his clenched fist. "Good luck out there," he taunted back, feigning a jerk of the rod as if he were setting the hook.

Bill Murphy's smile quickly morphed into a contemptuous sneer as he continued to walk down the dock toward the *Trust Me*.

With tensions high and the rivalry between Jason and Bill Murphy deepening, the *Family Tradition* cast off shortly afterward through Choctawhatchee Bay toward the East Pass for a 12:00 PM shotgun start. When Cricket reduced speed for the minimum wake zone by the Destin Bridge, Soda and Jason were in the salon with Katie and Mr. Gregory, making sure everything was secure and the cabinets were latched. Soda turned to Mr. Gregory and Katie and said, "Once we start runnin' fast out there, y'all need to just stay here in the salon because it ain't gonna be safe for you to go downstairs. If you need to use the head or grab somethin' down there, just tell us, and we'll have Cricket slow down."

Mr. Gregory and Katie nodded, exchanging anxious glances, unsure what to expect.

As the tournament boats paraded out of the East Pass, waves in the Gulf crashed against the outer jetty rocks, sending sprays of water shooting high into the air like confetti tossed in celebration as the droplets drifted toward them.

The waves at the pass were always higher because of the shallower water there. With the tide going out, the waves surged even higher, with some reaching heights of 8 to 10 feet. Cricket carefully maneuvered the *Family Tradition* through the treacherous waves, slowing down considerably to prevent the bow from crashing hard, which could damage the boat or injure the passengers.

Once out of the pass, the boats lined up for a shotgun start. The ocean was alive with frothy whitecaps scattered across the dark blue waves, mirroring the patches of white that spread across the stormy sky above. The *Family Tradition* team wore their navy-blue foul weather jackets, which boldly contrasted against the boat's white hull as they anxiously waited for the tournament to begin.

After a few tension-filled minutes, they finally heard the sound of a gun blast muffled by the wind howling at nearly 20 miles per hour from the southwest—the same direction the boats were traveling. As the vessels surged forward against the head sea, they crashed through the waves with an initial rush of excitement, racing to be the first to reach their chosen fishing destination. However, the teams' enthusiasm quickly waned after a few hard impacts from the waves hitting the bow, sending shudders through the boats and their passengers. Each vessel slowed slightly, their wakes quickly disappearing behind them, erased by the churn of the sea.

Mr. Gregory and Katie sat on the couch, visibly uncomfortable, bracing for each wave as the *Family Tradition* charged ahead. Meanwhile, Jason and Soda, accustomed to rough seas, casually moved about the cabin. Soda turned to Mr. Gregory and Katie and said, "We're gonna go up to the flybridge with Cricket. Y'all just holler if you need anything."

Although Cricket had zipped up the clear, flexible vinyl panels mounted on the front and sides of the flybridge—referred to as curtains— the rear remained open, allowing mist from the ocean spray to swirl through the air, making everything damp.

After Soda and Jason climbed up to the flybridge, they gazed out at the tumultuous sea, where huge walls of water were being pushed out from each side of the bow as the boat cut through the swells. Soda chuckled, "I don't know about four to six—this looks more like six with an occasional eight!"

"Yeah, it's a little sporty for sure!" Cricket replied, a mix of laughter and tension in his voice as he throttled back the engines for a moment to prevent launching off the backside of a particularly large wave.

The radar screen on the dash displayed the positions of the boats around them, along with Automatic Identification

System (AIS) transmissions for each vessel, which included the boat's name. The *Trust Me* was the largest boat in the tournament and had raced ahead, leading the pack. After roughly an hour, Cricket noticed that two boats displayed on the radar were headed back to Destin: *On the Hunt*, a 75-foot vessel, and the *Mississippi Kid*, a 65-foot vessel.

Cricket grabbed the boat's VHF radio microphone and raised it to his mouth, the coiled wire stretching from the dashboard. He then hailed his friend, the captain of the vessel *On the Hunt*, saying, "*On the Hunt*, I see y'all are headed back. Everything alright? Over."

"Yeah, we've got a couple of seasick anglers on board. It don't look like it's gonna get any better for 'em anytime soon, so we're headin' back in." He then continued, "The *Mississippi Kid* is right behind us. They broke somethin' slammin' into these waves that caused a bunch of their electronics to go out, so they ain't gonna be able to fish either. Over," the captain replied.

Cricket raised the mic, his expression tense. "Roger that. Hate to hear that, buddy. Y'all take care, and we'll see you in a couple of days. Over."

The captain called back, "Copy that. Good luck out there. Y'all be safe. Over."

"Thanks, Capt. Will do. Over and out," Cricket replied, easing the throttle back as the engines dropped to a low purr and another big wave rolled by.

They only had a few hours of daylight left to fish when they reached their first destination, the Petronius Oil Platform. One of the tallest freestanding structures in the world, the Petronius stood over 2,000 feet high from the ocean floor to the tip of its flare boom. Its barn-red base jutted from the dark blue water and appeared exceptionally narrow compared to the massive multilevel industrial platform above that housed over 200 full-time workers and included a helicopter landing pad.

When they arrived, Cricket positioned the boat on the up-current side of the rig, ready to start fishing down sea—going with the waves. The wind was still blowing at twenty miles per hour, with occasional gusts even higher, pushing the boat along as Cricket set the speed to 7 knots, roughly 8 miles per hour. Meanwhile, Jason and Soda quickly deployed the lures and teasers.

Mr. Gregory and Katie stepped outside briefly. The hoods on their matching navy-blue foul weather jackets drawn tight. They stood and marveled at the sheer size of the Petronius megastructure and its ability to withstand the harshest sea conditions. However, the weather quickly drove them back to the shelter of the salon as they waited for a fish to bite.

Jason and Soda remained in the cockpit, staring at the lures as they porpoised in a mesmerizing manner along the surface of the large, dark blue, frothy swells behind them. The lures would submerge and re-emerge in a rhythmic dance—diving for a few seconds, launching into the air, and then descending again with streams of bubbles trailing behind them.

The boat was in the trough between two large waves when something unexpectedly caught Jason's attention. He thought he saw a shadow under the left short rigger lure. The lure was at eye level with him, about a third of the way down from the top of the wave directly behind the boat. Leaning forward, he squinted to get a better look, unsure if it was just his mind playing tricks on him. The shadow continued to grow darker as it drifted up inside the wave. Suddenly, Jason noticed the electric glow of a marlin's fins—the fish was aiming directly at the lure.

"Marlin!" Jason shouted excitedly. "Left short rigger!"

Soda's eyes grew wide as he watched the fish emerge from a wall of water at eye level with him, exploding in a violent attack on the lure. In an instant, the line snapped free from the outrigger clip, cutting through the air as it tightened and began pulling the drag with a resounding "ZZZzzzzzzz..."

"Fish on! Fish on!" Soda yelled.

Jason rushed to the salon door, flinging it open and shouting, "Fish on!"

Mr. Gregory and Katie were shocked to hear that they were already hooked up with a fish. "You've got this one!" Mr. Gregory encouraged Katie.

Katie raced to the fighting chair, where Soda stood ready to hand her the reel. As she snapped the harness on to the reel, the marlin leaped into the air from the crest of a wave. They watched, wide-eyed, as the 300-pound fish soared 15 feet above the wave trough before crashing down with an enormous splash.

"Whoa!" they all shouted in unison. As they rushed to bring in the teasers and other lure lines, the fish made a few more leaps, but none were quite as spectacular.

With all the lines clear, Cricket began backing down on the fish. The waves crashed forcefully against the transom, spraying water into the air and drenching everyone. Water spilled over the coverboards, flooding the deck ankle deep.

"Get him, Katie!" Jason encouraged her excitedly.

Katie gave him a quick smile, while she continued to wind the reel handle frantically to regain line.

Jason grinned from ear to ear as he stood ankle-deep in the flooded cockpit, the boat backed down on the marlin. He exchanged a quick, excited glance with Soda, knowing this was the type of experience he had yearned for.

Soda leaned in toward Jason and said, "This fish ain't big enough to weigh in, so try gettin' a hand on the leader as quick as you can to get the points for catch and release."

Jason nodded, understanding the importance of his task.

To qualify for points in the billfish catch and release category, the tournament rules required teams to provide an uninterrupted video recording of the fight's conclusion. This recording needed to clearly show several key elements: the species of billfish caught, the leader connection either touching the tip of the rod or being touched by a team member, the GPS location with date and time, and the tournament designator issued at registration (a blue rubber bracelet in this case). Finally, the video had to capture the moment the billfish was released, ensuring it was no longer hooked to the line.

Although the boat had a camera mounted in the flybridge that Cricket used as a backup, the primary catch and release video recording was a small waterproof camera held by Soda on a lightweight pole several feet long.

After an intense 15-minute battle, Katie managed to bring the leader near the boat. With the video recording ready, Jason stretched out across the transom to grab the leader and quickly pulled it in toward him, making a clean double wrap with his right hand.

"Fish caught!" Soda yelled as Jason pulled the powerful marlin toward the boat, making precise wraps of line around his hands. Sensing that the fish was about to jump, Jason braced his knees under the gunnel and held on tight. Since Katie had successfully caught the fish when Jason touched the leader, they only needed to film the release to earn points for catch and release. In a flash, the marlin jumped straight up into the air in front of them. Everyone cheered as the fish shook its head wildly before crashing down with a huge splash. The fish hadn't broken the line with its powerful leap, so Jason quickly continued to wire it, making perfect wraps until he pulled it alongside the boat.

After getting video of the fish from above and even underwater, Soda pointed the camera at the designator on his wrist, then quickly moved to the GPS screen mounted on the port side of the mezzanine. He then handed the camera to Mr. Gregory to film the release after he tagged it. Once the fish was released, the boat erupted in cheers. Cricket called down from the flybridge, "Nice work, everybody! It's always good to break the ice on the first day!"

They didn't catch any more marlins during the limited daylight they had left. However, they were thankful for the smooth start in catching and releasing their first marlin, despite the rough weather. The initial success left them hopeful for more good luck to follow.

That evening, Cricket began the journey through the rough seas to their next fishing destination—an oil platform further southwest called Thunder Horse. It had four massive, columns painted barn-red that rose high from the water, supporting the industrial platform and helicopter landing pad above. As they approached Thunder Horse that night, it resembled a small, vibrant city shining brightly in the darkness, with countless lights dotting its exterior. Cricket kept the *Family Tradition* safely at a distance from the rig as they waited for the next day of fishing to begin.

Inside the salon, Soda was explaining the plan for the next day to Mr. Gregory and Katie. "So tomorrow, we're gonna be doin' some live bait fishin', which is usually more productive for us than trolling lures around the rigs. Y'all can sleep in until it's time to start fishin' around daybreak, but Cricket, Jason, and I will be up around three AM tryin' to catch bait."

"How big are the tunas?" Mr. Gregory asked.

Soda replied, "Well, I usually like to fish with ones about five pounds or so, but I've used some tuna as big as twenty pounds before."

Mr. Gregory and Katie's eyes widened in shock at the size of the tuna used as bait.

Soda continued, "In fact, a few years ago, we won first place at Bay Point with an eight-hundred-pound marlin that we caught using an eighteen-pound tuna as bait." With a twinkle in his eye, he chuckled, "Big baits catch big fish!"

Mr. Gregory nodded with a subtle smile and said, "Well, it sounds exciting. I'm looking forward to seeing how the live baiting works out for us tomorrow."

Katie nodded in agreement, captivated by the tantalizing idea of catching a tournament winning marlin on such an enormous live bait.

With only about four hours of sleep, 3:00 AM came early for the crew. Katie had slept on the couch due to the rough seas, so the men were quiet as they made their coffee in the galley, careful not to wake her.

Not wanting to waste a minute, Cricket moved the boat closer to the brightly lit Thunder Horse rig so they could catch bait. Compared to the massive rig that loomed above them, the 62-foot *Family Tradition* seemed minuscule.

The cockpit was lit by an array of bright lights, known as spreader lights, along with powerful underwater lights that illuminated the water all around, fading into darkness about 50 feet away.

As they stepped outside into the brightly lit cockpit, they were greeted by the striking sight of several flying fish soaring at head height behind the boat. The dark blue and silver bodies of the fish gleamed under the glow of the spreader lights. Caught in the draft created by the high winds, the fish were momentarily suspended in the air, shifting their wing-like fins side to side to stabilize their flight before diving back down. At least a dozen of the fish had landed inside the cockpit overnight and were lying lifeless on the floor, having failed to return to the water.

After clearing the deck of dead flying fish, Jason and Soda set out to catch bait. They each used a large spinning reel with a metal diamond jig lure. It didn't take long for Jason to hook his first fish.

"There he is!" Jason exclaimed as the rod bowed under the intense pressure of the fish fighting. Once Jason brought the fish to the boat, they could see it was a blackfin tuna weighing roughly five pounds. Blackfin tuna have a solid black back that abruptly changes to a narrow yellow stripe running along their body from head to tail, while the rest of the body is a shiny silver color.

Soda stood ready with a dip net that had a rubberized coating to minimize damage to the fish. "Got him!" Soda exclaimed as he lifted it into the boat.

"You really gotta baby these fish to keep 'em lively," Soda told Jason. "If they're bleedin' or hit the deck for any reason, just go ahead and throw 'em back because they ain't gonna make good bait."

Jason nodded and carefully took the fish from the dip net, being mindful not to drop it.

The *Family Tradition* was equipped with ten tuna tubes located at the back of the boat, designed to keep bait alive. The tubes stood vertically and were built to keep water constantly flowing across the gills of the tuna placed inside. Normally, the tubes were hidden from view by a removable section of the coverboard. With the cover removed and the water flowing, Jason carefully placed the blackfin in the tube. Its tail extended just above the waterline, ready to be pulled when the time came.

Over the next hour, Jason and Soda continued to fill the tuna tubes with blackfins ranging from five to eight pounds in size. Mr. Gregory briefly came out of the salon to say good morning and check out the bait before returning inside to finish his coffee.

As daylight quickly approached, the tuna bite gradually slowed down. The baitfish typically moved closer to the cover of the oil rig at sunrise, fearing the larger predators that would soon come to feed. Cricket turned off the underwater lights and began driving the boat away from the oil rig. Suddenly, he shouted, “I’m marking a large fish about three hundred yards out. Y’all, get ready to drop a bait!”

Jason and Soda quickly prepared to drop their first bait, getting the necessary tackle, including an 80W setup rigged for live-baits. When the boat was directly above the fish, Cricket yelled, “Drop ’em!”

Jason grabbed one of the tunas by the tail and pulled it out of the tube, so that Soda could attach a massive circle hook that stretched the width of his palm. As Jason held the muscular tuna tight, it thrashed wildly, its body thumping against his chest while he struggled to keep a grip on it. After a brief moment of intense flailing, the fish eventually calmed down.

To attach the hook, Soda inserted a small, narrow stainless-steel dart through the tuna’s nose and into its mouth. The dart was connected to a short loop of braided line that, when pulled up, would cause the dart to pivot 90 degrees, locking it against the roof of the tuna’s mouth. The circle hook was then secured to the other end of the braided line loop. Soda was skilled at the process and completed it swiftly.

With the hook in place, Jason dropped the tuna overboard, and almost immediately, it began to rapidly dive down away from the boat.

The sudden pull on the line was fierce, so Soda kept his fingers firmly on the spool, allowing the tuna to pull line out while preventing a backlash. After a frantic dive into the darkness, the tuna paused, momentarily ceasing its powerful pull on the reel. Soda grabbed the line from the rod tip and pulled it toward him, feeling every vibration telegraphed through the line. He sensed the powerful tuna swimming steadily, unaware of the hungry predator lurking nearby.

Suddenly, the tuna began to pull on the line erratically, clearly fleeing something it feared lurking in the darkness. In an instant, the line was snatched from his hand with immense power and began racing from the reel. Soda allowed the fish to take line, keeping his fingers on the spool to give it time to eat the big bait and ensure the circle hook was deep within its mouth.

Suddenly, the fish stopped pulling line from the reel. With intense focus, Soda carefully studied the subtle jerks of the rod tip. With years of experience, he knew the marlin had the tuna in its mouth like a dog clutching a bone and had stopped to try to turn the bait headfirst to swallow it.

"That's right, eat it down," Soda said quietly as he envisioned what was taking place underwater. He loosened his grip on the spool to reduce the resistance on the line, giving the fish time to adjust the big bait in its mouth.

As the line began to pull steadily from the reel again, he knew the hook was exactly where it needed to be. He slowly adjusted the drag lever forward. The rod bent over, and the reel started to scream "ZZZzzzzzzz..."

"Fish on!" Soda shouted gleefully, adrenaline coursing through him.

Jason rushed to the salon door and flung it open. “Fish on!” he said in a hushed but urgent tone to Mr. Gregory, careful not to wake Katie on the couch.

Stunned that they were already hooked up with a fish, Mr. Gregory set his coffee mug down and quickly followed Jason outside, where the action was unfolding.

As Mr. Gregory sat in the fighting chair, the warm, subtle orange and red glow of sunlight began to emerge on the horizon, vividly contrasting with the dark blue water and sky.

The marlin had already pulled out a hundred yards of line and jumped repeatedly behind the boat. Its sleek silhouette was barely visible in the morning twilight as it soared through the air, each leap punctuated by a faint white splash as it crashed down.

Since they didn’t have any teasers or lures out, Cricket was able to begin backing down on the fish right away. The waves were still roughly four feet high, so he was careful to keep from crashing the transom into them too hard. Jason and Soda stood ankle-deep in water that surged over the coverboards, fully immersed in the thrill of the moment as spray rained down on them after each impact.

Mr. Gregory wound the reel handle with determination, the rhythm of his movements matching the adrenaline coursing through him. The thrill of the chase fueled his excitement, energizing him far more than the coffee he had been drinking just moments earlier. As the first rays of dawn illuminated the water, his heart raced while he watched the fish leap into the air, attempting to shake the hook from its mouth.

Finally, after 15 minutes of relentless battling, he felt a wave of satisfaction as he saw the leader line coming up to the boat, signaling that victory was within reach.

With the sun just above the horizon, Jason made his first wrap. It was a spectacular sight to watch Jason battle the fish by hand as it leaped into the air repeatedly, splashing down in front of them. They estimated the fish to weigh roughly 350 pounds. However, it was clearly too short to boat, so Soda went to work capturing video of the catch-and-release.

Mr. Gregory beamed with excitement as the fish swam away. It had been an amazing morning, and they were just getting started.

After a brief pause celebrating their catch, Jason and Soda set out deploying one live bait on each side of the boat to troll around the rig at approximately 2 knots, which is a little over 2 miles per hour. The live-bait lines were run from the 80W setups to clips on each outrigger, which were pushed out about two-thirds of the way to the end.

Soda attended to the reel on the left rigger, while Jason managed the reel on the right rigger. Each of them sat on the side of the boat and used their fingers to keep constant pressure on the spool. This technique allowed the drag to be set low enough for a marlin to easily eat the bait with minimal resistance while preventing the large baits from pulling line as they were trolled behind the boat.

For the next couple of hours, they slow trolled around the rig, searching for marlin. It was around 7:00 AM when Katie emerged from the salon. She looked rested and ready for the day ahead, with her hair pulled tight into a ponytail.

She greeted Jason and Soda with a cheerful, "Good morning."

Jason and Soda responded in unison, "Mornin'!"

Soda added, "You missed some exciting action this mornin' at daybreak. We caught and released a blue just as the sun was comin' up!"

Surprised, Katie replied with disbelief, "Really? No way!"

Soda chuckled, "Yeah, really! You slept right through it, *sleepyhead*!"

Katie shouted up to the flybridge, "Dad, did you really catch a blue marlin this morning?"

"Yeah, we're tied one to one now!" Mr. Gregory playfully replied.

Katie stood there with her mouth open, stunned that she had slept right through the action.

Distracted by the friendly banter, Jason was caught off guard when the right rigger line suddenly snapped free from the outrigger. The fish struck the bait like a freight train, yanking the line with such tremendous force that the spool backlashed. With the immense force of the fish swimming away, a locked spool would undoubtedly lead to a broken line and the loss of the catch.

Jason tried to maintain light pressure on the spool to prevent the backlash from worsening, but he had to be careful not to let his fingertips get caught in the rapidly moving loops of line. Several larger loops rhythmically slapped against the side of the reel housing, the sound echoing in his ears as the line flew from the spool. He watched anxiously, holding his breath, as the loops became fewer.

When the last loop finally disappeared, a wave of relief washed over him, thankful that he hadn't lost the fish—or a fingertip. Slowly, he pushed the drag lever forward, causing the circle hook to roll securely into the corner of the fish's mouth.

Sensing the increased drag pressure, the fish immediately skyrocketed from the water, shaking its head.

"Fish on!" Soda cheered, while Katie and Mr. Gregory shouted, "Whoa!" in unison, their voices bursting with excitement.

Jason let out a deep sigh of relief. Although he had recovered from the situation, the stress of the situation rattled his nerves.

Katie turned to her dad, her face flushed with excitement. "I've got this one!"

Jason swiftly moved the rod to Katie, who was ready in the fighting chair. Meanwhile, Soda had brought the other bait to the boat, allowing Cricket to start backing down on the fish.

The fish stayed up top, jumping repeatedly. Too short to weigh in, the marlin appeared to weigh roughly 300 pounds based on their visual estimation. It put on an incredible display of dazzling acrobatic jumps that had everyone in the boat cheering with excitement.

Despite the rough seas, the team was able to catch-and-release the fish in under 20 minutes, giving each other high fives as it swam away.

They had secured their third successful catch-and-release for the tournament. With plenty of time left, they began to feel a surge of excitement about potentially scoring high enough to place in the catch-and-release category. Soda and Jason quickly deployed more baits, eager to see if their luck would continue.

For the next few hours, they continued to troll without a bite. Cricket marked a few fish down deep, but they were unable to raise them. Making matters worse, three other boats competing in the tournament had shown up, also trolling live baits near the rig in pursuit of the same fish.

With each passing moment, Cricket grew more restless, eager for another marlin bite. Around 11:00 AM, he turned to Soda and Jason and told them, "Let's make a run." It was their cue to pull in the bait and prepare to move to the next fishing spot.

The two baits they brought in were barely swimming and lacked the action needed to effectively attract a marlin. As they tossed them overboard, Soda said to Cricket, "We need to make bait if you see any at the next spot. We're down to four."

"Making bait" was a common phrase among marlin fishermen, referring to the process of catching bait. Every minute spent making bait during the day meant less time to catch a marlin. The difficulty of catching bait during daylight hours only added to the stress of the situation.

Cricket nodded, recognizing the need for more bait, his jaw tightening as he took a deep breath and considered his options one last time. He then set a course for their next fishing destination, an oil platform called Thunderhawk.

The seas continued to settle, dropping to 3-foot waves. This allowed Cricket to make better time traveling to the Thunderhawk, minimizing the loss of fishing time. The Thunderhawk had four massive yellow square columns that held up the huge platform above, contrasting distinctly against the surrounding blue water and sky.

As the *Family Tradition* approached the Thunderhawk, Cricket carefully watched the sonar, looking for marlin or bait. He saw that most of the bait was holding close to the rig. He told Soda and Jason, "Go ahead and drop 'em."

Soda and Jason quickly deployed two fresh tunas while the boat cruised slowly down-sea alongside the rig. Suddenly, the short rigger snapped free without pulling any drag from the reel. When Soda reeled in the line, he found that the leader had been cut, showing signs of having been bitten by a toothy type of fish.

Soda held up the leader as he looked at Cricket and said, "Looks like either a shark or a barracuda cut us off."

Suddenly, the right fishing rigger snapped free without any drag being pulled from the reel. Jason reeled in the line to find only the head of the tuna remaining attached to the circle hook.

Frustrated and knowing they were down to two live baits, Cricket told them, "Y'all keep the lines up while I take a quick look around to see if I wanna stay here or not." He continued to scan the area while Jason and Soda stood ready. As the boat turned to head up-sea, Cricket shouted, "I'm marking a fish up ahead, south of the rig. Y'all get ready to make a drop."

Eager to catch the fish, Cricket wasted no time steering the boat straight toward it, his excitement unmistakable as he shouted, “Drop ’em!”

Everyone watched with anticipation as Jason dropped the bait overboard. Soda sat on the side of the boat by the 80W setup in the rod holder. With his fingers gently pressed against the spool, he let the tuna pull line freely as it dove deep beneath the boat.

Cricket’s voice suddenly rang out with excitement, “It’s going for the bait!”

Soda’s expression shifted abruptly to intense concentration. Gripping the fishing line, he tried to read the steady tugs from the tuna, visualizing the struggle unfolding below the surface.

After a minute passed, Soda and Cricket exchanged glances, surprised that the fish hadn’t taken the bait. “Anything?” Cricket asked.

Soda shook his head. After waiting another brief moment, he yanked the line upward, trying to provoke a reaction from the tuna, and it worked. The fish began to pull on the line with strong, erratic tugs, exciting the larger predator. Suddenly, a powerful tug jerked Soda’s hand down, prompting him to release the line.

Sensing the large fish had swallowed the tuna, he let it run for several seconds before pushing the drag lever forward, driving the circle hook tight into the corner of its jaw.

The rod began to bend, but strangely, the line pulled from the reel with a slow and steady ZZZZZZZZZZ sound.

After watching the fish's reaction to being hooked, Soda turned to Cricket, with a puzzled look, and said, "The fish is on, but it's acting more like a shark, not really doing much."

"Alright, let's put some heat on it and see if we can get it to come up to the surface," Cricket said, putting the boat in reverse to follow it as it slowly swam away.

Soda moved the reel to the fighting chair where Mr. Gregory sat ready to battle the mystery fish. After Mr. Gregory strapped his harness to the reel, Soda told him, "Alright, Mr. Gregory, go ahead and push the drag all the way to strike and start winding on him as fast as you can."

Cricket slightly increased the boat's speed in reverse, chasing the fish as Mr. Gregory cranked the reel handle.

With a puzzled expression, Soda glanced at Jason and shrugged, unsure what kind of fish they had hooked as it slowly swam away.

After a few minutes, they could see the fishing line starting to rise in the water, signaling that the fish was coming to the surface.

Suddenly, Cricket's voice rang out excitedly, "It's a marlin! Get ready to grab the leader!"

The blue marlin was short and stocky, propelling itself away from the boat with powerful steady strokes of its thick, muscular tail. Soda guessed it weighed at least 400 pounds based on its appearance, but it didn't look long enough to be boated.

The engines roared to life as Cricket charged in reverse toward the fish. Mr. Gregory reeled frantically, struggling to keep up while waves crashed hard against the transom, drenching everyone in the cockpit with spray and flooding the deck with water up to knee height. Jason saw the leader coming up fast, so he positioned himself to grab it while Soda scrambled to get the camera ready, wading through the water.

"Got the leader!" Jason yelled as he grabbed the line. He then started frantically trying to keep up with the boat backing down on the fish, hastily making alternating wraps around his hands and throwing the excess line on each side of him. Suddenly, the fish darted to the left, pulling Jason from one side of the boat to the other across the flooded deck. He locked his knees against the left corner of the boat but wasn't confident he had a solid footing. As the fish skyrocketed from the water, Jason decided to dump the wraps from both hands, unaware that the line had coiled around his right forearm amidst the chaos. Since the wrap on his right hand couldn't come completely free, the line slid down from the thick leather pad on the top of his glove to the thinner leather on the fingertips. As the fish came splashing down, the line pulled with such tremendous speed and force that the friction cut through his shirt and the thin leather fingertips, slicing into his skin and leaving a searing burn.

Unable to let go, he gritted his teeth and braced himself against the deck as the 200-pound test leader line tightened around his forearm and fingertips with crushing force, stretching to its limits. Suddenly, there was a sharp "Kapow!"—like the crack of a small-caliber gun. The heavy leader line had snapped, letting the fish swim away while Jason winced in pain, shaking his right hand.

"You alright?" Soda asked, his voice heavy with concern. The others stood nearby, their expressions a mix of worry and anticipation as they waited for Jason's response.

"Yeah, the leader got me pretty good, but I'm fine," Jason replied, downplaying the excruciating pain as he examined the cuts on his forearm and fingers. Despite his casual demeanor and the fact that it was their fourth successful catch-and-release, a heavy mood of concern hung in the air. Everyone was grateful that nothing worse had happened to him. They went about their tasks, searching for another marlin that day, but their efforts proved unsuccessful.

That night, Cricket drove the boat to another rig a short distance away, closer to home, called Blind Faith. The rig platform was supported by four massive columns that jutted from the sea, their lower portions painted bright red.

After only four hours of sleep, Cricket, Soda, and Jason were up again at 3:00 AM. They didn't talk much as they slowly sipped the extra strong black coffee that Cricket had made. Their eyes looked tired, and their movements were more sluggish than the day before as they quietly waited for the caffeine to kick in.

Around 3:30 AM, Jason and Soda started jigging for bait, filling the tubes one after another with blackfin tuna. The cuts on Jason's right fingers from the day before made his hand feel stiff and were constantly aggravated by the salt water and fish slime.

As daybreak illuminated the horizon, they settled into a steady rhythm, slow-trolling live tunas around the rig. Cricket marked several large fish deep below, but despite their efforts, they were unable to entice them into investigating the baits.

Around 10:00 AM, Cricket shouted down to Jason and Soda, "The major feeding time is around ten-thirty. If we don't get a bite by eleven-thirty, I'm gonna make a run somewhere else while we still have a little time."

By 11:00 AM, Cricket overheard on the VHF radio that the *Trust Me* had hooked up with a fish, possibly putting them in the lead for the catch-and-release category. The pressure mounted as he realized he needed to find a marlin that would bite or decide to move to another spot. Staring intently at the map display on the dash, he weighed his options. The thought of losing valuable time by relocating nagged at him. He was leaving behind a spot teeming with bait and large fish he had marked, likely marlins.

Yet, something inexplicably drew his attention to a patch of water on the up-sea side of the rig, roughly a mile and half away. In a leap of faith, he decided to trust his instincts. Turning to Soda and Jason, he said, "I'm going to run a little further up-sea. Y'all get ready to drop some fresh baits."

After arriving in the area of interest far from the rig, he spotted a school of baitfish that made him feel good about his hunch. Jason and Soda put out two fresh tunas as bait, both weighing roughly 8 pounds, hoping to entice a marlin as they slowly trolled the area. Just a short while later, Cricket spotted two large fish swimming near another school of bait and shouted, "I'm marking two good-sized fish up ahead!"

Soda and Jason sat eagerly next to the reels, using their fingers on the spools to restrain the lively tunas as the fish tried to swim deep, struggling against the pull of the boat. As the boat trolled past the fish they had marked, Cricket's voice rang out, "One of the fish is coming up on the left rigger! Get ready, Soda!"

Soda's eyes widened, and his heart raced as he braced for the bite.

Cricket's voice rang out again, "The other fish is coming up on the right rigger! Get ready, Jason!"

Jason glanced at Soda with a huge grin, eager for the action to begin.

Both baits began racing toward the surface, frantically trying to escape. They darted back and forth in vain, splashing wildly as the boat dragged them forward. Suddenly, there was an explosion of water on each side of the boat as the marlins thrashed their bills and devoured the sizable tunas with ease.

Line raced from both spools at a blistering pace while Jason and Soda applied gentle pressure with their fingers to keep the reels from backlashing. Once they were confident the marlins had the hooks in their mouths, they gradually moved the drag levers forward, causing the rods to bend over, and the reels to join in a high-pitched chorus together "zzzzzzzzzz..."

Mr. Gregory and Katie watched from the flybridge with a mix of excitement and disbelief that they had hooked up with two marlins. Cricket turned to them, urgency evident in his voice. "Mr. Gregory, I need you to put on the stand-up harness. Katie, I need you to get positioned in the fighting chair."

Jason turned to Soda, grinning with excitement, and exclaimed, “It’s a double header!”

Wide-eyed with concern, Soda watched as both marlins leaped into the air, swimming toward each other. His voice tense, he called out, “More like double trouble! They’re crossing the lines! We need to swap positions!”

Worried that the crossed lines could cause them to lose one or both fish, they frantically pulled the reels from the rod holders and moved toward each other.

“Which line is on top?” Jason asked, his voice tight with anxiety.

“Hold the rod tips together!” Soda urged him.

They lifted the rod tips next to each other, trying to determine which line was on top.

“Mine’s on top—go under!” Soda called out.

Jason quickly ducked under Soda’s line and moved to the left rigger side, where Mr. Gregory waited, strapped into a stand-up harness. Once both Katie and Mr. Gregory were ready to battle the fish, the engines roared to life as Cricket put the boat in reverse, chasing after them. Suddenly, the fish began swimming toward each other again, leaping into the air repeatedly.

“They’re crossing again! Bring the rod tips together!” Soda shouted.

Mr. Gregory brought his rod tip over to Katie’s, while Soda and Jason nervously tried to determine which line was on top.

“His is on top!” Jason yelled.

“Go behind the fighting chair, Mr. Gregory!” Soda called out.

As Mr. Gregory moved to the right side of the cockpit, his fish unexpectedly turned and began leaping toward the boat at lightning speed.

Soda frantically shouted to Cricket, “Go forward! Go forward!”

The engines abruptly shifted gears, and the boat surged ahead, leaving a frothy plume of whitewash in its wake.

“Just hold tight, Katie,” Soda said as her marlin continued to speed away from the boat, pulling drag. He quickly turned to Mr. Gregory and yelled, “Reel, Mr. Gregory! Reel! Reel! Reel!”

Suddenly, Mr. Gregory’s marlin turned back toward their left, perpendicular to them, still pulling drag from the reel.

Soda and Jason looked on with anxious expressions as Cricket turned the boat to starboard, circling directly toward the fish and creating an immense bow in the fishing line as it dragged through the water.

As soon as marlin stopped pulling drag from Mr. Gregory’s reel, Soda yelled, “Reel! Reel! Reel!” With determination etched on his face, Mr. Gregory cranked the reel handle, battling the fish without the aid of the fighting chair and testing his resolve.

“You got this, Dad!” Katie cheered as she kept the pressure on her own marlin, waiting for her turn to battle it into the boat.

Soda leaned toward Jason and said, “Neither fish is big enough to boat, so just get your hand on that leader as fast as you can, then break it off so we can go after Katie’s fish before we lose it!”

Caught up in the intensity of the moment, he no longer noticed the pain from the cuts on his right hand as he slipped on his wireman gloves. Jason's heart pounded, and his breathing grew heavy as the leader line inched closer with each crank. Stretching his body across the transom, he grabbed the leader and made his first wrap, then a second. With his arms pulled in and knees locked against the side of the boat, he braced himself as the fish began to swim downward, pulling with incredible force. Every muscle in Jason's body was clenched tight, shaking with effort when suddenly he jerked back as the line snapped beneath the surface.

"Another catch-and-release!" Soda cheered, holding the camera high. "Let's go get the other one!"

Katie's marlin had stopped pulling drag from the reel, making it easier for Cricket to back down and help her quickly regain line. The crew exchanged excited glances as they watched the leader line approach, knowing that this fish might secure them first place for catch-and-release.

Jason reached out, grabbing the leader. "Got it!" he exclaimed, making his double wrap and pulling forcefully against the fish. In an incredible burst of speed, the marlin launched itself completely out of the water, shaking its head back and forth. When it crashed down, its head turned toward the boat, and it began jumping repeatedly toward them.

"Forward! Go forward!" Soda shouted, panic in his voice.

Cricket quickly thrust the throttle lever forward, causing everyone to brace themselves to avoid falling. Suddenly, there was a loud "shwack!" as the marlin's bill smashed against the top of the coverboard on the transom. The fish had nearly landed in the cockpit but fell back into the water, making a huge splash. Jason grabbed the leader, holding tight as the fish dove down. He could feel the line stretching to its breaking point. With a sudden snap, the force on the line released, and the marlin disappeared into the depths.

Cheers erupted on the boat as the initial shock and worry on their faces transformed into exhilaration. Soda exclaimed, "That's six catch-and-releases!" He patted Jason on the shoulder and gave Katie a high five, then exchanged a brief look of relief with Cricket, grateful that the fish hadn't landed in the boat.

The seas continued to calm as the day went on, settling around two feet high by the time they headed back. Although they didn't catch any more marlins, spirits stayed high as they enjoyed the smooth ride home, knowing they had a good chance to win in the catch-and-release category. Amid the laughter and chatter of the others on the boat, Jason and Katie exchanged brief glances, their eyes lingering a moment longer than necessary—a quiet acknowledgment of their shared triumph and the attraction they were still keeping hidden from the rest of the crew.

As they entered the protected waters of the East Pass, approaching the Destin Bridge, Jason and Soda proudly hoisted six small white flags on the starboard side of the boat, each displaying an upside-down blue marlin image.

Katie squinted with a confused smile and asked, "Why are the marlins upside down?"

Soda told her, "A long time ago, fishermen started the tradition of flyin' the marlin flag when they boated a big blue marlin. Nowadays, people fly the flag upside down to show how many blue marlins they caught and released. And if you see a blue flag with a white marlin, that means they caught a white marlin."

"Oh," Katie responded, her eyes widening in surprise. She then asked, "The blue marlins are worth more points than the white marlins for catch-and-release, right?"

"Yeah, the blues are worth five hundred points, and the whites are worth two hundred points," Soda answered.

As the Family Tradition backed into its slip at Baytowne Marina, Jason spotted the *Trust Me* pulling up at the end of the dock. It was the only other boat flying six marlin flags. A broad smile spread across his face, and excitement surged through him as he counted five blue marlin flags and one white marlin flag. It was clear now—his team had secured the first-place position for catch-and-release.

Jason spent the next few hours mingling with fellow fishermen, exchanging stories about their trips and listening to the announcer's voice broadcast through loudspeakers, along with the crowd cheering as fish were weighed in. The awards were typically given the next morning after the weigh-in, but due to the delay in starting the tournament, they were distributing them that night.

Just after dark, the announcer's voice rang out, "Next, we've got the *Family Tradition*. Is the *Family Tradition* here? There they are! I see Captain Cricket and the rest of the team headed this way. As the boat's name implies, this is a family affair for them, with the owner, Mr. J.P. Gregory, and his daughter, Katie, serving as the anglers. The *Family Tradition* caught and released six blue marlins during the tournament, earning three thousand points, which puts them in first place for catch-and-release!"

The crowd was much smaller than usual, due to roughly a third of the boats dropping out of the tournament and the change in the weigh-in date. However, they gave a warm round of applause as the *Family Tradition* team walked onto the stage, and Katie accepted the plaque for the team.

After they finished with the photos, the announcer's voice rang out again, "Since we have y'all up here, don't go away quite yet. Next up, we have the Top Lady Angler award, which just happens to also be Katie!"

The crowd cheered even louder, with a few folks, including Bill Murphy, yelling, "Go, Katie!"

Shocked to have won the title of Top Lady Angler, Katie beamed with pride as she held up both awards. She turned and exchanged glances with Jason for a fleeting second, their eyes sparkling with unspoken adoration and their smiles widening in unison.

On the sidelines, surrounded by the cheering crowd, Bill Murphy's smile slowly faded, replaced by a mix of confusion and frustration as he watched their chemistry. Jealousy welled up in his blue eyes as he turned and disappeared into the crowd.

THE TIDES

After the *Family Tradition* team's thrilling victory in the Catch-and-Release Division of the Emerald Coast Billfish Classic, Mr. Gregory, Cricket, and Soda were busy sharing stories with fellow fishermen. Meanwhile, Jason and Katie slipped away for a leisurely stroll through the scenic Baytowne Wharf, planning to regroup with the rest of the team later.

Strings of lights crisscrossed overhead, casting a warm, inviting glow over the Wharf. Most of the lights were white, but a few colored bulbs—red, orange, green, and blue—added a festive touch. The lively sounds of music filled the air, blending with the cheerful chatter of vacationers enjoying the family-friendly atmosphere. Adults gathered at outdoor bars, sipping drinks and engaging in animated conversations, while children shrieked with delight as they soared down a zip line that stretched across a pond nearby, its surface reflecting the shimmering lights above.

Yet, despite their victory and picturesque surroundings, Jason noticed a hint of melancholy in Katie's eyes. As they strolled beneath a canopy of brightly colored rain umbrellas whimsically hung overhead, he turned to her and asked, "Is everything okay? You seem to have something on your mind."

Hesitantly, she replied, "Yeah. I was just thinking about my mom. I wish she could have been here for this." A laugh escaped her as she added, "You would have loved her! She was always so much fun to be around—always smiling and the life of the party."

"Sounds like you two were a lot alike," Jason said with a grin.

Katie nodded with a bittersweet smile, the warmth of the memory flickering in her eyes. "Yeah, she used to call me her mini-me." Suddenly, she remembered Jacob's surgery from the previous Friday and asked, "Oh, by the way, how did your dad's surgery go?"

"He seems to be doing okay, but he won't get the results of the biopsy back until sometime later this week," Jason replied.

As they passed a wooden gate leading to a fishing pier, Katie said, "Let's walk out there." With no one else around, they strolled side by side down the pier, which meandered above the waist-high marsh grass and extended toward the open water. They paused at a dimly lit spot overlooking the marina to their left, where the tournament was taking place. The black night sky above them was dotted with bright stars, and a gentle warm breeze whispered through the air.

Turning to him, Katie asked, "So, have you thought any more about things between us?"

Jason slowly moved closer to her, his gaze locking onto hers as he replied, "Yeah, I haven't been able to stop thinking about it." He then playfully grinned. "And I think you are definitely worth the risk of me losing my job, but I think I should wait until after the Grand Championship to tell Cricket. We have such a great team right now, and I don't want to miss sharing that experience together."

Katie smiled brightly. "I agree! You have to fish that tournament with us before you tell him!" As they stared deeply into each other's eyes, she said, "It'll be our little secret for now."

As if caught in each other's celestial orbit, their bodies slowly drew closer. Like the moon calling to the tides, the gravitational pull of their hearts overwhelmed them in a surge of desire that felt both fated and forbidden as their lips met.

The kiss lasted only a few seconds when suddenly Katie's phone vibrated, pulling her away from their enchanting moment. She glanced down at the screen and said, "It's my dad. He said they're headed this way to meet us for drinks."

With a shared smile, they slowly made their way back down the pier, fingers intertwined. As they reached the gate, they reluctantly let go of each other's hands, the warmth of their connection lingering even as they walked toward the bar to meet up with the rest of their team.

After settling in at a table at one of the crowded outdoor bars, Jason turned to Katie and said, "I'll be right back. I need to run to the restroom."

As Katie sat there alone, filled with excitement about her developing relationship with Jason, Bill Murphy suddenly appeared, approaching her with a smile. "Hey, stranger. Celebrating your victory alone?"

Struggling to conceal her surprise, Katie laughed and said, "Hey, Billy! No, my dad and the rest of the team are about to be here."

Bill Murphy's demeanor shifted to a more serious tone as he asked, "So, is everything cool between us? I tried calling and texting you a bunch of times over the past few weeks, but I just sort of feel like you've been ghosting me for some reason ever since you and your dad flew back to Birmingham with me."

"I'm sorry, Billy. I've just been really busy," she said, hoping to ease the tension.

Bill Murphy nodded slowly, a flicker of uncertainty in his eyes. Despite his doubts, he told her, "Well, I'm having an after-party on my boat tonight. You should stop by." With a hint of hesitation and sincerity in his tone, he added, "I miss hanging out with you, Katie. I just feel like we have this connection that I don't have with other girls."

Caught off guard and unsure how to respond, Katie tried to let him down gently. "I'm sorry, Billy, but I can't hang out tonight..." Just then, Jason returned to the table.

"Hey, what's going on?" Jason asked awkwardly, trying to mask his surprise at seeing Bill Murphy.

Bill Murphy made no effort to hide his displeasure. "Oh, so you have time to hang out with your hired help but not me?"

"He's my friend, Billy," Katie replied, her tone laced with disbelief and frustration.

"Well, I thought we were friends, but I guess I was wrong," Bill Murphy shot back, his voice tight with anger. Cutting his eyes toward Jason, he sneered contemptuously, shaking his head as he turned away.

Just then, Mr. Gregory, Cricket, and Soda approached.

"Hey, Billy!" Mr. Gregory called cheerfully, but Bill Murphy didn't respond or make eye contact as he passed by.

Concern evident in his tone, Mr. Gregory asked Katie, "What's wrong with Billy?"

Katie replied hesitantly, "I think he wants to be more than just friends, but I don't feel that way about him." Her shoulders slumped, and a somber expression settled on her face at the thought of losing an old friend.

Mr. Gregory nodded thoughtfully, recognizing the difficulty of the situation for both of them.

As the team momentarily sat in awkward silence, a waitress approached with a friendly smile, breaking the tension. "Need some drinks?"

"Yes," Mr. Gregory answered with a smile. "Drinks are on me, everyone!"

Immediately, the atmosphere shifted as the team began placing their orders. They went on to enjoy the rest of the night, celebrating their victory. As they raised their glasses in a celebratory toast, Jason and Katie exchanged excited smiles, reveling in their success and relieved that they would only have to keep their relationship a secret for a little while longer.

The next day, back at Mr. Gregory's house, Jason and Soda got to work washing the boat and putting away tackle while Katie lounged by the pool. The team had planned to fish in the Bay Point Billfish Open tournament in Panama City that Thursday, just four days away. However, an urgent business matter arose for Mr. Gregory, requiring him to fly back to Birmingham.

Cricket was inside the house talking with Mr. Gregory, but eventually made his way down to the boat, telling Jason and Soda, "Since we're not gonna be able to fish the Bay

Point tournament this week, Mr. Gregory said we can take the next two days off."

"Alright!" Jason and Soda grinned. Although they were disappointed that they would be missing out on the tournament that week, they were happy to have off that Tuesday and Wednesday after their exhausting trip.

A short while later, Jason secretly texted Katie, "I have the next two days off. We should hang out."

Reclining on a poolside chaise lounge, Katie smiled as she texted back, "Definitely! What do you want to do?"

Jason replied, "There's a really cool place I want to take you on my boat, but the water's only deep enough to go there during high tide, which is around noon tomorrow. Can you meet me at my place around 10:00 AM?"

"Yes! Can't wait!" Katie texted back, followed by a kiss emoji.

That evening, after work, Jason stopped by his parents' house to check on his dad. When he arrived, he found his parents sitting at the end of the dock, watching the sunset.

As he walked along the old wooden pier, Jason noticed the tide flowing out. The bay water was dark, stained with tannins, and littered with seagrass and debris floating swiftly along the surface in the current. The heavy rainstorm a few days earlier had flooded the rivers and creeks, emptying muddy water into the bay, which flowed out through the East Pass and into the ocean.

Hearing his footsteps, his parents turned their heads to greet him in unison. "Hey, Jason!" His dad had a large bandage over the left side of his face.

"Hey! I just stopped by to see how you were doing, Dad," Jason replied.

Despite the bandage on his face, Jacob looked cheerful as he quipped, "Well, I've been better, but I suppose I could be worse! Come on, have a seat with us."

Jacob's upbeat demeanor brought a broad smile to Jason's face, and he felt relieved to see his dad in good spirits despite the significant surgery he had undergone just days earlier. As Jason sat down, he commented, "Man, the water sure is dirty. It was gorgeous earlier today when the tide was coming in."

Jacob chuckled. "Yep, the tides are a lot like life—the lows definitely make you appreciate the highs!"

Ellen chimed in, "So, how did your trip go, Jason?"

"Great! We won first place in the Catch-and-Release Division, and Katie won Top Lady Angler," Jason replied.

"That's terrific, Jason!" His mom responded lovingly, while his dad nodded approvingly.

Jason pulled out his phone to show them a group photo of the *Family Tradition* team, featuring Katie in the middle, proudly holding the plaques. Ellen's brows lifted slightly as she took in the picture. "Wow. She's really pretty! I'd heard you mention her name before, but I didn't realize she was so attractive."

"Yeah, she and her dad are super cool too. I really like working with them," Jason replied, his voice steady despite the intense feelings of attraction he was hiding.

As Jacob looked at the picture, he held the phone out away from him and tilted his head slightly upward to get a better view. "Yeah, she's easy on the eyes, alright," he said with a chuckle. "You don't see too many girls like that on a commercial fishing boat, that's for sure."

Jason and Ellen both burst into laughter at Jacob's comment, sharing a moment of lightheartedness.

As they returned their gaze toward the setting sun, Jacob asked, "Y'all fishin' Bay Point this week?"

Jason replied, "No. We were gonna fish it, but Mr. Gregory had some business come up that he needed to take care of in Birmingham. So, our next tournament is gonna be the Grand Championship over in Orange Beach. Y'all should drive over for the weigh-in!"

"Let's do that, honey!" Ellen said to Jacob, reaching out to hold his hand.

"Alright, sounds good to me. I'll make sure I ain't fishin' that weekend," Jacob replied.

"You plan on fishing again already?" Jason asked, his brow furrowing with concern as he glanced at his mom, who looked visibly worried.

"Yeah, I plan to run southwest this weekend if the weather holds up. Heard they've been catchin' a good grade of mingos out that way," Jacob said, excitement in his voice.

Jason's voice was tight with worry as he countered, "But Dad, we don't even know the results of your biopsy yet."

As the sea breeze gently surged, Jacob took a deep breath of the salty ocean air, filling his lungs. A smile crept across his face as he gazed out across the bay, listening to the distant calls of seagulls and the rhythmic sound of waves lapping at the shoreline.

With a steady voice, he replied, "Fear has robbed me of too much joy these past few weeks, but I ain't gonna let it do that no more. Nope. Nothin's gonna stop me from doin' what I love as long as I'm able."

Jason nodded gently, understanding his father's point of view. Despite the uncertainty that lay ahead, he and his parents watched the sunset over the bay, appreciating each precious moment together in a way they never had before.

The next morning, Jason waited anxiously for Katie to arrive at his townhome. His heart raced with excitement as he finally heard a knock at the door. When he opened it, she greeted him with a bright smile that lit up her entire face. "Hey-ey!" she said, her voice bubbling with enthusiasm as she stepped forward.

"Hey! Come on in!" he replied.

As Katie walked inside, she quickly scanned the sparsely decorated home. There was a single couch with a side table on each side and a worn coffee table in front of it. Between the living room and the kitchen was a round glass dining table with four chairs positioned around it. Several surfboards were propped up in one corner of the living room, while fishing rods and tackle were stored in another. "It's, uh, very spartan, but I like it," she playfully teased, causing Jason to roll his eyes humorously.

"Well, it was a bit of a fixer-upper when I bought it, so I haven't had a whole lot of money to put into furniture and decorations yet," Jason explained.

Katie's eyebrows raised in surprise as she asked, "You bought this place yourself?"

"Well, my parents helped me some with the down payment, but I saved just about every dollar I made for an entire year to afford it."

Katie nodded with her lips pressed together, clearly impressed by Jason's self-discipline and the remarkable achievement of buying and fixing up his own home. As she continued to scan the room, her eyes suddenly lit up. "Oh my gosh, I love that painting!" she said, stepping closer to get a better look.

Framed with weathered coastal wood, the painting displayed a vibrant blue marlin leaping from the water. An old man in a small boat struggled against the fish, the fishing line taut in his hands. At the stern of the boat, a small bird burst into flight, its wings outstretched, conveying a sense of freedom. Katie admired the artwork, her eyes catching a quote inscribed in the background that she read aloud: "But man is not made for defeat. A man can be destroyed but not defeated."

"Old Man and the Sea, right?" Katie asked.

Jason blinked in surprise. "Yeah, have you read it?"

"Yeah, my dad got it for us to read when we started to get interested in marlin fishing," Katie said. Turning her attention back to the painting, she continued, "I like how it shows the bird that landed on his boat. I remember reading that part."

Jason chuckled softly, clearly surprised. "Yeah, my buddy Matt painted this for me, and I asked him to include it."

"Your friend painted this for you?" Katie said, her eyes wide with astonishment. "Is he a professional artist?"

Jason replied, "No, he's actually a commercial fisherman, but ever since we were kids, he's just always been super talented at art. He runs a boat here in Destin called

Anything Goes." Jason sarcastically continued, "which is sort of ironic considering that's pretty much how he lives his life. He can be a handful sometimes, but I love the guy."

With a mischievous grin, Katie replied, "Can't wait to meet him!" As she glanced out the sliding glass doors onto the sunlit back deck, she asked, "Is that your boat out there?"

Jason motioned for her to follow him out back. "Yeah, come check it out."

His boat was an older fiberglass center-console skiff. It featured a single bench seat known as a leaning post, which was high enough to comfortably lean against while driving. The boat was weathered, with faded white paint from years of exposure to the sun and salt, but it remained sturdy. Designed for bay fishing, it glided effortlessly through shallow waters, only 6 to 8 inches deep, making it perfect for navigating the backwaters of the Intracoastal Waterway, where Jason planned to take Katie that day.

Katie laughed as she read the name of his boat. "*Sittin' Pretty*, huh?"

"Yep! You ready to cruise?" he asked.

"Let's go!" she replied, beaming with excitement.

After lowering the boat from the lift into the water, Jason and Katie cast off for a ride through the harbor toward the Destin Bridge. With their backs against the leaning post, Katie inched closer to Jason, causing a smile to spread across his face as they took in the sights and waved to other boats passing by.

When they exited the harbor and turned toward the Destin Bridge, they were greeted by the magical emerald-green waters of the incoming tide—a stark contrast to the murky, debris-filled outgoing tide, the day before. The incoming ocean water was crystal clear, revealing the white sandy bottom below, dotted with patches of seagrass.

Once they navigated through the no-wake zone by Crab Island, Jason pushed the throttle down, and the boat began racing across the smooth surface of the bay. The powerful growl of the outboard engine resonated around them as the wind whipped through their hair.

Eventually, they reached the spot Jason was eager to share with Katie, a stretch of undeveloped land on Santa Rosa Island. It was an expansive marshland teeming with wildlife, where waist-high needle rush grass framed a field of dead pine trees that had succumbed to the saltwater decades ago—a testament to the shifting sands of time.

The skeletal trees were light gray, bleached by years of sun exposure, while the marsh grass at their bases varied in color from green to gray. An enormous osprey nest was perched on one of the dead trees, its dark silhouette contrasting sharply against the brilliant blue sky.

"It's so pretty out here!" Katie said, as she scanned the area.

"Just wait. It gets better. There's a hidden spot back here called Pirates Cove," Jason replied. He then steered the boat into a secluded nook that wound through the marsh grass, hiding the entrance to a narrow creek. "The water is only deep enough to get back here during high tide." With a hint of mystery in his voice and a sly grin, he added, "Some of the old-timers in Destin say this is where the pirate Billy Bowlegs hid his treasure."

"Really?" Katie asked, her face lighting up with intrigue.

"Yep! But even if it's not true, it definitely holds a different kind of treasure," Jason said, guiding the boat carefully through the barely navigable water.

Slowly, Pirates Cove began to reveal itself. Majestic white sand dunes, untouched by human development, rose high against the southern shore, some towering as much as 40 feet above the water. Small scrub oaks and a few other hardy trees had made the dunes their home, creating a canopy of shade beneath them. Along the calm surface of the cove, a few mullet lazily leaped, glinting in the sunlight as they broke the surface.

Katie's expression brightened with amazement. "Wow! This is really beautiful, Jason." She then teased him, "I bet you take all your girlfriends back here, don't you?"

Jason replied, "Actually, I've never brought anyone back here before."

Sensing his sincerity, Katie reached for his hand. "Well, I'm really glad you decided to share this place with me. It's a treasure for sure."

Jason nodded and gave her hand a gentle squeeze. "I hope it stays like this forever."

After soaking in the timeless natural beauty surrounding them for a moment, Jason told Katie, "There is another type of treasure this place holds, but we're gonna have to hunt for it."

"Really? What is it?" she asked, curiosity lighting up her face.

Jason leaned in with a playful grin and humorously whispered, "This place is loaded with giant blue crabs!"

"Really?" Katie exclaimed, her eyes widening in excitement.

"Yep!" Jason replied as he reached for a net with a long wooden handle. Grinning, he added, "And we're gonna catch them old school style—with a dip net!"

Katie laughed, her enthusiasm infectious. "Okay! This sounds like fun! What do I have to do?"

"It's pretty simple," he explained. "You'll head to the bow, and when you see one, just scoop it up with the net. But you gotta be quick because these blue crabs are fast!"

"No problem! I've got this!" Katie replied confidently.

As Jason moved the boat closer to the shore, it wasn't long before Katie shouted, "Oh! I see one! Right over there!" She slowly reached out with the net, but just as it got close, the crab suddenly shot out from underneath, swimming quickly away.

"Aww! It got away!" Katie said, her tone laced with playful frustration. "But I'm definitely gonna catch the next one!" she reassured him.

Jason grinned. "I told you—they're quick!"

As Katie turned her gaze back to the water, she shouted, "Ooh! There's two of them right over there by the grass!"

The crabs had their claws raised aggressively, ready to fight, as they circled one another, waiting for the right moment to strike.

As Jason inched the boat closer, Katie quickly dashed the net onto one of the crabs, but it too shot out sideways, escaping her grasp. "Ah! Get back here!" she giggled, watching it swiftly swim away. She quickly spotted the other crab attempting to bury itself. The outline of its shell was barely visible through the sand.

With determination, Katie placed the net on top of the buried crab and began to drag it slowly toward her. As she did, the crab scurried from its hiding place, darting right into the net. "I got it!" she exclaimed, lifting it triumphantly. "Whoa! Look at the size of those claws!"

Like stunning jewels, the crab's huge claws were a rich sky-blue color, with bright white patterns on their interior resembling stratus clouds. Its cream-colored underbelly created a striking contrast against the dark blue claws and baby blue legs. The top of the crab's shell was a mottled mix of brown and deep green, with formidable red spikes adorning the outer edges of its shell and fierce pincers.

"That's a nice one!" Jason said as he took the net from her and shook the crab loose into his cooler. He teased, "Now all you have to do is catch about a dozen more, and we'll have enough for dinner!"

"Easy!" Katie said playfully.

"Okay!" Jason chuckled. "I like your optimism!"

The next crab Katie spotted was clinging to a patch of grass, and she easily scooped it up. Holding it up with excitement, she curiously said, "Look! The tips of the claws are red on this one!"

Jason replied, "Yeah, that's a female. You can tell by her red fingernail polish!"

"Are you serious?" she asked skeptically.

"Yes, I'm serious!" Jason said, laughing. As he reached for the net, he noticed that the female was carrying thousands of tiny bright orange eggs under her belly. "Look, this one has eggs, so we're not allowed to keep it."

"I didn't know they carried their eggs like that," Katie said with fascination as she examined it closely.

After Jason safely returned the egg-bearing female crab to the water, they continued to meander through the shallow marsh that afternoon. Laughter filled the air as they joked about each of Katie's failed attempts to catch a crab, and celebrated each success. Eventually, Jason told Katie, "Okay, so I have to admit, you did pretty good today. I'm impressed. But we still need a few more for dinner, so I'm gonna check the crab trap that I put out just in case you came up short."

"I can't believe you doubted me, Jason!" Katie teased, smiling playfully. "Although I'm offended, I'm also getting kind of hungry, so let's see what you got there, buddy!"

Jason reached down to grab a white buoy floating on the surface, then began pulling up the line attached to the trap. As he pulled the square-shaped trap, constructed from chicken wire, to the surface, five large blue crabs crawled around inside.

"Perfect," Jason said. "Just the amount we needed."

"Yes!" Katie said as she looked over the crabs.

Later that evening, back at Jason's house, he and Katie sat down to enjoy a candlelit dinner. Jason had cooked the crabs they caught and removed the sweet, succulent jumbo lump meat from the body, transforming it into delicious pan-seared crab cakes. He had also removed the claw meat, gently sautéed it in butter, and served it over a bed of delicate angel hair pasta.

"Wow, this looks and smells amazing!" Katie said. "Thank you for planning such an incredible day for us. I had so much fun."

"Me too," Jason replied, a warm smile spreading across his face as their eyes locked for a lingering moment.

After taking her first bite of the crab cake, she raved, "Oh my gosh, this is so good, Jason! Seriously, this is the best crab cake I've ever had!"

Jason laughed softly, delighted by her enthusiasm. "Thanks! It's a lot of work for a little bit of meat, but it's one of my favorite meals. My mom used to fix this for me growing up. The deal was that if I cleaned the crabs, she would cook them."

"Sounds like a smart woman!" Katie laughed.

With a playful smirk, Jason replied, "Yeah, I think you two will get along really well. She and my dad are actually planning to come to the weigh-in for the Grand Championship, so hopefully you'll get to meet them both then."

"Awesome!" Katie replied. "I've heard a lot about your dad, but tell me about your mom."

Jason gazed off with a subtle smile as he contemplated how to describe his mother. "Well, she's very patient and kind, and always full of encouragement. She grew up here in Destin and started dating my dad when they were in high school. Her family owned a lot of land in the area, including several rental properties that she helped manage. For the most part, she's been a stay-at-home mom and wife, taking care of me and Dad. But she still manages a few properties that she inherited and occasionally dabbles in selling real estate too."

Katie replied, "Well, I can't wait to meet her, and your dad!"

As they continued to enjoy their dinner, she asked, "So, what do you want to do tomorrow?"

"You up for some snorkeling?" Jason asked, a hint of excitement in his voice.

"Absolutely! That sounds fun!" Katie said, her eyes lighting up.

"Awesome! Let's meet back here tomorrow morning, and we'll take my boat. There are a couple of places I want to show you," Jason told her with a grin.

After finishing dinner, they kept chatting for hours, their conversation flowing easily as they explored each other's lives. Each revelation sparked curiosity, their eyes lighting up at shared interests and stories.

Late into the night, Katie glanced at her phone. "Oh my gosh! It's already one o'clock! I better get going—but I had so much fun today, and the dinner was amazing!"

Jason smiled. "I had a really good time too."

As they stepped outside into the warm, humid air, the bright full moon cast a silvery light across the driveway, illuminating their path.

Pausing by her car door, they stood face to face, holding hands. Jason leaned in, and they shared a gentle kiss.

After a moment, Katie said softly, "See you in the morning," before slowly pulling away and climbing into her car, her eyes bright and cheeks flushed.

Jason waved goodbye as he watched her back out of the driveway, a rush of exhilaration coursing through him.

The next morning, just before noon, Katie returned. Eager to go snorkeling, they cast off in Jason's boat and headed toward a stretch of rocks called the Finger Jetty, nestled just inside the East Pass on the east side.

"Wow! The water looks amazing today!" Katie said, glancing across the shimmering surface as they exited the harbor.

"Yeah, the tide's coming in until later this afternoon, so the visibility underwater should be really good too," Jason replied.

Once they reached the Finger Jetty, Jason tossed his anchor overboard, positioning the boat just a short swim away.

Suddenly, Jason's phone rang, and he saw it was his mom. His body tensed, knowing she was likely calling about his dad's biopsy results. Taking a deep breath to steady himself, he answered, "Hey, Mom. What's going on?"

Ellen's voice was filled with joy. "Well, your dad and I just wanted to tell you the good news. His biopsy results came back negative!"

Relief washed over Jason. "That's awesome, Mom!" He let out a deep sigh, his shoulders relaxing. "That just made my day!"

"I know! That's why we wanted to call and let you know as soon as we found out!" Ellen said.

In the background, Jason heard his dad's voice. "I still have to go back every six months for a checkup, but they said I'm cancer-free right now."

"That's great news, Dad!" Jason said, his tone full of reassurance.

"Yep! Sure is!" Jacob replied cheerfully.

Ellen added, "Well, listen, Jason, we have a few more people to call, but we wanted you to hear it first."

"Thanks, Mom. Love y'all," Jason said, his voice warm with gratitude.

"Love you, too," his parents replied in unison.

As he hung up, tears of happiness filled Jason's eyes. A tidal wave of emotions surged through him, washing away the stains of sadness and the murkiness of fear that had burdened his heart. He shook his head, laughing at himself for getting so emotional in front of Katie, but despite his efforts, warm tears cascaded down his cheeks.

Having overheard the good news, Katie stepped forward without a word and wrapped Jason in a tight hug. In that moment, holding her close and knowing his dad would be okay, Jason felt a rush of hope for a bright future filled with possibilities.

Jason took a deep breath to pull himself together and chuckled, "You ready to go snorkeling?"

Katie nodded gently, her eyes glistening with tears of joy. "I'm so glad to hear he's going to be okay," she whispered, hugging him tighter.

Basking in the good news, they slipped into the water and donned their masks and flippers. As they swam side by side toward the rocks, holding each other's hands, their bond felt stronger than ever. Schools of brilliantly colored fish darted around them, their vibrant hues creating a mesmerizing dance beneath the surface. They carefully navigated around a large pink jellyfish that floated gracefully nearby, its long tentacles trailing ominously behind it. To their delight, when they reached the end of the jetty, they spotted a small green sea turtle gliding gracefully by the rocks, adding to the magic of the moment.

With a shared sense of exhilaration, they continued to explore several of Jason's favorite snorkeling spots the rest of the day. Immersed in the underwater world of wonder, they marveled at the beauty of life in the crystal-clear waters of the incoming tide.

Later that afternoon, Jason and Katie returned to his townhome, still buzzing with excitement from the day's adventures. They settled onto the back deck, where Jason fired up the grill to cook some red snapper for dinner. The salty scent of the ocean mingled with the savory aroma of the grilling fish as they reminisced about the vibrant underwater scenes they had encountered. As the sun dipped below the horizon, their conversation ebbed and flowed, shifting seamlessly from stories of their past to dreams for the future, forging a shared vision of what could be. Beyond their physical attraction, they understood each other on a deeper level—overjoyed to have found kindred spirits in one another.

Though Jason had to work the next two days, he and Katie texted each other throughout the day. Since Mr. Gregory wasn't returning until Saturday, they eagerly made plans to meet each night. Jason was particularly excited to take her to a party Friday night at Norriego Point—the tip of the Holiday Isle peninsula, where he lived. Known affectionately as "The Point," this sandy stretch of beach on the southern side of the harbor entrance was a favorite hangout for Jason and his friends.

After work that Friday, Jason hurried home to shower and change into fresh clothes before driving his boat back to Katie's place. As he cruised through the harbor, the warm hues of sunset cast a golden glow on the horizon, painting the sky in shades of orange and pink. However, by the time he arrived, darkness blanketed the bay, prompting him to turn on his running lights—red and green on the bow and a single raised white light on the stern.

When Jason and Katie reached the party, the bows of a dozen small boats were already beached in the sand, side by side. More than twenty of Jason's friends had gathered there, most holding red plastic cups. Their voices mingled with the music playing from one of the boats, creating a lively atmosphere. The distant sounds of laughter and music from the bars and restaurants along the brightly lit boardwalk on the other side of the harbor added to the festive backdrop.

A young man with long blond hair pulled into a ponytail called out affectionately, "J-Bay!" as he strolled toward them. Barefoot and shirtless, he wore a pair of surf shorts and a shark tooth pendant necklace hanging around his neck. On his left wrist, he wore several bohemian style twine bracelets.

"Hey, Matt! What's going on, man?" Jason replied, clasping hands with him, before pulling him in for a quick hug. Turning to Katie, he added, "Matt, this is Katie. Her dad owns the boat I'm working on now. And Katie, this is Matt—he's the friend I was telling you about who painted that picture in my living room."

Katie's face lit up. "Oh! Hey, Matt. It's nice to finally meet you." She glanced at his shark tooth. "I like your necklace."

"Thanks! Nice to meet you too," Matt replied. Holding the shark tooth between his fingers, he dramatically added, "Yo, it's a crazy story how I got this! I was surfing one day when this ten-foot tiger shark came up and decided to chomp on my board. So, I started punching it in the head to show it what's up, and eventually, it left me alone. Then, when I got back to shore, I found this tooth stuck in my board, so I decided to make a necklace out of it."

Katie's eyes widened in shock at Matt's tale. "Really?" she asked, turning to Jason in disbelief.

Jason gave Katie a bemused grin. "He got it at a gas station down the road. I was with him when he bought it."

"Bruh!" Matt said, laughing. "Why you gotta mess up my story like that, man?"

Katie playfully slapped Matt on the arm as he turned to run away. "Come on, we've got a full keg!" he urged. With his arms raised, he shouted to the others, "Where my party people at? It's time to get our drink on and make some bad decisions!"

Jason chuckled, telling Katie, "I told you he was a handful."

Katie shook her head, smiling, as they followed Matt toward the others.

One by one, Jason introduced Katie to his friends, and she quickly blended in, her laughter mingling with the cheerful chatter and playful banter that filled the night air. When she spoke, his friends leaned forward, their eyes bright with interest, nodding enthusiastically at her words. The camaraderie enveloped her like a warm embrace, making her feel cherished and included. With every shared story and genuine smile, it became clear that this group was more than just a collection of friends—it was a tight-knit family, welcoming her with open arms and making her feel as though she belonged to something truly special.

While Katie was wrapped in conversation with some of the other girls, Jason briefly broke away to refill his cup. As he poured, Matt strolled up beside him, a wide grin on his face. “Bruh, that chick’s a unicorn! You hookin’ up with her?”

Jason chuckled nervously, glancing around to ensure no one was listening. “Yeah, but you can’t tell anyone yet. Seriously, dude—Cricket will fire me if he finds out. I’m planning to tell him after the Grand Championship, but you gotta keep it on the down low until then.”

“My lips are sealed, bruh!” Grinning playfully, he raised his cup to toast Jason. “My man!”

Later that night, as the party waned, Jason drove Katie home in his boat. Away from the bright lights of the harbor, Katie noticed a luminous glow in the water behind the boat. “Oh my gosh! Look, the water is glowing!”

Having seen it many times before, Jason casually responded, “Yeah, it’s caused by bioluminescent plankton. Pretty cool, huh?”

“Yeah, I’ve heard of it, but I’ve never actually seen it before,” Katie remarked with amazement.

The night felt enchanting as they held hands under the canopy of stars, the bioluminescent glow in the water trailing behind the boat as they approached Katie’s home. At her dock, Jason leaned in for a kiss goodnight. The moment felt magical as they held each other in a passionate embrace—a feeling that would linger with him as he drove home, lost in thoughts of their future together.

The next day, Katie's friends from school came to visit, and her father returned home. Her friends planned to stay with her for the Fourth of July holiday. Although Katie spent the day with them, she and Jason texted frequently, exchanging playful messages and making plans to meet up that night at Tripletails.

As evening approached, Jason and Matt headed to Tripletails in Jason's boat. When they arrived, they spotted the girls at a table in the lively outdoor bar area, overlooking the harbor. After quick introductions, Katie turned to Jason and said, "I was just about to go to the bar to buy a drink. Y'all want to come with me?"

"Yeah, sounds good," Jason replied. Leaning in, he quietly added, "But Matt's not twenty-one yet."

Grinning, Matt said, "It's all good, though!" Pulling a miniature bottle of rum from his shorts pocket, he added, "I brought my own!" The group erupted in laughter as Matt continued, "Just get me a Coke, J-Bay!"

While Matt stayed behind with Katie's friends, Jason and Katie headed to the bar. Unbeknownst to them, Bill Murphy and a group of his friends had just arrived and were walking toward Katie's friends.

Clearly intoxicated, Bill greeted the girls, saying, "What's up, ladies! Long time no see!"

"Hey, Billy!" Evie replied cheerfully. Several of the other girls greeted him warmly as well, while Jessica gave him a cold smirk and a half-hearted wave.

"Do you know Matt?" Evie asked. "He's one of Jason's friends."

Bill laughed. "Does he look like someone I would know?"

"Excuse me?" Matt responded, shocked at the audacity of his insult.

Standing at the bar, Jason turned and saw the tense encounter unfolding between Matt and Bill. He knew he had to act quickly to keep things from escalating.

With a slight slur to his words, Bill said, "Listen, bro, these girls are out of your league. You need to leave before you embarrass yourself even more than you already have by wearing that ridiculous necklace."

Just as Matt began to lunge toward Bill Murphy, his fists clenched, Jason leaped in front of him, raising his hands. "Whoa! Whoa! Whoa! We're not looking for any trouble tonight, buddy."

"Nah, bruh!" Matt said, fury blazing in his eyes. "I don't know who this punk thinks he is, but he ain't gonna clown me like that!" Looking over Jason's shoulder, he sarcastically said to Bill Murphy, "Hey, bruh, you need to stop embarrassing yourself and give those tiny pink shorts back to whatever twelve-year-old girl you borrowed them from."

With a sneering expression, Bill Murphy scoffed. "They're salmon color, you idiot!"

With a mocking laugh, Matt shot back, "Well, at least we both agree they're fishy!"

As the tension in the air thickened, Katie hurried over to Jason, positioning herself in front of Bill Murphy. "Y'all just stop," she insisted, her voice firm yet pleading.

Bill smirked, leaning back slightly. "Wow, Katie. You have really lowered your standards for the type of people you hang out with. You're better than this."

Angered by his comment, Katie shot back, "No, I'm better than hanging out with people who talk down to anyone who doesn't have as much money as they do."

Suddenly, two large men wearing black T-shirts that read "SECURITY" appeared. "Is there a problem here, folks?" one of them asked, scanning the group.

Bill Murphy shook his head with a smirk. "No problem. We were just leaving." He cast one last look of disappointment at Katie, then turned away, his friends falling in step behind him.

Despite Bill Murphy and his crew leaving, the heated exchange hung over the group like a dark cloud. Even Matt, usually full of energy and ready to party, was eager to head home early that night.

However, the next day brought a fresh beginning. With the sun shining brightly in a clear blue sky, Jason and Matt met up with Katie and her friends at the beach.

The girls had their brightly colored towels spread across the powdery white sand, side by side. A radio placed nearby played music, though it was muffled by the sound of the sea breeze and the rhythmic crashing of waves against the shore.

While some of the girls lounged on their towels, soaking up the sun and working on their tans, Katie and Jessica eagerly joined Jason and Matt, excited to try out the boogie boards they had brought along. Standing in the warm, crystal-clear water just above their waists, the four of them bobbed gently over the small waves. They scanned the horizon, searching for the perfect wave to ride, anticipation building with each swell.

"Okay, here comes a good one!" Jason called out. With the boards pressed against their stomachs and hands gripping the top edges, they lunged forward, kicking their legs fiercely. Suddenly, the wave began to carry them along effortlessly. The boys grinned widely while the girls squealed with delight as they raced forward, dropping down the face of the wave. As the wave crashed behind them, it transformed into frothy white-water, pushing them all the way to the shore.

Katie stood up in the knee-deep water, beaming with excitement, her board trailing on a coiled leash attached to her wrist. After wiping her eyes, she laughed. "That was so much fun!"

"I know!" Jessica replied, turning to make her way back out into the surf, clutching her boogie board tightly. "Come on, let's go again!"

They rode wave after wave that afternoon, playing carefree in the water together. Jason and Katie had told their friends about their secret relationship and made little effort to hide it that day. Their friends could see the undeniable connection between them and were happy to witness them falling in love.

Eventually, even the other girls joined in, taking turns riding the boogie boards. While they continued to ride the waves, Jason and Katie slowly drifted a short distance away, floating face to face with their knees bent, their heads just above the wave tops.

Glancing back, they saw Matt getting along with Katie's friends, the girls laughing at his crazy antics.

Katie tilted her head slightly, watching them with a smile. "They seem to be getting along well," she said. "We should do this again."

"Definitely," Jason replied, his grin lingering for a moment. Then his expression darkened. He shook his head, thinking about the tense exchange between Matt and Bill Murphy the night before.

"I still can't believe how your spoiled trust fund buddy, Bill Murphy, talked to him last night."

Katie drew back slightly, her expression puzzled. "I know Billy was out of line, but what does him having a trust fund have to do with it?"

Jason exhaled sharply. "Because he's an arrogant, entitled kook who's never had to work for anything."

Katie's brow furrowed, her voice carrying a note of challenge. "I have a trust fund. Does that make me a bad person?"

Jason looked away, instantly aware of his misstep. "No," he said regretfully. "I didn't mean it like that."

After a brief pause, Katie said with a softer tone, "I think it's normal for parents to want to help their kids. Even your parents helped you buy your townhome, right?"

Jason nodded, realizing her point. "Yeah."

Katie flashed a playful smile. "So, you still like me even though I'm a trust fund baby?"

Jason chuckled, some of the tension lifting. "Yeah, I guess I'll make an exception—but don't get cocky, alright?"

A grin spread across her face. "Oh, I'm very cocky," she said, splashing water at him.

He lunged forward, laughing, and caught her hands beneath the surface. Although there were still plenty of people on the beach, he was confident there was no one around they needed to hide from. He pulled her in closer, their lips meeting for a quick kiss.

With the tension between them lifted and Jason a little wiser than before, they rejoined their friends, spending the rest of the day together, playing in the waves.

When it was finally time to leave, everyone's skin was salty, sandy, and kissed by the sun. Though they were exhausted from the day's fun, none of them wanted it to end—especially Jason and Katie.

The next day, Jason returned to work, and he and Katie continued their charade of pretending to be just friends around Cricket, Soda, and her father—a challenge that grew increasingly difficult. When the Fourth of July holiday finally arrived, Mr. Gregory joined Katie and her friends on a trip to Crab Island aboard the *Family Tradition*. The scene was a spectacle to behold, as thousands of boats dotted the shallow sandbar while helicopters and planes buzzed overhead. The tide was coming in, revealing deep emerald-green hues in the depths, gradually fading to an almost crystal-clear clarity in the shallows, where the sandy white bottom was visible beneath the surface.

Smoke billowed from the grill where Jason cooked burgers and hot dogs, the savory scent making everyone eager for a bite.

As the festivities continued throughout the day, Katie and her friends swam and lounged on the floating mat behind the boat, their laughter and playful chatter creating a vibrant atmosphere of fun. As evening approached, they stayed to watch the fireworks show near the harbor entrance. While Mr. Gregory, Cricket, and Soda sat upstairs in the flybridge, Jason remained below, standing in the mezzanine beside Katie and her friends, hidden from their view.

As the powerful booms of the fireworks echoed and bright lights burst in the sky, Katie gently placed her pinky next to Jason's. Their fingers intertwined for just a moment, and they exchanged nervous but excited smiles. Change was coming—and they knew they'd only have to keep their relationship a secret a little while longer, until after the Grand Championship.

THE GRAND CHAMPIONSHIP

Dressed in a suit and tie, a local TV anchor announced to viewers, "Billed as the greatest show in sport-fishing, the Blue Marlin Grand Championship began today in Orange Beach. Sixty of the best billfishing teams in the Gulf will compete over the next three days for more than one and a half million dollars in prizes. This was the scene outside of the Perdido Pass today just before noon, with teams lined up, eagerly awaiting the shotgun start."

The camera cut to the tournament emcee on a boat, holding a VHF radio mic to his mouth as he excitedly counted down: "Five, four, three, two, one, go!" A gun blast suddenly rang out as another man fired a shotgun from the bow of the boat. Circling above, a different camera crew in a helicopter captured breathtaking aerial footage of the tournament boats racing off to their fishing destinations across the slick, calm ocean, where the glassy surface mirrored the sky of that perfect bluebird day.

The camera returned to the newscaster, who continued, "Some of these boats may travel nearly a thousand miles in pursuit of victory, while others might find success as close as forty miles away. For spectators, the highlight will be on Saturday at The Wharf from five to eight PM. Two giant

Jumbotron screens on each side of the weigh-in scale will ensure that everyone can witness the drama unfold as teams weigh in their fish, hoping to win the largest fishing tournament payout—in the Gulf."

Later that afternoon, the *Family Tradition* arrived at their first stop—the Petronius drilling platform. They had hoped to replicate the good luck they had experienced during their previous tournament there, but this time they had company—three other tournament boats were also fishing the same rig. While the other boats set out to catch bait near the Petronius, the *Family Tradition* began trolling lures, eager to be the first to hook a marlin.

Unfortunately, fishing turned out to be tougher than anyone had anticipated. No blue marlins were caught that first day at the Petronius or anywhere else as the teams battled the stifling summer heat and humidity.

For Jason, the heat and humidity weren't the only things making the day feel steamy. He struggled to keep his eyes off Katie, who wore a vibrant purple bikini paired with cutoff jean shorts and flip-flops. Occasionally, they exchanged flirty glances—each look a risky yet exhilarating move with others close by.

Despite not catching a marlin, the atmosphere on the boat stayed cheerful and lively. The others were blissfully unaware of the budding romance between Katie and Jason, seeing only two friends savoring the day, sharing laughter and camaraderie. Yet, their connection was undeniable. Katie, usually brimming with cheer, seemed to glow even brighter in Jason's presence. Her laughter was more vibrant and infectious, fueled by their growing bond and the thrill of the tournament.

As night fell, Jason took his turn at wheel watch to give Cricket a chance to shower. The ocean surface was smooth as he navigated the boat through the darkness toward their next stop—the Thunderhorse oil rig. Traveling at 12 knots (roughly 14 miles per hour), the airflow offered little relief from the hot evening air. Suddenly, he heard someone climbing the ladder to the flybridge behind him.

"Hey-ey," Katie said softly, smiling as she reached the top of the ladder.

"Hey," Jason replied, his face lighting up at the sight of her.

"I just want to see how things are going up here," Katie said as she walked toward him.

"Better now that you're here," he replied with a playful grin.

Without another word, they melted into a passionate kiss at the spot where their lips had first met. Their hearts pounded in the stillness of the night, each thud echoing like a drumbeat that reverberated through their bodies. In that moment, there was no fear of what the future might hold. There was only their irresistible, even if impulsive, desire to be together.

Suddenly, they heard the salon door open and close, followed by the sound of someone climbing up the ladder. Quickly, they let go of each other's hands, trying to hide their surprise.

It was Cricket. He cheerfully greeted them. "Thanks for watchin' the wheel for me, J-Bay." With a hint of surprise in his voice, he asked, "What are you doin' up here, Katie?"

"Oh, I uh—I just wanted to see where we'll be fishing tomorrow," she replied, her voice steadying.

"Well, we're gonna try fishin' Thunderhorse in the mornin'. Hopefully, we'll have some luck there like we did on our last trip!" Cricket excitedly replied. He then eagerly pointed out several other oil rig locations marked on the screen where they might fish in the coming days. Katie listened intently, genuinely interested in Cricket's game plan. However, she briefly exchanged smiles with Jason, relieved they hadn't been caught.

The next morning, with only a few hours of sleep, the crew woke at 3:00 AM to begin catching bait. When Jason stepped outside into the muggy morning air, he was immediately struck by the sight of five other tournament boats already catching bait around the brightly lit Thunderhorse rig. Frustration crossed his face when he recognized one of the boats—the *Trust Me*.

While Jason and Soda jigged for tuna, schools of squid darted in and out of the brightly lit water behind the boat with spectacular speed, fleeing predators below. Although the tuna were plentiful that morning, so were the sharks and barracudas. They struggled to land even half the blackfin tuna they hooked, as lines were cut and fish were often bitten in half.

They finally filled the tuna tubes with fresh bait just as daybreak arrived. The sun's warm golden light spilled across the water, casting shimmering reflections on its glassy surface. A few wispy clouds lingered on the distant horizon, tinted with soft hues of pink and orange, hinting at the promise of a beautiful day ahead.

After swiftly deploying a live bait on each side of the boat, they set out trolling at a steady 2 knots, competing with the other tournament boats to be the first to find a marlin.

It wasn't long before something with sharp teeth clipped off the bait on Soda's side. He sighed in frustration as he finished reeling in the line and noticed the jagged edges where it had been cut. Turning to Cricket, he called out, "Got sharked!"

With no time to lose, Soda quickly replaced the tackle and deployed another live bait, hoping that this time a marlin would find it.

By 10:00 AM, they had lost a total of four baits to toothy critters. Making matters worse, Cricket was having a hard time getting a clear picture on the Omni sonar and hadn't marked a single marlin. He told the others, "There's too much sonar interference with all these boats scanning the same area. I'm gonna move a bit farther up current to see if that helps. Hopefully, the sharks and barracudas won't be as bad farther away from the rig either."

By 11:00 AM, the temperature had soared, and the sun beat down relentlessly on Jason and Soda as they sat by the reels, hands resting on the spools, waiting for a bite. Eventually, they decided to don their gaiters to protect their faces and necks from the searing summer sun. Still, despite their best efforts, the suffocating heat enveloped them as they sat in the direct sunlight, with no shade to provide relief.

The sweltering heat was also taking its toll on the live baits, making them lethargic and slowly killing them. One bait died in the tube, and another expired as they trolled, leaving them with only four baits: two in the water and two still in the tubes.

Suddenly, Cricket's voice rang out sharply, "I'm marking a fish! It's straight ahead, a hundred feet down!"

The team perked up with excitement, eager to catch the first fish of the trip. Each member waited in anticipation, hoping the live baits trolled above would entice the marlin to rise from the depths.

After the baits passed over the area, Cricket turned to the others, a hint of disappointment in his voice. "It's not comin' up. I'm gonna circle around and make another pass." He began to slowly turn the boat in a wide arc back toward the fish, careful not to pull the baits too quickly, which could further stress the fish and cause them to perish.

As he maneuvered the boat, Cricket noticed the *Trust Me* speeding toward the location of the marked fish. "What are they doing?" he exclaimed, disbelief and frustration etched on his face. Although it wasn't strictly against tournament rules, it was generally considered disrespectful to encroach on another team's pursuit of a fish.

The *Trust Me* raced in front of the *Family Tradition*, abruptly stopping directly over the marked fish. On the back deck, a camera crew and four mates were focused on the action, along with Bill Murphy, who watched from the upper mezzanine level. Each mate wore a bright yellow long-sleeve shirt and black headphones with mics extending in front of their mouths, allowing them to communicate with each other and the captain.

As one of the mates quickly dropped a live bait overboard, Soda erupted, yelling, “Hey, we were workin’ that fish! Y’all need to back off!” He and Jason threw their arms up in frustration.

Cricket grabbed the mic of his VHF radio, his voice tense and angry. “*Trust Me*, this is the captain of the *Family Tradition*. We were actively pursuing that fish. Over.”

The *Trust Me* captain responded caustically, “Copy that, *Family Tradition*. You WERE pursuing this fish, and now we are pursuing this fish. Glad we got that squared away. Over and out.”

Cricket’s face flushed with anger as he seethed at the audacity of the *Trust Me* moving in on the fish they had found first.

Standing near Cricket and Mr. Gregory in the flybridge, Katie watched in disbelief. “I can’t believe he’s doing this,” she muttered under her breath, narrowing her eyes at the sight of Bill Murphy. It felt like a vindictive betrayal of their friendship and a blatant violation of the unspoken rules of respect among fellow fishermen. She glanced down at Jason, who looked back, shaking his head angrily. “This isn’t fair,” she said, her voice trembling on the verge of breaking.

Beside her, Mr. Gregory remained calm and composed. He turned to Cricket, who was gripping the wheel with white knuckles, his face flushed. In a measured tone, Mr. Gregory asked, “Is that allowed under the tournament rules?”

Trying to restrain his emotions, Cricket blurted out, “It ain’t against the rules, but that doesn’t make it right.”

Mr. Gregory nodded gently, his expression unwavering as he accepted the situation with an unsettling calm.

Suddenly, the fishing rod on the *Trust Me* bent sharply, and line began to peel away. "Fish on!" one of the mates shouted. Another mate turned toward the *Family Tradition* and yelled, "We're hooked up with a fish! Y'all need to back up and give us some space!"

As the *Family Tradition* slowly backed away, a heavy silence enveloped the team, their hearts sinking with the weight of lost opportunity. They watched Bill Murphy position himself in the fighting chair, waving them goodbye with a smug grin. In the distance, the silhouette of a massive marlin erupted from the water, leaping into the air multiple times. Each time it crashed down, it sent colossal splashes cascading around it. A puff of black diesel smoke rose into the air as the powerful engines of *Trust Me* roared to life, backing down on the fish.

Unable to bear watching it any longer, Cricket turned to Soda and Jason. His voice was heavy with disappointment as he slowly said, "Let's make a run."

The mood among the team was somber as they raced across the slick, calm water that afternoon. No matter how fast Cricket drove, they couldn't shake the haunting feeling that the *Trust Me* team had stolen their chance to catch a large marlin—one that could have won them prize money and possibly even first place in the tournament.

As they approached their next stop, the Blind Faith drilling platform, they spotted two tournament boats already on the scene: the *Reckless* and the *Roll On*. Both were slow trolling live baits around the platform. The teams on board were old friends of Cricket and Soda, greeting them warmly over the radio. Despite the friendly banter, everyone maintained a respectful distance while fishing, understanding the unspoken rules of the tournament.

Hoping to find a marlin away from the rig, as he had during their previous tournament, Cricket searched the same section of water where they had scored a double-header. The water was dotted with patches of sargassum, some broken into small pieces and scattered across the surface. This forced Jason and Soda to continuously clear the grass from their lines as they trolled, further stressing their already weary baits and causing them to die even faster.

Before long, they had exhausted the live baits they had caught that morning, prompting the team to search for more blackfin tuna close to the rig, losing precious daylight hours in their pursuit of a marlin. With a heavy cloud of despair still hanging over them, silence enveloped the boat as Jason and Soda struggled to restock the tuna tubes, losing several of the baits to the lurking sharks and barracudas.

When it was time to begin trolling again, Cricket moved well away from the rig and other boats.

Hoping for a change in perspective, Katie climbed from the flybridge to the top of the boat tower. Although it was only a small change in elevation, the view seemed dramatically different. She began to smile softly as she scanned the surrounding water from her new vantage point high above, captivated by the serene and stunning scenery of the sea. The vast expanse of blue water seemed to stretch endlessly, inviting her into its tranquil embrace.

Suddenly, something caught her attention in front of them. “Dolphins!” she called out excitedly. Mr. Gregory stood up for a better look, a warm smile appearing on his face as he saw a group of five dolphins racing toward them.

Cricket, however, clearly frustrated, turned to Jason and Soda. “Bring those baits in, quick!” he ordered.

Jason and Soda cranked the reel handles as fast as they could, skipping the tuna across the surface. Just as the baits neared the boat, one of the dolphins lunged forward, grabbing Jason’s fish and clutching it in its mouth like a dog bone. With a burst of speed, it barreled away from the boat, racing nearly a hundred yards. Katie looked alarmed when she heard the sound of the drag “ZZZzzzzzzz...” Deeply concerned, she leaned over the back rail and asked Cricket, “Is it hooked?”

Cricket shook his head. “No, they’re too smart to get hooked. Dolphins can see exactly where that hook is on the bait with their echolocation.”

Suddenly, the drag stopped. Jason cranked the reel handle with all his might, skipping the bait across the surface and trying to reel it back in. The dolphin remained where it was, waiting and watching as if challenging itself in a playful game. As the bait approached the boat, the dolphin charged forward, racing toward them with incredible speed. Just as Jason was about to pull the fish from the water, the dolphin snatched it up again, making another blistering hundred-yard dash before letting the bait go once more.

This time, the dolphin playfully leaped from the water, circling around the bait while emitting a series of sharp, rapid clicks and whistles that sounded like laughter: "eE, eE, EEEEE."

Jason threw up his hands in frustration. "Come on! Really?"

From the top of the tower, Katie playfully teased Jason, laughing as she said, "Oh my gosh! That's so cute! It wants to play fetch with you, Jason!"

Despite his irritation with the dolphin, he couldn't help but smile at Katie poking fun at him. Her words sparked laughter among the rest of the team, their smiles contagious as they watched the spectacle unfold.

Leaning over the rail, Katie continued to tease him, "You better be nice and play with him, Jason. That dolphin is a sign of good luck for us!"

Jason smiled and emphatically shot back, "THAT DOLPHIN IS DEFINITELY NOT A SIGN OF GOOD LUCK!"

With a flirtatious smile lighting up her face, Katie confidently replied, "The trip isn't over, Jason Baymont! Just wait and see!"

Jason laughed and shook his head as he turned his attention back to the rod and reel. He watched the dolphin in disbelief as it continued to jump around the bait, its expression one that everyone would later agree looked like it was smiling.

The dolphin eventually grew bored with Jason's reluctance to engage in its playful game. It casually swam up to the bait, snatched it with ease, and left behind only a small portion of the head attached to the hook. It then joined its friends as they disappeared beneath the surface in the distance.

Though they had lost another bait, Katie's lighthearted teasing brought a much-needed lift to their spirits. They continued their search for marlins around the rig for the rest of the day, but without any luck. Cricket marked a few fish on sonar, but they were unable to raise them even with their freshly caught live bait.

As the sun dipped toward the horizon that evening, the crew was down to just two baits trolled behind the boat. When Jason saw the small blackfin tuna on his side dragging lifelessly along the surface, a sinking feeling settled over him—maybe this just wasn't their lucky trip. With frustration creeping into his voice, he told Soda, "Well, it looks like this bait is dead, and there's not enough time to catch more before sunset." He shook his head in disbelief and frustration as he continued, "Our luck has been terrible this trip. Something's gotta change."

Soda optimistically replied, "Well, tomorrow's a new day. Luck is important, but we've just got to stay consistent, being meticulous in everything we do. That way, when an opportunity does come our way, we're ready for it."

With frustration evident in his face, Jason nodded, acknowledging Soda's point. Suddenly, a smile began to tug at the corner of his mouth as he exclaimed, "That's it, Soda! We need more opportunities—more shots at the marlins." Pausing for a moment to collect his thoughts, Jason continued, "What if we hunted for them with the sonar while pulling the teasers at eight knots instead of slow trolling live bait at two knots? That would let us cover four times as much ground with the time we have left. Plus, we wouldn't lose as many baits to the sharks, barracudas, and dolphins. When we find a marlin on the sonar, we can just turn on the electric reels to bring the teasers in. Then, you and I can get a live bait ready to drop on it. If the fish doesn't bite, we keep moving and search for another one."

Soda's brow furrowed, a puzzled expression appearing on his face as he considered Jason's idea. "You're suggestin' we only pull the teasers and not use any lures?"

"Yeah, exactly!" Jason replied. He then explained, "It takes too much time to pull in all five lure lines and the teasers just to drop a live bait on a fish that might not bite. But if there happens to be one up top that we can't see with the sonar, at least we'll have a chance to attract it with the teasers. Then we could drop a bait behind the boat for it. What do you think?"

Soda looked deep in thought before hesitantly responding, "I don't know, Jason. It sort of makes sense, but we've just never fished like that before. Cricket's the one responsible for puttin' us on the fish, so it's really up to him as the captain. I just don't think he's gonna want to try somethin' we've never done before in our biggest tournament of the year."

Jason's shoulders slumped as he let out a long, weary sigh, the weight of Soda's words settling heavily on him. He gave a quiet nod, his expression a mix of resignation and understanding.

Seeing Jason's disappointment, Soda shrugged and said, "Well, the worst he could say is no. I guess it wouldn't hurt to ask." With a wide grin, he motioned for Jason to follow him up to the flybridge, adding, "Come on, let's go run it by him."

With renewed optimism, Jason followed Soda, hopeful that Cricket might like the idea. However, after Jason shared his thoughts, Cricket slowly shook his head, a pained expression crossing his face. "I don't know, fellas. I like the idea of covering more ground, but I'm not sure about pulling teasers without any lures. If we're trolling, we might as well put a couple of lures out."

Hoping for a compromise, Jason said, "What if we put a lure on the center rigger? It's out of the way, and I could pull that one line in while Soda gets ready to drop the live bait."

Cricket considered Jason's suggestion, his lips pressed tightly together in thought. Weighing his options, he finally said with a sarcastic smile, "Well, I don't think we can do any worse at this point, so we'll give it a try."

Smiles spread across Jason's and Soda's faces as they heard Cricket's response. Their spirits lifted at the thought that this new approach to searching for marlins might offer them more chances to catch a money-winning fish before time ran out.

The team went to bed early that night, worn out from two grueling days of fishing in the stifling summer heat. Although they were weighed down by the disappointment of their lost opportunity with a huge marlin, they clung to the hope that the next day would bring a much-needed change in luck.

At 3:00 AM, the crew woke up to begin their day once more. Their eyes were weary as they softly grumbled, "Mornin'," to each other, reaching for their coffee cups and filling them with piping hot brew. No one was in a talkative mood, so they simply sipped from their mugs, each lost in thought about the day ahead.

After Cricket finished his first cup of coffee, he walked back to the pot and poured himself another. Leaning against the counter, he turned toward Jason and Soda, clutching his cup. His face was pensive and distant as he spoke steadily. "Word over the radio is that the *Trust Me* is currently in first place with that marlin they caught yesterday. It weighed in at seven hundred and twenty-two pounds."

Jason and Soda let out soft sighs of frustration. At a loss for words, their faces mirrored a mix of anger and disappointment. Cricket pressed his lips together and nodded to himself as he stared blankly into the coffee mug in his hand. Then he continued calmly, "And they were so confident that they had brought in the winning fish that they didn't even bother goin' back out. They just spent all night partyin', celebrating their victory early."

A smile crept across Cricket's face as he said, "Fellas, I think it's about time we go catch a giant marlin, win a bunch of money, and, most importantly, knock Team *Trust Me* off the top of that leaderboard."

Soda and Jason chuckled softly, their fatigue fading as they straightened their backs with renewed vigor. They nodded in unison. "Let's do it!"

Fueled by their determination to dethrone Team *Trust Me* from the top of the leaderboard, they quickly sprang into action. After filling the tuna tubes with fresh bait, the crew set out on a relentless pursuit, focused on finding a marlin that would beat Bill Murphy and his team. Following Jason's suggestion, they cruised at a steady 8 knots (roughly 9 miles per hour), towing four teasers alongside the center rigger lure. The boat sliced through the water, swiftly covering the area around the Blind Faith oil rig. They made several drops at the locations where Cricket had marked large fish but moved on when the fish refused to bite—knowing there was no time to lose.

As the morning wore on, the temperature soared even higher than the previous two days, causing the baits to perish more quickly. After checking the tubes, Soda sighed heavily while shaking his head upon discovering that two more baits had succumbed to the heat. He called up to Cricket, holding up the lifeless tunas for him to see. "We lost two more," he said. "We're down to three live baits. This heat's really gettin' to 'em."

Cricket nodded in frustration as he considered his next move, aware that they were running out of time and bait. He needed to find a new spot quickly—somewhere he could reach in time to potentially catch a big fish and make it back for the weigh-in. According to the tournament rules, boats had to return to The Wharf for the weigh-in via Mobile Bay, reaching the demarcation line in Sailboat Bay by 6:00 PM. Their return by the deadline would be confirmed by official tournament spotters. As Cricket studied the boat's navigational screen, which displayed the locations of all nearby oil rigs, an idea suddenly struck him.

"Y'all go ahead and pull everything in. I wanna try fishin' this new drill ship to the east that Mick was tellin' me about a few weeks ago. It's a pretty good run from here, but at least we'll be closer to Orange Beach for the drive back."

Sitting in the flybridge with Cricket and Mr. Gregory, Katie asked, "What's a drill ship?"

Cricket replied, "It's kinda like an oil rig, but it's a giant ship that uses a dynamic positioning system to keep it over the drilling site. Oil companies use 'em to drill exploratory wells in deep water. This one's drillin' in a spot that's just over two thousand feet deep."

"Oh," Katie replied, her face lighting up with genuine amazement—a reaction mirrored by Mr. Gregory.

Later on, as they traveled toward the drill ship, Cricket's eyes suddenly lit up, and he pointed toward the horizon. "Look! There's a pod of whales!" he exclaimed. In the distance, the majestic creatures broke the surface, their dark backs glistening in the sunlight as they dove and resurfaced in a rhythmic dance. Water shot up from their blowholes like geysers, and the droplets sparkled in the sunlight as they cascaded back down into the ocean.

"I didn't know there were whales out here!" Mr. Gregory exclaimed, his voice filled with wonder as both he and Katie gasped in astonishment.

"That's so cool!" Katie exclaimed.

Turning to Cricket, Mr. Gregory asked, "What type of whales are they?"

"Sperm whales," Cricket replied. "They're amazing creatures! I read that they can dive over ten thousand feet deep and stay underwater for up to ninety minutes."

The team watched in awe, marveling at the magic unfolding before them. Laughter and excitement erupted on the boat, lifting their spirits as they shared this incredible experience together. The sight of the whales was like a breath of fresh air, rejuvenating their hearts and reminding them of the ocean's beauty and wonder.

When they finally arrived at the drill ship, they were pleased to find that no other fishing boats were in sight. The cobalt blue water was dotted with patches of golden-brown sargassum, teeming with life. Flying fish leaped from the water, soaring in every direction as their boat sped by. Not far away, a massive weed line stretched toward the horizon, extending as far as the eye could see.

Katie and Mr. Gregory gazed in awe at the size of the drill ship, which featured a large, industrial-looking tower midship and a helicopter landing pad on its bow.

Soda shouted up to Cricket, "Is that the same drill ship we fished in Green Canyon last year?"

"Yeah, they moved over here about a month ago," Cricket replied.

Soda turned to Jason with a grin. "We caught some good fish off it last year in Green Canyon. Maybe we'll have some luck fishin' it here too."

Jason took a deep breath, scanning the new location. It looked promising. A smile crept across his face, fueled by the hope that this spot might finally bring them the change in luck they needed.

Soda addressed Cricket and Jason, "There's too much grass to pull the dredges through here, so let's just put out the bridge teasers and center rigger. We'll still have to shag grass a good bit, but at least we'll be pullin' somethin' in the water."

Jason and Cricket nodded in agreement with Soda's plan.

Cruising at 8 knots, Cricket was able to quickly survey the area with sonar, searching below the sea grass-covered surface for a marlin. It wasn't long before he spotted a blip on the screen and shouted, "I'm marking a nice-sized fish up ahead! It's just over a hundred and fifty feet deep!"

Instantly, their faces brightened with optimism. Jason quickly pulled a tuna out of the tube, only to find it had died in the brief time since he last checked it. The next one he grabbed was also dead. When he reached for the remaining fish, he discovered it was nearly lifeless. Soda and Jason exchanged glances. Their expressions reflected a mix of disbelief and frustration.

Soda called out to Cricket, "We're down to one live bait, and it's barely kickin'. What do you want us to do?"

Feeling the time crunch, Cricket sighed in frustration, shaking his head at the disappointing news. After a brief pause to consider his options, he hesitantly replied, "I'll head back closer to the drill ship so we can try to make bait. I just hope this fish stays around long enough for us to get another shot at it."

After leaving the marked fish, Cricket found a large school of bait holding close to the drill ship. It wasn't long before Jason excitedly said, "I'm on!" As the rod bent sharply, the fish unexpectedly started pulling drag from the reel. He added, "Feels like a good one!"

Suddenly, Soda grunted, "I got a nice one too!" His rod bent over, and line began to peel off the reel, a sure sign that he had hooked a large bait.

As they both fought their fish toward the boat, Jason's fish suddenly stopped fighting after a sharp pull. With a puzzled expression on his face, he said, “I’ve still got something on, but it feels like dead weight.” Once he brought the fish closer to the boat, they could see he had the head of a 20-pound yellowfin tuna with a cookie-cutter bite mark where the body had been. A shark had eaten everything but the head in a single bite.

“Hurry! Grab the net!” Soda urged as he fought a similarly sized yellowfin, determined to get it to the boat before a shark could dine on it as well. The tuna began circling beneath the boat, turning its body sideways to resist Soda’s intense effort to bring it up. Jason watched anxiously as the fish, with its long, brightly colored yellow sickle-shaped fins, inched closer to his reach with each heave of Soda’s rod.

Finally, seeing that the fish was within reach, Jason reached down with the net, but the fish quickly darted away, pulling out several more feet of line and escaping Jason’s grasp. Soda continued to pull hard on the fish, the rod bending under the immense pressure as the fish pulled down. Seeing the fish within reach again, Jason thrust the net in front of its nose, and it darted right in.

Cheers erupted as Jason triumphantly lifted the fish into the boat. Soda chuckled, “I don’t think I’ve ever been this excited to catch a small yellowfin!”

Cricket chuckled and said, “Yep! Sometimes a yellowfin like that is lunch, and sometimes it’s bait! Today, it’s bait! Y’all get that thing bridled up while I try to get back on the marlin!”

Katie and Mr. Gregory watched in wonder as Jason and Soda rigged the relatively small 20-pound yellowfin tuna—a fish that can reach over 200 pounds—as a massive live bait. Holding the fish against his chest, Jason struggled to maintain his grip as the muscular tuna thrashed its tail, shaking its entire body violently.

After driving back to the area where he had first spotted the fish on sonar, it wasn't long before Cricket shouted, "I found it! It's straight ahead and still about a hundred and fifty feet deep."

Just as Soda finished connecting the circle hook to the tuna, Cricket called out, "It's right below us! Drop 'em!"

Like a torpedo lobbed overboard, the tuna entered the water with a splash and began racing down deep beneath the boat, pulling line from the eighty-wide at a frantic pace.

Cricket focused intently on the sonar screen as he watched the large live bait dive directly toward the much larger fish below. Suddenly, with a surge of excitement, he shouted, "It's coming up! Get ready!"

Soda and Jason looked on with intense focus, knowing this was the shot they had been waiting for—and likely their only chance at a marlin before returning to the docks. Their meticulous attention to detail and all their preparation had been for this exact moment.

Suddenly, the tuna stopped pulling line, and the rod tip ceased moving. There was a long, silent pause as everyone waited with bated breath for the bite. Soda watched the rod tip closely. It jerked softly once, and then again. Abruptly, the rod tip bent down, and line pulled away from the reel with such tremendous speed that Soda had a hard time keeping pressure on the spool with his fingers. He wanted to ensure the fish had the extremely large bait and circle hook deep in its mouth, so he let it run a little longer than normal, just to be sure. Then, he slowly began pushing the drag lever forward. The rod bent under the immense pressure, and the drag quickly gave way, creating a sound that brought smiles to all their faces—"ZZZzzzzzzz..."

"Fish on!" Soda cheered.

Jason's eyes bulged with surprise as he listened to the line pulling from the reel, producing a sharp, high-pitched whine unlike any he had heard before.

Soda's face lit up upon hearing the distinctive sound of the reel. With his eyebrows raised and a wide grin spreading across his face, he turned to Jason and heartily exclaimed, "Big game!" confident that they had hooked a sizable, potentially prize-winning fish.

As the fish continued to speed away from the boat, staying submerged below the surface, Soda moved the rod and reel to the fighting chair where Katie sat. After she snapped her harness onto the reel, Soda gave Cricket a nod, signaling that she was ready.

The engines roared to life as Cricket began backing down on the fish in full reverse, cutting through the calm cobalt blue water dotted with scattered patches of grass. Eager to help Katie regain line, Cricket pushed the boat to its limits, chasing the fish in reverse like never before. A frothy plume of whitewash trailed behind them, extending two boat lengths past the bow as they raced toward the fish.

"Wait until it stops pulling drag, then wind it in as fast as you can!" Soda coached Katie.

Katie nodded, her smile brightening with excitement.

As the boat sped backward toward the fish, they approached a weed line that was thirty feet wide and extended as far as the eye could see in both directions.

Cricket shouted down to Soda and Jason, "There's no way around the weed line up ahead. We're gonna have to go through it. Y'all just make sure the grass doesn't bunch up on the line."

Soda clenched his jaw, clearly nervous about the grass creating too much drag on the line, which could potentially cause them to lose the fish.

As the fishing line moved through the dense mat of grass, the team watched with tense expressions. Some clumps of sargassum fell away easily, while others were ejected into the air as the line forcefully pulled through it. A sigh of relief washed over them when they saw the line break through the thick mat of vegetation.

Just as the back of the boat emerged from the weed line, the boat shuddered violently beneath their feet, and a loud grinding noise echoed around them.

Cricket quickly throttled back the engines, a tense expression on his face. "Sounds like we got somethin' stuck in the wheel!" he yelled, a term for the propellers often used by fishermen.

Soda's face showed a mix of disbelief and frustration as he looked over the side of the boat and saw yellow polypropylene rope floating alongside the boat and running directly toward the propellers. As the marlin continued to pull line from the reel at a blistering pace, he turned to Cricket and said, "We ran over some poly rope!" He quickly grabbed a straight gaff to pull the rope closer. Then he yanked as hard as he could to see if it would come free. Shaking his head, he said, "It's not comin' loose."

Cricket sighed, "We're gonna lose this fish if we can't get that rope free in a hurry!"

Jason rolled his eyes in frustration, knowing that someone would have to swim underneath the boat to cut the rope loose—and he was their best hope. Dreading the task of jumping into the shark-infested water, he took a deep breath, his heart racing, and said, "I'll do it. I've done it before on my dad's boat. Where's the mask?"

"It's in the storage compartment under the lower bunk in the crew's quarters," Soda quickly replied. "We'll try to slow the fish down with the drag, but it's gonna spool us if we don't get those props free in a hurry."

Jason rushed to the salon door, quickly shedding his shirt and flip-flops before stepping inside. He dashed downstairs to the crew's quarters, where the mask was stowed. After grabbing it, he remembered to remove his tool belt, swiftly unbuckling it and leaving it on the floor before hurrying back outside.

Standing by the open tuna door, Soda handed Jason a sharp serrated knife while Katie urged, "Be careful, Jason!"

Jason nodded, hiding his nervousness behind a calm facade. Taking a deep breath, he stepped off the back of the boat and into the water. As the bubbles dissipated around him, he spotted the propeller tangled in rope. The starboard side was more entangled, so he decided to cut that one free first.

Meanwhile, in the cockpit, Soda told Katie, "Alright, Katie. Go ahead and slowly move the drag lever forward to the strike position." Unfazed, the fish continued to pull line from the reel at a blistering pace.

Positioning his back against the hull for support, Jason looked down at the propeller as he worked to free it with the serrated knife. He briefly glanced past the propeller into the boat's shadow, which seemed to stretch endlessly below him into the dark blue abyss. Rays of light danced around its periphery. He tried to stay focused on sawing through the tough rope, pulling loop after loop away from the propeller, but his mind raced with thoughts of sharks lurking nearby. As the shadows shifted beneath him, a surge of panic coursed through his body. Unsure whether the shadowy movements were sharks or mere illusions conjured by his anxiety, he realized he couldn't hold his breath much longer.

He glanced toward the back of the boat, ready to leave, but hesitated. If he could just free this one piece of rope, he might be able to move to the other propeller on his next dive and still have a chance to catch the marlin. Gripping a loop of rope with his left hand, he sawed forcefully with the knife in his right. Each stroke was frantic, and his determination quickly turned to desperation as he hacked at the frayed strands. Suddenly, the blade sliced through the rope and cut deep into his left thumb. He dropped the knife and the rope, grunting from the pain as blood welled from the cut. The shiny knife blade fluttered down, reflecting light as it sank into the darkness below him. Desperate for air and bleeding, he rushed out from under the boat. As he broke the surface, he gasped for breath and quickly swam to the tuna door, shouting, "I need another knife! Hurry, I need another knife! I dropped the other one!"

As Jason held onto the boat in front of the tuna door, blood from his hand mixed with the water, spreading across the deck.

Katie's eyes widened as she noticed the blood. "Jason, you're bleeding!" she exclaimed, her expression filled with worry.

"Yeah, I cut my hand, but I'm alright," he replied, still breathing heavily while he treaded water, his legs gently kicking below him.

Soda rushed to a storage compartment, grabbing another knife. "I don't have another serrated one, but this one should be plenty sharp enough." He placed the straight edge fillet knife on the deck near Jason's hand and asked, "You sure you're okay?"

"Yeah, I'm fine. How much line do we have left?" Jason asked.

"About a quarter of a spool," Soda replied, his expression tense. "It slowed down a little bit, but it ain't stopped pullin' drag. I'm afraid if we put much more heat on it right now, it might break the line."

Jason nodded, knowing they didn't have much time left. He grabbed the knife, took one last deep breath, and dove down. As he swam toward the port-side propeller, his mask began to fog up, making it increasingly difficult to see.

With his back to the boat's hull, he began cutting at the rope again. Although there was less to remove, the rope was wedged deeper between the shaft and the propeller, making it harder to pull out. With his vision blurred, his left hand injured, and the straight-edge knife ill-suited for the task,

Jason struggled to cut through the tough rope. Suddenly, he saw something move to his left.

A jolt of panic surged through him as he jerked his head to look, knife raised and ready to defend himself. The sound of his pounding heartbeat echoed in his head as he tried to see through the foggy mask. When the object finally came into focus, he realized it was merely a long, coiled section of rope tangled with sargassum drifting by.

While his heart was still pounding, he felt a wave of relief that it wasn't a shark. He quickly shifted his focus back to the snared propeller, aware that he was running out of air and the reel was running out of line. With one last forceful slice, the blade cut through the final strands of rope. He looked for any remnants that could tangle around the propellers, then kicked his legs furiously, propelling himself toward the surface while pulling the rope with him.

Jason wasted no time pulling himself up through the tuna door, eager to get out of the water. He shouted up to Cricket, "Both props are free!" He then pulled the rope aboard, coiling it and placing it out of the way.

A look of relief washed over Katie's face when she saw that Jason was safe, even as the marlin continued to strip line from her nearly empty spool.

"Nice work, J-Bay!" Cricket exclaimed as he and Mr. Gregory gave him a proud nod.

Focused on the reel, and with concern in his voice, Soda warned, "We're gonna get spooled if we don't get some line back soon!"

Cricket quickly fired up the engines and thrust the throttle into reverse, once again pursuing the fish.

No longer hearing the drag being pulled, Soda shouted, "Reel, Katie! Reel! Wind as fast as you can!"

Jason, Cricket, and Mr. Gregory joined in, cheering her on. With their support ringing in her ears, Katie couldn't help but smile as she cranked the reel handle furiously, determined to catch the massive marlin and hopefully bring back a prize-winning fish.

Jason grabbed his *Family Tradition* T-shirt and slipped on the flip-flops he had taken off in front of the salon door. After putting them on, Soda leaned in and asked, "How's your hand?"

"It's fine," Jason responded, holding his hand up for Soda to see.

Wincing as he inspected the fresh deep cut across the top of Jason's thumb, Soda said, "Well, at least you ain't bleedin' too bad anymore." With a concerned expression, he asked, "You want me to wire this one?"

"Nah," Jason replied with a reassuring wink. "I'll just grab a bandage from the first aid kit. It'll be fine, really." Not wanting to dwell on his injury, he quickly shifted his attention back to cheering for Katie. "Come on, Katie! You've got this!"

With nearly 1,000 yards of line out, Katie cranked the reel tirelessly as the fish swam aggressively away, her heart racing with exhilaration. After roughly 20 minutes, she had recovered all but about 100 feet of line. Her face beamed with excitement, knowing the fish was close. However, the marlin had moved beneath the boat, rendering the backing-down technique ineffective.

She cranked the reel handle, lifting herself from the fighting chair. Using her body weight, she leaned back with the rod, determined to bring the fish up. However, the marlin wouldn't budge. As she returned to a seated position, the drag gave way in short bursts, producing the sound: "ZZZ...ZZZ...ZZZZ..."

Minutes turned to hours as the battle wore on in the steamy summer heat. She occasionally gained a foot or two of line, only to have the marlin quickly take it back, jerking the rod tip down forcefully until it regained its position.

Cricket watched the fish closely on the sonar, studying its position beneath the boat. A sudden shift in color marked where it was holding—a boundary between the warm surface water and the colder depths below, known as the thermocline.

He turned to the others, jaw tight. "It looks like it's holding right on the thermocline."

Nearly three hours after being hooked, the marlin showed no signs of tiring. It stubbornly remained in the cooler depths of the thermocline, unaffected by the warm water above. Meanwhile, the summer sun blazed down relentlessly, sizzling against the backdrop of oppressive humidity, clearly taking a toll on Katie. Glistening with sweat, her once-quick movements had become slow and labored. With each unsuccessful attempt to raise the fish, her excitement waned, giving way to frustration and physical fatigue.

"Just keep the pressure on it, Katie. You're doing great," Soda urged, trying to lift her spirits.

With concern in his voice, Cricket told them, “We don’t have a whole lot of time left to boat this fish. We need to head back within the next hour, or we’re not gonna make it back in time for the weigh-in.”

Katie’s shoulders slumped, and tears filled her eyes. Doubt filled her as she questioned whether she could catch the fish in time for the weigh-in. The thought of letting her team down visibly weighed on her.

Jason turned to Katie, speaking in a reassuring tone. “You can do this, Katie. There’s still plenty of time to catch this fish. Just remember, it’s only a hundred feet away. You just have to put a little more pressure on it.”

Soda chimed in, “That’s right. You just gotta put a little more heat on it, that’s all. We need to get it out of its comfort zone in that thermocline. Go ahead and move the drag lever up to thirty-four pounds.”

Katie nodded, taking a deep breath to muster her strength before pushing the drag lever forward. She cranked the reel handle, positioning herself upright and leaning back with the rod. The pressure on the line created a high-pitched, rhythmic sound: “Tink, Tink, Tink...” punctuated by short slips of the drag: “ZZZ...ZZZ...ZZZ.”

With each second ticking by, the pressure to raise the fish mounted. Soda knew that time wasn’t on their side, but he was also worried about possibly breaking the line. With a nervous expression crossing his face and a tinge of hesitation in his voice, he said, “Alright, Katie. Go ahead and move the drag all the way to sunset and try again.”

After adjusting the drag, she began using her body weight to pump the rod. The team grimaced as they listened to the line emit an increasingly high-pitched "Tink, Tink, Tink..." sound, signaling that it was being pushed to its limits. However, this time, the fish reacted. Sensing the increased strain, it jerked the rod down fiercely, pulling Katie forward.

Caught off guard, she feared she might be yanked overboard. Quickly, she grasped the chair with both hands, bracing herself against the intense force of the fish pulling on the reel attached to her harness. With every ounce of strength, she pulled herself back toward the chair in a fierce game of tug-of-war. This time, the drag didn't slip. The rod tip slowly inched upward, bringing the fish with it. She repeated the process, gripping the chair tightly and using her body weight to pump the rod, inching the fish out of its comfort zone within the thermocline.

After several more powerful pumps of the rod, they could see the line moving up in the water column away from the boat. "It's comin' up!" Soda shouted gleefully.

A wave of excitement swept through everyone on board as they erupted in cheers, watching the massive blue marlin burst from the water, sending an explosion of spray in all directions. With three-quarters of its body rising high above the surface, it fiercely shook its head before splashing back down. The fish made several more attempts to shake the hook loose, raising its massive head partially out of the water each time.

Cricket thrust the throttle in reverse and began backing down on the fish as it leaped away from the boat repeatedly.

Determined to catch the marlin in time for the weigh-in, Katie used every last ounce of energy she had to wind the reel handle, quickly closing in on the leader line.

Jason's heart pounded as he watched the leader line inch closer, almost within reach. The cut on his thumb throbbed inside his wireman gloves but he pushed the pain aside, caught up in the excitement of the moment. He exchanged a brief smile with Soda, who stood ready with the massive flying gaff. This was the biggest fish he had ever had a chance to wire, and it was potentially worth a considerable amount of prize money.

As he reached out to make his first wrap around the leader line, he felt the intense pull of the fish and the line tightening around his hand. Suddenly, a wave of panic surged through him when he realized he was missing his tool belt, where he kept his mate saver knife. He had left the tool belt in the crew's quarters when he retrieved the mask. Soda's voice echoed in his head: "This is called a mate saver knife. Always keep one of these on you. Alright?"

Knowing there was no room for error and no time to grab the mate saver knife, Jason quickly made his second wrap with precision. In that brief moment, everything else faded away, and it was just him against the marlin with everything on the line. Time seemed to slow as he battled the powerful creature, muscles straining and heart racing, laser-focused on pulling it closer to the boat.

Suddenly, the fish shot to the surface, its body halfway out of the water, shaking its head. Jason held on tight, bracing his knees under the gunnel, every muscle in his body straining against the pull of the fish as it crashed back down.

With a determined expression on his face, Jason swiftly made several more wraps, pulling the marlin closer as it dragged him down the length of the transom toward the starboard side. The fish turned and started swimming alongside the boat, prompting Cricket to shift into forward gear.

Jason felt a wave of relief as he watched the marlin begin to swim on its side. Its once vibrant color had faded to a bronze hue, marked by blotches of white, signaling that it was tired and on the verge of defeat.

Finally, as the marlin came within reach, Soda swiftly drove the giant flying gaff into the fish's head. After detaching the pole, he gripped the rope tightly, struggling against the powerful fish as it thrashed its tail, sending water spraying into the air, drenching both him and Jason.

While Soda and Jason continued to pull the marlin toward the boat with all their might, Cricket rushed down from the flybridge and stuck a second flying gaff into the marlin just behind the dorsal fin. With that final blow, the fight with the fish was over. However, the team was still in a race against time to bring it aboard and reach the demarcation line in Sailboat Bay by 6:00 PM.

The three men shouted short commands to each other as they strained to maneuver the marlin toward the tuna door. Grunting with effort, Cricket shouted, "Grab the meat hook, Mr. Gregory—we're gonna need an extra hand with this one!"

After getting the bill of the marlin lined up with the door, Cricket counted, "One, two, three, pull!" They heaved the marlin forward, repeating the process multiple times before finally getting it completely into the boat. The men were exhausted and sweating profusely, but they exchanged smiles, briefly admiring the size of the marlin.

With no time to pause for celebration and still breathing heavily, Cricket checked his watch and said, "It's gonna be close!" Turning to Mr. Gregory, he added, "We're about to test out the top end on this boat!" He hurried up to the flybridge to start driving back.

Meanwhile, Soda said to the others, "Let's measure it before we move it into the fish bag." He explained as he took the measurements, "Sometimes this estimate is a little high, and sometimes it's a little low, but it's almost always within ten percent of the actual weight." After measuring the fish's length and girth, Soda used a formula—length times girth squared divided by 800—to estimate its weight. A wide grin spread across his face as he exclaimed, "Seven hundred and twenty-five pounds! If we make it back in time, there's definitely a chance this fish could win first place for biggest marlin!"

A spark of excitement crossed Katie's face as she asked her dad, "How much money would we win for first place?"

Mr. Gregory grinned and calmly replied, "Well, based on what I put in the Calcutta, it would probably be a little over half a million dollars."

They all exchanged cautious smiles, fully aware that they first had to make it back in time.

Soda spoke up nervously, "Let's get this fish in the bag before it loses any water weight in this heat. I don't want to take any chances. I've lost tournaments over a few ounces before."

The men quickly sprang into action, carefully moving the massive fish into the bag. They sprayed it with water, placed wet towels over it, and packed the bag with ice to minimize water loss.

While Cricket drove the 62-foot *Family Tradition*, slicing through the slick, calm waters of the Gulf at an impressive 52 miles per hour, the rest of the team buzzed with nervous excitement in the salon.

Katie's jaw dropped. "I can't believe this marlin could be worth over half a million dollars!" She turned to Soda, her voice brimming with curiosity. "Is this the biggest marlin tournament in the world?"

"No, the White Marlin Open is the largest billfish tournament I know of, but it's held over on the East Coast," Soda replied. "The white marlins don't get real big. I'd say the winning fish is usually under ninety pounds, but the payout for first place is somewhere over five million dollars. They've also got smaller payouts for the biggest blue marlin, tuna, mahi, wahoo, and swordfish."

Mr. Gregory and Katie exchanged astonished glances, their expressions lighting up at the thought of such a huge payout.

"I've fished it a few times," Soda continued. "It's a blast, but you're up against over four hundred boats, which makes it tough."

Intrigued, Mr. Gregory leaned in. "When is that tournament?"

"It's usually in early August," Soda answered.

Turning to her dad, Katie's excitement bubbled over. "We should fish it, Dad! It could be our last trip before I start school!"

After a moment of considering the potential payout and the allure of a new East Coast fishing destination, a subtle smile crept across his face. "Okay," he said. "I'll check with Cricket to see what we need to do to make it happen."

Jason and Soda exchanged enthusiastic smiles, their minds racing with possibilities for the upcoming adventure.

Nearly three hours after they had boated the marlin, shouts of joy erupted from the team as they crossed the demarcation line at 5:50 PM, making it back in the nick of time. With a mix of exuberance and disbelief, they continued toward The Wharf, knowing that Katie's fish could potentially knock Team *Trust Me* from the top of the leaderboard and secure them first place in the Grand Championship.

When the *Family Tradition* finally arrived and backed into the dock, they were met with a huge crowd gathered near the weigh-in area. In the distance, the Ferris wheel loomed large, its vibrant colors contrasting with the sprawling condominium behind the stage, where balconies overflowed with spectators eager to catch a glimpse of the unfolding drama. At the center of the stage stood the towering white scale, flanked by the massive stainless steel marlin statues and the elegantly arched breezeway behind it. The excitement in the hot evening air was electric, heightened by the pageantry of the event. Somehow, this experience felt even grander than their previous visit for the Orange Beach Classic, transforming into a spectacle that truly lived up to its reputation as the greatest show in sport-fishing.

As the team carted their marlin toward the weigh-in area, they passed a long row of palm trees patriotically adorned with strings of red, white, and blue lights. Suddenly, the voice of the tournament's host and emcee boomed through the crowd: "Next up, we have Team *Family Tradition* weighing in a blue marlin! Wow! Looking at the size of that fish, I've got to tell you, it's gonna be close between them and Team *Trust Me* for first place blue marlin!"

As the tournament emcee and his female co-host interviewed Katie and her dad, a dedicated team of tournament staff worked diligently to unload the marlin. They hoisted the massive fish by hand, pulling on a heavy rope that ran through a block and tackle pulley system. Although an electric motor would have simplified the task, the old-fashioned method using muscle added to the spectacle of the event.

Meanwhile, Jason anxiously watched as they raised the marlin up the scale tower. Scanning the sidelines, he saw that they were surrounded by friends from the other tournament boats, all cheering them on. He also spotted his parents, waving proudly at him, his dad sporting a large bandage over his left cheek. Nearby, Team *Trust Me* stood clad in their bright yellow shirts. Some members looked nervous, while Bill Murphy stood confidently with a smirk, shaking his head at the others, convinced they would maintain their lead.

Working the crowd, the emcee exclaimed, "Alright, it looks like our weighmaster is ready to reveal the weight of this blue marlin. Are y'all ready? Make some noise if you're excited to see this fish's weight!" The crowd erupted in cheers, their anticipation building as they awaited the announcement of who would claim first place.

"And the weight of the blue marlin brought in by team *Family Tradition* is..." Suddenly, flames erupted from the top of the tower and from the mouths of the stainless-steel marlin statues on either side. White smoke billowed dramatically behind the tower, creating a breathtaking spectacle. As the excitement peaked, the emcee's voice rang out, "Seven hundred and twenty-three point five pounds! Team *Family Tradition* takes first place in the Blue Marlin Grand Championship!"

The sound of the crowd was deafening as Team *Family Tradition* embraced each other with high-fives and hugs, overwhelmed with joy. On the sidelines, Bill Murphy shook his head angrily, having slipped to second place. In frustration, he turned to leave, pushing his teammates out of his way.

As the team lined up in front of their marlin for photos, each member was handed a bottle of champagne. Standing side by side, Jason and Katie exchanged excited and affectionate glances just as the emcee's voice rang out again, "Okay, now that we've got the whole team up here, I need everyone in the crowd to help make some noise one more time as we crown this year's Blue Marlin Grand Champion, Team Fam—i—ly Tra—dition!"

The team shook their bottles vigorously, spraying champagne into the air and all over each other. The moment was pure joy—a celebration of their hard work and dedication. Once again, flames shot high into the sky from the top of the tower and the marlin statues, while white smoke billowed dramatically behind them. The crowd responded with enthusiastic cheers and applause, joining in the euphoria of the team's triumph.

As the celebration on stage wound down, Jason signaled for his parents to join him at one of the outdoor bars set up on the premises. After his parents greeted Jason and Soda with hugs, congratulating them on their team's victory, Jason excitedly introduced them to the rest of the team. "Hey everyone, this is my mom and dad!"

Katie's face lit up with joy as she greeted them, her signature warm smile and Southern accent shining through. "Hey-eh!" she exclaimed, wrapping her arms around each of them in a heartfelt embrace, as if they were family.

Initially surprised by Katie's warmth, Jacob and Ellen exchanged glances, their expressions shifting from astonishment to delight. Ellen chuckled as she returned Katie's hug. "Well, you certainly know how to make someone feel welcome!"

As Jason watched his parents blend in with the team during introductions, he was filled with a profound sense of joy and belonging. Everything felt perfect in that moment. Yet, a knot of worry tightened in his stomach. He knew he would soon have to tell Cricket about his feelings for Katie, and the thought loomed over him like a dark cloud. As laughter echoed around him, Jason took a deep breath, determined to navigate the complexities of friendship and love at another time. For now, he would savor this moment, but he knew the conversation he dreaded would need to happen soon.

With drinks in hand, their laughter echoed through the air, growing livelier as they recounted the day's thrilling events to Jason's parents and fellow fishermen, including Bear and Skip, who had stopped by to offer their congratulations. Bear and Jacob, long-time friends, hadn't seen each other in years. Their faces lit up with excitement as they greeted one another and shook hands firmly.

Jacob was completely absorbed in the camaraderie that enveloped him. His face lit up with every dramatic twist in the stories, and he laughed heartily at the playful antics, reveling in the joy of friendship.

Sitting next to Jacob, Ellen enjoyed the lively chatter, but her gaze kept drifting to Jason and Katie. She couldn't help but notice how they shared glances and laughter. Recognizing the familiar spark of attraction between them, a knowing smile spread across her face.

Later that night, after the bar closed and all their friends and family had departed, Jason and Katie slowly made their way back to the boat. There wasn't anyone in sight, but the distant sounds of after-parties on several boats lingered in the air.

Walking side by side, Katie turned to Jason, her eyes shimmering with excitement. "I still can't believe we won!"

"I know!" Jason replied, stopping to take her hand. "And now that the tournament's over, we don't have to hide anything anymore."

He pulled her close, and they embraced in a passionate kiss, completely lost in the moment, free from the worries that had once loomed over them.

Suddenly, Katie pulled back, her expression shifting to concern. "Wait! What about the White Marlin Open? You have to come with us! Maybe we should wait just a little longer."

Jason's brow furrowed as uncertainty flickered across his face. The thought of keeping their relationship a secret for several more weeks weighed heavily on him. Reluctantly, he replied, "I guess it wouldn't hurt to keep it a secret a little while longer."

They slowly released their embrace and continued on their way, their minds racing with what lay ahead, unaware that they were being watched.

In the shadows, a gruff looking man with dark hair and a thick shaggy beard lingered at a distance, snapping pictures of them with a professional-looking camera fitted with a long lens. After a moment of focused observation, he lowered the camera and pulled his phone out of his pocket to dial a number. A sinister smirk spread across his face as he said in a deep, low voice, "Hey boss, I got somethin' I think you're gonna want to see."

THE BILL

Two days after winning the Grand Championship, Jason was back in Destin. It was late afternoon when he pulled into the driveway at his parents' house. As he stepped out of his truck, his mother greeted him from the front door. "Well, hey there, Jason! I didn't expect to see you today!"

"Yeah, I thought I'd just stop by to say hi," he replied.

Ellen wrapped him in a quick hug. "Well, I am so glad you did! Come on in."

As Jason stepped inside, he saw his dad, who had removed the bandage from his face, revealing a long vertical scar with prominent stitches.

"Hey, man! What's going on?" Jacob asked, excited to see him.

"Hey, Dad! Not much," Jason replied, returning his father's hearty embrace. Carefully examining the scar on his face, he continued, "Looks like your cheek is healing up nicely." With a teasing grin, he added, "That's gonna make a good-looking scar!"

"Yeah, it looks alright," Jacob chuckled.

Jason continued, "Well, I just left the boat and figured I'd swing by. Soda and I were getting things ready for our fishing trip tomorrow."

Jacob and Ellen exchanged surprised looks. "Are you fishing another tournament already?" Ellen asked.

"No," Jason replied. "Mr. Gregory and Katie want to go fun fishing tomorrow. It's just gonna be a quick day trip, so I'll be back tomorrow evening."

"What are y'all goin' after?" Jacob asked as he sat down in his recliner.

"We're gonna fish for white marlin using light tackle to prep for the White Marlin Open next month," Jason explained. "It sounds like the bite has been pretty hot lately at the Elbow. We heard the *Sunrise* went six for six on whites yesterday, and the *One Eighty* went three for five on whites and caught a sailfish too."

"Nice! Well, I hope y'all get into 'em," Jacob replied. "I tell ya, man, you work with some great folks. For the past two days, all Ellen and I have talked about is how much fun we had with y'all the other night."

"Yeah, we definitely have a good team," Jason replied. However, a flicker of concern crossed his expression as he thought about his relationship with Katie and how Cricket might react if he found out.

"Y'all headin' out first thing in the mornin'?" Jacob asked.

"Yeah, we'll probably leave around five-thirty, but I've gotta be at the boat by four-thirty to help Soda get a few things ready before we go."

Ellen gave him a hopeful look. "Do you want to join us for dinner, Jason?"

"Well, I would, but I've gotta go in a little bit to get ready for Matt's birthday party. He turned twenty-one today, so we're throwing him a party at Tripletails tonight," Jason replied.

Ellen tilted her head slightly, a curious smile forming. "Is Katie going with you tonight?"

Jason tried to suppress his smile, sheepishly replying, "No," as his eyes darted about.

"Well, I think she is just lovely. Why don't you ask her to go with you?" she suggested.

"It's complicated, Mom," Jason replied, a hint of frustration in his voice.

Ellen met his gaze with a knowing look, her expression softening. "The rest of your team doesn't know, do they?" she asked gently, her heart aching for him as she understood the pressure he felt. She could see the conflict in his eyes, the way his shoulders seemed to sag under the weight of unspoken emotions.

Jason's expression blanked for a moment, caught between the urge to confide his feelings to his mom and the instinct to continue hiding his secret. After an awkward pause, he sighed deeply, and replied, "No."

Puzzled, Jacob furrowed his brow and scrunched the side of his face. "I'm confused. What are we talking about?"

Ellen laughed softly, shaking her head. "Honey, Katie and Jason like each other, but the rest of his team doesn't know yet."

Jacob turned to Jason, his expression a mix of surprise and curiosity. "Really?"

"Yeah," Jason said with a hint of hesitation and a restrained grin.

Not quite grasping why this might be a problem, Jacob said, "Dang, son! She's beautiful, rich, and likes fishin'? I gotta tell you, man, I'm impressed!"

Jason laughed, appreciating his dad's enthusiasm, but then he sighed and explained, "Thanks, Dad. But the problem is, Cricket warned me on my first day to keep it professional with her. If he finds out we've been seeing each other, there's a pretty good chance he's gonna fire me."

"Oh," Jacob replied, now understanding the gravity of Jason's predicament.

Jason continued, "I was gonna tell him after the Grand Championship, but then Mr. Gregory decided to fish the White Marlin Open. I just feel like if I tell him now, I'll lose my job and the chance to fish in the biggest event of the season."

Jacob took a deep breath and sighed. With a pensive expression, he told his son, "If you think being honest is gonna cost you too much, just wait until you get the bill for regret. It'll be a whole lot worse if he finds out from someone else."

Jason slowly nodded, processing the weight of his dad's words. He knew what he needed to do, but the fear of losing his dream job and the chance to fish the White Marlin Open loomed over him like a dark cloud. After taking a deep breath to steady himself, a determined expression settled on his face as he told his father, "I'll tell him tomorrow—when we get back from fishing."

Later that evening, after heading home to shower and change into fresh clothes, Jason cruised over to Tripletails in his boat. The sun was setting, casting a warm glow over the harbor, while the air remained hot and humid. The outdoor bar buzzed with energy, filled with laughter, clinking glasses, and the upbeat music of a live band, creating a perfect backdrop for Matt's lively birthday party.

As Jason approached the bar, Matt spotted him and called out, "J-Bay! What's up, bruh?"

"Hey, Matt! Happy birthday!" Jason replied, clasping hands with him before pulling him in for a quick hug.

"Dude! I still can't believe y'all won biggest marlin at the Grand Championship! That's crazy, man!" Matt exclaimed.

"Yeah, I'm still shocked myself, to be honest," Jason said, shaking his head in disbelief. "You should have seen Bill Murphy's face when we won! It was priceless!"

"Dude! I wish I could have been there to see that!" Matt replied with a mix of satisfaction and envy. "That guy is such a kook!"

"Yeah, no kidding," Jason agreed, shaking his head with a smile.

Leaning in with curiosity, Matt asked, "So, does Cricket know about you and Katie yet?"

"No, I'm gonna tell him tomorrow," Jason replied, a hint of reservation creeping into his voice. He could already feel the weight of the conversation looming over him.

Matt chuckled. "Well, listen, after he fires you, I need you to put in a good word for me, ok? I need that job, yo!"

Jason smirked and said sarcastically, "I feel so much better about it now!"

"You know I'm just joking!" Matt teased, rolling his eyes. "He's not gonna fire you! But—if he did, all I'm sayin' is, hook me up, bruh!"

Jason shook his head, a grin spreading across his face at Matt's playful ribbing. The bar was alive with energy, the warm glow of lights casting a festive atmosphere as friends gathered to celebrate. Despite the nagging concerns about how things would go with Cricket the next day, Jason pushed those thoughts aside, determined not to let them spoil his night. With drinks flowing and laughter mingling with the upbeat music, he immersed himself in the joy of the moment, savoring every toast and shared story in celebration of Matt's birthday.

However, as the evening wore on and he finished several drinks, Jason sensed it was time to go. Matt was still at the bar waiting for another drink, so he made his way over to him. Giving his friend a friendly pat on the back, he said, "I gotta run, Matt, but happy birthday, buddy!"

"Come on, J-Bay! It's still early. One more drink!" Matt urged, his enthusiasm infectious.

"Matt, I've got to be at the boat by four-thirty for an all-day trip. If I leave now, I'll only get six hours of sleep," Jason replied, trying to sound firm.

"Dude, it's my birthday. One more drink!" Matt pleaded. "Y'all are just going fun fishing tomorrow anyway. It's not like it's a tournament or anything."

Jason sighed, relenting. "Okay, one more drink, but then I seriously have to go."

"Yes!" Matt exclaimed, throwing his arm around Jason's neck and pulling him in close. He turned to the bartender and cheerfully shouted, "We need two more drinks over here!"

As the bartender handed them their beers, Jason raised his bottle in a toast. "Happy birthday!"

Just as Matt tapped his bottle to Jason's, his eyes suddenly grew wide. A group of attractive women around their age had walked up to the bar directly behind Jason and were glancing their way. A wide grin spread across Matt's face. "Dayum!" he exclaimed, staring wide-eyed at one of the girls with long, dark brown hair pulled tight into a ponytail.

When she flashed him a smile, Matt shot her a playful smirk. "How you doin'?"

The woman smiled brightly. "I'm good. So, is it really your birthday?"

As the bartender placed the bill for their drinks on the bar, Matt said in a playful, teasing tone, "Yeah! You should buy my drink for me!"

She laughed with a broad smile, her eyes sparkling with amusement. With a hint of mischief in her voice, she replied, "Okay." Cheerfully, she turned to the bartender and said, "Put his drinks on my tab." Looking back at Matt, she stared deep into his eyes with a flirtatious smile.

Matt's eyes widened in shock, a mix of surprise and delight flooding his face. He turned to Jason and whispered, "I'll be honest, I didn't expect that!"

Quickly, Matt shifted his focus back to the young woman with a wide grin. "By the way, I'm Matt, and this is Jason. What's your name?"

"I'm Miranda. Nice to meet you, Matt," she said, her smile bright and playful. Her eyes locked onto his, completely ignoring Jason, which added an intense spark to the moment.

Meanwhile, her friend with long blond hair had her sights set on Jason. "You look so familiar. Were you part of the team that won the Blue Marlin Grand Championship this past weekend in Orange Beach?"

"Yeah," Jason replied, his eyes narrowing slightly in surprise that she recognized him from the tournament. "I'm a mate on the *Family Tradition*. We won biggest marlin," he added proudly.

"That's so cool!" she exclaimed. "I thought you looked familiar!" A radiant smile spread across her face as she introduced herself. "I'm Mindy."

"I'm Jason. Nice to meet you, Mindy," he replied politely, maintaining a friendly demeanor while consciously trying not to hint at any romantic interest.

One of the girls enthusiastically exclaimed to her friends, "Hey! We need a group picture!" She then turned to a nearby stranger and asked the woman to take their photo. As the girls lined up, Miranda turned to Matt, waving him over with a friendly smile. "Hey! Y'all come get in the picture with us!"

"Alright!" Matt replied eagerly. He noticed Jason hesitating, so he urged him on, "Come on, dude. You've got to get in the picture too!" With a playful tug, he pulled Jason by the arm.

Matt wrapped his arms around the shoulders of Miranda and one of the other girls, positioning himself between them and grinning from ear to ear. As Jason hesitantly moved to the end, the blonde repositioned herself next to him, slipping her hand around his waist and pulling him closer, her smile bright and confident.

Jason tried to disguise his discomfort as the lady taking the picture counted down. "Three, two, one, cheese!" While the camera flashed multiple times, the blonde turned and kissed Jason unexpectedly on the cheek.

"Whoa!" Jason exclaimed, pulling away in surprise. He attempted to laugh off his irritation, forcing a smile that barely concealed his unease as he asked, "What are you doing?"

"I just thought you were cute. That's all," Mindy replied, her tone playful. She and Miranda then shared a quick, amused glance as if they were in on a joke together.

Miranda turned to Matt and said, "Hey, we've got to go meet some friends, but I'm sure we'll see you later on." With a bright smile, she added, "Happy birthday!" She then swiftly turned and walked away, waving goodbye along with the other girls.

"Wait, where are y'all going?" Matt asked, his voice full of disbelief. He turned to Jason, clearly confused. "What just happened, man? One minute she seemed really into me, and then she just up and left! I don't get it."

As they watched the girls walk away, Matt slowly lifted his right arm and sniffed his armpit. After a few cautious whiffs, he checked his left armpit. Not detecting any offensive body odor, he shrugged with a bemused expression.

They both chuckled and resumed their conversations with other friends at the bar, the warm atmosphere buzzing with laughter and chatter. However, a short while later, as Jason finished his drink, he glanced across the bar and spotted the same girls laughing and dancing with Bill Murphy and several of his friends. A sense of unease washed over him.

Seeing that something was bothering Jason, Matt asked, "What's wrong?"

His voice tinged with frustration, but trying to be discreet, Jason replied, "Those girls we were talking to earlier are over there with Bill Murphy."

Matt glanced over, and there was Bill Murphy, raising his drink and smiling directly at them.

Matt lifted his drink toward Bill Murphy, giving him a single nod and a forced grin. He turned to Jason, trying to disguise his unease, and said, "I really don't like that guy."

"Yeah, me neither," Jason muttered, feeling a mix of irritation and concern. Having finished his drink, he told Matt, "Hey, I gotta go, man, but I'll call you when I get back tomorrow."

After saying farewell to the rest of his friends, Jason left Tripletails in his boat. The water was smooth as glass, reflecting the shimmering stars above as he motored home across the harbor. Yet, an uneasy feeling lingered in the back of his mind about the encounter with the girls, especially knowing they were friends with Bill Murphy.

Suddenly, his phone vibrated. He pulled it from his pocket and saw it was a text from Katie—a screenshot of the blond girl kissing him on the cheek. Her message read: "The girl you were hooking up with tonight tagged our boat name in her posts. I can't believe you would do this to me."

Jason immediately tried calling her repeatedly, but each time, his call went straight to voicemail. He texted her back: "I didn't hook up with that girl. I can explain everything. It's not what it looks like. Please call me back so we can talk."

But Katie never called or texted him. Back at home, he paced restlessly, consumed by anxiety over losing her. Fury raged inside him, aimed squarely at Bill Murphy, whom he was convinced had orchestrated the photo with the girls. Once in bed, he tossed and turned, getting very little sleep.

When his alarm went off at 3:30 AM, he haphazardly pressed stop instead of snooze, desperate for just a few more minutes of rest. However, exhaustion quickly pulled him back under, and he drifted back to sleep.

He was later jolted awake by the insistent vibration of his phone. It was Soda calling. He grabbed the phone and squinted at the screen—4:50 AM. Panic surged through him as he answered, his voice still groggy. "Hey, Soda. Sorry, man. I overslept."

"Alright, well, try to hurry. Cricket's gettin' agitated, and you need to be here before the owners arrive," Soda said.

"Yeah, I'll hurry. I'll be there in just a little bit." After hanging up, he rushed into the bathroom and caught a glimpse of himself in the mirror. His eyes were puffy and bloodshot, and a painful throb pulsed in his head.

When Jason arrived at the boat just before 5:20 AM, Cricket greeted him with a sarcastic, "Glad you could join us."

Jason apologized, "Sorry, I overslept somehow."

After settling in, Soda leaned in and discreetly said, "You're lookin' a little rough this mornin', buddy. Too much to drink last night?"

Jason sighed, his head drooping. "Matt's birthday party was at Tripletails last night, and I stayed out a little later than I should've, but there's some other stuff going on too."

"Everything alright?" Soda asked, with his brow raised, concern evident in his expression.

Jason paused for a moment, then said in a serious tone, "There's something I need to talk to you and Cricket about when we get back tonight."

With a sincere tone in his voice, Soda said, "Alright." He then gave him a reassuring nod and a pat on the arm.

Just then, Mr. Gregory and Katie approached the boat. "Mornin', fellas," Mr. Gregory said as he greeted the crew. Katie offered a quiet "Good morning" of her own but avoided making eye contact with Jason. While Mr. Gregory climbed up to the flybridge with Cricket, Katie quickly slipped through the salon door, leaving an awkward silence in her wake.

It was nearly 6:00 AM by the time they made it out of the East Pass on their way to the Elbow. As Cricket drove, he noticed a text from an unknown number. When he opened the message, he was surprised to see a picture of Jason and Katie embracing in a kiss. The message read: "Thought you should know that your mate is hooking up with the owner's daughter behind your back."

Cricket nervously glanced at Mr. Gregory, who was staring out across the water. He quickly closed the screen on his phone and turned to look at Jason in the cockpit. As Cricket returned his focus to the horizon ahead of them, he struggled to restrain his feelings of frustration and disbelief.

A little over an hour later, they arrived at the Elbow. Jason and Soda wasted no time deploying teasers and 30W reel and rod setups rigged with ballyhoos. They ran one line from each side of the boat out to the outriggers, and they deployed another two lines directly off the back, known as flat lines. The flat lines were positioned closer to the boat than the outrigger lines and could be quickly dropped back, similar to a pitch bait, if a fish came in after the teasers.

The seas were calm that morning, accompanied by a gentle breeze from the north. At first glance, it seemed like the perfect day for fishing. However, as they settled in, everyone began to notice an unwelcome nuisance that arrived with the northern winds—biting black flies.

Blown out to sea by the breeze, the black flies sought refuge on the boat, tormenting the team with bites that felt like sharp needles piercing their skin. They swatted at the pesky insects, shifting their bodies to keep the pests at bay. Katie had briefly joined her dad and Cricket on the flybridge but quickly retreated to the comfort and safety of the salon.

Despite the annoyance of the black flies, Mr. Gregory was clearly excited about the prospect of catching his first white marlin. The area they were fishing was teeming with flying fish, a promising sign for the day ahead. It wasn't long before, seemingly out of nowhere, a white marlin seized the ballyhoo being trolled on the left rigger, pulling the line from the clip and peeling it away from the spool with a satisfying "ZZZzzzzzzz..."

"Fish on!" Soda cheered as the white marlin leaped from the water. It was an average-sized white marlin for the Gulf, weighing roughly 60 to 70 pounds.

Mr. Gregory quickly raced down from the flybridge. He snapped on a belt known as a "gut bucket," designed for stand-up fishing with lighter rod-and-reel setups, such as the 30W reel. Instead of attaching to the reel like the seat harness used with 80W setups, the gut bucket featured a shallow cup at the front to secure the rod butt, preventing it from digging into his waist during the fight.

After adjusting the belt, a look of pure excitement spread across Mr. Gregory's face as Jason handed him the rod and reel. The line raced away from the spool, pulling drag as the fish sped off, leaping into the air repeatedly.

Katie heard the commotion from inside and stepped out the door of the salon to see what they had hooked. As she quickly scanned the horizon, she saw the fish putting on a dazzling display, leaping from the water again and again. Her face lit up with excitement as she joined the rest of the crew cheering her dad on.

While Mr. Gregory fought the fish, he occasionally stomped his foot or swatted at a pesky black fly that landed on him. Despite the distraction, he was clearly reveling in the excitement of light tackle fishing. With the rod grasped firmly in his hands, bent under the steady pull of the fish, he confidently moved around the cockpit, following it as it raced from one side of the boat to the other.

After roughly ten minutes, he brought the leader line close enough for Jason to grab it. Jason's movements were labored, but he steadily made several wraps around the leader line, pulling the fish toward him. Suddenly, a sharp pain shot through the back of his right leg. "Ouch!" he exclaimed, stopping his foot abruptly as he tried to shake off the fly that had landed on him. Refocusing his attention on the fish, he made a couple more wraps, but then felt a bite on top of his left foot. "Damn it!" he muttered as he stomped his foot again and tried to swat it away, his frustration evident as he began to pull the fish aggressively.

Soda attempted to lighten the mood, joking, “Those aren’t the kind of bites we were hoping for today, are they?”

Mr. Gregory was the only one who chuckled, responding with a grin, “No, I think we could do without those types of bites!”

After pulling the fish alongside the boat, Mr. Gregory leaned over the side to pose for a quick photo with his catch. The team then congratulated him, giving him high fives to celebrate his first white marlin.

Jason briefly smiled at Katie, hoping for an opportunity to reconnect. However, as their gazes met, she rolled her eyes, and her smile instantly vanished, replaced by an annoyed expression.

Unbeknownst to them, Cricket was watching closely from the flybridge. Frustration and disappointment crossed his face as he witnessed a situation he had hoped to avoid. “Let’s get those lines back out,” he said tersely to Jason and Soda before returning his gaze to the horizon.

Soda sensed that something was amiss. He knew Cricket was annoyed about Jason showing up late and looking like he had been out all night, but there seemed to be something more troubling simmering beneath the surface.

Despite the excitement of Mr. Gregory catching his first white marlin, an undercurrent of tension hung in the air as they redeployed the lines. However, soon after positioning the lures and teasers, they were thrilled by the satisfying sound they had been hoping for: “ZZZzzzzzzzz...” A fish had struck the ballyhoo on the left rigger.

As Soda adjusted the drag, ensuring the fish was securely hooked, it leaped spectacularly from the water. “It’s a sailfish!” Cricket shouted excitedly from the flybridge.

In a surge of adrenaline, Soda rushed to hand the reel to Mr. Gregory, who stood poised with a gut bucket strapped around his waist, grinning with excitement at the opportunity to catch a sailfish.

Even Katie couldn’t help but smile. Her heart raced with excitement as she watched the fish leap into the air. Weighing roughly 50 pounds, it had a long, slender body—dark blue on top and silver below—with a striking light bronze stripe down the middle. Electric blue radiated from the vertical stripes on its sides and fins. As the sailfish thrashed from side to side, attempting to shake the hook, its majestic dorsal fin unfurled, revealing stunning shades of blue adorned with small dark spots dotted throughout.

Without the usual tournament pressure to land the fish quickly, Mr. Gregory took his time battling it, savoring each moment and clearly relishing the sport of light tackle stand-up fishing. After an intense struggle, he brought the fish close enough for Jason to grab the leader line and complete the catch.

Aside from the annoyance of a black fly buzzing around his ankles, Jason wired the fish in with relative ease, bringing it alongside the boat quickly.

Wearing a glove to protect his hand, Soda held the fish by the bill, then reached down with his other hand and extended its tall dorsal fin for everyone to see. Katie and Mr. Gregory stood in astonishment, their faces illuminated with wonder as they admired the fish's magical colors and magnificent sail.

After Katie snapped a few photos of her dad with the fish, Soda carefully released it. With a few swift strokes of its tail, the fish swam away, disappearing into the blue.

With a cheerful grin, Soda turned to Mr. Gregory. "If you catch a third billfish species today, like a blue marlin, you'll join the Grand Slam club!"

The term "Grand Slam" is significant for anglers, representing the impressive feat of landing three different species of billfish in a single day—a challenge few achieve. Anglers strive for this coveted goal to etch their names in the record books of the International Game Fish Association (IGFA).

"Really?" Mr. Gregory asked, the excitement clear in his voice.

"Yeah! We don't usually catch a lot of blues this close in, but you never know!" Soda replied with a sparkle of excitement in his eyes.

Katie exchanged an eager glance with her dad. "Well, if y'all hook another white marlin or sailfish, I want to catch one!"

"Alright!" Soda responded, matching her excitement.

Despite the occasional nuisance of black flies swatted away by Katie and Mr. Gregory, the two sat in the mezzanine, eager to catch their next fish. Meanwhile, Jason and Soda positioned themselves next to the reels, ready for the next bite.

However, sleep deprivation and the alcohol Jason had consumed the night before were taking a heavy toll on him.

The sweltering summer heat wrapped around him like a thick blanket, making it even harder to concentrate on fishing. Sweat trickled down his brow, and with each passing moment, his eyelids grew heavier. Occasionally, a sudden twitch would course through his body, which he tried to conceal from the others, as he fought the urge to doze off.

Suddenly, Cricket shouted, "Right rigger!" Looks like another white!"

Katie's face lit up with excitement at the chance to catch her first white marlin.

Jason snapped out of his daze and watched as the fish closed in on the bait. When the marlin grabbed it, the right rigger clip snapped free, and the line whizzed through the air, pulling tight. As the line began to peel away from the spool, Jason pushed the drag lever forward, hoping the hook would catch securely in the fish's mouth. However, just as quickly as it had struck, the sound of the drag fell silent, leaving him stunned.

"Damn it!" Jason groaned quietly, realizing he had missed the fish. As he reeled in the line, he saw that only the head of the ballyhoo remained on the hook.

"*Sancocho*!" Soda exclaimed with a teasing grin and a slight Spanish accent. The term is often used by billfishermen to poke fun at an angler who has missed a fish, leaving only the head of the bait on the line.

However, Cricket chimed in with a frustrated tone, "You've got to let 'em eat it, Jason!"

As Jason reached out to grab the hook, a black fly landed on his foot, biting him sharply. "Ouch! God damn it!" he exclaimed, swatting it away.

"Language, Jason! Language!" Cricket quickly scolded him, shaking his head.

Jason clenched his jaw tightly, frustration seething within him as he grabbed another ballyhoo to rig.

Hoping to lighten the mood, Mr. Gregory said, "Hey, don't sweat it, Jason. That's why they call it fishin', not catchin', right?" He turned to Katie, expecting her to agree, but instead she replied, "I'm going back inside," her tone laced with annoyance.

Mr. Gregory and Soda exchanged puzzled glances, unsure why the mood on the boat had soured so quickly over one missed fish.

An awkward silence hung over the boat as they trolled across the calm blue water, the minutes dragging on like hours under the oppressive swelter of the sun. Jason felt miserable, teetering on the edge of his breaking point. Fatigue and anger coursed through him, his frustration simmering like a pressure cooker ready to explode. Each bite from the relentless black flies felt like a potential last straw, their irritating buzz amplifying his growing impatience.

Suddenly, Soda's voice erupted through the stillness. "Marlin!"

The announcement of a marlin instantly ignited a spark of excitement in Jason, pulling him from the depths of his gloom and into the thrill of the chase. As he looked out, scanning behind the boat, he saw the fish barreling toward the right bridge teaser. Its dorsal fin was raised high above the surface, slicing through the water and creating a wake in its path. It quickly closed in on the squid chain teaser, thrashing its bill in a frenzied attack.

"It's a blue! It's a blue!" Cricket shouted excitedly as he turned on the bridge teaser reel, pulling the teaser away from the fish.

Jason sprang into action, dropping the right flat line bait back into the water. His heart pounded as he watched the fish swallow the bait. He free-spooled the reel, giving the fish time to eat—he didn't want to take a chance on losing another one. Then, he slowly pushed the drag lever forward, and the reel screamed with a loud "ZZZZzzzzzzzz..."

The boat erupted with cheers as the blue marlin leaped into the air, shaking its head with the hook securely lodged in the corner of its mouth.

Jason handed the rod and reel to Mr. Gregory, then hurried to help Soda pull in the other lines.

Although it was a smaller blue marlin, roughly 250 pounds, it dwarfed the white marlin and sailfish they had caught earlier.

When Katie opened the salon door, Mr. Gregory excitedly exclaimed, "It's a blue marlin!" Her face lit up with joy, knowing that if her dad caught this fish, he would achieve a grand slam.

Once the other lines were cleared, Cricket began backing down aggressively on the fish. Based on experience, he knew Mr. Gregory would need all the help he could get using the lighter 30W tackle, and the longer the battle continued, the less likely they were to land the fish.

Mr. Gregory beamed as he cranked the reel handle. "Whoa!" he shouted as the fish made several spectacular leaps directly behind the boat before disappearing below the surface. A moment later, it leaped again, this time several hundred yards to the right, having traveled at a blistering speed underwater in what felt like mere seconds.

Cricket turned the boat sharply in pursuit, water crashing against the transom and spraying into the air. After roughly ten minutes of battling the fish, it was only fifty yards from the boat, still racing away near the surface.

"Come on, Dad! You've almost got it!" Katie cheered.

To count as a caught fish and complete the Grand Slam, all Jason had to do was touch the leader. He watched anxiously, his eyes fixed on the line, waiting for the marlin to come within reach. Suddenly, the fish erupted from the water in a vertical leap right in front of them, then dove back down, disappearing for a moment. When it resurfaced, leaping into the air again, it was headed straight for them. Time seemed to slow as Jason watched in horror, realizing the bill was aimed directly at Soda.

Soda barely had time to flinch as the marlin crashed over the side of the boat, teetering back and forth on the transom, thrashing its tail. The marlin's large, round eye looked around wildly, just inches from Soda's face. Gritting his teeth, Soda shoved the marlin back with all his might, grunting with the effort.

As the marlin tumbled back into the water, Jason yelled, "Soda! Are you alright?"

Breathing heavily and in shock, Soda scanned his chest and noticed a hole in his shirt near his left bicep. Blood began to soak through the fabric of his *Family Tradition* T-shirt and drip down his arm.

Everyone stood frozen for a moment, staring at Soda while the fish raced away, the sound of the drag filling the air like a warning siren, "zzzzzzzzzz..."

At first, he didn't realize he had been stabbed. But with each passing second, the pain intensified, making him wince as he leaned against the transom for support, fighting to stay upright. He turned ghostly pale as a pool of blood began to form at his feet on the deck.

Cricket's eyes widened with worry as he shouted, "Hurry! Cut the line. We've got to do something to stop the bleeding!"

Not wanting to wait another second, Mr. Gregory threw the rod and reel overboard and rushed to Soda's side. He quickly used a towel Jason handed him to wrap Soda's arm and apply pressure to the wound. Then he and Jason helped move him inside, where he could lie down on the couch.

It was a tense hour-long ride as Cricket pushed the boat to its limits, racing toward Pensacola, the closest place where Soda could receive medical attention. Despite their relationship troubles, Jason and Katie exchanged concerned glances, united in their worry for their dear friend.

Cricket had notified the Coast Guard of the accident, and by the time they arrived at the dock, an ambulance was already waiting to rush Soda to the hospital. Mr. Gregory had also arranged transportation for the rest of the group, so they quickly piled into the vehicle and headed to the hospital as well.

Mr. Gregory sat in the front passenger seat while Jason, Cricket, and Katie squeezed into the back. Katie found herself in the middle, sandwiched between Jason and

Cricket. An uncomfortable silence enveloped them, thick with tension. Jason stared out the side window while Katie kept her gaze straight ahead. Cricket tapped his fingers on his knee—worried about Soda and struggling to suppress his frustration toward Jason. The camaraderie that once defined their friendship felt distant, replaced by a heavy unease as they raced toward the hospital.

Once they arrived at the hospital, Jason, Katie, Cricket, and Mr. Gregory spent the next couple of hours in the waiting room, anxiously awaiting news. As they sat there, Jason replayed the moment over and over in his mind. Though the accident wasn't his fault, he knew he hadn't been at his best that day and wrestled with whether there was anything he could have done differently to protect his friend.

When the doctor finally emerged to give them an update, they all stood up, worry visible on their faces as they eagerly awaited news about Soda.

"Hey, everyone," the doctor said with a friendly smile as he approached. "I've got to say, this is my first time treating someone stabbed by a blue marlin, but the good news is he's going to be just fine. He'll need to take it easy for a while, of course, as he heals, and he'll need to take the antibiotics I've prescribed to help prevent any bacterial infection. But I expect him to be fully recovered in no time."

A wave of relief washed over them as they heard the good news.

The doctor continued, "We're going to keep him here overnight to monitor him, but you all can go visit him now if you'd like. I'm sure he'll be glad to see you."

As the doctor turned to leave, he paused and said in a serious tone, "You know, your friend is quite lucky. If that marlin had stabbed him just a little to the right, it could have been much worse."

They nodded, fully aware of just how fortunate their friend was. As they entered Soda's room, relief washed over them that he was okay and that his injury wasn't worse. Each greeted him with wide smiles, brightening the sterile environment.

Soda lay in his hospital bed, hooked up to an intravenous (IV) drip and surrounded by the rhythmic beeping of machines. His face lit up at the sight of his friends, but he seemed eager to escape the confines of the hospital. Despite the cold, clinical setting illuminated by bright fluorescent lights, the warmth of camaraderie filled the space as they crowded around him.

"How you feelin', buddy?" Cricket asked, his voice full of concern.

"Better than I was! That's for sure!" Soda replied, lifting his arm to reveal the wound, which resembled a large bullet hole stitched shut. "They got me stitched up pretty good."

Jason grinned. "Yeah, looks good. You'll be back to fishing in no time."

"Well, I just hate that this whole ordeal ruined the trip. Don't tell your dad I had to be rushed in for a little wound like this or I'll never hear the end of it," Soda joked, his grin infectious. "Jacob probably would've just stitched it up himself and poured some bleach on it!"

"I don't know, Soda. You were bleeding pretty bad. We're all just thankful you're okay, and that it wasn't worse," Jason replied, his tone turning serious. The others nodded in agreement, the weight of the situation lingering for a moment.

The group then began to share their animated memories of the astonishing incident. Laughter erupted when Cricket recounted how Mr. Gregory had tossed his rod and reel overboard while rushing to Soda's side—the fish still hooked, racing away with it underwater.

As the evening wore on and their laughter faded into comfortable conversation, Soda looked around the room and asked, "Did y'all get anything to eat yet? I know you must be starving by now."

"Not yet," Mr. Gregory replied. "We'll probably grab something here in a little bit and then come back to see you."

Soda waved his hand dismissively. "Well, listen, I'm fine. Y'all don't have to come back to the hospital tonight on my account. You should head back to Destin so you can get some fresh clothes and catch a good night's sleep. Seriously, it's only an hour's drive by car to come back in the mornin'."

Mr. Gregory paused, considering his options. After a moment, he said hesitantly, "Alright, but we'll drive back over first thing in the morning. Okay?"

"Yeah, sounds good to me," Soda replied. "I'll be about ready to bust out of here by then, whether they like it or not!" His playful confidence lightened the mood, making everyone laugh before they said goodbye to him for the night.

After leaving the hospital, they headed back to the boat and made their way to Destin. The ride home was quiet. It had been a long day for everyone, but they were comforted by the thought that Soda would be all right. When they arrived at the dock, Mr. Gregory and Katie said goodbye and headed to the house while Jason and Cricket stayed behind to take care of a few things on the boat.

As they finished up, Cricket's irritation grew as he thought about Jason disobeying all three of the rules he had given him. Unable to contain his frustration any longer, he said, "Jason, there's something I need to talk to you about."

"Yeah, sure. What's going on?" Jason replied, his expression tightening with concern.

"Someone sent me a picture this morning that looks like you and Katie kissing." He held out his phone for Jason to see. "Is it true you've been hookin' up with her behind my back, even after I specifically asked you to keep it professional?"

Caught off guard, Jason stared at the picture, unsure of who had sent it to Cricket or how to respond. Hesitantly, he replied, "Yes, but Cricket, it's not like I did it on purpose. It just sort of happened. I was going to tell you and Soda today when we got back from fishing."

"Yeah, sure you were," Cricket sneered, shaking his head in disappointment. His anger and frustration built as he continued, "And you show up to work late this morning, lookin' like you'd been partyin' all night. Then you had the nerve to use the Lord's name in vain on the boat after I told you not to do that either!"

He paused for a moment to collect his thoughts. "I can't have someone workin' for me that I don't trust, Jason. I'm sorry, but you're not fishin' with us anymore. I'm gonna have to let you go. If you've got any personal stuff on the boat, go ahead and get it now." He then turned abruptly and walked away.

Jason's shoulders and head dropped, devastated by the news. After collecting his belongings from the boat, he made his way to the driveway where his truck was parked. It had been a terrible day. His eyes were weary and full of heartache as he struggled to hold back the tears. Just as he reached his truck, Katie opened the front door. "Jason, can we talk?"

As she approached, she noticed he was upset. "Are you ok? What's going on?" she asked, her voice heavy with concern.

"I just got fired. That's what's going on. Someone sent Cricket a picture of us kissing after the tournament last weekend," Jason replied, shaking his head in disbelief.

"Really?" she said, blinking in disbelief.

"Yeah, and I guarantee it was your old buddy Bill Murphy," he said, anger seething within him.

"Why do you think it was Billy?" Katie asked with a confused expression.

"Because he's the one who set me up with that picture of the girl kissing me on the cheek last night, Katie! And somehow, he got a picture of us kissing last weekend and sent it to Cricket."

Katie gave him a doubtful look. "It's just hard for me to believe he'd do all that."

"Oh! But I guess it's easy for you to believe I'm lying," Jason snapped, his anger flaring.

"That's not what I'm saying, Jason," Katie said apologetically, frustration creeping into her voice.

"I just got fired from my job, Katie! Unlike some people, I don't have a trust fund to pay all my bills. I actually have to work for a living," he said sharply, his words cutting deep.

Katie flinched at his comment, her expression shifting to a mix of pain and disbelief. Tears welled up in her eyes as she struggled to process his harshness.

Realizing he had gone too far, Jason's tone softened. "I'm sorry. I didn't mean that."

Unable to respond, Katie shook her head, tears streaming down her cheeks as she abruptly turned to leave.

"Wait, Katie, I'm sorry!" he pleaded as she stormed away, slamming the door behind her. Jason sighed heavily, his head dropping in despair.

THE BACKLASH

The next morning after the ill-fated "fun fishing" trip, Jason was still grappling with the shock of Soda being stabbed by the marlin, getting fired by Cricket, and his relationship woes with Katie.

Hoping to mend things with Katie, he tried calling her, but the line rang without an answer. A knot of anxiety twisted in his stomach as he sent her a text: "I'm sorry about last night. Please call me so we can talk." The message showed as delivered, then marked as read. Suddenly, he noticed the cursor indicating she was texting back. A flicker of hope sparked within him that he could work things out between them.

Katie replied: "You told me I was worth the risk of losing your job, but last night, you sure didn't act like it. I think we both need some time to figure out what we really want. I'm not ready to talk to you yet."

Jason's heart sank as he read her words. He let out a heavy sigh, closed his eyes, and drooped his head, feeling the weight of her disappointment hit him hard.

Unsure of what to say to Katie or do next, he messaged his dad to let him know he needed to talk. He had told his parents about Soda's accident the day before but hadn't mentioned being fired or his problems with Katie.

Jacob replied that he was working on the *Vanessa*, so Jason said he would meet him there. When he arrived that morning, the air was already hot and humid, with barely a breeze. Most of the charter boats had set out fishing for the day, leaving their slips along the dock empty. With morning rush hour over, the harbor was peaceful and calm. Seagulls soared above, their cries filling the air. Pelicans floated serenely on the water, while herons wandered slowly along the boardwalk. All of the birds eagerly awaited the fishermen's return, each hoping to get their share of scraps from the day's catch.

As Jason walked toward the *Vanessa*, he spotted his dad on the back deck inspecting a metal cylindrical device with gears on one end. Sweat soaked through his shirt, and smudges of grease stained his hands and forearms.

Jason greeted him, "Hey, Dad. Whatcha up to?"

After wiping the sweat from his brow, Jacob said, "Replacing the starter again. I tried to crank her up this mornin' and all I heard was click, click, click, click, click." He shook his head in frustration and continued, "I don't know why this darn thing went out again. I just replaced it last year." He then asked, "What's going on with you? Is Soda okay?"

"Yeah, Soda's good. Mr. Gregory and Cricket drove over to Pensacola this morning to pick him up and bring him home," Jason replied.

"You didn't want to ride over there with 'em?" Jacob asked curiously.

"Well, that's actually what I came to talk to you about," Jason said, his expression tense. "Cricket fired me yesterday."

The left side of Jacob's face tightened as he winced at the bad news. "I hate to hear that, son, but you did the right thing by tellin' him about you and Katie."

"Actually, someone sent him a photo of us kissing before I got the chance to tell him," Jason replied, remorse creeping into his voice.

Jacob's head dropped and he nodded softly, acknowledging the outcome he had feared.

Jason continued hesitantly, "I also stayed out a little too late for Matt's birthday party the other night and showed up late yesterday morning looking a little rough."

Jacob pursed his lips and blew out a quick, "Whew!" His eyes flickered in disbelief.

Jason's shoulders sagged, regret clear in his eyes, as he continued, "And I lost my temper while we were fishing and said, 'God damn it,' even though he had asked me not to use the Lord's name in vain when he first hired me."

Jacob's eyes widened in shock. "Anything else?" he asked, clearly hoping the answer was no.

"Well, Katie's also mad at me and doesn't want to talk to me right now, but that's about it," Jason replied, his eyes shifting around.

Jacob nodded slowly, his brow furrowing deeper as he absorbed the extent of Jason's problems. "Well, son, it sounds like you've got yourself one hell of a backlash." After pausing for a moment to gather his thoughts, he continued in a slow and steady voice, "You know, sometimes when that fishin' line is all knotted up on the spool like a dang bird's nest, it can look almost impossible to untangle. But if you just tackle one knot at a time and you're real careful, sometimes you can get that mess straightened out. You just gotta be patient. And if you're not having any luck with one knot, you might have to stop and work on another for a while before coming back to it. You know what I mean?"

Jason nodded with a reflective expression, understanding his dad's metaphor for the situation.

Jacob sighed deeply. "But as you know, sometimes those knots get dug in so deep, or the line gets kinked so bad that you don't really have any choice but to cut all that line out and re-spool. Now, I hope you can work this mess out—I really do—but just remember, son, you got bills to pay. So, at some point, you gotta get back to fishin'—even if it's not on the *Family Tradition*." Jacob paused briefly before adding, "You can always come back to work on the *Vanessa*."

Jason nodded, appreciating his dad's advice and offer to work on the *Vanessa* again, but the thought of going back to commercial fishing and no longer being able to work with his team on the *Family Tradition* filled him with dread. Anger bubbled up inside him as he blurted out, "This is all Bill Murphy's fault. I was going to tell Cricket and Soda everything when we got back to the dock yesterday, but this guy is doing everything he can to try and ruin me."

Jacob met his son's gaze steadily. "I don't know anything about this Bill Murphy fella, and I'm not saying whatever he did was right, but if you want to fix things between you and your team, the first thing you're gonna have to do is take accountability for the mistakes you made, learn from 'em, and be damn sure not to repeat 'em."

Jason gave a slow nod as the weight of his dad's words sank in. He realized that to have any chance of undoing the mess he had made, he would have to confront his mistakes head-on, one at a time.

Sensing he had told Jason what he needed to hear, Jacob asked, "So, did you see that tropical storm that formed south of Cuba?"

"No, I guess I must have missed that with everything going on yesterday," Jason replied, a hint of surprise in his voice.

"It's forecasted to become a Cat Three once it makes it into the Gulf. Looks like it's gonna do a bank shot off the Yucatán Peninsula and head toward Apalachicola. The seas are fixin' to start pickin' up tomorrow, so nobody around here'll be headin' out fishin' for the next few days," Jacob told him.

Jason nodded thoughtfully, aware of the storm's implications and knowing they would be getting some rough weather in Destin as well.

After spending a little more time with his dad, Jason said goodbye, giving Jacob a hearty hug and thanking him for his advice. As he walked away from the Vanessa, he passed the spot where Soda had first offered him the job as a mate. He recalled Soda saying, "You know how I said I'm gonna need a second mate on this new boat? ... Well, I told Cricket and the owner that you were the guy we needed."

Jason's shoulders sank under a wave of regret as he thought about how badly he had messed up such an incredible opportunity. Just as he reached his truck, his phone vibrated in his pocket. It was Soda calling. Jason swallowed hard, his throat tightening as he answered the phone.

"Hey, Soda. How you feelin'?" Jason asked, trying to keep his tone light.

Soda cheerfully said, "A little sore, but not too bad, all things considered!" Then, with a hint of concern in his voice, he continued, "I was actually callin' to check on you. Cricket told me about what happened."

Jason rubbed the back of his neck. "Yeah, I messed up pretty bad. I just want you to know that I'm really sorry about not telling you and Cricket sooner about Katie and me. That was what I wanted to talk to you and Cricket about when we got back from fishing."

Soda said kindly, "I ain't worried about it, Jason. When Cricket told me about you and Katie, I figured that was what you wanted to talk to us about—and I told him that—but he was still a little worked up about everything."

"Yeah, I don't know if he's ever gonna trust me again after all the mistakes I made," Jason responded, his voice heavy with regret.

"Well, let me try talkin' to him some more and see if I can get him to change his mind," Soda replied. "Obviously, he was pretty stressed about me gettin' injured yesterday, so I'm sure that factored into his frustration as well."

Jason said, "Thanks, Soda. Does Mr. Gregory know?"

"Yeah, Cricket told him too. We were both a little surprised, as you can imagine, but he didn't seem to be bothered by it or anything. I'm sure he just wants Katie to be with someone who makes her happy and treats her right."

Jason sighed in frustration. "Well, unfortunately, Katie's also upset with me and doesn't want to talk to me right now," he said, his voice heavy with resignation.

"Ouch! Sorry to hear that, buddy." Soda chuckled. "Boy, when you mess up, you mess up right!"

"Yeah, tell me about it," Jason replied.

"Well, I don't think there's a whole lot I can do to help you with Katie. You're gonna have to work that one out on your own. But I'll give Cricket a call in a little bit and let you know how it goes," Soda continued.

"Alright. Thanks, Soda," Jason said with a grateful tone.

Later that evening, as the sun dipped below the dark purple clouds on the horizon, the rest of the sky blazed with deep reds and fiery oranges. The air felt still and thicker than usual, even for late July. The usual chorus of birds around the harbor had fallen silent, their absence amplifying the eerie stillness.

Standing on his back porch and looking out across the harbor, Jason felt his phone vibrate once, indicating that he had received a text message. He pulled out his phone and saw a text from Soda: "Cricket seemed to be warming up to the idea of giving you another chance after we talked, but you need to talk with him in person. He'll be at the boat tomorrow morning if you want to stop by."

A wave of relief washed over him at the thought that Cricket might give him another chance. He quickly typed back, "Thanks, Soda! I'll stop by and speak with him tomorrow." However, that feeling was short-lived as he imagined the difficulty of facing Cricket while still uncertain about the future of his relationship with Katie.

The next morning, Jason arrived at Mr. Gregory's house. Although the hurricane was still far from making landfall, the wind had already picked up, with occasional gusts shaking the tops of the palm trees in the yard. Before heading to the boat to face Cricket, he decided to see if Katie would give him a chance to talk.

After knocking on the door, Mr. Gregory opened it, greeting him warmly. "Hey, Jason! What's going on?" His eyes narrowed slightly in surprise, aware that Cricket had let him go and that Katie was upset with him.

"Hi, Mr. Gregory. Is Katie home?" Jason asked, his eyes darting nervously from side to side.

Mr. Gregory shook his head. "No, sorry, Jason. She's not here right now," he replied, his tone steady.

Jason nodded slowly, his shoulders slumping. "Well, I came over to apologize to Cricket. I'm sure you heard about him firing me."

"Yeah, he mentioned it to me yesterday," Mr. Gregory said, his expression serious yet sympathetic.

Glancing down, Jason continued, "I feel like I owe you an apology too." He took a deep breath, straightening up as he met Mr. Gregory's gaze. "I just want you to know that I really appreciate you giving me the chance to work on your boat and everything you've done for me. I love this job, and I love working with our team, but I also fell in love with your daughter. She's just unlike any girl I've ever met, and I can't stop thinking about her." He paused, his frustration evident. "I know I messed up, and I'm really sorry for how things turned out, but I never meant any disrespect to you or to hurt her. I hope Cricket will give me another chance, but if it comes down to choosing between this job and Katie, I'm gonna choose Katie—if you'll allow me to date her." Jason waited nervously for his response.

Mr. Gregory studied him intently, gently nodding. "Choosing your heart over a job is a bold and difficult move, Jason—one I'm very familiar with. I don't have a problem with you dating Katie if you two are able to work things out. And as for working on the boat, Cricket is the captain. He does the hiring and firing of the crew, and his word is final." He then added with a reassuring smile, "But I'll put in a good word for you."

Jason's expression softened with gratitude. "Thank you, Mr. Gregory."

Motioning toward the boat with a tilt of his head, Mr. Gregory said, "Good luck with Cricket," and with an encouraging wink, he added, "And Katie too."

With his confidence buoyed by Mr. Gregory's support, Jason made his way behind the house to the boat. However, the closer he got, the more tense and nervous he became.

Cricket stood at the helm, leaning over the dashboard as he intently studied the weather displayed on several electronic screens, concerned about the approaching hurricane. When he saw Jason walking toward the boat, he slowly descended the ladder to the cockpit, his expression serious but not angry.

"Hey, Cricket," Jason greeted him.

"Hey, Jason. I understand you wanted to talk to me," Cricket replied.

Jason stared at the ground, guilt weighing heavily on his expression. "Yeah. I just wanted to tell you that I'm sorry, and I don't blame you for firing me. I know I messed up, and I have to live with that. I just hope that one day you'll be able to forgive me and trust me again. If you're willing to give me a second chance, I'd love to work for you again. But—I can't change how I feel about Katie. If I have to choose between her and this job, I'm gonna choose her. You deserve the respect of me telling you that, not hiding our relationship behind your back. I wanted to tell you sooner, but I guess I was just afraid of letting you down and losing the chance to work with this amazing team."

Cricket's eyes slowly drifted to the horizon as he took a deep breath and sighed. Returning his gaze to Jason, he said, "I was your age once and made plenty of mistakes too. In the Bible, it says: 'Forgive one another, as God in Christ forgave you.' I believe that is the gospel, Jason, and I forgive you. But you and Katie having a romantic relationship complicates things."

He then dropped his head and continued, "I never told you this before, but about fifteen years ago, I was captain of a boat called the *Southern Girl*. And I, uh—well, I ended up hookin' up with the owner's daughter."

Jason's eyes widened in shock at Cricket's revelation.

Lifting his head to look at Jason, he continued, "Things were really great between us for a while, but then we started bickering constantly, and it just soured the whole mood for everyone on the boat. I ended up having to leave the boat because of it."

Cricket sighed. "The other day, I was upset that you broke the rule I gave you about keeping it professional with Katie, but I could also tell that y'all were fighting about something, and it brought back a lot of painful memories that I don't really want to relive on this boat."

Jason nodded, gaining a newfound appreciation for Cricket's perspective as he considered the implications of his relationship with Katie on the rest of the team.

Relating to each other in a way they never had before, both men settled into a comfortable silence. The tension between them had dissipated, even though it was still unclear if Jason would get a second chance to work on the boat.

Eventually, Cricket broke the silence, saying, "It looks like we're gonna get some epic surf later today thanks to that hurricane that formed in the Gulf."

"Yeah, head-high groundswell and wind from the north cleaning it up. I'm stoked!" Jason said, his enthusiasm building.

"You should come paddle out with me," Cricket suggested, his tone sincere and encouraging.

"Yeah, definitely! I'd love to," Jason responded.

Later that afternoon, Jason and Cricket met up at the beach on Okaloosa Island, just across the Destin Bridge. Condominiums lined the shore, each featuring a wooden boardwalk that cut through the powdery white sand dunes leading to the water. As they made their way to the water's edge with their surfboards in hand, the beach grass and sea oats atop the dunes bent beneath the force of the steady breeze, their tips fluttering like ribbons. A few surfers dotted the water further down on both sides, but Jason and Cricket had this specific stretch of beach all to themselves that day.

Exchanging smiles, they looked out at the head-high waves rolling toward the shore, beautifully spaced apart. The hurricane was to the east, causing the winds to flow from north to south while the waves traveled in the opposite direction. As a result, the waves had smooth faces that arched high overhead, many forming picture-perfect barrels with wisps of ocean spray blowing off their crests.

Not wanting to waste a minute of this epic opportunity, they quickly began paddling out. As Jason ducked his board under the first wave, a surreal peace washed over him as the sound of the ocean flowing by him filled his ears. He emerged from the backside of the wave, feeling renewed, as if his soul had been cleansed, erasing his worries. He took in a deep breath, filling his lungs with the salty air, energizing him as he paddled out.

By the time he made it past the last break, there was no past and no future. There was only the present—with he and Cricket sitting on their boards, staring out across the ocean at the oncoming sets of waves and searching for the right one. It wasn't long before Cricket spotted a wave he wanted to catch. He began paddling gently at first, positioning himself at just the right spot. As the wave approached, he paddled fiercely, gaining speed.

For a moment, Cricket disappeared from Jason's view as the wave passed by, but then his head became visible just above the wave's crest. He was up!

Jason yelled at the top of his lungs, cheering Cricket on with a hearty, "Yeww!"—a common surf slang called out to share the stoke of riding the waves.

Cricket quickly disappeared from view behind the wave. Taking a deep breath, Jason returned his gaze to the oncoming swells, trying to read the subtle ways they built up as they approached, searching for the right one.

Finally, Jason spotted his wave. He began paddling slowly at first, then with a burst of speed, paddled as fast as he could as the wave started to push him toward the shore. Feeling the wave carry him, he quickly jumped to his feet, his legs bending and arms extending out to balance as he dropped down the face of the wave.

Cricket was paddling back out and saw Jason drop in on the wave, yelling, "Go, J-Bay!"

Jason quickly turned toe-side down the wave, watching as it began to curl over him, just above his head. He crouched low, racing through the pipeline of water as it closed in around him. Just before it closed out with a crushing force, he shot out the other side, a burst of water spray shooting out behind him.

Cricket threw his hands up in the air, fists clenched tight, cheering, "Yeah!"

Jason beamed with excitement as he reunited with Cricket, just past the second sandbar where the waves were breaking.

"That was the craziest barrel I've ever seen, J-Bay! I wish I had gotten that on camera!" Cricket exclaimed.

"I know!" Jason replied, the thrill of the ride still coursing through his veins. He flashed a grin at Cricket, "That wave was perfect!"

They continued to surf that afternoon, catching wave after wave and having fun cheering each other on. Occasionally, one of them got barreled, but none were quite as spectacular as Jason's first wave.

As the sun dipped low in the storm-gray sky, they met back on the shore, carrying their boards. Both men were exhausted but grinning from ear to ear. The wind had picked up, and strong gusts caused the sugar-white grains of sand on the beach to pelt their ankles as they walked back to where they had parked.

"That was one of the best sessions I've had anywhere!" Cricket exclaimed. "I'm glad we finally got the chance to surf together, J-Bay."

"Yeah, me too!" Jason replied, walking beside him.

With a sincere tone, Cricket told Jason, "You know, with Soda only having one good arm right now, I could really use an extra hand tomorrow taking the boat to The Ditch. We're gonna ride out the storm there if you're up for it."

"Yeah, definitely," Jason responded, a mix of surprise and excitement lighting up his face. Even though he was unsure about his long-term prospects of working on the boat, he knew it was a good chance to rebuild the trust he had lost with Cricket.

"The Ditch" was a nickname locals used to describe a narrow stretch of the Intracoastal Waterway that connects Choctawhatchee Bay to West Bay in Panama City Beach. With its high banks, The Ditch provided shelter from intense hurricane winds and storm surges, making it a favored refuge for captains looking to minimize the risk of damage to their boats.

The next morning, Jason met Cricket and Soda at the boat. The wind had intensified significantly overnight, causing the tops of the palm trees to flutter like flags in a fierce gale. Although the water in Joe's Bayou, where the boat was docked, was still relatively calm, Choctawhatchee Bay churned with whitecaps, creating a tumultuous scene.

Even though the hurricane was projected to make landfall far to the east of Destin, Mr. Gregory was acutely aware of how unpredictable hurricanes could be. To protect his home, he had secured the house with storm shutters before he and Katie flew back to Birmingham the day before.

Soda wore a sling on his arm, immobilizing it to relieve pressure on his injury and allow time for healing. He did what he could to help, but both he and Cricket were grateful to have Jason on board.

Jason was also glad to be back on the *Family Tradition* with them, even though reminders of Katie surrounded him. Memories of her flooded his mind. When he looked at the tower, he remembered her beaming with excitement on their first trip, waving to the other boats as they passed by. Seeing the fighting chair reminded him of her radiant smile when she caught her first fish—a beautiful bull dolphin. He also recalled her excitement and pride when she landed the giant marlin that won them first place in the Grand Championship. Glancing at the flybridge, he remembered their first kiss. The vibrant memories felt like sunlight piercing through the cloudy gray sky above him, illuminating the joy they had once shared while simultaneously serving as painful reminders of his loss.

Despite the water being choppy, the short ride across Choctawhatchee Bay was smooth. It didn't take them long to reach the narrow section of the Intracoastal Waterway that snaked through the landscape, flanked by towering banks. The Ditch was already crowded with a variety of boats lining the shoreline—sportfishing vessels, sailboats, houseboats, trawlers, and many other cabin boats—all seeking refuge from the impending storm.

As they slowly navigated the narrow waterway, they eventually spotted an open area on the north side of the channel with plenty of space to tie up. They dropped two anchors from the bow and one from the stern, solidly securing the boat in place. Just as Jason finished securing the last anchor, he looked up and saw the *Trust Me* pulling into the empty space downstream from them.

"You've got to be kidding me." Jason mumbled to himself. Although he was relieved not to see Bill Murphy, he was still annoyed that they had chosen to pull up next to them.

The four crew members of the *Trust Me*, wearing bright yellow shirts and black radio headsets, quickly set about executing a plan similar to that of the *Family Tradition*. They dropped two anchors from the bow and one from the stern. Neither team acknowledged the other with so much as a wave.

As the morning wore on, a few more boats filtered through the maze of moored vessels, including a forty-foot sailboat named *Let It Go*. The owner positioned his boat between the *Family Tradition* and the *Trust Me*, throwing a single anchor from the bow. He then motored away on his dinghy, leaving the *Let It Go* behind.

Despite the wind blowing hard above the high bank tops, the ditch remained calm and uneventful that afternoon. Jason even broke out the small portable boat grill, cooking lunch for everyone.

"Man, that Conecuh sausage smells good!" Cricket exclaimed. Smoke billowed from the grill, and the savory aroma filled the air as Jason removed the links and placed them on a wooden cutting board at the foot of the mezzanine. The board had a container of pimento cheese, a jar of Wickles Original Sweet and Spicy Pickles, and a sleeve of saltine crackers.

"Now, what do you call this again?" Soda asked curiously.

"Southern Charcuterie," Jason replied, slicing several small pieces. "Alright, so the first thing you do is spread pimento cheese on the saltine cracker, then top it with a slice of Conecuh sausage and a Wickles pickle."

Soda wrinkled his nose, his expression clearly skeptical. "I ain't a big fan of sweet pickles."

"Me neither! But you gotta try it! Somehow it just works!" Jason insisted, handing him and Cricket a loaded cracker.

Both Cricket and Soda exchanged doubtful glances as they inspected the unusual combination.

They raised their crackers in a toast and popped the entire hors d'oeuvre into their mouths.

After several chews, they nodded at each other.

Cricket's mouth was still full, but he managed to mumble, "That's good! Real good!"

A wide smile crossed Soda's face as he said, "Darn! That's right tasty! I like that, Jason! It's sweet, savory, smoky, spicy, and has just the right amount of crunch! I like that a lot!" He reached for another cracker with a determined expression. "I'm gonna have to fix me another one of those!"

Cricket chimed in, “Me too! That’s good stuff, J-Bay! Good idea!”

Jason flashed a quick smile. “I thought y’all might like it.”

They continued to enjoy Jason’s Southern Charcuterie lunch special, relishing the carefree moment together. However, the storm was expected to make landfall that night, and everyone knew that was when the worst weather would arrive.

As evening fell, the wind shifted direction and howled through The Ditch. Jason, Soda, and Cricket were safely sheltered in the salon, but the tension hung thick in the air. Cricket was glued to the weather updates, his brow furrowed with concern.

Meanwhile, Jason sat on the couch, fingers hovering over his phone as he tried to craft the perfect text to Katie. He was determined to patch things up between them. He typed: “Hey, Katie. Not sure if you heard, but Cricket asked me to help him and Soda take the boat to The Ditch to ride out the storm tonight. Cricket and I went surfing yesterday and had a great time. Things are good between us again, and it feels great to be back on the boat. But honestly, everything here just reminds me of you. I’m grateful Cricket is giving me a second chance, but I told him if I have to choose between this job and you, I’m choosing you.”

Jason’s thoughts were interrupted as Cricket turned to him and Soda. “Looks like the eye of the hurricane is still on track to make landfall in Apalachicola. But one of the feeder bands is about to hit us, so we’re about to be in for some bad weather.”

Jason and Soda exchanged tense glances, their worry evident. Even though the high banks of The Ditch surrounded them, an uneasy feeling lingered, knowing hurricanes had a way of throwing surprises.

With the storm bearing down, Jason quickly finished the message, adding, "The worst part of the storm is coming soon, so I have to go, but I just wanted to let you know that I miss you and I love you." He pressed send, his heart racing with a mix of hope and anxiety.

With the large feeder band rapidly approaching, Jason told Cricket and Soda, "I'm gonna check the lines again to make sure everything's holding tight."

As he stepped outside, he immediately noticed that the sailboat next to them was drifting steadily closer to the *Trust Me*. After checking the lines securing the *Family Tradition*, Jason opened the salon door and told Cricket and Soda, "The lines are holding good, but it looks like the anchor on the sailboat next to us is dragging."

Cricket and Soda joined Jason in the cockpit, watching as the sailboat drifted closer to the *Trust Me*. It moved slowly at first, but then picked up speed as the anchor completely lost its hold. With nothing to restrain it, the sailboat crashed into the side of the *Trust Me*, jolting the crew into action as they rushed outside to see what was happening.

Lightning flashed overhead, followed by a deafening crack of thunder and sheets of rain pouring down. Jason, Soda, and Cricket quickly ducked just inside the salon but poked their heads out the door, eager to witness the chaos unfolding before them.

Meanwhile, the captain of the *Trust Me* barked orders to his mates, who scrambled to place buoys between the sailboat and the hull. But their efforts seemed futile as the sailboat slid down the length of the *Trust Me*. Even from a distance, the sound of metal bending, breaking, and scraping against the fiberglass hull was unmistakable. The mast of the sailboat eventually snagged on the anchor line running from the bow of the *Trust Me*, holding it in place, but the boats continued to collide sharply against each other.

The mates struggled through the torrential downpour and howling winds, tying ropes to buoys and tossing them between the two boats. Just as it seemed they were making progress, a rumbling sound filled the air. Faint at first, it grew louder, like the jarring sound of a train at full speed—it was the unmistakable roar of a tornado, and it was close. Debris flew overhead, raining down around them as the rumbling intensified.

One of the mates shouted, "Go, go, go!" They turned to traverse the boat's massive bow, each step cautious on the wet surface as the rain pummeled them, making it difficult to see. Suddenly, a tree branch hurtled through the air, striking the man farthest behind. He was knocked overboard, crashing onto the deck of the sailboat below before tumbling into the water.

Fear gripped the remaining crew as debris rained down around them. They hurried toward the salon, casting desperate glances back at their teammate, who floated face down in the strong current, drifting toward the *Family Tradition*. Each glance was filled with dread, believing they were powerless to help him.

Jason watched wide-eyed as the man drifted face down toward them, his bright yellow rain jacket barely visible. Before Cricket or Soda could say a word, Jason swiftly shed his shirt, slipped off his flip-flops, and jumped overboard, swimming as fast as he could to save him.

Cricket raced up to the flybridge, shouting to Soda, "I'll grab the life ring! Open the tuna door for him!" After pulling the life ring and rope out from under the bench seat cushion, he quickly dashed back down, ready to throw it to Jason.

Soda and Cricket struggled to see through the heavy rain as they waited anxiously by the tuna door, water dripping in their eyes and distorting their vision. They couldn't see the tornado, but they could hear it loud and clear, along with the sound of trees snapping high above them on the bank and the debris crashing to the ground.

When Jason reached the man, he quickly flipped him over, keeping the man's head above water. The man had short dark hair and appeared to be in his late twenties. Jason used one arm to hold the man while using his other arm to swim back to the boat. Debris continued to rain down around them, splashing against the water's surface and occasionally striking one of the boats near them.

"Grab the ring!" Cricket shouted, his voice barely cutting through the deafening roar of the tornado, as he hurled it toward Jason.

After Jason grabbed the life ring, Cricket quickly pulled him toward the back of the boat. With urgency, he helped hoist the man up through the tuna door, where the man began coughing up water. Together, Cricket and Jason grasped an arm each and rushed him into the safety of the salon, their hearts racing. The sound of the tornado began to fade behind them, vanishing as quickly as it had appeared out of nowhere.

Once inside, they helped him onto the couch. “Are you okay?” Cricket asked the man, concern etched on his face.

The man nodded weakly, but his face contorted in pain as he gingerly shifted his position. “What happened?” he asked, his voice strained.

“There was a tornado that passed by, and you got knocked overboard, but J-Bay swam out to save you,” Cricket explained, pointing to Jason who was still panting out of breath, exhausted from the exertion of swimming the man back.

“You risked your life to save me?” the man said, turning to Jason with a surprised expression, his brow furrowed in disbelief.

“Yeah. I couldn’t just stand there and watch you drown like your teammates,” Jason replied, his tone serious.

The man winced as he tried to sit up straighter, the ache in his body a harsh reminder of the danger he had just escaped. “Thank you,” he said, his voice filled with gratitude, though tinged with the pain still coursing through him.

“I’m just glad you’re okay,” Jason told him. “By the way, I’m Jason, and this is Soda, and Cricket is the captain. What’s your name?”

“Clint,” the man replied. “I know who all of you are.” He chuckled softly, though still clearly in pain. “I hear Mr. Murphy cuss Jason’s name just about every day.” He continued, “Who’d’ve thought the guy my boss says is such a terrible person would risk his life to save me when my own crew wouldn't do the same?"

Jason's voice was firm but gentle. "Well, you're safe here now, and that's what matters."

As Cricket and Soda nodded in agreement, Cricket said, "I'll radio your captain and let him know you're okay, and that we'll drop you off with them tomorrow once the storm has passed."

Soda added, "I'll get him a towel and see if we've got some dry clothes he can change into."

Jason was soaking wet, so he went downstairs to change in the crew's quarters. As he pulled out his dripping wet wallet and keys from his pockets, he suddenly realized he had lost his phone. "My phone..." he sighed. "It must have fallen in the water." His head drooped in frustration, leaving him anxious about whether Katie had responded to his message.

That evening, they all made small talk late into the night as the storm passed by without any additional surprises. Clint slept peacefully on the couch that night, feeling sore yet grateful to be alive.

The next morning, the sky was surprisingly clear of clouds, with only a light breeze rustling the treetops high on the banks. A few once-tall old-growth pine trees had been snapped in half, their yellowish-white wood exposed at the break, twisted and mangled.

Although tree limbs and debris were strewn all around them in the canal, the *Family Tradition* had emerged unscathed. The *Trust Me*, on the other hand, had deep gashes along its hull, with several sections of fiberglass smashed by the sailboat that was still stuck at the end of its bow.

Jason, Cricket, and Soda were up early, drinking coffee in the galley recounting the night's crazy events. Clint was noticeably quiet as he sat on the couch sipping his piping hot coffee. Clint's gaze was distant, and he appeared lost in thought.

"How you feelin' over there, Clint?" Cricket asked.

Clint smiled faintly. "Pretty much sore everywhere, but I'm okay."

"Well, looks like things have cleared up, so we can drop you off on the *Trust Me* in just a little while," Cricket told him.

Clint hesitantly asked, "Would it be alright if I rode back with y'all?" Shaking his head, he sighed, "My karma has been terrible ever since I joined that team, and I don't want anything to do with them anymore."

Cricket blinked in surprise, then nodded. "Sure, that won't be any problem at all."

"Thank you," Clint said gratefully. With a heavy expression, he added, "There's something I need to get off my chest."

Cricket, Soda, and Jason listened intently as Clint turned to Jason and told him, "Mr. Murphy was bragging the other day about how he paid some girls to take a picture with you and your buddy, and he even had one of them kiss you to stir up trouble between you and Katie. He's obsessed with doing everything he can to stick it to you and ruin your reputation. He even hired a guy to follow you around and try to dig up dirt on you. That's how he got the picture of you and Katie kissing that he sent Cricket. I heard him say you would never work on the *Family Tradition* again, but I'm glad that wasn't true, because I might not be here right now if it was."

The news confirmed what Jason had suspected all along. "Thanks for sharing that with us, Clint," he replied, keeping his voice steady.

Meanwhile, Cricket and Soda exchanged glances, their faces reflecting a mix of surprise and anger. "I'll radio the *Trust Me* and let 'em know you'll be riding back with us," Cricket added firmly.

A short while later, with Clint on board, the *Family Tradition* set off for the ride back to Destin. The water was calm, but Cricket took his time, keeping a close eye out for loose lumber and logs washed into the bay by the storm surge or tossed by the tornado that had passed by.

When they arrived back at Mr. Gregory's house, Clint thanked them all again for risking their lives to save his—especially Jason. While Soda headed home and Cricket drove Clint to his vehicle, Jason decided to stop by his parents' house. Since he had lost his phone, he wanted to check on them and share his intense experience at The Ditch.

As Jason pulled his truck into the driveway, he saw his dad hammering on the dock behind the house, repairing a board that had come loose.

"Hey, Dad!" Jason called out. "Looks like the dock made it through another hurricane without too much damage."

Jacob replied, "Yeah, this one board come loose, but I'd say it held up pretty good." He then added with a wide smile, "It's a good thing we built it strong and anchored those pilings deep!"

"Yep," Jason said, his eyes shining with admiration for his father and everything he had taught him over the years, as they walked back toward the house.

Jacob asked, "So, how did things go at The Ditch? I tried callin' you this mornin', but it went straight to voicemail."

"Well, I've got quite a story for you. We had a tornado pass by last night, and I ended up losing my phone when I jumped in the water to save a mate who was knocked overboard from Bill Murphy's boat—the guy I was telling you about the other day."

"Really?" Jacob exclaimed, his voice filled with disbelief and shock.

"Yeah, and the guy I saved spilled the beans in front of Cricket and Soda about everything Bill Murphy has been doing to try and stick it to me," Jason replied.

"Dang, Son! Let's go inside where I can have a seat and hear all about this! I might have to pop me some popcorn! This sounds like a good one!" Jacob said, laughing as he clapped Jason on the back.

Once inside, Jacob and Ellen settled into the living room, captivated by Jason's story. Despite his recent mistakes, their pride swelled as they recognized that he had done the right thing in the face of danger. They understood he wasn't perfect—no one is—but the strong principles and deeply ingrained moral values they had instilled in him had given him the strength to save a man's life. Much like the sturdy dock he and his father had built together, Jason had a foundation that would weather the tests of time and the many storms he would face.

That evening, Jason returned to his townhome. Without his cell phone and with no landline, he felt cut off from the world. He wondered if Katie had responded to his text message but knew he would have to wait another day to find out.

He sat there alone, lost in his thoughts about Katie. A smile tugged at the corner of his mouth as he remembered the first time she came to his townhome, their time together cruising around the bay on his boat, and the lively party at The Point.

Suddenly, he heard a knock on his front door. Not expecting anyone, a look of surprise crossed his face as he got up from the couch and walked to the door. When he opened it, his expression shifted to shock. “Hey, Katie.”

“Hey,” she replied warmly, though with a hint of nervousness.

“I wasn’t expecting you,” he told her as his surprise expression turned to a smile.

“I heard about what happened at The Ditch, and I just felt like I needed to see you in person,” she said.

“I’m glad you did. I would have called or texted you, but I lost my phone,” Jason explained.

“I know. Cricket told me. He told me about everything that happened.” With a wide smile, she added, “He also told my dad that you’re definitely going with us to the White Marlin Open.”

“Yes!” Jason said softly, playfully restraining his enthusiasm as he raised his arm to his chest, clenching his fingers into a celebratory fist.

Katie laughed softly at Jason's antics, but her expression turned more serious as she looked deep into his eyes and said, "I just want you to know that I'm really sorry for not believing you at first about Billy, and..." Katie stepped forward, pulling Jason in. "I love you too, Jason Baymont." As they embraced in a passionate kiss, the warm ocean breeze wrapped around them like a soft caress, accompanied by the faint sound of waves crashing against the distant shore.

THE WHITE MARLIN OPEN

A few days after Jason finally untangled the massive backlash in his life, he found himself right back where he belonged—aboard the *Family Tradition* with his team. The boat was docked behind Mr. Gregory's house, and everyone was gathered in the galley, discussing their game plan for the White Marlin Open tournament, their anticipation building as they prepared for the challenges ahead.

"So, this tournament's gonna be a little different from what we're used to fishin' in the Gulf," Cricket said, leaning against the kitchen counter while the others sat at the bar and dinette. "We'll be fishin' against close to four hundred boats—and most of 'em will have the home-field advantage, fishin' their favorite spots."

He grinned. "But if we happen to get lucky, the payout for the biggest white marlin is expected to be over four million dollars."

Smiles of excitement spread through the team as he continued. "And although we'll be primarily fishin' for whites, the payout for the biggest tuna is around one million, and the biggest blue marlin is worth over half a million. So, needless to say, we'll have the eighty-wides ready, just in case!"

"One big difference though is that this tournament lasts for five days, but we can only fish three of 'em. On the days we fish, we have to stay within a hundred nautical miles of the Ocean City sea buoy and can only put our lines in the water from eight in the morning to three-thirty in the afternoon, then we have to head back in. We can't deploy the omni sonar before eight AM, either."

He scratched the back of his head. "I'm not sure which three days we'll be fishin' yet, but I'll be keepin' an eye on the weather as we get closer to the tournament to see which ones I think will give us the best shot."

"When do we leave?" Mr. Gregory asked.

"Well, it's gonna take us about five days to run the boat up there, assuming the weather holds. But for y'all I guess, it depends on if you and Katie want to ride with us, or if y'all plan to fly up there and meet us?" Cricket said.

"Traveling by boat sounds like an adventure. I think we'll come along for the ride." With a reserved smile, Mr. Gregory added, "There is one particular harbor I'd like to stop at, though."

Katie's face lit up. "Key West?"

Mr. Gregory gave her a nod, his smile broadening.

"Yes!" Katie exclaimed, which caused the men to chuckle while they exchanged enthusiastic glances.

The crew spent the next several days loading the boat with provisions and preparing for their great migration from the warm waters of the Gulf to fish the cooler waters of the Atlantic off the coast of Ocean City, Maryland.

After leaving Destin, both the temperature and their anticipation rose with every degree of latitude they traveled south. The seas were smooth, creating an enjoyable ride that allowed them to make good time on their first day. They stopped overnight in Venice, Florida, to refuel before continuing early the next morning.

As they approached the Keys, the water gradually transformed into a stunning turquoise, resembling a postcard from paradise. When they finally arrived in Key West later that afternoon, the moment felt truly magical. Sailboats, yachts, and fishing boats cruised gracefully through the crystal-clear water surrounding the island. Next to the marina, two enormous cruise ships loomed over Mallory Square, where thousands of passengers had disembarked, eager to embark on their island excursions.

Though the harbor docks were crowded with boats, a dockhand in a white polo and khakis waved Cricket over, pointing toward their slip.

Once the *Family Tradition* was secured, the crew stepped off the boat and into the steamy bustle of Key West. Just beyond the marina entrance, shaded by a swaying coconut palm, a golf cart awaited them—arranged by Mr. Gregory. As they climbed in, Katie glanced at the map in her hand. "Let's start with the butterfly sanctuary, then the lighthouse, Hemingway's home, and finish at the Southernmost Point. This is going to be so much fun!"

"Sounds good," Mr. Gregory replied. He pressed the gas pedal, and the small engine sputtered to life, carrying them into the colorful chaos of Old Town. Roosters crowed, sunburned tourists wandered the sidewalks, scooters darted through traffic, and horns honked in a lively symphony of sounds.

"Now that's not something you see back home," Soda called out, pointing to an iguana sunbathing lazily on a low stone wall. Its tail dangled over the edge while a hen and three fuzzy chicks pecked around the grass nearby.

Their first stop, the Key West Butterfly and Nature Conservatory, felt like stepping into a fairytale. Inside the glass-enclosed oasis, lush tropical plants thrived, brilliant butterflies fluttered all around them, and the soft chatter of exotic birds filled the air. Pink Caribbean flamingos glided gracefully through shallow pools, adding to the vibrant scene. Suddenly, a bright blue butterfly landed on Cricket's head, drawing a round of laughter from the others.

With broad smiles still on their faces, they eventually made their way to the Key West Lighthouse, just a few blocks away. Climbing the narrow spiral staircase, they were slightly winded by the time they reached the top, but the reward was worth it. Stunning views from the lantern deck stretched over the homes and swaying palms, all the way to the sea. As they soaked in the scenery, Katie exclaimed, "Look! There's Hemingway's house!" Her excitement was contagious as the team gazed out at the stop they had all been eagerly anticipating.

After making their way back down the winding stairs, they walked to Hemingway's home, strolling alongside the rustic red brick wall that guided them to the entrance. The midday sun blazed overhead as they approached the house, but upon stepping into the courtyard, the heat surrendered to the shade of towering palms and tropical trees. The house rose majestically amidst the lush foliage, resembling a monument with its white walls and yellow-green shutters flanking tall arched windows. A wide wraparound porch and balcony, supported by elegant black wrought-iron pillars and railings, completed the picturesque scene.

A stillness enveloped the place, interrupted only by the slow, slinky movements of Hemingway's famous six-toed cats. One lounged lazily on the porch, while another meandered down a narrow path, gently brushing against a hibiscus flower.

"Looks like they've got the run of the place!" Soda chuckled as another cat with wide paws leapt effortlessly onto the porch, sprawling out in the shade.

As they made their way onto the porch and stepped inside, they were greeted by a comfortable coolness, with fans whirring in each room—a welcome relief from the oppressive heat and humidity outside. The air inside had a distinct scent—like old books, heartwood, and the smell of history.

A soft-spoken woman with short gray hair clad in a teal linen shirt, smiled warmly as the group filed into the front parlor. "Welcome to the Hemingway Home," she greeted them. As another cat strolled gracefully across the floor, she laughed softly. "And yes, all of these cats are indeed descendants of Snow White—the original six-toed cat given to Hemingway by a ship's captain. You'll find them just about everywhere here." She added, "I'll be giving a tour in about thirty minutes if you'd like to wait, or you're welcome to explore the house on your own."

Since they were short on time, Mr. Gregory replied, "Thanks, I think we'll walk around ourselves."

"That'll be just fine. Go right ahead," she said, gesturing for them to continue.

Room by room, they wandered through the house, each space revealing layers of Hemingway's life. They moved slowly, soaking in the rich details of the antique furnishings and decorations that made the house feel both curated and lived-in. Black-and-white photographs lined the walls: marlins he had caught, African game he had harvested, and cherished moments shared with friends. Each image spoke of a life lived boldly—steeped in adventure, competition, and camaraderie.

They paused longest in front of a wall with a wooden ship's wheel in the middle, surrounded by photos of Hemingway, marlins, and his beloved boat, *Pilar*. Beneath the photos, encased in glass, sat a small-scale model of the boat. To its side sat a small portable typewriter placed on top of a small suitcase used to transport it. They lingered, studying the boat and feeling humbled by what Hemingway had achieved with it, which inspired generations of offshore anglers, including themselves.

Eventually, they made their way to his writing studio—a space where discipline and imagination met to create many of his works. Bookshelves lined the walls, filled with novels, their spines faded and cracked with age. A mounted deer head hung proudly on the wall, accompanied by other trophies and artifacts from his far-flung adventures. At the center of the room stood a small wooden table, a vintage black typewriter resting on top, with a single chair placed beside it.

"Is this where he wrote *The Old Man and the Sea*?" Katie asked, glancing around the room.

Jason shook his head. "No. He wrote most of his earlier work here, but he wrote *The Old Man and the Sea* when he was living in Cuba."

"He lived in Cuba?" she said, her eyebrows raised.

Mr. Gregory nodded. "Things were a lot different in Cuba back then. He lived here in Key West for about eight years, then moved to Cuba, where he spent the next twenty-one years."

"Oh," Katie said, her surprise mirrored in the expressions of Cricket and Soda as they quietly continued exploring the room.

Through one of the windows, they caught a glimpse of the pool outside and eventually descended the back steps into the garden to see it. It was unusually large, 24 feet wide and 60 feet long.

Katie crouched down, smiling as she traced a line of tiny six-toed paw prints indelibly pressed into the concrete walkway.

Nearby, Jason spotted a coin embedded in the patio and bent down to examine it, squinting in curiosity.

Mr. Gregory said, "I read that Hemingway's wife had this pool built while he was off covering the Spanish Civil War. It cost around twenty thousand dollars back then—which would've been over four hundred thousand today. The story goes that he was so upset about the price that he told her she'd spent all but his last penny on it. Then he tossed that last penny at her feet and said she might as well have it too. It's been there ever since."

"She got his last red cent!" Soda quipped, drawing a round of chuckles from the crew.

They lingered a moment longer around the pool, soaking in the beauty of their surroundings, then made their way out through the garden and back to the street.

"That was really cool," Katie said, still smiling from the visit.

"Yeah, I'm glad we stopped here," Mr. Gregory replied. The others nodded in agreement, each sharing their favorite parts of visiting the historic home.

"Are y'all ready to go to the Southernmost Point?" Katie said excitedly.

The guys shifted their eyes, hemming and hawing in a way that was anything but earnest—it was obvious they didn't really want to go.

"Come on! Y'all don't want to take a picture in front of the Southernmost Point?" Katie urged.

Mr. Gregory delicately let her down. "I think we're ready to get a drink at one of Hemingway's old hangouts, Sloppy Joe's. But why don't you and Jason go without us and then meet up with us later?"

"Okay, fine!" Katie playfully lamented. "Well, after we go there, I want to watch the sunset at Mallory Square!"

"Okay. Sounds good," he replied. "You two have fun, and we'll meet up for dinner."

After parting ways with the others, Jason and Katie made their way to the Southernmost Point, a popular tourist attraction, joining a long line of eager visitors waiting to snap photos at the iconic landmark.

The oversized concrete marker—designed to resemble a navigational buoy—stood at the corner, painted in thick bands of black, red, and yellow, each separated by narrow white stripes. Near the top, a conch shell and the words *"The Conch Republic"* paid tribute to Key West's famously independent spirit. Below that, it read:

90 Miles to Cuba
Southernmost Point
Continental U.S.A.
Key West, FL
Home of the Sunset

Once they had taken a few quick photos, Jason hailed a pedicab—a human-powered tricycle with a carriage that offered a fun and romantic way to explore the sights on their way back to Mallory Square to watch the sunset.

As they settled into the carriage, the lively atmosphere of Key West enveloped them. They glided past charming homes adorned with vibrant pastel colors, their inviting porches draped with hanging ferns and colorful flower boxes. Lush tropical gardens spilled over with hibiscus flowers in shades of pink, yellow, and orange, alongside vivid bougainvillea blossoms in hues of magenta and purple. Each turn revealed the island's unique charm, making their ride feel like a delightful journey through paradise.

When they finally arrived at Mallory Square, they decided to swing by the boat first—just a short walk away. Despite the steady breeze, the heat had taken its toll, and they wanted to freshen up before watching the sunset and meeting the rest of the team at Sloppy Joe's.

After showering and changing into clean clothes, they hurried to leave the boat, eager not to miss the sunset. Near the end of the dock, they came across an old man, fishing around the pilings off the stern of his sailboat. His boat had a clean white hull, and its name, *The Last Line*, was painted navy blue on the transom. As they approached, the man hooked a fish. Joy sparked in his eyes as he reeled it in with a light spinning rod and reel. After a short fight, he brought the fish—just over twelve inches long—skipping along the surface before landing it in the boat.

Despite his scruffy stubble and casual attire, he had a distinguished presence and a friendly smile. A faded red baseball cap sat atop his head, with strands of white wavy hair peeking out from beneath. His eyes twinkled, hinting at the stories he could tell.

"Nice one!" Jason said.

"Yeah, it'll make a fine dinner tonight! These mangrove snappers are good to eat—fun to catch too!" the old man beamed.

Jason smiled back. "I used to catch and cook them all the time when I was a kid. We call them black snappers back home."

"Oh, yeah? Where's home?" the old man asked, his curiosity piqued.

"Destin," Jason replied.

A nostalgic expression crossed the old man's face. "Ah, Destin. I've been there a time or two—beautiful place!"

"Where are you from?" Jason asked.

"Well, I was born in Mississippi but spent most of my life wandering from place to place. I went to Paris for a while, lived in London, New York, and at least a dozen other places. But that was all a lifetime ago. Now, this boat is my home, and I move where the wind takes me." With a distant gaze, he added, "Still searching for something, I suppose..."

Jason and Katie gave understanding nods.

"So, is this your first time in the Keys?" he asked.

"Yeah. We're traveling to Ocean City, Maryland, for a fishing tournament and stopped by for the day," Jason replied.

"Tournament fishing, huh? Sounds exciting. Although it looks like you've already found a keeper, if you ask me," the old man said, tilting his head toward Katie and giving Jason a wink.

Jason grinned and pulled Katie close. "Definitely." Despite having just met, the two men seemed to share a kind of kinship common among those who chase fish and dreams. With a warm smile, Jason offered a fisherman's farewell: "Well, safe travels and tight lines. I hope you find what you're searching for."

The old man's eyes softened, as if seeing a younger version of himself. "You too, young man." As they exchanged friendly waves, his parting words rang like a goodbye and a gentle reminder: "Have fun."

With the old man's words still echoing in Jason's head, he and Katie meandered hand in hand toward the edge of Mallory Square. It was just before 8:00 PM, and the cruise ships that had dominated the waterfront earlier had long since pulled away, leaving behind a clear view of the sea and

Sunset Key to the northwest. Sailboats glided across the water, silhouetted against the molten sky, where streaks of orange and lavender bled into the blue hues like a watercolor dream.

The square pulsed with life. Laughter and applause echoed off the old brick walls of nearby buildings as street performers spun fire and balanced atop unicycles.

They passed a group of men that looked like castaway pirates from another century. Despite their tattered clothes and scruffy beards, their voices rose in beautiful harmony as they shook maracas and tapped tambourines. One had a bright green parrot perched on his shoulder, bobbing along with the beat.

Nearby, folding tables displayed local art and handmade crafts—beaded jewelry, driftwood carvings, painted conch shells, and countless other offerings.

Jason and Katie stopped at a wooden cart heaped with green coconuts, their husks stacked in a messy pyramid, palm fronds jutting upward like sails. A barefoot man in a frayed straw hat chopped the tops off coconuts with a machete, his movements practiced and rhythmic. With a grin, he handed one to Katie, then Jason, each with a straw poked into the center. Jason pulled a few bills from his pocket and handed them over with a nod of thanks, then raised his drink toward Katie in a toast.

As the sun slipped lower, the crowd edged closer to the seawall. Jason gently squeezed Katie's hand as she leaned her head against his shoulder. It was like watching the sunset from the end of the earth—somehow marking more than just the end of another day. A collective hush settled over the square just as the final sliver of light disappeared beneath the horizon, followed by a ripple of applause that slowly faded into the hum of conversation and laughter.

Jason turned toward Katie, the glow of the fading sky reflected in her eyes. They didn't have to say a word—just smiled, knowing whatever came next, they were in it together.

After basking in the moment, Jason glanced at his watch. "You ready to catch up with the others?"

Katie nodded, her eyes gazing into his, before taking the last sip from her coconut.

They made their way back through the vibrant chaos of the square, weaving through the crowd, hand in hand. The music from Duval Street grew louder with each step until the familiar neon glow of Sloppy Joe's came into view, casting a flickering light onto the sidewalk.

Inside, the bar was alive with energy as people sang along with a cover band playing Jimmy Buffett's "Margaritaville." Mr. Gregory, Cricket, and Soda had already claimed a table near the back and waved them over.

As Jason and Katie slid into open seats, Katie exclaimed, "Oh my gosh, y'all! That sunset was amazing!" Jason nodded in agreement, still soaking in the moment.

While she chatted with her dad, sharing all the details of what they had seen, Jason glanced around the bar. The walls were lined with old photos, neon signs, and nautical relics. Ceiling fans stirred the air, and flags from all over the world draped across the rafters above them. A large stuffed marlin hung high above a cluster of black-and-white photos of Hemingway, catching Jason's eye. Rich with history, it was easy to imagine Hemingway sitting at the bar with his friends, sharing fishing stories and laughter.

Turning to Cricket and Soda, Jason asked, "So what's the biggest marlin y'all ever caught?"

They both paused, thinking for a second.

"I guess it was that eight-hundred-pounder we caught at Bay Point a few years back," Soda said, while Cricket nodded in agreement.

With a hint of pain in his expression, he continued, "Though we did lose a marlin one time that was a lot bigger than that eight-hundred-pounder. You don't supposed to call it a grander unless you weigh it in, so we always round down and call it a nine-fifty out of respect for those that have—but that fish probably would've crossed the mark."

Cricket nodded, a distant look in his eyes. "Yeah, we've caught a lot of good fish over the years, but that one still haunts me. Some people spend their whole lives—and sometimes even their fortune—searching for a fish like that." Turning to Soda with a grin, he added, "One day we'll catch a grander though."

"Yep," Soda replied, his gaze distant, nodding gently.

Breaking the heaviness of the moment, Katie said, "Catchin' a grander would be cool and all, but all I can think about right now is bringing in a white marlin worth four million dollars!"

The table erupted in laughter, smiles spreading all around. The team continued to enjoy their time together that night in Key West—filled with stories, cold drinks, and the shared thrill of chasing dreams.

The next morning, the team cast off, gliding through the enchanting tropical waters. Soon, everyone settled into the flybridge, soaking in the breathtaking island scenery while sharing stories about their favorite moments spent in Key West. With blue skies overhead and a warm, salty breeze blowing in their faces, the possibilities felt endless, stirring excitement for the days ahead as they cruised the open water.

As they rounded the southernmost tip of the island and began heading north, the deep blue stretched endlessly ahead. Jason slipped into a daydream, his gaze drifting toward Havana, Cuba, just beyond the horizon. He imagined Hemingway's villa, Finca Vigía, nestled among the palms, its windows thrown open to the Gulf breeze, the clack of a typewriter echoing faintly through the still morning air. It felt surreal, being this close to the waters Hemingway once roamed. He pictured the great author at the helm of *Pilar*, prowling these very currents in search of marlin, tuna, and the kind of truth he could capture in prose.

Katie's voice cut softly through the quiet, pulling Jason from his thoughts. "It's crazy how fast the water changes. It was so clear and tropical just a few miles back—now it's this deep blue, like it is back home sometimes."

Cricket replied, "Yeah, this is part of the Gulf Stream—it flows out of the Gulf, runs up the East Coast, and then crosses the Atlantic toward England. In fact, it's such a strong current that sailors have been using it since the early fifteen hundreds to shave a few days off the trip back to Europe."

Still looking out across the water in front of them, Katie said quietly, "Wow, I didn't know water from the Gulf went all the way up to Europe."

Cricket added, "Yep, it's also the reason why England is a lot warmer than similar latitudes in Canada or Russia."

Still astonished by how people had been navigating the Gulf Stream for over 500 years, Jason shook his head. "It's mind-boggling to me how captains used to navigate these waters without all the electronics we have nowadays."

Cricket nodded. "Yeah, I could do it if I had to, but it's definitely a lot safer out here knowing the ocean bottom and getting real-time weather updates."

Mr. Gregory and Soda nodded in agreement, their eyes wide—aware of the countless shipwrecks along that stretch of coast. As they glided along the smooth seas, the team quietly reflected on those who had traveled the same waters long before them, all in search of something. Drawn not to a specific destination, but to the crossroads of the Gulf Stream, where profit, adventure, and the unknown waited on the horizon.

They spent the next several days skirting the coast, stopping only to refuel. Long stretches of open water passed beneath them, broken now and then by the silhouette of another fishing boat in the distance or the shape of a massive container ship on the horizon. Occasionally, a playful pod of dolphins paced them just off the bow before peeling away and vanishing beneath the surface.

The long days at sea settled into an almost meditative rhythm, with the steady hum of the engines in the background. They would wake early, share stories and laughter as they traveled along, then gather around the table for dinner each night. There was an unspoken ease that developed from logging so many miles together on the water. There was no rush, no pressure—just time together unfolding at sea, where even the quiet moments felt shared. They were not islands unto themselves, but a tight-knit team that felt more like family with each passing day.

However, when they reached Harbour Island Marina in Ocean City, Maryland, the contrast in pace was striking. The scene was electric. In the distance, a Ferris wheel rose above the rooftops, while rows of gray-and-white condos lined the marina, their sharp rooflines and chimneys giving off a distinctly East Coast charm. Fishing boats packed every slip. Their outriggers stretched skyward like a ceremonial saber arch, silently saluting the teams walking beneath them as they prepared to battle for bragging rights, record purses, and a shot at offshore glory. Vendors had filled the area with rows of white tents stocked with gear, apparel, and everything in between. Part festival, part pilgrimage, the waterfront teemed with spectators, while camera crews and satellite trucks from major networks stood poised to broadcast the event to audiences around the world.

As they neared the harbor, Soda drew in a deep breath. "Man, even the air smells different here. Smells like cold water, crab cakes, and clam chowder!"

The others laughed, their eyes bright with excitement as they took in the sights and smells themselves.

Cricket called out, "Hey, check it out—that's Michael Jordan's boat over there, the *Catch 23*."

Katie's voice rose, caught between disbelief and excitement. "Michael Jordan? As in the basketball player?"

Cricket laughed. "Yeah, Michael Jordan—the GOAT. Y'all didn't know he marlin fished?"

"No!" Katie said, as Jason and Mr. Gregory shook their heads, equally stunned. Each of them shifted side to side, hoping to catch a glimpse of the famous athlete.

"He's got a really good team. They're gonna be tough to beat," Cricket added.

Though they didn't get to see Michael Jordan, the team was still riding high with excitement as Cricket backed into their slip. After Jason and Soda secured the boat, they set out to explore the area, stopping for a local tradition—the famous Orange Crush drink. They waited in line at a crowded dockside tent serving the cocktails and had just taken their first sip when two fishermen passed by. One of them did a double take when he saw Katie, recognizing her and the rest of the team.

With a thick New Jersey accent, the younger man said, "Hey! Didn't you guys just win that big tournament down in the Gulf? Team *Family Tradition*, right?"

Katie beamed. "Yeah! We won biggest marlin at the Grand Championship."

"Yo! That was a good fish." He tapped the older man walking beside him on the shoulder, clearly excited. "Hey, that's Team *Family Tradition*! They won biggest marlin at the Grand Championship in the Gulf."

The older man gave them a quick once-over, clearly unimpressed. Speaking in the same strong Jersey accent, he said, "Yeah? Well, there's no oil rigs here and you can't use live baits in this tournament, so... good luck." He turned abruptly and continued on his way.

The younger man gave a quick wave and a friendly grin as he followed after him. "Good luck," he said over his shoulder.

The team gave the young man a quick wave goodbye, then sipped their drinks through straws, exchanging glances—a silent acknowledgment that they were no longer on their home turf.

Weaving through the crowd as they enjoyed their drinks, they explored vendor booths and local shops. All around them, fishermen greeted each other with booming voices and hearty handshakes, their accents sharp and distinctly northern. Though it shared many similarities with tournaments back home, the scene at Ocean City carried a noticeable shift from the slow southern drawls and easy banter of the Gulf Coast. Everything there felt faster and louder—deeply rooted in the pride and long-standing traditions of the Northeast.

As the sun began to dip behind the marina, they found a tucked-away seafood joint with a patio strung in white lights that twinkled like stars. A chalkboard menu out front boasted crab cakes, fresh oysters, and fish tacos. Inside, the air buzzed with the lively roar of chatter as people feasted on platters of fresh seafood and clinked glasses over tournament talk.

After the team finished dinner, they made their way back to the *Family Tradition*—stomachs full and spirits high. To their surprise, the temperature had dropped significantly.

Katie crossed her arms, a slight shiver running through her. “I can’t believe how cool it is.”

“Feels great,” Mr. Gregory replied.

“I know!” Cricket replied, as Soda chimed in, “Definitely a welcome change after that heat in the Keys!”

Once inside the salon, Cricket said, “I’ve been watchin’ the weather, and it looks like the seas are gonna start pickin’ up Thursday and keep gettin’ worse through Friday. So fishin’ Monday through Wednesday will be our best bet.”

“Sounds good,” Mr. Gregory said, the team’s excitement evident.

The crew spent the next day preparing for the tournament, while Katie and her dad continued exploring the area—sightseeing, shopping, and soaking up the atmosphere.

Everyone turned in early that evening, knowing they had an early start ahead, and three intense days of fishing to follow.

It was still dark the next morning as they passed the inlet buoy and headed to their first spot, a stretch of deep water known as Poor Man’s Canyon.

Unfortunately, they weren’t the only ones with the same idea—nearly sixty boats were already scattered across the area as they began trolling.

“Looks like a parking lot out here,” Jason said to Soda.

“Yeah,” Soda replied, eyes scanning the area. “But this is a good spot. We’ve done well here before.”

Throughout the day, the radio crackled with captains reporting their catches. One boat, just a few miles away, called *Big Rig*, announced they’d landed a white marlin estimated to weigh over eighty pounds—a sizable fish that could easily win prize money.

The crew occasionally spotted plumes of diesel smoke from boats backing down on fish, but for them, not a single bite came their way.

Jason and Soda looked frustrated. They adjusted lines, double-checked their rigs, but nothing seemed to help. At 3:30 p.m., they promptly removed their lines from the water, per tournament rules, and the team began making their way back to the marina empty-handed.

At the docks, fishermen proudly brought their catches to the scale, the crowd cheering around them.

Though Mr. Gregory and Katie didn't seem bothered, the crew was clearly disheartened that they didn't even get a bite.

"I can't believe we got skunked," Jason said.

"Yeah, we were in the right place though," Soda said. "That boat *Big Rig* that was fishin' by us is in first place right now with the one they caught—it came in at eighty-six pounds."

Cricket sighed. "Well, we've got two more days and a lot more water to fish."

Jason and Soda nodded softly, hoping the next day would bring a change in luck.

On day two, the team was up early again—this time headed for a place called Baltimore Canyon, roughly 70 miles offshore.

After deploying the trolling spread, it wasn't long before they heard that satisfying sound they'd been waiting for: "ZZZzzzzzzz..."

"Fish on!" Soda cheered as a white marlin exploded from the surface in a flash of silver. It was a small one—roughly 40 pounds—but the team was ecstatic to have hooked their first white marlin of the tournament.

Katie raced down from the flybridge. She snapped on the gut bucket belt, locked the 30W rod butt into place, and began battling the fish standing up. She moved around the deck, following the marlin as it put on a dazzling display—leaping from the water again and again. Katie's face lit up with excitement as the crew cheered her on.

It didn't take her long to bring the leader line within Jason's reach.

"Is it big enough?" she asked as he brought it alongside the boat.

Soda shook his head. "No, they've gotta be over seventy inches, and this one looks a little short."

"Hey, at least we broke the ice!" Cricket called down, smiling.

After releasing the fish, they continued trolling. It wasn't long before they hooked another, and then another, eventually landing a total of six white marlin. Unfortunately, none were big enough to weigh in, and before they knew it, 3:30 PM had arrived.

Although they didn't have a fish to bring back, spirits were high as they returned to the docks, hopeful their luck would only get better on their final day of fishing.

The next morning, the crew was up at 3:00 AM, sipping coffee in the galley. With his voice still groggy, Soda asked, "Where are we headed, Cricket?"

Cricket rubbed his tired eyes. "Well, there are some blue water eddies from the Gulf Stream about ninety miles out. Thought we'd give that a shot today."

Soda grinned. "Well, I guess since that water comes from the Gulf, we'll have the home turf advantage."

Cricket chuckled. "Yeah, maybe." After finishing his last sip of coffee, he stretched his arms and yawned. "Alright fellas, let's go catch a big fish and win a bunch of money."

Jason and Soda chugged their remaining coffee. Slowly, they stood up, their bodies still stiff. "Let's do this," Jason said, his voice groggy but determined.

Later that morning, they reached the blue-water eddies of the Gulf Stream. The skies were clear, and the sea stretched smooth and glassy in places, broken only by the gentle undulation of long, slow swells. Faint lines of surface slicks traced the eddy's rotation—subtle signs of the powerful currents flowing beneath. Below, microscopic plankton shimmered like flecks of glitter, dancing in the shafts of sunlight that disappeared into the depths.

A sense of reverent wonder filled Soda's voice as he said, "I know we're a long way from home, but there's just somethin' about this water that feels familiar."

Jason raised an eyebrow, a playful smirk on his face. "It's definitely pretty—I'll give you that."

"I'm tellin' you, Jason, I've got a good feelin' about us fishin' this Gulf Stream," Soda said, his eyes bright with excitement.

"What do you think about putting out a couple of lures on the eighty-wides, just in case there's a blue marlin out here?" Jason asked, his expression hopeful.

Soda scanned the horizon, narrowing his eyes. “Yeah, that sounds like a good idea. You never know what we might run into out here.” He glanced down, considering their options. “Let’s keep the two flat lines, push the other two out to the long rigger position, and run the two eighty-wides in the short rigger position.”

With the plan set, Jason and Soda waited for the clock to strike 8:00 AM, then quickly deployed their teasers and the six fishing lines. Meanwhile, Katie and Mr. Gregory joined Cricket in the flybridge as he began searching for fish with the omni sonar.

The day unfolded slowly, the beautiful blue water stretching endlessly around them. The lures on the short riggers skipped rhythmically over the ripples, their movement hypnotic as the hours slipped by. While Cricket steered the boat and scanned the horizon, Mr. Gregory sat beside him in the flybridge with a paperback in hand. Every now and then, he paused to gaze out at the water, quietly reflecting on a passage before turning the page.

Katie lounged in the mezzanine, scrolling through her phone and chatting with Jason and Soda, who kept steady watch on the spread. Every so often, they adjusted a lure that was off-track or had picked up a strand of sea grass. Around 1:00 PM, a distant flock of birds was seen diving sharply into the sea, sending a jolt of anticipation through the crew. Though no fish followed, the moment served as a quiet reminder that everything could change in an instant.

By 3:00 PM, with only half an hour left to fish, a sense of peace had settled over the team. Jason and Katie exchanged subtle smiles of resignation. They had given it their best, and although they hadn't weighed in a fish, it had been a memorable trip for everyone.

A short while later, Cricket's voice unexpectedly rang out, "I'm marking a fish up ahead! Y'all get ready!"

The news jolted Jason and Soda to attention, their bodies tense as they scanned behind the boat.

Cricket's eyes were still glued to the screen, watching and waiting to see if the fish would rise from the depths. "It's coming up!" he shouted. "Whatever it is, it's big!" He turned to look behind the boat, scanning the spread of lures and teasers. "There it is!" He shouted. "It's comin' up behind the left short rigger! It's a big blue! It's a big blue! Get ready!"

Like a submarine rising from the depths, its towering dorsal fin cut through the surface, while its massive dark body pushed a wall of water aside as it barreled toward the lure.

The fish quickly closed in, its fins radiating electric blue as it slashed its bill back and forth at the lure. With an audible snap, the line broke free from the outrigger clip, but an eerie silence followed.

A pained expression crossed Soda's face as he realized the fish had missed the lure.

"He's fading right! He's fading right!" Cricket called out. "Get ready, Jason!"

The marlin glided beneath the boat's wake and quickly zeroed in on the right short rigger lure chugging along the surface. It began to thrash its bill at the lure, just as it had with the other one. With a sudden snap, the line freed itself from the outrigger clip, and the eighty-wide's drag began to scream: "ZZZzzzzzzz..."

"Yeah!" the team cheered.

The marlin instantly erupted out of the water, raising its head just above the surface and violently thrashing side to side in an attempt to shake off the lure.

Jason clenched his jaw, holding his breath and hoping the hook would stay in place. A wave of relief washed over him as the fish disappeared below the surface, and the line continued to scream off the spool. The fish was still hooked—and hooked good.

Soda shouted up to Cricket, "She might be the one!"

Believing the fish could be the grander they had always wanted to catch, Cricket exclaimed, "We've been after a fish like that for a long time, buddy! Let's bring her on in!"

As the line continued to peel off the reel at a blistering pace, Katie positioned herself in the fighting chair. Filled with nervous excitement, she asked Soda, "How do y'all know it's a female?"

"Giant blue marlins like that are always females," Soda replied, his voice slightly shaky. He took a deep breath, trying to steady himself as he gazed out toward the fish. "I've never seen one this big."

Jason and Katie exchanged anxious smiles as he handed her the reel. After she secured the harness, Cricket quickly began backing down on the fish in full reverse. Water sprayed into the air like celebratory streamers as he chased the marlin for several hundred yards before it finally dove deep beneath the boat.

Eventually, the drag fell silent, and Katie was faced with the arduous challenge of raising the fish.

Cricket suspected they were in for a long fight and promptly radioed in their status—tournament rules allowed any boat still fighting a fish after the 3:30 p.m. deadline to continue until the fish was boated, released, or lost.

For the next three and a half hours, Katie made slow but steady gains. She tirelessly cranked the reel handle, winding herself up and using her body weight to pump the rod in an epic battle against the behemoth below. Each turn of the reel was a test of her strength and resolve, her muscles burning as she fought to bring the massive marlin to the surface.

Breathing heavily, Katie took a moment to rest and wipe the sweat from her brow. "What time is it?"

"Six thirty-five," Soda replied, his voice steady. "You're doin' great, Katie. Just keep the pressure on it."

Despite her fatigue, a proud smile spread across Katie's face. She glanced at the spool and saw it was nearly full—an encouraging sign that the fish was getting close. Just as she was about to begin cranking herself up again, the fish yanked the rod tip down, and line began dumping from the reel at a blistering pace.

Katie watched in disbelief as a hundred yards of line slipped away in mere seconds.

Amazed by the incredible speed of the fish, Jason let out a low whistle. "Whew!"

Soda turned to Katie, his expression serious and his voice low. "Big game," he said with an affirming nod.

Katie sighed, frustrated by the setback.

"Don't worry, Katie—you'll get that line back," Jason encouraged.

Hoping to help her out, Cricket called down, “Hold on, Katie. I’m gonna try adjusting the position of the boat. Maybe pulling from a different angle will help you get that line back a little quicker.”

Katie nodded, her expression weary but hopeful.

Cricket spun the boat around, eager to give her an advantage. But the fish quickly adjusted its course, thwarting his plans. After several more failed attempts to gain leverage, Cricket shook his head. “This fish ain’t having it. Every time I adjust the boat, it changes course, putting us right back where we started.”

A look of bewilderment crossed her face as she wondered how much longer this battle would last. Taking a deep breath, she exhaled slowly, realizing it was now just her against the fish.

Minutes stretched into hours as the sun sank lower on the horizon, casting a warm glow across the water. The gentle hum of the engine mingled with the rhythmic lapping of waves against the boat while Katie tirelessly cranked the reel handle. As the last rays of sunlight faded, a cool breeze began to stir, and the sky transformed from brilliant oranges and pinks to deep blues.

Nearly five hours into the fight, with stars twinkling overhead, Katie finally brought the fish within a hundred feet of the boat. The floodlights illuminated the cockpit like a stage, drawing all eyes to her as the tension mounted. Though the fish was close, Katie’s exhaustion was evident—her movements were slow and labored as she fought to continue on.

"Come on, Katie. You've got this, sweetie," Mr. Gregory encouraged. "Just think, this fish might be worth more than what we won in the Grand Championship."

A small smile tugged at the side of her mouth at the thought of catching another fish worth over half a million dollars. Still breathing heavily, she summoned the strength to crank the reel handle one more time.

"Yeah! There you go, Katie!" Cricket shouted from the flybridge. "I can't wait to see you at the weigh-in with this giant fish hanging next to you! I'm framing that photo!"

A soft laugh escaped her as she envisioned herself beside the giant fish, holding the oversized winning check, cameras flashing all around her.

"Most people will never see a fish this big, let alone catch one," Soda chimed in. "I know you're tired, but you just gotta dig deep and keep going."

Gritting her teeth, she cranked the reel handle again, eager for the battle to just be over. But as she leaned back, bowing the rod, the fish suddenly raced off as if there were no drag at all. She watched helplessly as the fish pulled out the hundred yards of line she had just worked so hard to gain, then abruptly stopped.

Katie's brow furrowed in disbelief. With such a powerful burst of speed, the fish didn't appear to be tired at all. She, on the other hand, felt utterly exhausted. It was a crushing blow to her spirit, and tears welled in her eyes as she stared hopelessly at the reel.

The crew exchanged tense looks, knowing that moments like this can break an angler's will to continue.

"Don't let it get in your head, Katie. You can do this," Jason said, followed by encouraging words from the rest of the crew.

But their voices sounded distant as doubts flooded her mind. What had begun as an exciting challenge now felt like pure agony with no end in sight. She slowly took her hand off the reel handle to inspect it, as a steady, sharp pain had settled in. When she turned it over, she saw that her fingers and palm were covered with blisters. Turning her left hand over, she noticed a few forming there as well from gripping the top of the reel.

The men winced at the sight of the blisters on her hands but hoped she would press on for the sake of catching the fish of a lifetime. In a caring tone, Soda said softly, "There's a pair of gloves inside if you want to try 'em. They might help."

Katie sat quietly for a moment, her face long and drawn as she stared at the reel. She wanted to quit, but the thought of letting her dad and the rest of the team down weighed heavily on her heart. With a quick nod, she signaled to Soda that she would try the gloves.

After putting on the gloves, she took a deep breath and began cranking the reel handle again. Her hands still hurt, but she pushed through the pain, fueled by her resolve to catch and kill this blue marlin.

Time passed painfully slow as she spent two more punishing hours bringing the fish back to the boat again. Some of the blisters on her hands had popped, and the gloves, soaked in salty sweat, rubbed against her raw skin.

Her entire body ached, making each heave of the rod increasingly difficult.

The rest of the team watched in tense silence, the initial adrenaline long since drained away. Occasionally, someone would pass Katie a water bottle or offer a quiet word of encouragement, but mostly, they just waited—watching the line.

Behind the boat, the underwater lights lit up everything within 50 feet of the boat. Both Jason and Soda peered over the transom, eager to catch a glimpse of the fish as Katie raised it from the depths.

Finally, Jason called out with excitement. “There it is!”

“I see her!” Soda said. “She’s on her side, Katie! She’s tired.”

By turning onto its side, the fish was able to use its massive width to increase drag, conserving its energy. For Katie, it was like trying to pull up a sheet of plywood horizontal through the water. As the marlin steadily paddled away from the boat with powerful strokes of its tail, its fins and body continued to radiate a brilliant electric blue.

Katie’s eyes stayed focused on the reel. She was glad to hear the fish was on its side—a tell-tale sign it was losing strength—but she struggled to find the energy to even smile.

Jason cheered her on. “Come on, Katie! Just a few more cranks, and I’ll be able to reach the leader.”

Katie strained with all her might to raise the fish. Every inch of line she gained was hard fought and felt more difficult than the last.

The tension was palpable as the swivel attached to the leader line slowly teetered back and forth, going in and out of the water. Like the front line in a grueling battle of attrition, Katie and the fish appeared to be at a stalemate, neither able to gain the upper hand.

Jason's heart pounded as he looked at the giant marlin swimming steadily beneath the boat, hoping his time to battle the fish would come soon. Meanwhile, Soda stood by anxiously with the flying gaff in hand, knowing he had to make his shot count or risk losing a fish of a lifetime. In the flybridge, Cricket watched nervously, his jaw clenched tight, ready to thrust the boat into action if needed.

"Just a little bit more, Katie. You're almost there," her father encouraged, his voice steady and full of loving support.

The rod doubled over as Katie leaned back, the drag holding firm under the incredible strain. Slowly, the fish began to relent, and the swivel inched above the water, closer to Jason's grasp.

"That's it, Katie! Just a little more, and I can reach the leader," Jason urged her, excitement lacing his voice.

However, Katie's moment of triumph was short-lived. Like a bolt of lightning, the fish sped away, pulling line as ferociously as it had on its first run. The sound of the drag sliced through the air with a heart-wrenching "ZZZzzzzzz..."

Katie watched in dismay as the line screamed off the reel, quietly mouthing, "No. Stop." Within seconds, the marlin had erased all of her hard-earned progress, leaving her no closer to catching it than she'd been five hours earlier. Tears streamed down her face as she shook her head. "I can't do this anymore," she said, her voice breaking.

As Katie sobbed, Mr. Gregory and the rest of the team sat in silence for a moment, torn between their worry for her well-being and their hope that she wouldn't quit.

Hesitantly, Mr. Gregory moved closer, his expression softening. "You don't have to do this if you can't go on. The money's not as important to me as you are."

Katie didn't respond. Her breathing was shallow, her face streaked with sweat and tears. Slowly, she let go of the reel handle. Her hand dropped to her side, fingers curled inward, cramping and stinging with pain. Though the rod was still secured in her harness, she was no longer fighting the fish. She closed her eyes and felt the burn in her lower back and the ache radiating through her entire body. The only sounds were the soft slap of waves against the hull and the low hum of the engines, steady and indifferent.

As Katie opened her tear-filled eyes, ready to surrender, a small bird suddenly fluttered down out of the darkness and landed on the starboard side coverboard.

Surprised, Soda said, "Where'd you come from, little fella?"

From above, Cricket called down, "It must've seen our lights and come over to take a rest. I had a bird like that stay with me all the way back to shore one time."

A smile spread across the other men's faces as they watched their unexpected guest hop along the coverboard, tilting its head in quick, curious movements as it inspected them and the boat.

"It must be lost," Soda said. "Warblers don't usually fly this far out—especially at night."

Jason's eyes widened. "That's a warbler?"

"Yeah, cute little bird, ain't it?" Soda replied fondly.

Jason's voice was quiet, almost reverent. "Katie... that's the same kind of bird that landed on Santiago's boat in *The Old Man and the Sea.*"

Katie could hardly see the bird through her tear-soaked eyes. Still sniffling, she wiped them away, and the small creature came into focus. It was looking at her curiously, extending its neck and tilting its head back and forth in a way that made her smile. She recalled the image of the bird taking flight in the painting at Jason's home, and the quote inscribed in the background: "But man is not made for defeat. A man can be destroyed but not defeated."

Suddenly, the rod jerked down, catching her off guard. She gripped the chair tightly, straining against the pull of the fish as the drag slipped in short bursts, "ZZZ...ZZZ...ZZZ."

Concerned for her safety, Mr. Gregory rushed in to assist her. "Here, let me help," he said.

"No, wait!" Katie exclaimed, extending her palm toward him. She quickly glanced back toward the bird and saw it had flown away. With surprise etched on her face, she slowly turned to face her father, shaking her head. As their eyes met, her shoulders lifted, and she told him confidently, "I wasn't made for defeat."

A proud smile spread across Mr. Gregory's face as the crew began cheering her on. "Yeah, Katie! Don't give up. You can do this!"

Yet, her expression shifted to sadness as she stared out towards the fish.

"What's wrong?" Mr. Gregory asked.

"I'm going to catch this fish, but I don't want to kill it," Katie replied. "I want to let it go."

Confused, Mr. Gregory replied, "But Katie, this fish could be worth over half a million dollars."

Tears began to stream down her cheeks. "It was never about the money when we decided to start fishing, Dad." Shaking her head, she continued, "This is no ordinary fish. I don't want to kill it. I want it to live."

Mr. Gregory watched Jason and Soda grimace at the thought of letting the fish go. Their faces reflected disappointment mingled with disbelief. He then turned to Cricket, who looked deeply conflicted as well.

Cricket sighed. "That fish is worth a lot of money, boss—at least to us it is."

Mr. Gregory nodded, acknowledging how much the money meant to the crew. As he looked at his daughter, he thought about the time he had lost with her and his wife while building his company. The moment hung heavy on him as he considered his options. With firmness in his voice, he told the crew, "I'll make it right and compensate you for the lost tournament winnings, but we're going to release the fish if that's what she wants."

The crew was relieved to hear they wouldn't lose out on the money, but they couldn't hide their disappointment at not being able to weigh in the giant fish for all to see.

As the news sank in and the weight of their emotions settled, something else slowly began to rise—a sense of camaraderie. The disappointment remained, but it was joined by something stronger: resolve. The fight wasn't over yet.

"Alright, Katie! Let's catch this fish!" Cricket called down.

With a warm smile and soft tone, Soda said, "Get 'em, Katie."

Jason nodded, a hint of understanding in his eyes. "Let's do this."

Drawing on a quiet, renewed strength, Katie continued to fight the fish, her expression steady—somewhere between fierce determination and calm resolve. With each pull on the line, she felt a surge of energy, as if the marlin's struggle were fueling her inner fire—to never give up, to never be defeated. The crew surrounded her, their cheers rising and falling across the vast emptiness of the ocean, with no other boat in sight. Time blurred beneath a canopy of stars and the crescent moon as the dance between Katie and the mighty marlin unfolded toward its conclusion.

Eventually, the marlin came back into view beneath the boat, its fins and body still radiating a brilliant electric blue.

The team watched with bated breath as the swivel broke the surface of the water, then continued to climb higher. Suddenly, the drag began to slip, but Katie quickly placed her hand on the spool, pushing the line to its breaking point.

The crew winced as the rod doubled over at an alarming angle, acutely aware that the line could snap at any moment under such pressure.

Straining against the fish, Katie closed her eyes and whispered, "Just let me catch you, and I promise I'll let you go."

After a few tense seconds, the rod tip slowly inched upward.

"That's it, Katie! Keep it coming!" Jason urged. "You're almost there!"

Sensing a shift in momentum, Katie wound the reel again, pumping the rod and lifting the leader within Jason's grasp.

After nearly ten brutal hours of battling the fish, the boat erupted in cheers as Jason grabbed the leader. "Fish caught!" Soda shouted.

Jason's knees were locked firmly under the gunnel as he made his first wrap. It was a terrifying amount of power to hold in one's hands, but he held firm, knowing there would be no dumping the line this time. Since they weren't boating the fish and Katie was in no shape to continue if it made another run, he braced himself to break it off.

Time seemed to slow as he watched the line angle upward in the water. Every muscle in Jason's body shook, straining against the immense force of the fish as it leaped gloriously in front of him.

Though it had appeared massive underwater, it looked even bigger in the air. The team's eyes widened in wonder as they watched the colossal beast shake its head in a magnificent display of power and defiance.

As the fish began to descend, Jason braced himself, knowing it would bring the full weight of its body to bear against him. His jaw clenched tight as the 400-pound monofilament leader tightened around his hand with crushing force. His arms and back strained as the line stretched to its limit, pulling him forward slightly—testing both him and every knot he had tied to perfection.

An explosion of water sprayed into the air, followed by a sharp “kapow” as the leader snapped and the fish vanished into the darkness.

The hum of the boat’s engines was the only sound as they quietly gazed out across the water, the image of the leaping marlin still vivid in their minds. Tears of joy streamed down Katie’s cheeks, while the team exchanged knowing smiles and gentle nods, reflecting on the moment without saying a word. Each second seemed to stretch as they absorbed the beauty of their shared experience—a fleeting encounter with nature that would forever bind them together.

Soda eventually broke the silence, playfully joking, “Well, that was the biggest nine-fifty I’ve ever seen!”

Laughter erupted from the team as they began giving Katie high-fives, congratulating her on the hard-earned catch and beaming with pride at what they had accomplished together.

It was just past 1:00 AM, and after a grueling ten-hour fight, Katie was utterly exhausted. A quick laugh escaped her as she wiped away the tears. “I think I’m ready to go inside and get some rest.”

With respect etched on their faces, the men watched as Katie slowly hobbled inside, her father helping her along the way.

While Katie and Mr. Gregory retired to their quarters, Cricket began the long drive back to port. After putting away the gear, Jason and Soda joined him on the flybridge.

“I still can’t believe the size of the fish!” Cricket exclaimed, his voice filled with awe.

"I know! I'm still shakin' a little bit," Soda said. "It had me rattled good."

"And how crazy was that when the bird showed up?" Jason added, his eyes wide in disbelief. "Nobody's ever gonna believe us about the size of that fish or the bird."

Soda grinned. "Actually, I got the whole thing on video."

"No way!" Jason exclaimed, his face lighting up with excitement.

"Yeah, I turned the boat's camera system on when I thought we were about to gaff it, and it just kept runnin' the whole time after that."

"Yes!" Jason shouted, pumping his fist in celebration while Cricket and Soda joined in the laughter, their spirits soaring.

As they navigated through the darkness, the men continued to discuss the astonishing events of the day, reliving each thrilling moment. By the time they arrived back at the docks, they were ready to climb into their bunks for some much-needed sleep, their minds still racing from the day's events.

The entire team slept in that morning, enjoying a well-deserved rest. It was just after noon by the time everyone finally stirred.

Still riding the high from Katie's incredible catch-and-release, they gathered in the salon in front of the boat's flat-screen TV to watch the video that Soda had recorded.

Sitting on the edge of their seats and leaning forward in anticipation, they exclaimed in unison, "Whoa!" as they watched the fish leap from the water with Jason straining against it, holding the leader. The room was filled with a whirlwind of chatter and laughter, each recounting their favorite moments. After watching several replays, Katie said, "Well, are y'all ready to go get some lunch? Because I'm starving!"

"Yeah," the men replied, nodding their heads in agreement. "Sounds good!"

As they headed toward the salon door, Mr. Gregory said, "I need to grab something from my room. I'll meet you outside."

When Mr. Gregory finally opened the salon door, he held three white envelopes.

"I know it was difficult letting that marlin go yesterday, so I want to give you this in appreciation of your hard work," he said, handing each crew member an envelope with their name written on it.

One by one, their eyes widened as they peered inside, each discovering a check. "Oh, wow! Thank you, Mr. Gregory!" Cricket said with a shocked expression.

"Yeah, thanks, boss!" Soda chimed in, grinning from ear to ear.

Jason was stunned. "Thank you," he replied, grinning in disbelief.

"You're welcome, and it's well-deserved," he told them in a sincere tone. "Last night reminded me that sometimes losing can mean winning." He then grinned and teased, "But most of the time, it just means losing."

"Daaad!" Katie exclaimed, her voice filled with playful exasperation, prompting a round of laughter from the crew.

Mr. Gregory quipped, "I'm catching the next nine-fifty we hook up with in a tournament—that's all I'm saying."

Katie shook her head, rolling her eyes playfully in response, as the men laughed heartily.

After pulling Katie in for a quick hug, Mr. Gregory exclaimed, “Let’s go get some food!”

After making their way onto the dock, the team walked side by side down the boardwalk, their lighthearted banter flowing effortlessly. Mr. Gregory asked, “So, if you could fish anywhere in the world, where would you go?”

“Oooh, that’s a tough one,” Cricket replied. “I guess if I could fish anywhere, I’d probably wanna try fishin’ for blue marlins out of Cape Verde, off the west coast of Africa.”

Soda grinned. “Kona! Fishin’ for blue marlins in Hawaii is at the top of my bucket list.”

Katie’s face lit up. “That’s where I want to go, Dad! Hawaii!”

“How about you, Jason?” Mr. Gregory asked.

Jason thought for a moment. “Australia sounds pretty cool. They’ve got big blue marlins and even bigger black marlins down there.”

A curious expression crossed Mr. Gregory as he replied, “Billfishing Down Under, huh? That does sound fun.”

DISCUSSION GUIDE

The sea always tells two stories: one on the surface, one below. These questions invite readers to dive deeper into the novel.

1. The quote by Thoreau at the beginning of the novel suggests that many people fish without realizing it is not the fish they are after. As you read *Bills*, what deeper reasons stood out to you that drive the characters to fish?

2. In Chapter 1, how does the story about billionaire Charlie Munger regretting that he waited too long to catch a two-hundred-pound tuna exemplify the tension between chasing wealth and pursuing meaningful experiences? How might this connect to the Thoreau quote?

3. Several chapter titles in *Bills* have layered meaning. Which one resonated with you most, and why?

4. How does *Bills* invite us to consider the double-edged nature of family traditions—sometimes a compass, other times an anchor? Have you ever felt pulled between the expectations of your family and the vision you have for your own life?

5. In what ways does the novel highlight the importance of trust and integrity?

6. What does the story suggest about the value of family and friends as we move through the tides of life—both good and bad times?

7. Which boat name was your favorite, and why? Did you notice any patterns or hidden meanings in the boat names throughout the book?

8. In Chapter 10, Jason meets an older man fishing from a sailboat named *The Last Line*. How do the man's parting words—and the boat's name—deepen the meaning of the place where they cross paths and reinforce the theme of pursuing your passion?

9. How did you feel about Katie's decision at the end of the novel? What circumstances or motivations might lead you to agree or disagree with her choice?

10. For readers familiar with *The Old Man and the Sea*, how do *Bills* and Hemingway's classic differ in their beginnings and endings? What themes do they share, and which themes feel unique to *Bills*?

If you enjoyed reading *Bills*, help spread the word!

- Tell a friend
- Leave an online review
- Snap a photo of the book and share on social media: tag @billsthebook and use #billsthebook

Thank you!

John Yelverton

www.ingramcontent.com/pod-product-compliance
Lightning Source LLC
Chambersburg PA
CBHW060810310726
48980CB00002B/293
* 9 7 9 8 9 9 9 2 4 7 7 1 1 *